PRAISE FOR JOE WEBER AND HIS ELECTRIFYING BESTSELLERS

DEFCON One

TOM CLANCY:
"One of America's new thriller stars...a blazing debut."

W.E.B. GRIFFIN:
"Thought provoking to everyone interested in the global balance of power."

STEPHEN COONTS:
"An ominous, nightmarish scenario...a must read."

SHADOW FLIGHT

HERBERT CROWDER:
"Starts off with a bang and never lets up...vivid battle scenarios and riveting action."

RULES OF ENGAGEMENT

His newest, most controversial novel of war...

"A writer who does what writers are supposed to do—tell a story!"—*The Wichita Eagle*

Rave Reviews for Joe Weber's
DEFCON One

*Other books by Joe Weber
available from Jove*

DEFCON ONE
SHADOW FLIGHT

RULES OF ENGAGEMENT

Joe Weber

JOVE BOOKS, NEW YORK

This Jove Book contains the complete text of the original hardcover edition. It has been completely reset in a typeface designed for easy reading and was printed from new film.

A glossary of technical terms and military acronyms appears at the end of the book.

RULES OF ENGAGEMENT

A Jove Book / published by arrangement with Presidio Press

PRINTING HISTORY
Presidio Press edition / 1991
Jove edition / December 1992

ISBN: 0-515-10990-8

Jove Books are published by The Berkley Publishing Group,
200 Madison Avenue, New York, New York 10016.
The name "JOVE" and the "J" logo
are trademarks belonging to Jove Publications, Inc.

PRINTED IN THE UNITED STATES OF AMERICA

10 9 8 7 6 5 4 3 2 1

Rules of Engagement *is dedicated to the memory of the thousands of brave Americans who gave their lives in the Vietnam War. May we never forget their sacrifice.*

Rules of Engagement *is also dedicated to The Red River Valley Fighter Pilots' Association (RRVFPA). RRVFPA was started in 1967 as a modest attempt to share tactics among pilots who had flown missions over the most heavily defended areas of North Vietnam. Out of respect for their fellow fighter pilots who died in combat, RRVFPA established a scholarship fund for the children of the men who made the ultimate sacrifice for their nation. From 1970 to the end of 1990, the Red River Valley Association granted 553 scholarships totaling $587,000. Sierra Hotel to the River Rats!*

Acknowledgments

Many people have contributed to the development of *Rules of Engagement*.

Thanks to my wife, Jeannie, who continues to be my most loyal fan, my best critic, and my closest friend.

Thanks to the captain and entire crew of USS *Ranger* (CV-61). Their gracious hospitality while I was on board is deeply appreciated.

Special thanks to Judy Holt for her tireless hours of effort, to Lt. Col. John Flaherty, USAF (Ret.), and to Larry and Vivi Hodgden for their undying support.

As always, the contributions of Presidio Press editor Adele Horwitz deserve special recognition.

RULES OF ENGAGEMENT

1

YANKEE STATION, GULF OF TONKIN

Marine 1st Lt. Brad Austin exercised his flight controls to the stops, then saluted the catapult officer and braced his head for the violent launch. He inhaled a deep breath of pure, cool oxygen and held it in his lungs.

The F-4 Phantom's twin turbojets produced an earsplitting roar as the cat officer leaned forward and touched the flight deck, signaling to fire the catapult.

The deck-edge operator, standing in the starboard catwalk of the mammoth ship, pushed the launch button and quickly ducked below the surface of the flight deck to avoid the superheated jet blast.

The fighter-bomber, howling in afterburner, snapped the holdback bar and hurtled down the deck in a cloud of swirling steam.

Austin's helmet was pinned to the ejection seat headrest as his eyeballs flattened under the 6-g cat shot. His normal body weight of 165 pounds had instantly increased to 990 pounds.

Austin's radar intercept officer, navy Lt. Russell Lunsford, gripped the sides of the rear cockpit and looked at the port catapult track. The ship and the ocean were vague blurs of gray and blue as the Phantom accelerated from zero to 170 miles per hour in two and a half seconds.

Clearing the starboard-bow catapult, Brad popped the landing gear lever up, accelerated straight ahead, then raised the flaps and scanned his engine instruments and master caution light. Everything looked normal. He left the Phantom in afterburner and started a rendezvous turn toward his flight leader, Cdr. Dan Bailey.

Rapidly closing on the squadron commanding officer, Austin inched the throttles out of burner and slid into the standard loose deuce tactical formation on Joker 204. Bailey gave his wingman a quick glance, then gently initiated a steeper climb.

Their mission was to fly target combat air patrol (TARCAP) for a strike group from the carrier USS *Intrepid*. The *Intrepid*, carrying a full complement of attack aircraft, had joined their carrier five days earlier.

The four A-4 Skyhawk jets and four single-engine, propeller-driven A-1 Skyraiders were going to attack a large industrial complex at Thai Binh, fifty miles southeast of Hanoi.

Brad Austin, an exchange pilot with the navy fighter squadron, concentrated on his flight leader as the two Phantoms climbed in radio silence. Dan Bailey, respected as one of the best fighter pilots in the navy, believed in professionalism and discipline. He used head nods, augmented with hand signals, to communicate until it was absolutely necessary to talk over the radios.

Austin, who was beginning his fourth month with the navy squadron, had volunteered for the assignment to the carrier air wing. He would remain with the fighter squadron for the duration of the cruise.

Russ Lunsford glanced at the lead aircraft and keyed his intercom. "Ah . . . Brad, I've got a heads-up for you. Word is that the skipper is giving you a look this ride . . . for section leader. I didn't want to say anything until we were off the boat and settled down."

Brad smiled. "Thanks, Russ. I figured something was up when the boss had me conduct the brief."

The flight leveled at 20,000 feet and contacted the KA-3B tanker. Four minutes later, Joker Flight eased into the stabilized position behind the large twin-engine Skywarrior. Both pilots filled their fuel tanks to capacity, then dropped away from the Whale and headed northwest to Thai Binh.

Austin and Lunsford, feeling the tension mount as they approached the coast-in coordinates, rechecked their armament switches. The two men purposely cinched their restraining straps to the point of being uncomfortable. If the pilot and his RIO had to eject, they could not afford to have any slack in their ejection-seat harnesses.

"You tucked in, Russ?"

Lunsford snugged his shoulder straps one last time. "Any tighter, I'd have gangrene."

Squinting through the early morning haze, the two fighter pilots saw the coast at the same time. They would be over land—feet dry—in three minutes. The crews went through their combat checklist as the shoreline passed under the Phantoms.

"Joker Two," Bailey radioed as the flight crossed the beach, "you've got the lead. You are now Joker One."

Brad had anticipated the command. "Joker One, copy. I have the lead."

The CO drifted off to the right side and slid behind the new flight leader. Bailey had a keen respect for the young marine aviator and often referred to Austin as his brother in green.

"Combat spread," Brad ordered, tweaking the F-4's nose down five degrees below the horizon.

Bailey, intently scanning the sky for MiGs and surface-to-air missiles, answered with two clicks from his microphone. The response was standard for a pilot who was busy or desired to keep radio chatter to a minimum. The veteran fighter pilot, who had a well-deserved reputation for rowdy behavior on the ground, was deadly serious in the arena of aerial combat.

The Phantoms leveled at 15,000 feet and Austin entered a left-hand pattern two miles southwest of the target. After three orbits around the area, the F-4 crews heard the rescue combat air patrol (RESCAP) flight call the strike leader. The four additional A-1 Skyraiders, referred to as Spads by their pilots, were circling low off the coast. Their job was straightforward. They had responsibility for protecting downed aircrews until a helicopter or an amphibious aircraft could rescue the men.

Austin and Lunsford continued the lazy circle as the lead Skyhawk pilot rolled into his bombing run. The morning sky suddenly filled with a barrage of 37mm and 57mm artillery fire, interspersed with hundreds of small-arms rounds tracking the diving aircraft.

Brad looked down to see three surface-to-air missiles rise from an emplacement next to the road leading into the target area. Two more SAMs lifted off from another position before a Skyhawk pilot scored a direct hit on the missile battery. The SAMs exploded, spraying flaming fuel and skittering across the ground in erratic maneuvers. Two of the missiles impacted a fuel storage tank, causing a blinding explosion.

The prop-driven A-1s strafed and bombed gun emplacements surrounding the industrial complex. The A-4 pilots varied their run-ins, dropping all their ordnance in one pass. The small attack jets disappeared in the rising smoke, emerging from the other side in steep, climbing turns.

Austin caught a glimpse of two buildings disintegrating in a series of bright explosions. The violent blasts sent visible shock waves across the ground.

"Russ, it looks like they hit an ammo dump, from the type of explosions down there."

"Yeah," Lunsford replied, snapping photographs as quickly as he could work his camera. "Probably why they have so much artillery around the complex."

The Skyhawks pulled off the target and raced for the shoreline, followed by the slower Spads. Antiaircraft fire arced through the air in dense streams of multicolored tracers. Six more SAMs lifted off and shot skyward. One missile detonated under a Skyhawk, but the aircraft continued toward the coastline.

"MiGs, eleven o'clock low!" Lunsford yelled over the radio as four sets of eyes focused on the position. The Communist fighters were below and slightly to the left of the Phantoms.

"Tally, tally," Brad replied, feeling his pulse pound in his neck. "Jokers, arm 'em up."

"Two," Bailey acknowledged, flipping his missile-arming switches to ON.

The five MiG-17s had launched from Phuc Yen airfield, situated twelve miles north of Hanoi, and had made a low-level, high-speed pass to the northeast of the sprawling city.

The MiG-17, code-named Fresco by NATO, was an aerial hot rod that had tremendous maneuverability. The MiG was smaller than the Phantom and two-thirds less gross weight. Although the MiG-17 was not a supersonic fighter, it could outturn the more powerful F-4. Armed with three 23mm cannons, along with rockets or heat-seeking Atoll missiles, the compact fighter was a formidable air-craft. The MiG-17 was hard to spot in the air, giving it the advantage of surprise. Conversely, the big Phantom emitted dark jet exhaust, which made it easy to see from fifteen to twenty miles away. Selecting afterburner was the only way to eliminate the F-4's telltale smoke.

The MiGs had remained close to the ground as they approached Thai Binh. The North Vietnamese pilots were attempting to foil the U.S. early-warning radar, call sign Red Crown, stationed aboard a navy cruiser in the Gulf of Tonkin. The lower the MiGs flew, the less likely they would be discovered in the usual radar ground clutter.

Brad Austin could see that the MiG pilots, flying almost 430 knots, were rapidly overtaking the strike group. It was his responsibility to protect the attack pilots.

"Let's take it down," Brad radioed as he pushed the throttles forward. "Goin' burner."

"Two."

The F-4s rocketed toward the MiG-17s as Austin radioed the strike leader. "Seahorse Lead, you have bandits at your seven o'clock, closing rapidly."

"Roger that!" the A-4 pilot replied, looking over his left shoulder. "How close . . . how much time do we have?"

"Jokers out of burner," Brad ordered before he answered the frantic Skyhawk pilot. "They're about four miles.

Suggest your flight do a hard in-place port turn; put 'em nose on and hose 'em down.''

"Copy," Seahorse Lead radioed as he looked back to his three charges. "Seahorses, port one-eighty, NOW!"

Austin and Bailey continued to close on the MiGs while the A-4 pilots completed a knife-edge reversal to face the bogies. Russ Lunsford stowed his camera and hunched down in his seat when a line of reddish white tracers shot past his canopy. The bright rounds, seemingly close enough to touch, tracked over the top of the canopy and disappeared in the gray haze.

"Got a lock, Russ?" Brad asked while he watched the Skyhawks, going in the opposite direction, flash over the top of the withdrawing Spads. He could see that the attack pilots were firing their 20mm cannons in a head-on pass at the MiGs.

"I've got one," Lunsford answered, concentrating on their quarry, "but the A-4s are going right through the middle of my sco—"

"Missiles!" Brad interrupted, seeing two surface-to-air missiles rise in a plume of gray-white smoke. He thumbed the radio button. "Joker—SAMs! Three o'clock low, comin' right up the pike."

"Joker Two!"

Brad shoved the nose over, trying to outmaneuver the weapons, but the missiles continued straight toward the Phantoms. Sensing an imminent collision, Brad squinted and prepared for the explosion. The first SAM flashed under the fuselage; the second missile screeched over the canopy without exploding. Shaken by the narrow escape, Brad felt the sweat on his brow.

"Holy shit!" Lunsford swore, breathing in gasps.

The radio frequency was chaotic with calls to break, jink, and dive. The antiaircraft fire seemed to intensify as two more SAMs accelerated toward the Phantoms, missing them by less than fifty yards.

Brad bottomed out near the ground at 630 knots and quickly selected HEAT. He cursed the lack of cannons on the navy and Marine Corps F-4s. Their Phantoms had been equipped to carry four radar-guided Sparrow missiles and four heat-seeking Sidewinder missiles.

Dan Bailey, flying 100 feet above the trees a quarter mile to the right of Austin, had also selected HEAT. He knew that the marine pilot was going to attempt to scatter the MiG formation.

The Communist pilots fired several missiles at point-blank range, narrowly missing the Skyhawks as the A-4s pulled into the vertical. Two MiGs broke away to pursue the A-1 Spads while the other three pilots snapped straight up to engage the A-4s. Heavy antiaircraft fire continued to rain across the sky, spewing flaming death through friend and foe alike.

Brad raised the nose of his Phantom and tracked the lead MiG chasing the Skyhawks. "Come on, lock on. Where's the tone? Gotta have a tone."

Lunsford, turning his head from side to side as he watched for other MiGs, saw the second pair of SAMs fly out of sight toward the Gulf of Tonkin. "Clear of SAMs!"

Recognizing that his closure rate to the first MiG was excessive, Brad pulled his throttles to idle. He heard the missile annunciator tone at the same instant.

"Got it!" Austin exclaimed over the intercom as he fired two Sidewinders. "Go . . . nail his ass."

The first missile shot out in front of the Phantom, completed a barrel-roll maneuver, and flew out of sight toward the horizon. Shoving his throttles into afterburner, Austin swore as the second Sidewinder left the rail. The heat-seeking missile guided straight for the MiG leader, exploding ten feet behind his tail pipe.

The black-orange explosion blew debris from the aft fuselage of the MiG-17, but the aircraft continued to fly as the pilot dove for the deck.

"Got him!" Brad shouted over the radio. He experienced a sudden surge of adrenaline. "Jokers go vertical!"

Bailey squeezed off a Sidewinder, selected afterburner, then pulled hard to bring the F-4s nose straight up. He saw the AIM-9 missile go ballistic, missing the third MiG by a wide margin.

Brad viciously rolled his Phantom, looking for their adversaries. He saw the telltale mist of leaking fuel from the MiG flight leader.

Russ Lunsford also spotted the lead MiG. "Brad, you got him! He's trailing smoke or fluid, but he's still flying that bucket."

Austin quickly glanced at the damaged Communist fighter. The MiG was nose low, accelerating to maximum speed.

"Yeah," Brad replied disgustedly, "running to Phuc Yen, their goddamn sanctuary."

"Joker Lead," Dan Bailey calmly radioed, "you got a good hit. They've disengaged—all down in the weeds goin' for broke."

"I have 'em," Brad replied as his F-4 accelerated through 470 knots. He scanned the sky toward the coastline. "Let's get the others . . . the two on the Spads."

"Joker Two."

Listening over the open (hot mike) intercom system, Lunsford could hear his pilot breathing rapidly.

Brad swiveled his head, checking for SAMs and MiGs, then searched for the A-1s and their predators. He saw the MiGs fire missiles at the Skyraiders seconds before the A-4 Skyhawks cleared the beach.

"Seahorse is feet wet. We're winchester." The Skyhawk flight leader had radioed Red Crown, the radar surveillance ship, that his four-plane division was over water and out of ordnance.

Brad, watching the A-1s jinking all over the sky, saw black smoke belch from the trailing Skyraider. The staggering Spad had narrowly escaped an air-to-air missile before flying through a concentrated burst of 23mm cannon fire from the first MiG.

Nine heavy projectiles had ripped through the Spad's engine cowling, shredding fuel and oil lines.

"Buckshot Four is hit!" the attack pilot radioed. "I'm hit—goin' down! I can't make the beach!"

Brad pulled hard to track the high MiG, released pressure

on the stick to unload the g forces, heard the annunciator growl, then fired his third Sidewinder.

"Shit!" Austin swore as the missile left the rail and tumbled underneath the airplane. He instantly punched off his fourth heat seeker.

"Lifeguard One, Lifeguard One, Joker Lead," Brad radioed as the missile made a tentative wiggle, then guided directly to the MiG and exploded off the fighter's right wing. "We need RESCAP—repeat, we need RESCAP! Buckshot Four is down!"

Surprised that his target was still flying, Austin watched both MiGs turn hard into the F-4s. He executed a high yo-yo and flinched when Dan Bailey, in afterburner, flashed by a scant forty feet away.

"Wilco, Joker," the rescue combat air patrol leader replied. "Lifeguard up. We're buster with a Sea King in trail—have you in sight."

"Go with a Sparrow!" Brad said to Lunsford as he whipped the Phantom over and pulled 7 g's. The snug-fitting anti-g suit felt as though it was going to crush his legs and squeeze his abdomen in half. He had to work fast to set up a shot on the second MiG.

"We've got . . . ," the RIO began, then hesitated when his throat tightened with fear. "I've got to have some separation to get a lock."

Brad yanked the Phantom into a vertical roll, floating inverted over the top of the climb. "Okay, these gomers aren't amateurs."

Austin saw Bailey, nose up and inverted, a split second before the CO fired a Sidewinder. The missile tracked straight to the MiG's tail pipe, exploding in a pulsing, red-orange fireball that blew the aircraft apart in a shower of pieces.

Bailey snapped the big fighter into a gut-wrenching displacement roll. His RIO, Lt. Cdr. Ernie Sheridan, witnessed the front half of the MiG-17 tumble out of the blast. He was amazed to see the nose landing gear extended. The canopy had separated, but the pilot remained in the cockpit.

Sheridan watched, fascinated, as the MiG spun counter-clockwise to the ground.

Brad saw the second MiG dive toward the airfield at Phuc Yen. He knew it would be impossible to hit the fleeing fighter with a Sparrow. The radar-guided missile would not be able to lock onto the low-flying MiG.

"The other MiG," Lunsford radioed, feeling relief sweeping over him, "is disengaging. He's in the grass at the speed of heat!"

"Roger that," Bailey replied, studying the sky and ground. He caught a glimpse of the retreating MiG, lowered the Phantom's nose, then saw the stricken A-1 Skyraider gliding to a forced landing.

"Jokers, let's join up," Brad radioed, sensing the visceral effects of the adrenaline rush. "We'll orbit the Spad until Lifeguard arrives."

"Two," Bailey radioed as he extended his speed brakes to slow his closure rate on the lead aircraft.

Austin and Bailey, stealing glances at the crippled Skyraider, continued to search the hazy sky for MiGs. The A-1 pilot had slid his canopy open in preparation for the engine-out landing.

Brad looked back at the Spad. He was startled by the flames flowing down the left side of the aircraft.

"Buckshot Four," Austin radioed frantically. "You're on fire! You've got fire coming down the fuselage—your port side!"

"Copy!" the pilot replied in a tight voice. His propeller was slowly rotating as the engine spewed flames along the blackened fuselage. The aviator cocked the Skyraider into a steep side slip to keep the fire away from the fuselage.

The other three Spad pilots, who had not seen the fire in their search for MiGs, formed a wheel around their squadron mate as he flared to land the burning plane.

The pilot, who had elected to land gear up, floated over the uneven field, then crash-landed in a shower of earth and metal. The A-1 bounced into the air twice, then settled into a long slide.

Austin, flying 1,500 feet above the ground, banked into a

gentle left turn and watched the Skyraider plow to a grinding halt.

The pilot, fighting to extricate himself from the smoke-filled cockpit, dove over the right side of the aircraft as flames licked the canopy. He crawled a few feet, then stumbled to his feet and ran sixty yards before kneeling to rest. He looked around, frantic to find some form of concealment. The singed pilot was more than a mile and a half from the Gulf of Tonkin.

Brad, closely monitoring the sky in all quadrants, continued in a circle while the RESCAP flight leader contacted Buckshot 1.

"Ah . . . Buckshot Lead, Lifeguard with a full load. I've got a tally. We'll be overhead in two minutes."

"Copy, Lifeguard," the relieved flight leader responded as he watched his downed pilot. "He looks okay . . . moving across this field toward the eastern tree line."

The escaping pilot energized his survival radio and called his flight leader. "Jim, this is Clint. Do you copy?"

The Spad leader keyed his mike. "Roger that, loud and clear. Are you okay?"

The downed pilot stopped and looked up at the A-1s. "I'm okay. Just a few minor burns. Should I head for the beach, or stay put and wait for the helo?"

The radio remained quiet for a few seconds.

"Clint, head for that tree line east of you and take cover. We'll get the helo in as soon as we can."

"Okay," the pilot replied, running toward the thick vegetation. He heard his Skyraider explode as he reached the row of trees.

Brad checked his internal fuel-quantity indicator, knowing that they had to depart for a tanker soon. The gauge showed 2,600 pounds remaining.

"Joker Two, say fuel."

"Two point three," Bailey replied, deliberately placing Austin in a position to make a decision. The young marine aviator could continue to provide cover for the Spads, at the risk of losing two Phantoms, or depart for the safety of a tanker.

Suddenly, antiaircraft weapons opened fire from the edge of a small village. The 37mm guns were reinforced by a company of North Vietnamese regulars hiding across the road from the dwellings.

Brad could see dozens of AK-47s winking at him from under the trees. The gunfire was intense and concentrated directly in front of the screaming Phantoms.

"We're taking fire!" Sheridan radioed as the bright red tracer rounds flashed over their F-4.

"Joker Two, let's go upstairs," Austin radioed as he shoved his throttles forward and raised the F-4's nose fifteen degrees.

"Two," Bailey replied, then immediately added, "Uh, oh, I'm hit!"

Brad turned his head to see his CO. "Okay, Jokers, we're getting out of here!"

"Brad," Bailey radioed in a terse voice, "look me over."

"Wilco."

The Phantoms were streaking over the white-sand beach as Austin drifted under Bailey's damaged airplane. He could see four holes stitched from aft of the auxiliary air doors forward to the wing roots. Brad stared at the fuel pouring out of the second and third holes. The heavy spray was streaming directly under the jet exhaust.

"Brad," Lunsford said quietly over the intercom, "the skipper is in deep shit."

"Yeah . . . we may be too," the pilot replied, keying his radio transmitter. "Joker Two, you have a fuel leak. Say fuel state."

Bailey scanned his fuel-quantity indicator as Brad eased out to the right of the stricken Phantom.

"Good Lord," the CO radioed, not believing his eyes. "Two point one, and it's going down fast. Let's get to a Whale, ASAP."

"Roger," Brad responded, leveling off to accelerate at their present power setting. "Skipper, whatever you do, don't go into burner."

"Wilco," Bailey replied, watching the fuel quantity drop below 2,100 pounds.

Ernie Sheridan remained quiet, repeating the silent prayer that had always been a source of strength for him. The devout petition, the RIO fervently believed, had guided him through many tight situations.

Brad keyed his mike again. "Switch Red Crown."

"Two switching."

Austin changed his radar transponder, known as an IFF (identification friend or foe), to emergency, switched radio frequencies, and pressed the transmit button. "Red Crown, Joker Two Oh Seven, feet wet with an emergency."

There was a short pause, tempting Brad to transmit again, before the ground-control intercept (GCI) radar controller answered the call.

"Copy, Joker Two Zero Seven. Squawk One Four Zero Four and say type of emergency."

Brad inhaled and let his breath out slowly. "My wingman has a severe fuel leak. We need vectors to a tanker. He has eight minutes of fuel remaining."

"Roger that, Two Zero Seven. Stand by."

Brad felt his pulse quicken. The CO did not have time to stand by. He and Ernie Sheridan would be in the water in a matter of minutes if they could not plug into a tanker.

"Joker, we hold you in radar contact. Come starboard to one one zero. The Whale will be at your twelve o'clock, sixty-five miles, angels two four zero. Cleared to switch frequency."

Brad did not acknowledge the radio call in his hurry to contact the KA-3B. "Snowball, Joker Two Oh Seven. My wingman has seven minutes of fuel left. Request you rendezvous with us ASAP."

Austin knew the tanker crews did not like to leave the refueling track and fly north; especially without a fighter escort.

"Copy, Joker Two Oh Seven," the Skywarrior pilot replied as he shoved his throttles forward. "Say angels."

Brad scanned his instruments, noting his fuel and altitude. "We're at your twelve o'clock, sixty miles at eight thousand. We can't afford the fuel to climb."

The radio remained silent a moment.

"We're coming downhill," the KA-3B pilot said in a calm voice as he eased the tanker's nose down. "Be with you in four minutes."

Dan Bailey keyed his radio mike. "Snowball, Joker Two Zero Four. Suggest you bottom out at eight thousand in three minutes and start a one-eighty. We'll come aboard as soon as we have a tally."

"Wilco, Joker."

Brad glanced at his fuel-quantity indicator, then watched the second hand sweep slowly around the eight-day clock. Time seemed to stand still as the two flights raced toward each other. Another minute passed as Austin and Bailey searched the horizon.

"Joker Two, say fuel state," Brad said into his sweat-soaked oxygen mask.

"Nine hundred pounds," Bailey replied at the same time that Austin caught a glimpse of the KA-3B commencing the rendezvous turn.

"Tally!" Brad radioed in an excited voice. "I have a tally at eleven o'clock, in a port turn."

Three seconds passed before Bailey saw the tanker.

"Joker Two has the Whale. Probe coming out."

Brad extended his refueling nozzle and glanced at Bailey's Phantom. Joker 2 had his probe in the open-and-locked position.

"Joker's cleared to plug," the tanker pilot said. "We have the drogue out, indicating two-fifty. We'll increase the speed after you're aboard."

Austin clicked his mike twice and concentrated on the join-up. The Phantoms had a closure rate on the KA-3B in excess of 160 miles per hour. The fighter pilots would have their hands full trying to slow down in the last few seconds before they rendezvoused.

Brad watched the tanker fill his windshield. The F-4s were less than 400 yards from the Skywarrior. "I'm moving out to the side, Skipper."

"Roger," Bailey replied, pulling his throttles back. "Idle and boards."

Brad clicked his mike, reduced power to idle, and

extended his speed brakes. The two Phantoms, although slowing rapidly, were about to fly past the tanker. Brad moved farther to the right and cross-controlled the F-4 to avoid a collision.

"Goddamnit!" Lunsford swore as the fighter yawed sideways. "I'm gonna jump out of this sonuvabitch if you don't get it under control."

"Relax," Brad replied as the tanker's wing tip stabilized twenty feet to the left of the F-4.

"Snowball," Bailey radioed, standing his Phantom on its side, "pick it up to three hundred knots."

"Roger."

Brad watched closely as Bailey stopped cross-controlling and rolled the thirsty fighter level. The CO moved smoothly toward the basket on the end of the fuel hose, then suddenly fell back.

"I've flamed out!" Bailey radioed. "Snowball, toboggan and maintain the speed you have!"

"Wilco," the tanker pilot replied as he lowered the nose. He held the aircraft in a twenty-degree dive and eased the throttles back.

Bailey's General Electric J-79 engines were still wind-milling, providing hydraulic power to the flight controls during his chase after the basket.

"Jesus Christ," Lunsford said over the intercom. His breathing was labored. "Come on, boss, get in the basket. Get it . . . nail it . . ."

Bailey rammed the drogue, knocking it aside twice. Brad called out altitudes as the three aircraft plummeted toward the Gulf of Tonkin. "Five thousand three hundred . . . five . . . four point six . . . four . . . three point five . . . three . . ."

Lunsford watched Ernie Sheridan reach over his helmet for the ejection-seat handle. "Don't pull it," he said to himself. "Don't blow the skipper out of the driver's seat."

Brad released his mike switch when the CO mated with the basket and shoved the drogue forward.

"Fuel flow!" the tanker pilot radioed, sounding as if he was hyperventilating.

Brad looked at his altimeter and keyed his mike again. "Two point four . . . two . . . one point seven—"

"Light off!" Bailey said as Austin and Lunsford saw a ball of red-orange flame shoot out of the right tail pipe of the Phantom.

"I'm pulling out!" the tanker pilot radioed, easing the Skywarrior level at 400 feet above the water.

"I've got . . . the starboard engine on line," Bailey said in gasps. "Let's start a shallow climb . . . get some altitude so I can get an air start on the other engine."

Emotionally drained, Ernie Sheridan lowered his hands and slumped in his seat.

"Roger," the KA-3B pilot responded in a voice one octave higher than normal. "We'll drag you to the boat."

"Joker One," Bailey asked as the three aircraft climbed through 1,700 feet, "how's your gas?"

Brad looked at his fuel indicator and fudged. He did not want to add any additional pressure to his CO. "I'm fat, Skipper. Take your time."

"Fat, my ass," Lunsford said sarcastically over the intercom. "Just out for a Sunday drive . . . no problem."

The radios remained quiet while the flight climbed to 8,000 feet. Brad, staring at 1,100 pounds of fuel remaining, was beginning to feel uncomfortable. He glanced at Bailey's Phantom. It was still streaming kerosene at an alarming rate.

"Okay, Snowball," Bailey radioed, "I'm showing three grand. I'm going to back out and try an air start."

"Roger."

Bailey's probe slid out of the basket. "Brad, jump in there and grab a quick drink."

"I'm on it," Austin replied, moving smoothly behind the Whale. "Joker One is plugging."

Brad inched his throttles forward and placed his nozzle in the basket. He shoved the hose forward until the fuel started flowing.

"Fuel flow," the tanker pilot confirmed.

"Concur," Brad responded, then watched the internal fuel-quantity indicator climb. The precious fluid surged into his dry tanks. When the fuel gauge showed 2,200 pounds,

Austin backed out of the basket and again moved out to the right. "Thanks for the gas."

"Roger."

Brad caught a glimpse of the CO as he hurtled past the tanker. Bailey was in a high-speed dive, windmilling his left engine in an attempt to relight the J-79. He pulled out 2,000 feet below Austin.

"I've got 'em both on line," Bailey radioed, speaking in a slower, calmer voice. "I'm going to plug again."

Brad watched Bailey climb back to the tanker, then called the carrier. "Checkerboard Strike, Joker Two Oh Seven."

The carrier air-traffic controller answered without hesitation. "Joker Two Zero Seven, Strike. We have been informed of your emergency. We're shooting another tanker. You'll have a ready deck on arrival. Your signal is charlie on arrival."

Austin was relieved. They were cleared to land on arrival. His radio navigation instrument, the TACAN, had locked onto the carrier's homing beacon. They would be over the carrier in eleven minutes. Brad switched back to the tanker frequency.

"Joker Two, we're charlie on arrival. You will land first, an we've got another tanker on the way."

"Copy," Bailey replied as he continued taking on fuel. "You're doing a super job . . . for a jarhead."

Brad's oxygen mask concealed his grin.

2

The last aircraft on the carrier in the scheduled launch cycle was sitting on the waist catapult when the Air Boss heard about the inbound emergency.

He waited until the A-4 Skyhawk was safely airborne, then ordered an emergency pull forward of all the airplanes on the fantail. The next aircraft-recovery cycle was not scheduled for another twenty-five minutes. Seven airplanes had to be quickly moved from the area behind the arresting-gear wires.

The Air Boss, in Primary Fly (Pri-Fly), the control tower on the carrier, gave commands over the 5-MC loudspeaker system to the flight-deck crew. The men responded in a well-orchestrated, fast-paced effort to clear the landing area.

The blue-shirted aircraft handlers scurried around the deck, moving planes to the bow. Two "hot suit" members of the crash crew donned silvery asbestos garments, topped by see-through fire-retardant helmets.

The plane-guard helicopter landed and was immediately hot-refueled with the engine running. After fresh pilots had strapped in, the Kaman Seasprite "angel" lifted off and flew along the starboard side of the carrier. The rescue swimmer, clad in a full wet suit, sat in the helicopter's open door with his legs hanging down.

Belowdecks, medical corpsmen were prepared to treat the inbound flight crews. Topside, four seasoned corpsmen waited for the crippled Phantom to appear. Between the quartet of medical experts, they had helped rescue twenty-seven aircrewmen.

18

The tension was felt through the carrier as the flight-deck crew received continuous updates on the position of the F-4s. Every minute was critical for the aircraft handlers.

Brad listened while the second KA-3B checked in on tanker frequency. The Whale, flying at full power, started a tight rendezvous turn and glided into position off Bailey's left wing. The hose and drogue were already reeling out when the tanker stabilized next to the Phantoms.

Russ Lunsford was impressed by the skill of the Skywarrior pilot. "That guy is shit hot."

"Yeah, both of the Whale drivers are good," Brad replied as he wiped the perspiration from under his chin. He keyed his radio transmit button. "Snowballs, let's go approach frequency. We're getting close in."

"Copy."

"Wilco."

"Joker Two."

Brad looked at the CO and switched to approach. He listened to the controller while Bailey deftly unplugged from the tanker and moved over to the second Skywarrior. The CO, trailing a steady stream of jet fuel, coasted into position behind the KA-3B and nimbly plugged the bobbing basket on his first attempt.

"Approach, Joker Two Oh Seven with you at twelve miles." Brad could see the carrier's churning wake.

"Joker Two Zero Seven, approach. The Boss wants Two Zero Four to begin his approach abeam the carrier."

Brad looked at Bailey. The CO gave him a thumbs-up.

"Jokers, copy."

The four aircraft, descending slowly to 600 feet, were flying toward the bow of the carrier. They were in a perfect position to land out of the downwind alignment.

"Joker Two," Brad radioed when the TACAN indicated eight miles. "Let's dirty up."

"Roger," Bailey responded as he unplugged from the tanker and dropped back fifty feet. "Thanks, Snowballs. I owe each crew a case of spirits."

"We'll take you up on that. Catch a three wire." The

tankers added full power and climbed straight ahead to orbit the carrier.

Brad directed his attention to Bailey, waiting for him to stabilize in formation. "Gear . . . now."

The CO dropped his landing gear in sequence with his flight leader, then lowered his flaps and arresting-gear hook. Bailey's Phantom, with the exception of the streaming fuel, looked normal to Austin and Lunsford.

"Gear down," Brad informed the controller.

The pilots and their radar-intercept officers, about to land their jet fighters on board an aircraft carrier, felt their heartbeats accelerating. The task was considered to be one of the most dangerous operations in aviation.

"Two Zero Seven," the controller said in a laconic voice, "extend downwind and turn in at five miles."

"Wilco," Brad replied, running through his landing checklist.

The two Phantoms passed abeam the ship at the same time that the approach controller switched them to the landing-signal officer.

The LSO, standing on a platform on the port side of the four arresting-gear wires, braced himself against the thirty-two-knot wind. He could see a trail of frothy white jet fuel streaming out of his commanding officer's F-4.

Lieutenant Nicholas Palmer, newly qualified squadron LSO, keyed his hand-held radio receiver. "Skipper, you're lookin' good. Keep it coming."

Bailey remained quiet, concentrating on his angle of attack. Navy and Marine carrier pilots did not refer to their airspeed indicators for landing information. They were trained to fly at optimum angle of attack.

The CO added power, rounding the ninety-degree position from his final lineup. The center angle-of-attack doughnut lighted again, indicating that the F-4 was "on speed."

Nick Palmer, considered one of the squadron's "hot sticks," watched the approach with a critical eye. He saw the Phantom go slightly low but waited for his CO to catch the mistake. "Call the ball."

The "meatball," located behind the LSO platform, was a

bright yellow-orange light between a horizontal row of green reference lights. The highly visible light provided the aviators with a visual glide slope to the flight deck. If the pilot allowed the ball to rise above the datum lights, he was high. If the ball went low, he was in danger of striking the aft end of the carrier, the flight-deck round-down. If the pilot kept the ball centered all the way to touchdown, he would theoretically snag the third arresting-gear wire.

Seeing the meatball come into view, Bailey concentrated on lineup and angle of attack. The LSO could see the amber yellow "on speed" light shining brightly from the CO's nose-landing-gear door. The angle-of-attack indication that the pilot saw on his glare shield was displayed simultaneously by one of the three lights on his nose-gear door.

"Phantom ball," Bailey radioed. "Two point one."

In the squadron ready room, located directly below the flight deck, Bailey's men watched their skipper on closed-circuit television. The pilots and radar-intercept officers, sitting quietly, stared at the screen as the damaged F-4 grew larger. The tension mounted as the crippled aircraft approached the fantail of the carrier.

High on the flight-deck side of the island superstructure, sailors crowded "vulture's row" to watch the tense drama unfold. They could hear the distinctive high-pitched howls from the jet engines as Bailey jockeyed the throttles to keep the ball centered. The Phantom, racing toward the end of the carrier deck, continued to spew a long stream of jet fuel.

"Power," Palmer cautioned, leaning backward in the buffeting wind. "Give me a little power."

Brad Austin, listening to the LSO, decided to start his turn early. He banked the Phantom to the left, twisting his head around to see the carrier. He knew that the CO was about to cross the ramp.

Palmer watched the F-4 begin to settle. "Power!"

The Phantom's engines shrieked as it passed over the round-down and slammed into the flight deck. The tail hook caught the number four wire as Bailey, out of habit, went to full power in case the hook missed all four arresting-gear cables.

"Off the power!" Palmer shouted as he turned to follow the howling fighter. He could see that the F-4 had trapped.

A nanosecond later, the aft flight deck erupted in a blazing inferno. The Phantom's superheated exhausts and screeching tail hook, showering sparks along the steel deck, had touched off the jet fuel pouring out of the damaged aircraft. The F-4 charged up the flight deck, stopping close to the forward edge of the angle deck.

"Fire on the flight deck!" the Air Boss yelled over the 5-MC loudspeaker. "Lay down foam!"

Bailey yanked the throttles to idle cutoff and flipped off the electrical switches as the Phantom was pulled backward by the arresting-gear wire. The pilot stomped on the brakes after the steel cable had fallen from the tail hook.

Bailey glimpsed the pandemonium on the flight deck as he hit the canopy-open switch. "Get out! Let's go, Ernie!"

Austin, three miles behind the carrier, stared in shocked disbelief. "Holy shit! The flight deck is on fire. The skipper must have crashed."

Lunsford remained silent, leaning to his left side to see the carrier through the pilot's windshield.

Bailey and his RIO, about to jump over the side of the burning Phantom, were hit by a powerful stream of fire-retardant foam. The impact knocked them back into their ejection seats as the two hot-suit rescue personnel slapped metal ladders against the cockpits.

The thick white foam covered the Phantom, but the conflagration quickly spread underneath the belly of the blazing F-4.

Bailey and Sheridan stumbled down the side of the burning Phantom, then slipped and fell in the gooey foam. The rescue team, aided by two corpsmen, helped both officers to their feet and whisked them away to the safety of the island.

Sheridan heard a muffled explosion a second before the Air Boss shouted over the flight-deck loudspeaker.

"Bring Tilly over!" the commander ordered, concerned about the missiles still attached to the Phantom. "Shove the aircraft overboard!"

The huge yellow pushmobile lurched forward and lumbered across the flight deck. Tilly, a monstrous combination of crane and bulldozer, plowed into the fiercely burning fighter. The impact collapsed the F-4's landing gear as the aircraft slid sideways, then hung precariously over the catwalk before plunging inverted into the water.

"Foul deck! Foul deck!" the LSO radioed to Austin. "Take it around, Two Oh Seven."

"Wilco," Brad responded as he passed over the stern of the ship. "Did they get out?"

"That's affirm, Joker," Palmer said as he surveyed the damage to the landing area. The fire had been extinguished and the men were rapidly clearing the deck. "I'll be able to take you on the next pass."

"Copy," Brad replied, then keyed his intercom. "Jesus, that was close."

Russ Lunsford inhaled a deep breath of pure oxygen and unsnapped one side of his mask. "Yeah. Flying with you guys sure as hell is not boring."

Turning downwind, Brad rechecked his landing gear—down and locked, flaps extended, and arresting hook down. He continued the approach, turned crosswind, called the ball, crossed the fantail on speed, and engaged the number three arresting-gear cable.

The F-4 screeched to an abrupt halt, then rolled back five feet. When the wire dropped free, Brad added power and taxied to the starboard-bow catapult. He waited for the aircraft handlers to secure the Phantom to the rolling flight deck, then shut down the engines.

Austin and Lunsford opened their canopies and breathed in the salty breeze. The fresh air smelled good. They sat in quiet exhaustion as curious deck crewmen pointed to the numerous bullet holes in the F-4 Phantom.

Slowly removing his crash helmet, Brad watched his plane captain run across the deck toward them.

3

The ready room was noisy and crowded. When Brad and Russ walked through the hatch, immediate silence descended. All eyes shifted to the sweat-soaked pilot and his RIO.

Bradley Carlyle Austin wore the insignia patch of his former Marine Corps fighter squadron. It denoted that he was an F-4 Phantom Phlyer. Twinkling hazel eyes highlighted a tanned face and trim physique. Brad was five feet ten and 165 pounds. Known as a gregarious officer with a quick wit, he enjoyed the company of his fellow pilots and RIOs. They, in turn, respected their solitary ''jarhead'' for his straightforward personality and excellent flying skills.

A graduate of the Naval Academy, Brad Austin had majored in aeronautical engineering. He had also been a member of the swimming team, and competed as a platform diver. Graduating with honors, he had resisted his father's wishes by accepting a commission in the Marine Corps.

His father, Vice Adm. Carlyle Whitney Austin, USN, was a proud Annapolis alumnus who firmly believed in tradition and loyalty. The three-star flag officer had vociferously opposed his son's decision not to pursue a career in the naval service.

Brad's senior year at the academy had been marred by the prolonged quarrel with his father. The more incensed his father had become over his decision, the more determined Brad had become to chart his own course.

The past holiday season, when Brad had worn his marine dress blue uniform home, had been a strain for the entire

Austin family. When again pressed by his father, Brad had made it clear that it was his decision, and his decision alone, to pursue a career path of his own choosing.

What he had not disclosed was the fact that he did not want to serve in the same service as his father. Brad had always bristled at the insinuations that his father would ensure a smooth career path. Furthermore, how could he possibly explain to the admiral that he genuinely liked the Marine Corps?

Lieutenant Russ Lunsford, tall and lanky with stooped shoulders and thinning blond hair, was considered one of the better RIOs in the squadron. The twenty-seven-year-old bachelor had an intellectual air about him, underscored by his methodical approach to every facet of his life. Lunsford made a constant effort to keep his personal world, including his impeccably clean stateroom, as neat and predictable as possible. Naturally nervous, he hid his apprehensiveness behind a pretense of hardy self-assurance.

Although Russ Lunsford was competent technically, he had never quite adjusted to the hostile environment of aerial combat. Everyone liked the former college basketball star but knew not to approach him when he became moody. His worst emotional swings generally manifested themselves two to three hours before a combat mission.

It was common knowledge that Russ Lunsford was not overly fond of flying, even with the best pilots in the squadron. The few individuals who knew about Lunsford's past attributed his acute nervousness to the fact that he had washed out of advanced fighter–attack pilot training. Whatever the reason had been, he remained an extremely uneasy crew member.

Lieutenant Jon O'Meara approached Brad as Lunsford closed and secured the hatch. O'Meara was a quintessential Irishman, full of mirth and always boisterously confident. He was two inches shorter than Brad, with short-cropped red hair and dancing blue eyes.

O'Meara's pranks had become legend before the air-group commander had censored him for singing an indecent song in mixed company at the officers' club. The lewd rendition of "Shagging O'Leary's Daughter" had not been well received by the admiral's wife.

O'Meara's look asked the question. "What the hell happened out there?"

Austin dropped his helmet, flight gloves, and kneeboard in one of the high-backed crew chairs. "We got our asses shot off covering a downed Spad driver. How's the skipper and Ernie?"

Lieutenant (junior grade) Harry Hutton, the squadron duty officer, placed his hand over the phone he had just answered. Hutton was at a desk next to Brad. "I'm talking to Scary McCary now." McCary was Dr. Lloyd McCary, the squadron flight surgeon.

O'Meara saw the XO stand. "I'll stop by your pit later. I'd like to hear all the details."

"Well," Brad exhaled softly, "it wasn't pretty." O'Meara nodded knowingly and went back to his flight-planning table.

The executive officer, Cdr. Frank "Rocky" Rockwood, stepped around his chair and walked down the center aisle toward Brad and Russ. He sat down on the arm of a chair next to the two men. "Are you guys okay?"

Brad unzipped his torso harness. "Yessir, just a little post-flight shakes."

Rockwood pulled a cigar out of his shirt pocket and lighted it as Austin and Lunsford unzipped their g suits. "Tell you what . . . why don't you two go get a bite to eat and a cup of coffee. We'll get with Jocko for a debrief when the skipper is released from sick bay." Jocko was Lt. Cdr. Jack Carella, the squadron operations officer.

Brad folded his g suit over his helmet. "Sir, I really need to talk to you and Commander Carella now. It was my fault that the skipper got hit."

A hush settled around the back of the compartment. Lunsford glanced at Austin, then busied himself with his flight gear.

Rockwood, not the typical executive officer who acted as the CO's hatchet man, placed his hands on his knees and studied Brad. "Okay, I'll grab Jocko and we'll go to my stateroom."

Austin nodded his head. "Yessir."

Rising to his full six feet two, the partially bald Rockwood started up the aisle toward Carella. He had almost reached the operations officer when the cherubic-faced Hutton, holding his hand over the phone receiver, leaped out of his chair.

"The CO and Dirty Ernie—Commander Sheridan—have been released. They're on their way to the ready room."

Applause and cheers filled the long, narrow briefing room. The CO was considered to be one of the good guys, and Ernie Sheridan, the senior RIO in the squadron, was a happy-go-lucky friend to everyone.

Brad felt a burning sensation in the pit of his stomach. The more he thought about the mission, the more convinced he became that his judgment had been faulty.

Lunsford leaned closer to Austin and spoke in a hushed voice. "It wasn't your fault. What the hell do you expect to gain by taking the blame for—"

Lunsford stopped in mid-sentence when Frank Rockwood and Jack Carella started toward them. The XO and the operations officer looked like Mutt and Jeff characters. Rockwood lived up to his nickname in appearance. He was a solid, well-muscled 205 pounds. Big for the average fighter pilot.

A devoted husband and father of three teenage daughters, Rockwood centered his life around his family. Always a gentleman, he was a blend of natural leader, gifted aviator, and superior intellect.

Jack Fierro Carella, a compact and dark-complected man, had curly black hair and piercing dark eyes. His nasal Italian accent had not changed since his boyhood in Philadelphia. The Temple University graduate had been a rough-and-tumble street fighter in his blue-collar neighborhood. He took his squadron job seriously and was considered tough but fair.

Unsmiling, Carella walked up to Brad. "What's on your mind, Mister?"

Brad knew that Carella called him mister out of habit. Junior officers in the navy were addressed by their rank, mister, or sir. Marine officers were addressed by their rank, or sir.

Frank Rockwood spoke before Brad had a chance to open his mouth. "Jocko, let's wait until the CO gets here. He may want to speak with Brad and Russ alone."

"Yes, sir," Carella replied, then turned to face Austin. "Just one question. Can you confirm that the skipper knocked down a MiG?" The room suddenly became quiet again.

"Yes, sir," Brad responded, then fell silent as shouts of joy and loud clapping filled the small space.

The hatch leading to the passageway opened and the yelling, whistling, and clapping intensified as Cdr. Dan Bailey and Dirty Ernie Sheridan stepped into the crowded ready room.

The din of celebration increased as everyone tried to get through the throng to shake hands with the MiG killers. The pilots and RIOs slapped Bailey and Sheridan on their backs, whooping with happiness. The carrier had been conducting their operations from Yankee Station, off the southern coast of North Vietnam, for seventeen days and the Jokers had the first confirmed MiG kill.

Brad stood to the side, unsure of what he should say or do. Lunsford waded into the cluster of men and offered his congratulations to the victorious crew.

Frank Rockwood, seizing an opportunity to say a quiet word to the CO, spoke quickly about Austin's feelings of guilt. Bailey acknowledged his XO, shook more outstretched hands, darted a look at Brad, then made his way toward the marine aviator. He steered Russ Lunsford along with him while Sheridan followed.

Brad, feeling a pang of trepidation, watched the CO approach. Bailey looked jubilant, as did Ernie Sheridan. Lunsford showed no emotion.

The smiling CO stopped between Austin and Lunsford, then grasped the pilot's right wrist and the RIO's left wrist. Like a boxing referee, he raised their arms over his head and addressed the ready room crowd. "These guys also deserve a round of applause. They have a probable on their record, and they did a hell of a job this morning." Everyone cheered again while the CO shook hands with Brad and Russ.

"One other note," Bailey announced loudly. "You're looking at a new flight leader—our token marine and junior section leader, First Lieutenant Austin."

The CO stepped away as various members of the squadron congratulated Austin and Lunsford. The handshakes and slaps on the shoulders expressed genuine feelings of praise.

Bailey waited for the right moment, then stepped close to Brad and Russ. He looked straight into Brad's eyes and spoke quietly. "The XO says you have something on your mind, Lieutenant."

Harry Hutton interrupted before Brad could reply. "Skipper, they got the Spad driver out. Shot up a couple of helos, but he's on his way back to the *Intrepid*."

The celebration masked Bailey's words as he addressed Austin and Lunsford. "You guys drop your gear in the locker room and join me in my stateroom in fifteen minutes."

"Yes, sir," the two men replied in unison.

Brad and Russ quickly stowed their bulky survival gear, crash helmets, oxygen masks, .38-caliber revolvers, g suits, and kneeboards. They showered in record time, then donned fresh uniforms and reported to Bailey's stateroom. Brad knocked on the door.

"Come in," the CO invited as he opened the safe mounted in the bulkhead at the back of his fold-down desk.

Brad opened the door and entered the room, followed by his RIO. Frank Rockwood and Jack Carella sat on the bunk next to Bailey's desk chair. The cabin was cramped but not as confining as the junior officers' quarters.

"Have a seat," the CO said, motioning to the two gray straight-backed chairs next to the far bulkhead.

Bailey's tanned face was distinguished by pronounced crow's-feet and a dimple in his square chin. He had a salt-and-pepper crew cut and a pronounced southern drawl.

He read extensively and could quote with equal ease from Chaucer's *Canterbury Tales* or the comic strips.

Earning his wings the hard way, Bailey had parlayed a private pilot's license, combined with two years of junior college, into a NAVCAD appointment. As a naval aviation cadet, Dan Bailey had distinguished himself throughout every phase of flight training.

Graduating second in his class, Bailey had proudly accepted his commission and the accompanying gold bars. His fiancée, and former high-school sweetheart, had pinned on his coveted wings of gold.

After the graduation ceremonies, Ens. Dan Bailey and Karla Jane Cooper had married at the base chapel. They had enjoyed a brief honeymoon, marred only by an unexpected mechanical failure in Dan's 1949 Chevrolet. The drive shaft had dropped to the pavement four blocks from the church. For years Dan and Karla, along with their twin sons, had laughed about the incident.

Dan Bailey was revered by all the officers and men of the squadron for his professionalism and leadership qualities. He was respected most for his genuine consideration for every man under his command.

Brad and Russ sat down while Bailey placed a stack of reports in his safe and closed the door. The XO and the operations officer remained quiet.

Bailey turned around, smiling pleasantly. "Care for a cold Dr. Pepper?" Both men, seeing that Rockwood and Carella had a can in their hands, accepted the soft drinks.

"Okay, jarhead," Bailey said, "what's bothering you?"

"Well, sir," Brad began, watching Rockwood and Carella out of the corner of his eye, "I feel like it's my fault that you . . . that we got nailed. I led us too low over the downed Spad."

Bailey raised a hand. "Wait a minute. Brad, you're one of the best pilots in the squadron. And besides being a natural stick, you have good logic and leadership skills. If you didn't possess those traits, the Marine Corps would not have allowed you to come out here, and I would not have made you a flight leader."

"Yes, sir," Brad responded awkwardly. He was openly embarrassed, especially in the presence of his backseater.

Rocky Rockwood swallowed the last of his soft drink and tossed the empty can in the trash. "Hey, Brad, you're doing a super job—got a probable kill, too. The only mistake you've made is joining the wrong service." The friendly barb broke the tension.

"Austin," Carella said in a businesslike tone, "the skipper briefed me on the mission. You didn't do anything he would not have done."

Brad nodded his head.

"One thing to remember," Bailey offered, finishing the remains of his Dr. Pepper. "There is no safe altitude in our type of mission. If you're high, the SAMs and triple-A will come after you. If you duck down in the weeds, the Cong and everyone else with a rifle or rock will use you for target practice. As a section leader, Brad, you have to constantly evaluate your situation and make a judgment call. It's that simple."

"Yes, sir," Brad replied, having forgotten his drink.

"Hey," Rocky said in his usual carefree manner, "we know you marines are trained for close air support, but just cover your ass. You don't have any guns to keep the little bastards' heads down."

Brad managed a chuckle, finally relieved of his anxieties. "Thanks, I appreciate the advice."

"Both of you," the CO said, smiling, "are contributing a lot to the squadron. Enough said . . . so get the hell out of here and go have a drink."

The junior officers' eyes gave away their secret. They, along with every flight-crew member in the squadron, had liquor stashed in their private safes. Although navy regulations prohibited having alcohol on board a ship, the breach of rules was overlooked for those men who flew off the carrier, endured the stress of combat engagements, then had to land on the pitching, rolling deck again.

Bailey grinned at the two men. "Just keep it confined to your staterooms."

"Yessir," they answered, stepping out of the stateroom.

After leaving the CO's quarters, Brad returned to the ready room to check the flight schedule. His friend and roommate, Harry Hutton, was just finishing his stint as the squadron duty officer. Hutton, who still looked like a peach-faced high-school sophomore, was exuberant and full of unrestrained energy. Brad always enjoyed his company.

The majority of the flight crews had gone forward to the dirty-shirt wardroom, leaving the ready room almost deserted. Hutton was leaning back in his chair with his hands clasped behind his head. His feet were propped up on the deck, and a coffee mug was balanced precariously on his stomach.

"Hey, MiG killer," Hutton said as his marine friend entered. "Letsqueet," a Harry translation of "let us go eat."

"Will you cut the MiG killer shit?" Brad said, unamused. "I got a probable. He was packin' cheeks north the last time I saw him."

"Okay, already," Harry replied, picking up a rough copy of the new flight schedule. "You're going to get another shot at it tomorrow. The XO told Jocko to schedule you and Nick together for a BARCAP. He said, and I quote, 'The skipper wants the two hot sticks to fly together . . . best chance to bag a MiG.' End quote."

Brad looked at the proposed schedule. "Great, but they've got me leading."

Harry grinned his infectious grin. "Yeah, that'll piss off my man, the egotistical asshole." Hutton was Nick Palmer's RIO.

The two-man flight crews were not allowed to room together. If a crew went down, their respective roommates would have the responsibility to arrange for their personal belongings to be shipped home. There was an additional unwritten rule. It would be the roommate's obligation to send a letter, apart from the commanding officer's, to the closest relative.

"Well," Brad said with a sigh, "this should be interesting . . . having Nick Palmer on my wing."

"Oh, yeah, you can count on it," Harry responded, picking up his pen. "You hungry?"

"No, not really," Brad replied, glancing at the two pilots playing acey-deucey at the back of the room. "The skipper told me to go have a drink."

Hutton's face lit up. "You mean a drink-drink?"

"Yeah," Brad said quietly. "You want to join me?"

Harry displayed his toothy grin. "Is a skeleton's ass skinny?"

4

Brad and Harry were settled back, discussing the morning's MiG engagement, when Nick Palmer knocked on their stateroom door. An inch short of six feet, the athletic-looking Palmer was a movie idol type from his light brown hair to his perfect white teeth. A graduate of Princeton University, Palmer was the oldest son of a wealthy manu-facturing mogul.

Nick Palmer and Harry Hutton, both bachelors, had shared living quarters prior to their squadron's deployment to the Gulf of Tonkin. The well-furnished apartment, dubbed the snake ranch, had been the center of many noisy and disorderly parties. A bevy of young, attractive women had made the apartment, along with the swimming pool, their favorite gathering place.

"Mind if I come in?" Palmer asked, stepping into the cluttered stateroom.

"Pull up a chair," Brad replied, feeling a little uneasy. On his second cruise, Nick the Stick Palmer was considered to be the best pilot in the squadron. "Care for a shot of the good stuff?"

"Sure," the LSO responded, accepting a fresh glass from Brad. "I see that we're flying together tomorrow."

Austin poured a liberal amount of vodka into the ward-room iced-tea glass, then added water and a half dozen ice cubes. Harry Hutton had brought a small bucket of the precious frozen liquid from the wardroom.

"The skipper," Hutton said to his pilot, "is the one who scheduled the flight."

Palmer lighted a cigarette and sipped his drink. "Thanks. This hits the spot."

Brad leaned back against his fire-resistant flight suit hanging on the bulkhead. "Have you got any suggestions for a new kid on the block?"

Nick chuckled, shaking his head. "No. It sounds like you're doing okay on your own."

"Yeah, Nicko," Harry chimed in, "the gyrene is a half MiG ahead of us."

Palmer laughed good-naturedly, then leaned into Hutton's face. "Well, wise-ass, why don't you drive tomorrow and I'll sit in the backseat. That should be worth the price of admission."

Brad tilted his chair forward. "Seriously, Nick, you've got a lot more experience than I have. Any assistance will be greatly appreciated."

"Well," Palmer said, settling back in his chair, "Jocko showed me an interesting maneuver that he believes can bag a gomer eight out of ten times. After he pulled it on me, I believe he's right."

"The negative-g trick," Harry said, now that Nick was letting his little secret out. Palmer, who had wanted to be the first Joker pilot to down a MiG, had sworn Hutton to secrecy. A highly competitive person, Nick did not want anyone else to have the same advantage.

Palmer ignored Hutton. "What you do is let the MiG driver get on your six, then turn into him just enough so he can pull inside of your radius."

Brad looked perplexed. "Jesus, you're leaving yourself wide open if the guy is halfway good."

"Wait a minute," Palmer said, snuffing out his cigarette. "Patience and timing are the key elements. You've got to have confidence in yourself to pull this off."

In characteristic fighter-pilot style, Palmer raised his hands to demonstrate the maneuver. "When the gomer pulls inside of you, you push the stick forward, staying in the same angle of bank. When you see the MiG disappear from sight below your canopy, you snatch 8 g's back into the turn and roll over the top in the opposite direction from your original turn. Most of the time your bandit will be confused when you disappear under his nose without rolling your aircraft.''

"I think," Brad said, hanging onto every word, "I see the picture. When the MiG snap rolls to follow your push maneuver, you're coming back through his line of flight too fast for him to follow."

Palmer smiled, raising his glass. "Exactly. Before he can react, you've popped your boards and rolled up and over him. You're now in a position to take advantage, or disengage if you have any doubt about the outcome.''

"Jesus," Brad said, replaying the tactic in his mind. "That's definitely an unorthodox maneuver, especially using the speed brakes.''

"Yep," Palmer responded knowingly, "but it works. Jocko did it to me coming back from a BARCAP, and I took the bait. When I snapped over, the son of a bitch flashed by me in a blur, with a lot of kinetic energy.''

Almost giggling, Hutton butted in. "Next thing Ace here knows, Jocko is on our six.''

Brad stifled a laugh. He was amazed that Harry still had all of his original teeth.

"Well," Palmer said sarcastically, "since we're airing our laundry now, why don't you tell Brad about how you identified an air force Phantom as a MiG?''

Unable to resist, Brad laughed.

"Tell him," Palmer continued, "about how excited you were to lock on with a Sparrow, until I saved your dumb ass from knocking the poor bastards out of the sky. Great pair of eyes, kid.''

Undaunted, Hutton swallowed the last sip in his glass. "So, I made one mistake this year.''

"Oh, yeah," Palmer replied, shaking his head. "We would have had the entire goddamn air force after our asses.''

Brad appreciated Palmer's effort to form a closer friendship with him. He seemed to be very genuine. "Nick, why don't you lead out and I'll lead back, until I have more experience?''

"Naw, you go for it. You're a hell of a lot better than you give yourself credit for."

Feeling a tinge of embarrassment, Brad got up and rinsed his glass. "Nick, I'd like to try your negative-g maneuver on our way back tomorrow. I've always been taught that speed—lots of it—is the key to winning, and living to fight again."

"That's basically true," Palmer replied, feeling a closeness to the less experienced Phantom pilot. "But intimidation and unpredictability are the keys to survival. You've got to know your aircraft, and push it to the limits of its capability, and your capability."

Brad sat down, not taking his eyes off the seasoned fighter pilot.

"A lot of people," Palmer continued, "are afraid of the Fox-4. They're afraid to take it to the edge, or over the edge. To get the most out of the Phantom, you need to keep your speed above four hundred thirty knots, and fight below thirty thousand feet.

"If you can get a MiG to jump you at an altitude below fourteen thousand feet, you're in the prime F-4 envelope. The Phantom, as I'm sure you've discovered, turns like a lead sled at higher altitudes."

Austin acknowledged with a smile and a nod.

"What about the MiGs?" Brad asked, intrigued by Palmer's knowledge. "What are their weaknesses and strong points?"

Hutton was also interested in the discussion.

"The seventeen is flight-control limited, or so we've heard. If the gomer pushes it past four hundred thirty knots, he's on the verge of losing control. That's about all I know, except it turns on a dime."

Unusually candid, Palmer appeared to be pleased that Austin was interested in his experience. "I don't know that much about the MiG-19, but the twenty-one is a thirteen-hundred-mile-per-hour rocket. The twenty-one pilots basically use slash-and-run tactics."

Palmer thought for a moment. "We'll work at tactics on each flight. The primary thing to remember is that if you place second in this league, you're dead. Nail 'em quick, and get the hell out of Dodge.''

"Thanks," Brad offered, having absorbed every detail provided by Palmer's insight. "I'm looking forward to flying with you tomorrow.''

"Yeah," Harry grinned, "he's a real treat.''

"Hey, Brad," Palmer said, crunching on an ice cube and ignoring Hutton, "our contingent of marines is target practicing on the fantail. I think they're using M-16s. Suppose you could use your influence to get us a little firing time?''

Laughing out loud, Harry could not resist. "Shit, Palmer, you couldn't hit water if you fell out of a boat.''

Brad smiled, feeling a bond developing between the two pilots. "Sure. They've got a machine gun too. We can really put on a show with that little hummer.''

"Think they would allow us to tow Harry as a target?''

"How in the hell," Brad laughed, "did they ever team you two together?''

Harry blew Palmer a kiss. "Just lucky, I guess.''

5

Brad and Russ Lunsford walked out of the ready room, down the long passageway, and out onto the catwalk, then mounted the steps to the flight deck. The low, dirty gray clouds threatened rain. Not a good day for flying.

Stepping onto the gritty deck, Brad was mindful of the hazards that surrounded them. Planes and tractor tugs were in constant motion. Men in various colored shirts moved swiftly around the crowded flight deck, dodging jet exhaust, wings, wheels, jet intakes, and tugs. The deck crews stepped nimbly over and around airplane chocks, taut arresting-gear cables, tie-down chains, bombs and rockets, and thick hoses pumping thousands of gallons of the volatile jet fuel into the menacing-looking planes.

Brad remembered the day a sailor, caught in the inferno of a Phantom's jet blast, had been hurled over the side of the flight deck. The aircraft handler had fallen sixty-five feet to the sea. The plane-guard helicopter, flying along the starboard side of the carrier, had managed to rescue the severely injured youth.

Kneeboards and helmet bags in hand, Russ and Brad leaned into the blustery wind and walked forward to their Phantom, Joker 208. The F-4 sat ready, canopies open, fueled, and armed with two Sparrows and four Sidewinder air-to-air missiles.

Scanning their fighter-bomber, Brad smiled to himself. The Phantom was the meanest-looking airplane he had ever seen. It reminded him of a giant prehistoric bird, one with wing tips angled up and tail fins angled down. The tough-looking monster, packed with two huge General Electric J-79 engines, was a world-class record holder. The F-4 had already set a speed record of more than 1,600 miles per hour. The Phantom could also sustain a combat altitude of 66,000 feet, and zoom climb to 100,000 feet. The amazing airplane could carry a weapons load twice that of a World War Two B-17 bomber.

Brad performed a thorough preflight walk-around while Lunsford climbed into the backseat. The pilot checked the external fuel tank for security, then pushed against the missiles to ensure that they were tightly attached. Brad peered into the engine intakes, checking for anything that might be sucked into the powerful yet delicate engines. He looked carefully for any signs of fuel or hydraulic leaks, and checked for any loose or open panels.

The plane captain was responsible for making sure that the fighter was ready to fly, but Brad had the overall responsibility for the expensive aircraft. He noted that the right main-gear tire was almost smooth and had deep scuff marks on the side. He calculated that the tire was good for one or two more landings before it would blow out. What the hell, Brad thought, the maintenance officer had bigger problems.

Watching Nick Palmer check the security of his Sidewinder missiles, Brad climbed the fuselage steps to his cockpit. He closely inspected his ejection seat, looked down the row of aircraft being manned by other crews, then stepped into the cockpit and settled in his seat. The distinct odor of fuel, oil, and hydraulic fluid swept over him. This would be his environment for the next two hours.

The plane captain, a conscientious Wyoming teenager who aspired to be a rancher like his father, helped Brad and Russ buckle their parachute attachments and strap themselves to the hard-bottomed ejection seats.

Austin scrutinized the cockpit, carefully checking his instruments and the position of every switch, knob, gauge, lever, button, dial, and circuit breaker. One item out of place could spell disaster for the crew.

Brad firmly grasped the rudder-pedal adjustment lever

and tried to turn the crank. He placed both hands on it, but it would not budge. Phantom 208 had a history of rudder-pedal adjustment problems.

Leaning close to the plane captain, Brad yelled over the whipping wind and flight-deck noise, "Toby, I need the knockometer."

"Yes, sir," the blond-haired youth replied, then quickly scurried down the side of the fighter. He ran to the catwalk tool bin, grabbed a hammer, and raced back to the Phantom. He climbed the fuselage steps and handed the tool to his pilot.

"Thanks," Brad said, whacking the crank. The lever rotated ninety degrees, freeing the jammed drive gear. He handed the hammer back to the youngster. "The miracles of modern technology."

"Lieutenant," Toby Kendall shouted, bracing himself against the fierce wind, "be careful . . . and I hope you get one of them MiGs."

The plane captain could only visualize what it was like to be catapulted from an aircraft carrier, fly a sophisticated, high-performance jet fighter into aerial combat, then find the ship and land the complex aircraft on the small, moving deck. The men who helped the flight crews in and out of their cockpits had a deep respect and strong attachment to their pilots and RIOs.

"Thanks, Toby," Brad replied as he placed his helmet on and tightened the chin strap. Their plane captain climbed down the side of the fuselage as the signal to start engines blared across the flight deck.

Brad and Russ lowered their canopies to seal themselves from the jet exhaust fumes of the F-4s in front of them. Four of the Joker Phantoms would provide target combat air patrol while Austin and Palmer would provide barrier combat air patrol for the carrier. A standby F-4 was also manned in the event that one of the strike aircraft malfunctioned prior to being launched.

"You ready?" Austin asked as he initiated the engine start procedure.

Lunsford snapped the loose side of his oxygen mask to

his helmet. "All set. If we get lucky, they'll scrub the strike for weather."

Brad ignored the comment. He knew that his RIO, who prayed for mission cancelations, would do a good job when the chips were down.

After he had both engines running, Brad adjusted the three rearview mirrors mounted on the canopy bow over his head. They would allow the pilot to watch where he was going while darting quick glances behind him. Brad's most vulnerable position was directly aft of his fighter—the infamous six o'clock position.

Brad added a small amount of power and taxied out of his tie-down spot. Clear of Nick Palmer's Phantom, Brad lowered and locked his F-4's wing tips and followed the taxi director forward to the starboard-bow catapult. Austin brought the Phantom to a smooth stop behind the catapult blast deflector. He watched the A-4 Skyhawk in front of him go to full power, waggle his controls back and forth, then hurtle down the deck and climb toward the sullen clouds.

Brad rechecked his instruments and armament panel as the blast deflector was lowered. Following the taxi director, Austin moved forward until his nose gear went up and over the catapult shuttle. He immediately stopped while the green-shirted cat crews hooked the bridle harness and holdback bar to his heavily laden fighter.

A deck crewman held up a plastic-covered board indicating the fighter's total takeoff weight. The steam pressure of the catapult launch would be predicated on the gross weight of the Phantom. Brad looked at the board, which indicated 49,000 pounds. He gave the weight checker a thumbs-up and swept the control stick backward, forward, left, and right to see if the flight controls were working properly. The catapult officer checked under the Phantom and gave Brad the two-finger turn-up signal.

Shoving the throttles forward, Brad focused on the engine instruments, then selected afterburner and glanced at the end of the flight deck. "Harness locked?"

"All set," Lunsford replied in a slightly strained voice. "Don't screw up."

Brad placed his left hand on the catapult grip that prevented the throttles from being retarded during the violent launch. He again scanned the engine parameters, feeling the Phantom shudder under full power.

Placing his helmet against the headrest, Brad snapped a salute to the yellow-shirted catapult officer and waited for the powerful kick in the back. The cat stroke would render the pilot immobile during the launch. Four seconds elapsed before the Phantom blasted down the deck, settled precariously close to the water, then entered a climbing right turn.

Snapping the gear up, Brad could hear Lunsford breathing in short gasps through the open intercom system. "You gonna make it, sailor?"

Lunsford slowed his breathing rate. "Yeah. Palmer is off . . . good shot."

The Phantoms rendezvoused and joined on the tanker. Brad plugged the basket on his second attempt, filled his tanks to capacity, then backed out and drifted to the left so Palmer could top off his fuel load.

Tuned to the tanker frequency, Brad was surprised to hear the carrier call him on the 243.0 UHF Guard channel. "Joker Two Zero Eight, Checkerboard Strike on guard. Come up button seven."

This is unusual, Austin thought, sensing trouble. Or, he reasoned, the mission might have been canceled due to the rotten weather.

Brad dialed in the strike frequency. "Checkerboard Strike, Joker Two Oh Eight is up."

"Joker, Checkerboard. We've got a delay on strike . . . stand by one."

Brad clicked his mike twice, watching Nick Palmer slide out of the basket. The Whale reeled in the refueling hose and banked into a shallow left turn.

Palmer, who had also heard the call from Checkerboard, came up on button seven. "Joker Two."

"Copy," Brad responded seconds before the carrier talker called.

"Joker Two Zero Eight, Strike."

Brad keyed his mike. "Joker, copy."

"Joker," the controller radioed without emotion, "we're holding for a weather check. Your flight is directed to make a reconnaissance sweep over the target area."

"Horseshit," Lunsford said over the intercom.

Looking at the folded map section on his kneeboard, Brad glanced toward the coast. The dark, rain-swollen clouds looked ominous. "Wilco, Checkerboard. We'll relay through Red Crown."

"Roger that."

The primary target was the Vu Chua highway and railroad bridge north of Hanoi. The combination support structure was a vital link in the North Vietnamese supply chain. The flight crews were aware that the target had been given a high priority.

Brad checked in with Red Crown, discussed the weather reconnaissance mission, then descended to 100 feet as the coastline appeared. The two F-4s, traveling at 450 knots, went feet dry south of Cam Pho.

Brad guessed the ceiling to be 1,800 to 2,000 feet with five to seven miles of visibility. The strike group could squeeze in, but it would be tight. Continuing toward the bridge, Brad was startled when antiaircraft fire erupted from the hills on both sides of the low-flying fighters.

"Jokers," Brad radioed, "let's light the pipes and get the hell out of here. Come hard starboard, and watch the foothills. They're obscured by clouds."

"Two," Palmer replied, breathing heavily, "is tucked in tight. Pull as hard as you want."

The Phantoms, thundering over the gun emplacements, were hit by several rounds of fire as they rolled into the tight turn. Brad glanced back and forth at his annunciator panel. So far, so good.

"MiGs!" Harry Hutton shouted from the backseat of Joker 2. "They're . . . I see three of them comin' down the valley—right on our six! Ah . . . they're seventeens. Three Mig-17s!"

Brad, flying low and bleeding off airspeed in the turn, stole a quick peek. "Shit." He looked out ahead, knowing the MiGs were flying at terminal velocity. There was no escape. They would have to engage the rapidly overtaking MiGs.

"Nick," Brad called, looking back over his shoulder, "they're overrunning us. Idle and boards . . . NOW!"

Palmer yanked his throttles back to the stops and popped his speed brakes out. "Let's get down on the deck!"

"Doin' it," Brad replied, shoving his stick forward. "They're going to overshoot." The MiGs could not slow quickly enough to keep from overtaking the Phantoms in the narrow valley.

Hutton, seeing two of the three MiGs pull up in a climbing turn, radioed his friend. "Brad, you've got one comin' over the top . . . two o'clock high. The other two are running—I've lost them."

Slamming the throttles into afterburner, Brad retracted the speed brakes and reefed the fighter into a tight, climbing turn. He immediately reversed to the left, squarely on the MiG's tail.

The North Vietnamese pilot, painfully aware of his error, dove for the edge of the gently sloping hills. His two wingmen had disappeared in the low overcast.

Palmer pulled up in a sweeping wingover. "You've got him, Joker. Shoot! Shoot!"

Inhaling sharply, Brad and Russ were squashed into their seats under the heavy g load. Their faces sagged as they felt the onset of gray-out.

The MiG pilot banked hard, racing toward the other side of the valley. He was 400 feet above the ground when the Phantom, 2,000 feet behind and closing, flew through the MiG's powerful wing tip–generated vortices. The phenomenon was familiar to all pilots.

The Phantom, straining under the heavy g load, hit the twin horizontal tornadoes, shed the port Sidewinder missiles and ejector rail, then snapped inverted to a nose low attitude.

"Oh!" Brad groaned, shoving the stick forward while desperately pushing on the left rudder. He was upside down, petrified by the trees rushing up to kill him. He was too terrified to utter a sound.

The F-4 twisted in a 7-g rolling pullout, then slammed through a stand of trees in an exploding hail of branches and debris.

"God . . . damn!" Brad shouted as the heavily damaged jet fighter, rolling upright, shot skyward. "Sweet mother of Jesus . . . we're alive." His heart hammered so hard that he suffered chest pains.

Afraid to open his eyes, Russ Lunsford spoke in a low, reverent voice. "If I ever get back on the ground, I promise you God, I'll go to church every Sunday . . . I promise." He gulped a deep breath of oxygen. "Thank you, precious God."

Brad was startled by the master caution light and annunciator-panel lights glowing. The bright red fire-warning light caught his attention. He looked down at the engine tachometers and exhaust gas temperature indicators. The starboard engine was surging from the tremendous amount of debris it had ingested.

Brad could feel the vibration from the straining J-79. The powerful engine was quickly succumbing to the foreign-object damage. He retarded the right throttle to idle, then cutoff. The smoking, overheated turbojet ground to a shuddering halt.

Brad and Russ were looking over their shoulders, trying to locate the MiG-17, when they heard Palmer's excited voice.

"I've got him! Got a tone!"

Austin saw the MiG heading up the valley, scud-running beneath the overcast. Palmer, 100 feet below and 3,000 feet behind the MiG, fired two Sidewinders. Brad watched the first missile detonate in a brilliant flash to the right of the MiG. The second Sidewinder exploded under the fighter but failed to destroy the aircraft.

Swearing to himself, Palmer fired his last two heat-seeking missiles. His soliloquy continued unchecked as both Sidewinders, two seconds apart, detonated under the belly of the damaged MiG-17.

The blast blew off the tail of the fighter in a blinding flash. The MiG continued to fly momentarily, trailing vapor and smoke, before exploding in an orange-black fireball. The pilot ejected from the tumbling fuselage seconds before the burning MiG hit the ground. His parachute never had time to fully deploy before he slammed into the ground next to the remains of his fighter.

"I got him!" Palmer shouted over the radio. "Good kill!"

Brad pushed his left throttle forward and banked into a shallow turn to expedite the rendezvous with Palmer. "Nick, I've got major problems."

"Yeah," Palmer replied, trying to slow his breathing rate, "I saw you go through the trees."

Hutton keyed his radio. "Brad, we're coming up your port side. Let's get feet wet and back to the boat."

Austin looked at the lights on his annunciator panel and scanned his instruments. The airspeed indicator was inoperative. The PC-1 hydraulic system indicated zero pressure. The PC-2 was fluctuating and the utility system remained steady.

"Nick," Austin said, "take the lead and keep your speed below two-fifty. I've lost an engine and I don't have any airspeed indication. I've got a lot of buffeting and I don't want this baby to come apart."

"Roger," Palmer radioed as he pulled even with Austin's fighter and surveyed the damage. The right engine intake was crumpled and partially collapsed against the fuselage. The wings were dented and deeply scored, with long scrapes near the fuselage. "You need to send a thank-you card to McDonnell-Douglas."

Looking back at his wings, Brad was astounded by the extent of damage his aircraft had sustained. The leading edges of both wings were mangled. Pieces of tree limbs and leaves were embedded in or protruded from both wings. Brad had to bank the aircraft slightly to the right, while adding a touch of left rudder, to maintain coordinated flight.

Palmer crossed under the battered F-4 and stabilized in a loose parade formation. "You guys have the best camouflaged Fox-4 in Southeast Asia."

Scanning the left engine gauges, Brad inched the throttle

forward. "Nick, do you see anything that is an immediate threat? Any fluids?"

Palmer scrutinized the crumpled centerline fuel tank. "You've got a lot of damage, and fluid is leaking from a couple of holes. Your centerline tank is smashed beyond recognition. It's sort of canted to the side. I'd just leave well enough alone and not try to jettison it."

"Rog," Brad replied, watching Palmer move into the lead position. "Does it look like fuel or hydraulic fluid?"

"I can't really tell."

"Nick, I'm going to punch off my starboard pylon."

"Roger," Palmer replied, turning to watch Austin's right missile rack fall away.

Hutton looked back at the crippled fighter. "Jesus, Brad, it looks like you're flying a shrub."

Still shaking, Lunsford raised his helmet visor and keyed his radio switch. "How about canning the goddamn monologue, and get us back to the boat."

Palmer checked his airspeed at 250 knots, thinking about the MiG-17 he had just shot down. The reality was difficult to comprehend. "Jokers, switch to Red Crown."

"Switchin'."

Palmer waited for the shoreline to pass under him, glanced at his wingman, then called the radar picket ship. "Red Crown, Joker Two Oh Two."

"Joker Two Zero Two, Red Crown."

Turning in the general direction of the carrier, Palmer added power and started a gentle climb. "The weather over the target area is miserable and getting worse. Advise canceling the strike."

"Copy that," the controller replied. "Squawk One Three Three Seven. Do you need a tanker?"

"Stand by one," Palmer answered, looking over his shoulder at Austin. Nick Palmer believed they should get the damaged fighter on the carrier as quickly as possible, unless Austin needed fuel. Palmer would be tight on fuel, but he felt confident that he could fly to the ship without a problem. "Need any gas, Brad?"

"Negative. I've got enough to make the boat."

Palmer steepened the climb and reset his IFF. "Red Crown, we're okay on fuel, but my wingman has had a fender bender and we need a ready deck on arrival."

"Wait one," the controller responded, punching up another frequency. He contacted the carrier, relayed the weather information, and informed them about the inbound emergency.

6

The dimly lighted ready room had become crowded since the message about Brad Austin's plight had been received. The mood was somber, with the usual noisy banter replaced by a quiet uneasiness.

Dan Bailey rushed into the compartment, followed by Frank Rockwood. After they received a quick brief from the duty officer, both men hurried to Pri-Fly.

Bailey and Rockwood discussed the situation with the Air Boss, then the XO went below deck to the Carrier Air Traffic Control Center. He would listen to the radio conversations between the controller and the pilots. If anything significant happened prior to the time Austin contacted the Air Boss and the landing-signal officer, Rockwood would relay the word to Dan Bailey.

Brad and Russ meticulously went through their pocket checklists, discussing various emergencies they might encounter. Lunsford read the single-engine landing procedure while Brad replayed the drill in his mind. Landing on board an aircraft carrier with one engine secured was not an emergency procedure they actually practiced. A carrier-arrested landing was difficult enough with both engines operating. Landing the critically damaged fighter with an engine secured was something only a test pilot should have to do.

"Joker Two Zero Two, Red Crown."

"Joker Two Oh Two," Palmer replied, feeling the tension draining from his neck.

"You have a priority deck on arrival, and the strike has been canceled. Come port ten degrees. The ship is one one five for one zero five miles."

"Copy that," Palmer replied, then added, "we have a confirmed MiG kill. A MiG-17."

"Congratulations!" the exuberant voice replied. "We'll pass the word along to your ready room."

Brad keyed his mike. "Red Crown, Joker Two Oh Eight. Pass the word that Two Oh Two downed the MiG."

"Will do. Contact Strike out of two two thousand."

Palmer replied, "Roger, Red Crown."

The two Phantoms climbed to altitude while Austin and Lunsford prepared for the next phase of their harrowing flight—the single-engine carrier landing.

Nick Palmer, elated over his MiG kill, checked his altimeter. The instrument indicated 21,700 feet. Close enough. "Checkerboard Strike, Joker Two Oh Two with you out of two two thousand."

The response was immediate, as usual. "Roger, Two Zero Two. Drop Two Zero Eight on the ball, and we'll take you on the next pass. We have eight aircraft ahead of you, but we don't expect any delay."

Palmer acknowledged the radio call and leveled at 27,000 feet. He slowly reduced power to remain at 250 knots. His TACAN indicated seventy-two nautical miles to the carrier.

Brad was worried about two items—the weather at the ship and the slow-speed flight characteristics of his battered Phantom. The nose radome was shattered, exposing the crushed radar antenna and myriad wires. Two of the wing leading-edge slats, one on each side, had been ripped off. Austin could see buckled wing panels and exposed innards in the right wing. He also noticed that the wing tip was deformed.

Keying his radio, Brad called the carrier and asked for the current weather conditions.

"Joker Two Zero Eight, we have intermittent rain squalls with a ragged ceiling three hundred to four hundred feet. The visibility is varying between one half to one and a half miles."

"Copy, Checkerboard," Brad replied, then keyed his intercom switch. "You've been unusually quiet back there. Any problems?"

A pause followed before Russ Lunsford answered. "Yeah, I'm going to have to throw away my skivvies . . . if we ever get down in one piece."

Brad could tell by the tremor in Lunsford's voice that he was still unsettled by the frighteningly close brush with death. He wondered if his own voice had sounded strained over the radio.

Austin closely monitored his hydraulic gauges, fearful that the priceless fluids would leak out of the Phantom before they were safely on the carrier. If the F-4 lost all hydraulic fluid, the primary flight controls would lock, forcing the crew to eject.

"Nick," Brad radioed, "I need to perform a stability check. Let's descend to five thousand and see what speed I'll need to control this beauty."

"Reducing power now," Palmer replied. "Indicating two-fifty. Do you want to try extending your hook and flaps before we go into the soup?"

Afraid of having an asymmetrical situation, Brad thought about the split-flap possibility. He needed the flaps to reduce his final approach speed. "Sure. Here goes." Austin lowered his arresting hook and selected partial flaps. Everything worked as advertised.

The Phantoms rapidly descended into the rain and clouds and leveled at 5,000 feet. They slowed to 230 knots, then 220 knots, as Palmer radioed the speeds to Austin.

"Okay, Nick," Brad said, grasping the landing-gear handle, "I'm going to drop the gear . . . I hope."

"Wait," Palmer cautioned. "Wait a second. Your machine is really trashed. Let's not place any extra strain on anything at this speed. I recommend we slow to one-eighty and go for it. With the damage you've got, I'd leave the flaps where they are."

Agreeing with the more experienced Phantom pilot, Brad reduced power to match Palmer's F-4. They were flying in solid instrument conditions, blocking out the river of water

flowing over their canopies. Relying solely on Nick Palmer
to fly instruments, Brad ignored his instrument panel and
concentrated on flying formation with his leader.

"Russ," Brad said over the intercom, "if we have to
jump out, we've got plenty of time from five thousand."

"I've been ready . . . got everything stowed."

Fighting the insidious onslaught of vertigo, Brad intensified his concentration in an effort to reduce the sensation of
dizziness. Spatial disorientation was a constant threat to
pilots flying in instrument conditions. He studied Palmer's
Phantom and attempted to suppress the fear gnawing at him.
He did not want Russ Lunsford to know that his pilot was
anything but confident about the outcome of the flight.

"Okay," Palmer radioed, closely monitoring his airspeed
indicator. "I'm showing one-eighty. Let 'er go."

Brad said a silent prayer and yanked the landing-gear
handle down. He was rewarded by the clunk, clunk of the
main gears and the thud under the nose. "I show three down
and locked."

"Looks good," Palmer replied. "Let's see what your on
speed will be. Coming back on the power."

Reducing power, Brad stayed glued to Palmer's Phantom.
The vertigo was dissipating and he darted a glance at his
left-engine instruments, back to Palmer's F-4, then back to
the fuel-quantity indicator. The powerful turbojet was
operating smoothly and, to his relief, he had 2,900 pounds
of fuel remaining. Enough for a couple of approaches before
the Air Boss would have to rig the barricade.

"One-seventy-five," Palmer soothed. He gently moved
his throttles back. "One-seventy . . . one-sixty-five . . .
one-sixty . . . one-fifty-five . . . one-fifty . . ."

Brad felt the Phantom shudder, then the wings wobbled
as he shoved the left throttle forward.

"Shit!" Lunsford exclaimed as the fighter leveled out.
"We're going to be at least fifteen knots fast."

Adjusting the power, Brad spoke to his flight leader.
"Nick, I've gotta have one-fifty to touch down."

"Okay, partner," Nick said, peering at his smooth-flying

wingman. "I'll keep it on one-fifty-five . . . give you a cushion to the ramp."

Austin and Lunsford knew they would be attempting a single-engine landing almost twenty miles an hour faster than their normal approach speed. Adding to the difficulty was the fact that the angle-of-attack indexer was not working. The sensor had been sheared off in the violent collision with the trees.

Hutton, who had been quiet, watching the drama unfold, spoke to his roommate. "Brad, you can do it. Show the navy how the marines land a flying tree."

"What was it you said," Palmer radioed Austin, "about marine fighter pilots?"

Brad smiled to himself. "When we're out of ammo, we resort to ramming our bogies."

Lunsford nervously keyed his mike. "And you wonder— flying with that kind of mentality—why I'm a basket case."

Palmer and Hutton shared a laugh over their intercom but kept their comments to themselves. They both were concerned about Lunsford's increasing uneasiness.

Palmer talked to the carrier controller who would vector the flight to a position for an instrument approach to a visual landing. The radar operator steered the Phantoms to a point six miles behind the carrier, then turned them inbound to line up with the small flight-deck landing zone. He wanted the pilots to have adequate time to stabilize before they started their descent. "Reduce to your final approach speed."

"We're already there," Palmer radioed as the two aircraft flew into a heavy downpour. "Dash Two is damaged and can't slow below one-fifty-five."

The controller sensed a disaster in the making. "Copy. Understand that you're at final approach speed."

Twenty seconds elapsed before the radar operator again contacted the flight. "Approaching glide slope . . . up and on the glide slope. Begin your descent." Palmer eased the power back and followed the controller's calm instructions.

"You're on the glide path, left of course. Come right five degrees." Palmer made a very slight correction. His instrument scan was automatic from hundreds of hours of practice and five years of experience.

"You're on glide path, on course. The last aircraft has trapped. You have a clear deck."

"Roger, clear deck," Palmer replied, closely monitoring his rate of descent. They were descending through 600 feet in a heavy rain squall.

"On glide slope, on course," the controller advised without inflection.

Brad never took his eyes off Palmer's Phantom. Only seconds to go before they would see the carrier deck. He felt his pulse quicken. God, don't let me fail.

"Phantom ball," Palmer called, omitting his fuel state. He would have to trap on the next pass.

Darting a quick glance toward the carrier, Brad saw the dim meatball, then drifted away from his leader. "Two Oh Eight, ball, one point nine."

Palmer broke away, climbing back into the clouds as the LSO coached Austin. "You're fast and high. Get off the power! Get the power back!"

Brad inched the left throttle back and nudged the stick forward. The ball remained high as he approached the round-down. The Phantom, on the verge of stalling, shuddered as Brad shoved the throttle forward.

"Oh, shheeeit," Lunsford uttered at the moment the F-4 passed over the fantail of the ship.

"Bolter, bolter, bolter!" the LSO said, seeing that the Phantom was going to overshoot the landing zone.

The fighter ballooned over the four arresting-gear wires, went into afterburner on the left engine, touched the deck for a split second, then mushed into the air as Austin fought for control. He could feel the adrenaline shock to his heart. Brad knew that he could not reduce power on the approach because the aircraft would stall and crash.

The crippled fighter struggled for altitude as the LSO called, "Okay, five wire, settle down. You've got the best boarding rate in your squadron."

Determined to stay below the cloud deck, Brad was about to respond when the Air Boss called.

"Joker Two Zero Eight, we're going to barricade you. Two Zero Two, we're shooting a tanker. Anchor overhead at eight thousand and give us a tops report when you break out."

"Two Oh Two, copy," Palmer acknowledged, adding a small amount of power. His low-fuel state was becoming more critical by the second.

Brad leveled off under the ragged overcast. He flew in and out of the scud at 400 feet.

"Two Zero Eight," the Air Boss radioed, "extend downwind. We're rigging the barricade now. Say fuel."

Glancing at the fuel-quantity indicator, Brad could hear Lunsford trying to control his breathing rate.

"Two Zero Eight, one point six."

The radar-controlled approach had consumed more than a thousand pounds of jet fuel.

The LSO conversed with Austin for the next three minutes. He suggested a flat approach, due to the extra speed. Brad felt more comfortable having the carrier in sight during the entire approach.

Dropping out of heavy rain with a single engine, battle damage, overspeed, and low fuel was a carrier pilot's second worst nightmare. The worst would be to find yourself in the same situation at night.

"Two Zero Eight," the Air Boss radioed, "turn inbound. We'll be ready in less than a minute."

"Two Oh Eight, turning inbound."

Lunsford tilted his head back, eyes closed. "Austin, you better get your shit in one bag."

"Ready deck," the Boss radioed from high in Pri-Fly. "Bring it home."

Brad reduced power until the F-4 trembled, then added a nudge of throttle. His breathing became a series of gasps. Feeling claustrophobic, he ripped his oxygen mask loose and sucked in the refreshing ambient air.

"Phantom ball, one point one," Brad reported as he held the yellow-orange meatball a fraction below the centered position.

"Lookin' good," the LSO said calmly. "Stay with it."

Brad tweaked the power back and forth, nursing the damaged fighter toward the rainswept flight deck. He was twenty-five seconds from the round-down when the Phantom again shuddered.

"Keep it together," Lunsford said through gritted teeth.

Focused on survival, Brad blocked out every sensory input except the spot where he intended to land. Watching the deck rush toward him, he concentrated on his lineup and the meatball. He was committed to land on this pass.

Lunsford sucked oxygen. "Oh, merciful God . . . help us."

"Power to idle!" the LSO coached, using body English to work the Phantom down. "Raise your nose!"

Brad waited a second, then slapped the throttle to idle as the round-down flashed under the Phantom. He pulled back on the stick an instant before the fighter crashed into the flight deck, shearing off the nose gear.

A horrendous screech filled the cockpit as the F-4 slammed into the huge nylon-webbed barricade. Both men were savagely thrown forward into their harnesses as the fighter slewed to a sudden stop. The nose-gear assembly bounced over the tangled barricade, ricocheted off the angled deck, and splashed into the sea.

"Sonuvabitch!" Lunsford spat, then let out a sigh of relief. His tongue was bleeding from the inadvertent bite during the controlled crash landing.

Brad quickly shut down the left engine and started releasing himself from his restraints and hoses. He was vaguely aware of the frantic action taking place around his demolished airplane.

Two men scrambled up on the canopies and started pulling away the twisted nylon straps. Seconds later, Austin and Lunsford felt the brisk sea air sweeping over them as the canopies were raised.

A half dozen rescue personnel helped the stunned crew out of their destroyed jet fighter. Brad and Russ were led to a hatch in the island superstructure. They were surprised to see the CO standing inside the opening. He had watched the barricade landing from Pri-fly before rushing down to the flight deck.

"You guys okay?" Dan Bailey asked, clearly awed by the magnitude of the crash landing.

"I've been better," Brad answered, removing his helmet, "but I'm okay . . . physically."

Bailey looked at Lunsford, who had also taken off his helmet. The CO saw the trickle of blood in the corner of the RIO's mouth. "You look like you need to sit down."

"I'm okay, Skipper," Lunsford responded, rubbing his chest where the shoulder harness had bruised him.

The three men turned to look at the remains of Joker 208. The Phantom rested on the remains of its smashed nose cone. Brad noticed that the right main-gear strut had been driven up through the wing. The once sleek, fearsomely aggressive-looking fighter had been reduced to a heap of twisted metal.

The three watched the deck crew place a dolly under the Phantom's nose. Moving swiftly, the aircraft handlers towed the wrecked F-4 to the forward deck-edge elevator, then lowered the aircraft to the hangar bay. Joker 208 would become the squadron hangar queen, providing useful parts for the flyable aircraft.

Bailey turned to Brad and Russ. "I want both of you to report to Doc McCary. We'll get together with Palmer and Hutton later."

"Skipper," Lunsford said, wiping his face with the sleeve of his flight suit, "I don't need to see the flight surgeon. I need to see a shrink."

"You, along with the rest of us," Bailey replied as Nick Palmer's Phantom slammed onto the steel deck and snagged the three wire.

7

Brad Austin toweled himself dry and leaned over the washbasin. His eyes were bloodshot and puffy. The three small bottles of medicinal alcohol Doc McCary had given him, along with the seven hours of restless sleep, had not erased the image of the trees rushing up to kill him.

Walking down the passageway to his stateroom, Brad met his roommate, who was returning from dinner.

"You missed the celebration in the ready room," Harry Hutton said. "Palmer is now a legend in his own mind."

Brad brushed his close-cropped hair with a thin, fraying towel. "He deserves the recognition. He bagged a gomer . . . and got my dumb ass back to the boat."

Grinning mischievously, Hutton shook his head. "That was one hell of a show you put on. Have you been down to see that pile of shit?"

Stepping into the small berthing compartment, Brad set down his dopp kit. "No, and I really don't care to be reminded, okay? I almost killed Russ twice today."

Hutton sensed that his friend, normally easygoing and even-tempered, was not in the mood for jocularity. "Okay. The old man wants to see Nick, Russ, you, and me in his stateroom at nineteen hundred."

"I'll be there," Brad responded, opening his small closet. "What's for chow?"

Hutton sat down and casually propped his feet on the lower-bunk bed. "Chicken fried steak and smashed potatoes."

Brad glanced at Harry. "Smashed potatoes?"

"Wait till you see 'em."

Austin donned a fresh uniform shirt and slipped on a pair of razor-creased khaki trousers. He turned to the small washbasin, picked up his toothbrush, squeezed toothpaste on the bristles, and looked at Hutton's reflection in the mirror. "Something on your mind?"

"As a matter of fact," Harry said uncomfortably, "I do have something I'd like to mention. Two items, actually."

"Shoot," Brad replied, brushing vigorously.

Hutton remained quiet a few moments, contemplating how best to phrase his two topics. "First, the Air Boss didn't want to let you come aboard. He wanted you guys to fly upwind and jump out."

Rinsing his mouth, Brad again glanced at Hutton's image in the mirror. "Well, in retrospect, I would have to agree with him."

Hutton stood, walked over next to Brad, and leaned against the bulkhead. "The CO talked him out of it, because of the sea state. He was afraid both of you would drown before the helo could find you."

Hutton walked to the bunk and stretched out with his hands behind his head. "Bailey told the Air Boss that if there was anyone on the boat who could bring a Fox-4 aboard at a hundred fifty knots, it was you, his marine nutcase."

Brad wiped his mouth. "Nutcase?"

"Look, I'm only repeating what the XO and Carella said during Palmer's ready-room grab-ass."

Brad sat down at his small desk and leaned back. "I believe you had another item on your agenda."

Hutton sat up and put his feet on the deck. "We're friends, right?"

Brad nodded.

"Everyone likes you," Hutton continued, "but face it, you are somewhat of an enigma."

Brad Austin remained silent, showing no outward signs of emotion. For Harry, being serious was unusual and difficult.

"You're a marine fighter jock," Harry said carefully, "in

a navy squadron . . . and you're damn good. You and Palmer, one on one, would be a hell of a match.''

Austin looked at his watch. ''Are you trying to butter me up for a date or something? Throw it on the table.''

''Well,'' Harry began, then hesitated. ''I, along with some of the other guys, think you are pressing too hard.''

''Really?''

''Yeah, I really do. That remark you made a couple of days ago—in the ready room—when Dirty Ernie said something about feeling helpless the time that they had been surrounded by seven MiGs.''

''Go on,'' Brad prompted, leaning forward.

''You said something to the effect that you felt being surrounded was, in reality, just a better opportunity to bag more MiGs. That remark raised a few eyebrows.''

Feeling exasperated, Brad rubbed his sore neck muscles. The violent barricade engagement had whipped his head more severely than any trap he had ever made.

''Harry, let me set the record straight. I am not a warmonger, and I don't get any pleasure out of war, or killing people. I despise wars, and I despise the psychopathic tyrants who perpetrate warfare.

''I enjoy flying, and the Marine Corps spent more than a million dollars to train me to be a fighter pilot. I didn't expect to ever use my special skills, nor did I have a desire to shoot people.''

Hutton raised his hands. ''Enough. I know you better than anyone else, and you—''

''Wait a minute,'' Austin interrupted, feeling a need to vent his frustrations. ''Hear me out. I had my future planned, about ready to go to graduate school, when our illustrious buffoons in the White House decided to jump into this goddamned mess.

''I packed my trash, like I was ordered to do, and marched my ass over here. Now, after all the training and psyching myself emotionally, we have rules of engagement that had to have been developed by morons. Christ, the North Vietnamese have to be rolling on the ground in Hanoi laughing their asses off at our ineptitude.''

"Brad, my man," Hutton said, feeling the same disdain for the combat restrictions, "you can't change the course of this administration, so just take care of number one."

For weeks, the topic of conversation in the ready rooms, wardrooms, and staterooms had been the shackles imposed on combat operations. Many senior military commanders had been calling for maximum-effort attacks on the key components of North Vietnam's war-making machine.

"Harry, I can't shut off my mind and just waddle down the path of least resistance. Jesus, we're sitting here, basically throwing dirt clods at tanks.

"We've got the capability," Austin continued, incensed, "to blast the Communist regime into total submission using conventional weapons. We need to destroy their military complexes, electrical power plants, key industrial sites, petroleum storage facilities, transportation systems, bridges, air-defense installations, and—my favorite topic—airfields.

"But no," Brad persisted, "we have the 'McNamara War.' A goddamn piecemeal, half-assed effort that is confined to bombing a rail-repair shop, a power transformer, a couple of unimportant bridges, a small cement plant, and—if we haven't pissed the commies off too much with those devastating attacks—perhaps a truck depot or laundry facility."

"Hey," Harry said in his seldom-used, serious voice. "You need some chow, and I could go for another dessert. Let's go grab a bite, then we'll see the old man."

"All right," Brad replied, trying to suppress his anger at the fact that the aircrews were having to risk their lives on missions of little or no importance.

"Harry, tell me one thing. Am I crazy? Has my logic missed the brilliance of this scheme, or do I not understand the big picture?"

Hutton placed his hand on the doorknob. "Brad, I understand your frustration. I feel it, too, but I've buried my feelings because I don't have any say in what type of missions we will fly."

"I can't bury my anger." The bitter reply was very unusual for the easygoing pilot. "Harry, think about this.

We can now attack the MiG base at Kep but not the airfield at Phuc Yen. Right?"

"Right," Hutton replied, still holding the knob.

"So the resident genius in Hanoi moves all the operational MiGs to Phuc Yen, since we notified them that the MiG field was off-limits to our pilots. Absolutely brilliant planning."

Hutton remained quiet, then opened the cabin door. "Come on, shipmate, I'll buy you an after-dinner drink on the promenade deck."

Brad smiled at his close friend. "Seriously, Harry, it's a goddamn crime. We bomb targets into oblivion, then Johnson and McNamara decide that we should stand down for three weeks. During that time, as we all know, the gomers rebuild, resupply, and reload their missile launchers, to blow the shit out of us on the next round."

Seething, Brad tried to remain calm. "Aha, now our brilliant strategists in the White House decide—since Uncle Ho isn't cooperating, as usual—that we'll go back and bomb the same goddamn targets."

Brad clenched his fists. "We're being manipulated, and I don't like it. Harry, when you lose good people for stupid, totally preventable, unjustifiable reasons, I sometimes wonder if the real threat is in Hanoi or Washington."

The two men stepped into the passageway, shut the cabin door, and walked in silence for a few seconds.

"I'll tell you one thing," Hutton said in mock seriousness, "I know for certain."

Brad opened the hatch to the main fore-and-aft passageway under the port side of the flight deck. "What?"

"If President Johnson," Hutton said evenly, "had to fly in your backseat, the war would be over in a matter of minutes."

8

The evening movie was just beginning in the squadron ready room when Brad Austin and Harry Hutton reported to the CO's quarters. Brad adjusted his uniform and knocked.

"Come in," Dan Bailey invited, writing at his desk. His stateroom, although designed to accommodate only one person, was larger than the two-man rooms assigned to the junior officers.

Nick Palmer and Russ Lunsford were seated in two metal chairs against the bulkhead. They reminded Brad of two kids who had been sent to the principal's office.

Bailey motioned to his bunk. "Have a seat."

"Congratulations, Nick," Brad said as he and Hutton sat on the neatly made bed. "And thanks for getting us to the fantail."

"The MiG," Palmer replied earnestly, "should have been yours. You had him pegged."

Bailey set down his reports, including the operational loss of Austin's Phantom. He removed his reading glasses and turned to Brad.

"The XO is investigating my accident, so Jocko will handle your incident. He will go over the details with you later this evening."

"Yes, sir," Brad responded, seeing the indelibly imprinted picture of the trees rushing at him. He wondered if the sight of death only a split second away would ever fade from his memory.

At the request of the CO, Austin and Lunsford recounted

the facts pertaining to the encounter with the trees and the succeeding barricade landing.

Palmer and Hutton remained quiet, enthralled with the story. They had seen the tape of Brad's crash landing, shown over and over in the ready room, and still had trouble believing what they had seen. When the landing sequence had been detailed by Austin and Lunsford, the CO shut his cabin door.

"First," Bailey said, sitting back in his chair, "I want to again add my congratulations to Nick and Harry. However, and there always seems to be a 'however,' we need to chat about a few things."

Austin and Hutton nodded. Palmer and Lunsford felt a sense of uneasiness but remained quiet.

"I've addressed most of the squadron this afternoon, but I wanted to talk to the four of you in private." Bailey saw concern beginning to appear in Lunsford's eyes.

"Nothing major, gentlemen. Just a chat about philosophy and survival in our arena."

Brad relaxed, anxious to be candid with his skipper.

"I want to discuss," Bailey began, "our basic mission, how to accomplish the objectives as safely as possible, and the growing unrest and resentment over the current rules of engagement." Bailey's eyes, moving easily from face to face, detected an involuntary twitch on Brad's face.

"We are here to do our jobs as efficiently and safely as possible. Although Nick scored a kill, we can't afford to trade plane for plane. The squadron has two MiGs, but we've lost, for practical purposes, two F-4s."

Forcing himself to remain quiet, Brad shifted forward.

"We are not in a position," the CO said, "to question policy in regard to targeting, or how the course of battle is to be conducted."

Bailey leaned forward and focused on Austin. "Brad, I sense that a part of your aggressiveness is borne out of frustration. Would that be a fair assessment?"

Brad swallowed. "Sir, may I be candid?"

"That's why we are having this little discussion off the record."

"Skipper," Brad hesitated, "if someone could explain to me why we are being placed in a no-win position, I'd like to hear the reason. It's as if we are being told not to win the war, just keep playing the same game and get more people killed."

Hutton and Lunsford exchanged concerned glances. Austin was stepping over the line.

"Sir," Brad continued, "keeping military targets off-limits is insane, or so it seems to me." Austin sighed. "Yes, my frustration level is very high. We could easily flatten Hanoi and Haiphong, mine the harbors, then put a choke hold across their supply line. The war would be over very quickly.

"I keep hearing," Brad continued, "that our leaders in Washington don't want to upset the major Communist powers—the same people who are providing the weapons that are shooting us down."

The stateroom became deathly quiet. Palmer quietly cleared his throat.

Nodding his head in agreement, Bailey directed his words to both crews. "I have to agree with Lieutenant Austin that we are using only a fraction of our military capabilities."

Bailey picked up his pen and flipped it back and forth between his index and middle fingers. "I empathize with Brad—with everyone who shares the resentment for being placed in jeopardy for little or no gain. The four-star commanding our Pacific forces, along with every military commander in the chain of command, is resentful of the needless deaths."

The CO again leaned back, staring distractedly at the overhead before speaking. "I have two points to make. One, we are not in a position to question the politics involved in these decisions. I happen to agree with Brad that the military strategy being formed in the White House is incompetent— morally reprehensible—but I emphasize that we took an oath, reposing of special trust and confidence, to uphold the orders of our commander in chief.

"We will continue to do our jobs," Bailey hesitated,

"and pray that someone intervenes who has the wisdom and fortitude to win . . . or end this debacle."

Hutton glanced at his roommate. Austin appeared to be absorbing the frank conversation with a degree of understanding.

"The second point," Bailey continued, placing his pen down, "ties to the first. We have missions to fly, albeit with questionable targets, but missions just the same."

Inhaling deeply, Bailey gazed at the floor, exhaled, then moved his eyes from man to man. "I expect all of you to continue to be professional leaders, and duty bound. I want you to carry out your duties as safely as possible, and not let personal resentment cloud your logic."

"Yes, sir," Brad and Harry replied.

"Oh, one other item," Bailey said, remembering what he had emphasized to the flight crews in the ready room. "I don't want anyone trolling for MiGs. That is a violation of standing orders, and I will ground anyone who is caught hunting MiGs instead of flying the mission he was assigned."

"Sir," Brad said firmly, "we weren't trolling for MiGs. We'd been sent in to check the weather."

"I'm well aware of that. I reminded the rest of the squadron, and I am simply reminding you."

The silence made Brad uncomfortable.

"Now," Bailey said, standing, "I want all of you to get out of here so I can get some rest. We've got a double strike laid on for tomorrow."

The four junior officers stood when the CO got up from his chair. They respected him as a leader, pilot, and plain old-fashioned good friend.

Opening the door, Bailey turned to his men. "I intend for you to continue flying as a team. You're doing a hell of a job under difficult circumstances."

Brad Austin and Russ Lunsford sat in adjoining seats in the ready room. They had on their flight suits and were taking copious notes about the target combat air patrol they had been assigned. Across the aisle, Lt. Cdr. Lincoln Joshua

"Bull" Durham, the TARCAP mission flight leader, sat with his RIO, Ernie Sheridan. Dirty Ernie, the senior and most experienced radar-intercept officer in the squadron, rotated flying with the senior pilots.

Lincoln Durham, a friendly and sensitive giant of a man, had been an all-American tackle at Grambling College. After a brief stint with the Chicago Bears, Bull Durham had opted to join the navy and become a fighter pilot. The black aviator had graduated from flight school in the top ten percent of his class.

Jack Carella reminded the men about safety, then finished the brief and wished the crews good luck.

Brad and Russ followed Durham and Sheridan out of the ready room and down the passageway to the musty-smelling locker room.

Stepping over the hatch combing, Brad turned to his friend, Bull Durham. "How's your wife doing?" Cordelia Durham had returned to George Washington University to complete her master's degree in political science.

"Fine," Durham replied, working his combination lock. "I had a letter from her day before yesterday. Her studies are going well, but she is concerned about the growing number of war protesters. I guess it's really getting ugly."

Brad opened his locker and grabbed his g suit. "Has she had any problems in regard to you being a fighter pilot?"

"I don't think so. Cordy is not the type to say much about the war, or express an opinion." Durham paused. "Besides, she probably wouldn't tell me if she did—wouldn't want to worry me."

Brad slipped on his snug, inflatable g suit. "When is she graduating?"

Durham zipped his g suit around his waist. "The end of next month. I'm going to try to go home for her graduation, and surprise her."

"That would be nice . . . if you can get off this tub."

"Right."

"Tell her hello from the jarhead." Brad had met Cordelia Durham in Hong Kong during an extended port call. The quiet, gracious woman had flown over with four other squadron wives.

"I'll do that," Durham replied, sitting down to zip the legs of his g suit. He leaned closer to Brad, almost whispering. "Also got word last week that Cordy is pregnant."

Grinning, Brad stuck out his hand. "Congratulations, Papa San."

"Thanks," Durham laughed, shaking Austin's hand. "We're excited, to say the least."

9

Brad and Russ sat in their idling Phantom, waiting to taxi forward when the port blast deflector was lowered. Bull Durham, on the starboard catapult, went to full military power, then selected afterburner. Bright orange flames shot out of the twin tail pipes as the deafening roar swept over the flight deck.

Brad watched his flight leader snap a salute to the cat officer. Four seconds later, the F-4 thundered down the catapult, rotated, settled low over the choppy water, then climbed to the departure altitude.

Nick Palmer, ahead of Brad's Phantom, taxied onto the number two catapult while Jon O'Meara and his RIO, Mario Russo, taxied over the starboard-cat shuttle.

The green-shirted deck crewmen quickly hooked O'Meara's F-4 to the number one cat, then scurried out from under the heavily laden fighter.

Palmer went into afterburner and rocketed down the deck in a repeat of Durham's launch. The blast deflector was immediately lowered, allowing Brad to taxi onto the steaming catapult. He moved forward slowly and stopped when the nose wheel dropped over the shuttle.

Feeling tension taken on his fighter, Brad was coming up on the power when O'Meara's F-4 was fired. The Phantom, carrying a 600-gallon centerline fuel tank, erupted in flames when the fuel cell split open from the g force. The torrent of fuel, ignited by the blazing afterburners, swept the length of the cat track.

"Oh, shit!" Brad exclaimed as his fighter came up to full

throttle. He was afraid to reduce power in the event that his F-4 was fired intentionally, or accidentally.

O'Meara's F-4, trailing twenty feet of orange flames, hurtled off the deck and climbed unsteadily. O'Meara, hearing a frantic call from the Air Boss, jettisoned the ruptured fuel tank. Brad and Russ watched it tumble harmlessly into the water.

Billowing black smoke engulfed Brad's Phantom as the cat officer rushed up and gave him the catapult-suspend signal. Austin could hear Lunsford swearing in the backseat. Brad pulled his power to idle at the same moment the Air Boss yelled over the radio to shoot Austin's F-4.

"Sonuvabitch!" Brad swore, shoving the throttles forward again. The power was passing ninety-six percent when the Phantom squatted down and blasted the length of the catapult track.

"Stay with me, Lunsford!" Brad ordered as the afterburners lighted with a resounding boom. The F-4 settled low over the water, kicking up spray as Brad popped the gear lever up and tweaked the nose down to take advantage of the cushion of air between the Phantom's wings and the water. Lunsford held his breath and gripped the alternate ejection-seat handle between his thighs.

The compressed layer of air, known as ground effect, would allow the fighter to stay in the air until Brad had enough speed to climb. It was not in the book, but Brad knew it was their only chance to salvage the aircraft.

Slowly, Brad nursed the howling Phantom out of ground effect and started climbing. His left hand, holding the throttles in afterburner, was shaking.

"Goddamnit!" Lunsford shouted, gulping oxygen. "We've gotta be out of our goddamn minds."

Brad let the Phantom accelerate before switching to the carrier Strike frequency. He deselected afterburner, then waited while the controller explained to Durham what had happened during the launch.

O'Meara and Russo were holding overhead to trap after the launch was complete. The Air Boss, afraid that Austin's fighter might catch fire and explode, had fired the F-4 off the catapult. The fuel fire had been extinguished with only minor injuries to the deck crewmen.

"Joker Two Oh Three up," Brad radioed, calming himself while Lunsford, ranting over the intercom, continued to cast disparaging remarks about the Air Boss and his mother.

"Bring it aboard, Brad," Bull Durham acknowledged. "You doin' all right?"

"Roger that," Austin replied as evenly as possible. He was grateful that no one could see his shaking hands. "I have you at one o'clock."

"Copy," Durham said, then added, "you are now Dash Three."

Brad clicked his mike twice and spoke to his RIO. "Russ, let's get it together."

"I'm gonna kill that sonuvabitch," Lunsford responded, breathing unevenly. "He fired us before we were ready."

"Calm down, for Christ's sake. He was just doing his job . . . and we need to do ours, okay?"

Exhaling sharply, Lunsford looked at Bull Durham's airplane. "I guaran-goddamn-tee you one thing."

"What's that?" Brad asked absently as he approached the two Phantoms.

"You are never going to pull the power back again unless the cat officer is standing in front of the goddamn airplane."

Brad started to respond, then decided to discuss the incident after his RIO had had an opportunity to calm himself. At the moment, they needed to concentrate on their mission.

The three-ship formation climbed in silence to the KA-3B Skywarriors waiting for them, checked in on the tanker frequency, and then topped off their fuel tanks.

Departing the Whales, Joker Flight checked in with Red Crown and headed toward Thanh Hoa. The target would be an industrial site heavily defended by surface-to-air missiles and antiaircraft batteries. The three F-4s separated into a loose combat spread, with Austin in the middle 1,000 feet behind and 500 feet higher than Jokers 1 and 2.

Durham entered a wide orbit at 16,000 feet and listened

to another flight of Phantoms check in with the leader of the strike group.

Ninety seconds later, the lead A-4 pilot commenced his run-in from the southwest of Thanh Hoa. The sky suddenly filled with exploding AAA fire and SAMs. The fourth Skyhawk pulled off the burning target as the flight leader of the second group released his ordnance and snapped into a ninety-degree climbing turn.

Brad, constantly scanning the sky and ground, caught a glimpse of the number three Skyhawk at the instant it was hit by a SAM. The A-4 disintegrated in a brilliant fireball, raining flaming debris on the target. The pilot never had a chance to eject.

"MiGs!" Ernie Sheridan shouted over the radio. "Four MiG-17s at three o'clock low!"

The camouflaged MiGs, concealed by a thin cloud cover at 3,000 feet, had slipped into the area undetected. Passing 2,000 feet, the enemy fighters had been seen by the radar picket ship.

"This is Red Crown! We hold bogies climbing over the target. Repeat, we have bogies over the target."

Durham acknowledged the frantic call and rolled toward the rapidly approaching MiGs. "Jokers engaging! Drop tanks!" The three Phantom pilots simultaneously punched off their centerline fuel tanks.

Durham shoved the nose down, rolling to the right, and lined up for a head-on pass. The three fighter pilots saw the MiGs' 23mm cannons wink at them as the F-4s slashed through the Communists' formation. The MiG pilots broke in two directions, one section going low, the other two aircraft going high.

Bull Durham elected to go for the two pilots who had pulled up. "Hard starboard, goin' burner!"

The high MiGs went into a slow weave as the F-4s shot skyward. Durham, recognizing they were in danger of overshooting the MiGs, pulled his power to idle. "Jokers, go idle!"

Austin and Palmer had anticipated the call as they rapidly closed on the MiGs. They retarded their throttles and cracked open the speed brakes a few inches. Lunsford and Hutton were twisting their heads left and right, checking their sixes for the other two bogies.

"I'll take the one on the left!" Durham announced, then fired a heat-seeking Sidewinder. The MiG pilots, seeing the missile ignite, pulled into a diving high-g turn. The Sidewinder, unable to guide during the evasive maneuver, shot over the MiG and accelerated out of sight.

"The two on the deck," Hutton radioed in gasps, "are raising their noses!"

"Jokers, Showboat is engaging the low gomers!" The second Phantom target combat air patrol was entering the aerial fray.

"Roger, roger," Durham panted, violently rolling his Phantom to follow the diving MiGs. "They're running for their sanctuary . . . burners!"

The MiG-17s, flying close to 430 knots, were heading straight for Phuc Yen. The MiG pilots, diving steeply, had gained the knowledge that the U.S. missiles had a difficult time locking onto targets close to the ground.

The downside for the MiG pilots was the problem their aircraft had flying at high speeds close to the terrain. Not having hydraulically powered flight controls, the Vietnamese pilots had very little control authority. The faster they flew, the more aerodynamic resistance they encountered. Since the MiG pilot could not perform abrupt maneuvers, they were forced to run for safety once the Americans had the advantage.

"Cover us, Brad," Durham radioed as he bottomed out 100 feet above the ground. "Nick, take the one on the right."

Two seconds later, Palmer got a tone and squeezed the trigger. Nothing happened. "Sonuvabitch!" The Sidewinder remained on the launch rail while Palmer frantically checked his armament switches.

"Jokers!" the Showboat flight leader called. "You have two MiGs on your six . . . the ones who went low. We can't shoot—they're directly between us." Showboat Lead was afraid his missiles would hit Joker Flight.

Flying at 2,000 feet, Brad rolled his fighter, holding it inverted. "Joker Three is rolling in on the trailing gomers."

Durham heard the insistent growl of the Sidewinder tone. He fired the missile at minimum range, then experienced a chill as red tracers slashed by his canopy. The heat-seeking projectile arced up, then nosed down and flew into the ground.

Swearing to himself, Durham keyed his radio switch. "Nick, break hard starboard . . . NOW! Nose coming up."

Brad was closing on the trailing MiGs at 600 knots when the Showboat flight leader and his wingman fired their Sidewinders. Seeing the two smoke trails, Brad yanked his screaming fighter into an 8-g vertical climb. He rolled to keep the enemy in sight, then saw the trailing MiG-17 disintegrate and impact in the middle of a 37mm AAA emplacement. The other MiG pilot raced for the safety of Phuc Yen.

Keying his mike, Brad spoke icily. "Showboat, Joker Three. I'm on the same team, guy."

"Sorry, didn't see you."

Brad pulled through the top of his evasive maneuver and searched for Durham and Palmer. He spotted the two Phantoms at the same instant his flight leader called.

"Joker Three, rejoin and let's cover the strike group."

"Joker Three is at your five, closing," Brad replied, searching the sky for other MiGs.

The three F-4s accelerated to Mach 1.1 as they chased after the departing strike aircraft. The sky erupted with antiaircraft fire as they passed due north of Thanh Hoa. The white bursts looked like a fireworks display.

"SAMs! SAMs!" Harry Hutton yelled, blocking out Ernie Sheridan's warning call. "We've got SAMs at two and three o'clock!"

"Hard starboard!" Durham ordered, trying to outturn the missiles. The SAMs looked like flying telephone poles as they rapidly accelerated.

Brad was 300 feet behind Durham when the first SAM, turning hard, exploded next to his flight leader's right wing.

The F-4 flipped over on its back, then slowly rolled right side up. The second missile exploded above and behind Nick Palmer.

Momentarily paralyzed, Brad flew into the exploding debris from the first SAM. He and Russ Lunsford felt a vicious jolt, then became disoriented in the fog that had instantaneously filled the cockpit.

Seeing the master caution light glowing, Brad snapped his tinted helmet visor up. He quickly scanned his annunciator panel, noting that they were not in imminent danger, then searched for Durham and Palmer.

He was shocked to see Bull Durham's Phantom trailing a sheet of flames. "Joker One, you're on fire!"

There was no response from the burning fighter.

Palmer radioed a second later. "Bull, you've got fire—you're trailing fire from your belly!"

Still no answer from the blazing F-4.

"He's lost his radio," Lunsford said, noting the strange noise that had invaded their cockpit. He looked around, taking inventory, then stared in awe. "Brad! You've got a chunk of your canopy missing!"

Tilting his head back, Brad saw the jagged, grapefruit-sized hole at the forward right side of his canopy bow. His eyes darted back to Durham. "Joker One, do you copy?"

Brad's padded earphones remained quiet a moment before Palmer called.

"Three, you hanging in?"

Looking closer at his annunciator panel, Brad analyzed the lighted anomalies. One generator had been knocked off the line and numerous circuit breakers had popped. Austin reset the generator, then pushed in the circuit breakers. "Yeah, Nick, we're okay."

Durham's aircraft was burning furiously as the three Phantoms passed over the beach. Palmer and Austin closed in on their flight leader. Durham was busy, trying to get as far out to sea as possible. Each second meant a better chance for survival.

Glancing at Ernie Sheridan, Brad was astounded to see him leaning as far forward as he could wedge himself. The fire had engulfed the fuselage, melting the back of the RIO's canopy. Durham was aware they were on fire.

"Brad," Palmer radioed, "come up Red Crown."

"Switchin' Red Crown."

"Red Crown, Joker Two Oh Seven, emergency!" Palmer radioed, moving a safe distance away from Durham's intensely burning Phantom.

"Joker, say emergency."

"Red Crown, our flight leader is on fire," Palmer began, then stopped when the left engine of Durham's F-4 exploded, blowing off the tail.

Horrified, Brad held his breath while the blazing Phantom tumbled end over end. A half second later, Durham and Sheridan ejected from the wreckage of their fighter.

Nick Palmer banked steeply to the left to circle his former flight leader. Palmer was now Joker 1, with Brad as Dash 2. "Correction, Red Crown. They jumped over the side. We are orbiting over them now."

"We hold you in radar contact," the controller responded in a reassuring tone, "three miles offshore. We have helos on the way."

"Copy, Red Crown," Palmer replied, then talked to Austin. "Joker Two, say fuel state."

"Five point one," Brad replied, spotting activity along the shore. He watched Durham and Sheridan splash into the water. Both men quickly shed their parachutes and inflated their life rafts.

Completing another 360-degree turn, Brad was startled to see a North Vietnamese patrol boat leave a small dock. "Joker One, we've got a boat coming toward Bull and Ernie." Another minute passed as the patrol vessel continued toward the downed crew.

"Red Crown," Palmer radioed. "How far away are the helos? We've got company coming offshore."

"Stand by."

Brad talked to Lunsford during the pause. "Russ, I've got an idea. Over this cool water, we might be able to get a Sidewinder to lock onto the heat from that boat's engine."

"Jesus H. Christ," Lunsford said in a resigned voice.

"Do you lie awake at night figuring out new ways to get us killed?"

"Joker, Red Crown. The helos will be overhead in eight to ten minutes."

Palmer calculated the speed and distance of the fast-moving patrol boat. "We don't have that long."

Brad looked down and keyed his mike. "Nick, I'm going down after the boat."

"Are you crazy?" Hutton said before Palmer could reply. "You don't have any guns. They'll blow your ass out of the sky on the first pass."

"Roger," is all that Palmer said. He understood Brad Austin. They were both highly trained, motivated aerial hunters. When the pilots were confronted with what appeared to be an insurmountable obstacle, the two aviators would improvise to accomplish their objective. They were determined to take care of their brotherhood.

Austin carefully checked his armament panel and switches, selected HEAT, and rolled the Phantom inverted into a plummeting split-S maneuver. Brad pulled out of the dive at two hundred feet and circled the patrol craft, closing from the stern of the vessel.

Indicating 460 knots, Brad eased down to fifty feet above the water. Two machine guns opened fire from the patrol boat a second before Brad heard the familiar Sidewinder tone. He squeezed the trigger and watched in fascination as the missile climbed away, tucked down, then leveled out a fraction of a second before it slammed into the boat. The stern of the vessel lifted out of the water as the entire bridge area was blown off the hull.

"Shit hot!" Palmer shouted. "Fantastic!"

Brad snatched the stick back, rolling the aircraft inverted to view the devastation below. The patrol boat, now out of control, was heeling to port and rapidly decelerating. Austin rolled upright to check the whereabouts of Palmer's F-4, then rolled inverted again. The heavily damaged patrol boat was almost dead in the water, listing to port.

"Red Crown," Palmer radioed exuberantly, "my wingman has eliminated our problem."

"Copy, Joker. We have a tanker at your one one zero for fifty."

Palmer checked his fuel-quantity indicator. The gauge showed 4,700 pounds. "Joker Two, go gas up, and come back and relieve us."

"On our way," Brad replied, shoving his throttles forward to full military power. Passing 9,000 feet, Austin and Lunsford heard the rescue-helicopter pilots check in with Red Crown and Palmer.

Brad continued to monitor the frequency, anxious for the rescue effort to be successful. Three minutes later, Austin heard Nick Palmer tell Red Crown that the marine helicopters were over the downed crew.

Palmer circled another minute while he watched Durham and Sheridan struggle into their rescue collars, then radioed that Joker 1 was departing for the tanker.

10

Brad leveled the Phantom at 22,000 feet and extended his aerial fueling probe. He cast a glance to his right, then froze at the same time Lunsford saw the damaged refueling nozzle. The end of the tube was crushed and the tip was bent outward at an odd angle.

"Uh, Brad, we're out of the refueling business."

"I noticed."

Austin retracted the bent refueling probe, wondering what other damage they might have incurred from the missile explosion. He tilted his head back and inspected the hole in his canopy, then checked the oxygen control panel. The gauge, which indicated fifteen percent full, was showing a steady depletion.

Brad glanced at all of his instruments, then keyed the intercom. "You ready for some more good news?"

"Don't tell me anything," Lunsford said, waving his hands from side to side. "I don't want to hear anything bad. Just get our asses back to the boat."

Brad glanced at the oxygen gauge again. "We are going to be out of oxygen very shortly . . . must have severed a line."

Lunsford exhaled. "That isn't a problem—we'll be on the boat in a few minutes. Don't bother me with category-three bullshit."

"Hey," Brad responded, "I just wanted you to know what's going on, so you wouldn't be surprised."

Brad called the tanker pilot, explained that they could not

refuel, then called the carrier. "Checkerboard Strike, Joker Two Oh Three."

"Joker Two Zero Three, Strike."

"Two Oh Three is inbound with Two Oh Seven in trail. Two Oh Six went in the water, and the crew has been rescued."

Brad scanned the horizon while he waited for a reply. The dense black clouds and towering, fluffy white cumulus formations indicated the presence of heavy thunderstorms south of the carrier.

"Joker Two Zero Three," the controller said with a different pitch in his voice, "is directed to hit the tanker and marshal one five miles, angels one six on the three six zero." The instructions told Brad to enter a holding pattern fifteen nautical miles from the carrier at 16,000 feet. He would be due north of the ship.

"Checkerboard, Two Oh Three has damage. We are unable to tank, and I can't hold very long."

"Copy. Stand by."

While he waited for instructions, Brad studied the lightning flashes in the distance. The black clouds appeared to illuminate from within.

"Two Zero Three," the controller said over the unusual background noise, "be advised that we have a fouled deck. Your signal is bingo to Da Nang."

Brad stared at his fuel-quantity indicator. He might make Da Nang Air Base if he flew directly to the airfield. The only problem, Brad told himself, was that he would have to fly through the menacing-looking thunderstorms to reach Da Nang. There had to be another option.

"Checkerboard, I'm not sure we can make Da Nang. Do you have an estimate as to when the deck will be open?"

"Negative," the controller responded over the background noise. "A Zuni rocket ignited and hit two aircraft. We have a major fire on the flight deck. My guess would be forty-five minutes to an hour—possibly longer—before we can recover aircraft again."

"Copy," Brad replied as he sucked the last of the oxygen supply. "Two Oh Three is bingo Da Nang."

"Sonuva . . . bitch!" Lunsford exclaimed, feeling his neck and shoulder muscles tighten. "I must've been born under a goddamn curse. What have I done to deserve this shit?"

Adjusting the throttles for maximum fuel conservation, Brad snapped one side of his oxygen mask loose. He studied the thunderstorms blocking their only option. "Russ, better strap in tight. We've got to go straight through those boomers to make Da Nang."

Both men knew they did not have the fuel or oxygen to climb over the raging storms, let alone ascend to the Phantom's optimum cruise altitude of 39,000 feet.

"Have we got enough fuel?" Lunsford asked, snapping his mask loose.

Looking at the fuel-quantity indicator, Brad quickly calculated the distance to Da Nang against time of fuel exhaustion. "It'll be close."

"Goddamnit," Lunsford swore over the intercom. "Why me? Why does all this happen to me?"

Brad spoke slowly. "Hey, why don't you go see Scary McCary and get some tranquilizers or something? You're driving me crazy."

Lunsford bolted straight up in his seat. "I'm driving you crazy? You gotta be kiddin' me—I'm driving you crazy. I'm flying with a lunatic jarhead who goes through trees and shoots air-to-air missiles at boats." Feeling the onset of hypoxia, Lunsford sucked in a breath of air. "I'm driving *you* crazy . . . Jesus."

Brad chuckled to himself, then remained quiet a couple of minutes, hoping Lunsford would calm down. The RIO was still muttering to himself when they flew into the edge of the ominous-looking storm.

"Here we go," Brad announced as the Phantom was swallowed by the angry black clouds. He increased the cockpit lighting to maximum, then peered up at the hole in his canopy. The lashing rain flowed over the opening as if it did not exist.

The F-4 bounced and rocked as Brad fought to keep the fighter level. Lightning flashed, temporarily blinding him, a second before the aircraft was pounded by baseball-sized hail. Brad fixated on the engine instruments, fearful that the intense combination of hail and torrential rain might cause the engines to flame out.

"Holy shit!" Lunsford shouted as the Phantom shot upward in a powerful updraft, then slammed downward. "I'm beginning to feel light-headed."

Although their oxygen had been depleted, Brad had remained at 22,000 feet to conserve fuel. "Hang on," he said, glancing at his fuel-quantity indicator. "We'll be starting down in a few minutes." Austin also felt light-headed from the lack of oxygen at their altitude.

Gritting his teeth, Brad worked the stick and rudders to keep the aircraft level. Lightning flashed almost constantly as the Phantom sliced through the heavy rain and pounding hail.

Suddenly, the pitch-black darkness began showing signs of light. The severe turbulence slowly began to dissipate, and the hail ceased to bounce off the fighter. Seconds later, they flew out of the dark storm cell. The crew had an ephemeral moment of calm before they plunged headlong into another intense storm.

Looking on his kneeboard, Brad found the radio frequency for Da Nang approach control. He also noted that their fuel was dangerously low. Brad tuned the radio and rechecked his fuel gauge. It read 1,100 pounds.

"Da Nang approach, Joker Two Oh Three."

"Two Zero Three, Da Nang approach."

Brad winced when a bolt of lightning appeared to hit the starboard wing tip. "We're a navy Fox-4 with damage and emergency fuel."

"Roger, squawk three two five two and say angels."

Brad set the transponder code in his IFF and keyed his radio. "Thirty-two fifty-two, two two thousand."

"Joker Two Zero Three," the controller responded dryly, "I have you in radar contact. Be advised that we have severe thunderstorm activity in all quadrants."

Feeling his blood chill, Brad glanced at his fuel gauge and steeled himself for the instrument approach. Lunsford, who was swearing a blue streak in the backseat, was preparing for a controlled ejection.

The approach radar monitor waited for the gravity of the situation to sink in, then keyed his mike again. "Two Zero Three, continue present heading."

"Copy approach," Brad replied, checking his TACAN readout. The distance-measuring equipment broke lock twice, then registered forty-two nautical miles to Da Nang. Austin had purposely remained high in order to make an idle descent to the runway.

Swallowing to moisten his dry throat, Brad wrestled the flight controls to keep the bouncing fighter under control. The jarring turbulence increased as they neared the coastline, turning minutes into hours.

"Joker Two Zero Three, descend to seven thousand and turn left one six zero degrees."

Brad complied with the instructions, then switched to the ground-control approach radar operator when the Phantom descended through 14,000 feet. The unflappable GCA controller was a savvy veteran who had helped many pilots in the same predicament.

"Two Zero Three," the reassuring voice said, "keep it clean. I'll call one mile so you can dirty up."

Brad would leave his flaps and landing gear up to keep the Phantom aerodynamically clean.

"Descend to three thousand," the calming voice instructed. "Increase your rate of descent."

Looking at his altimeter and distance to Da Nang, Brad judged that adding another 500 feet per minute to his descent rate would place him at 3,000 feet two miles from the end of the runway. He increased pressure on the stick, checking the increase in descent rate on his vertical velocity indicator.

Taking a look at the fuel indicator, Brad felt a burning sensation in the pit of his stomach. The gauge showed 300 pounds of fuel remaining. Oh, God, please let us make it to the runway.

The rain increased as the Phantom jolted through another powerful storm cell. Passing 5,000 feet, Brad began slowing the steep descent. He was flying faster than he normally would at this point in an instrument letdown, but speed was his only chance to reach the runway.

"You're three miles from touchdown," the radar controller said in a conversational manner. "You're right in the ball park."

Brad shallowed the rate of descent even further, bleeding off airspeed. He heard the GCA operator call two miles as the F-4 settled onto the glide slope.

"You're up and on glide path," the controller radioed, then added, "come left five degrees . . . a mile and a half."

Cracking open the speed brakes, Brad glanced at the fuel-quantity indicator. It read zero. His palms were sweaty as he fully extended the speed brakes.

"One mile," the calm voice said, "dirty up."

Without acknowledging, Brad partially extended his flaps, waited until the airspeed decelerated to 220 knots, then dropped the landing gear and lowered full flaps at 170 knots. The Phantom leveled off for a moment.

"Going slightly above glide path," the controller said as Austin saw the runway lights through the pouring rain.

Transitioning to the landing attitude, Brad keyed his mike. "Runway in sight."

"Roger, take over visually," the controller replied with a hint of pride in his voice, "and have a good afternoon, gentlemen."

"Thanks," Brad responded as he felt the rain coming through the hole in the canopy. He added power to stabilize his speed at 135 knots, crossed the end of the runway, then pulled the throttles to idle as the main gears touched the rain-soaked ground.

The tires, inflated to 225 pounds per square inch, hydroplaned a moment before slicing through the pools of water on the runway. The Phantom rapidly decelerated, sending showers of water spraying in every direction.

"Thank you, God," Lunsford exclaimed. "Austin can take over now."

Brad rolled out, switched to ground control as he turned

off the runway, then added a nudge of power to taxi. The left engine surged, then flamed out, followed twelve seconds later by the right engine.

Ignoring the steady rain pouring on him, Brad keyed his radio. "Da Nang ground, Navy Two Oh Three has flamed out on the taxiway."

Lunsford, slack-jawed with a wide-eyed expression, sagged in his straps. "Un-goddamn-believable."

11

The muddy jeep came to a stop in front of the Da Nang Officers' Club. Brad and Russ got out, thanked the staff sergeant for the lift from Operations, then studied the air base and surrounding area.

Da Nang, the second-largest airfield in Vietnam, had been located near the ocean. The unspoiled white beaches were right out of a travel brochure.

Soaked by the suffocating heat and humidity, Brad looked to the northeast. The rain had abated, affording him a spectacular view of "Monkey Mountain" protruding from the sea. He paused a moment, following two fighters banking over China Beach.

The air base was teeming with aircraft from all the services. Marine F-4s and A-4 Skyhawks, flying close air support and strike missions, were constantly taking off or landing. Scores of helicopters clattered over on their way to the "Marble Mountain" airfield.

Concertina wire was strung on both sides of the chain-link perimeter fence that surrounded the busy air base. People in every conceivable style of dress and uniform scurried about the base in a strange disorderliness.

Turning to Lunsford, Brad pulled a piece of paper out of his pocket and noted the name. Master Sergeant Horace Grevers. "Let's go to the package store first. Grevers is a scotch drinker who is going to be mighty surprised before he leaves the GCA shack."

Brad had phoned the radar controller who had talked him down. The sergeant was still on duty, but a coworker had told Brad that the veteran controller liked scotch. The grateful pilot was going to send a case of premium spirits to his new friend.

The two men walked into the small package store, paid for a case of Dewar's, made arrangements to have the scotch delivered to the radar site, then headed for the officers' club and a cold beer.

Austin had had their Phantom towed to the sprawling ramp where the divert aircraft were parked. The F-4 had been refueled, and a tarp had been secured over the front canopy. Both men had left their flight gear in the cockpits.

Brad had sent a message to the carrier from Operations, detailing the extent of the damage to Joker 203. The return message directed him to fly back to the carrier the following morning. They had an overhead time of 0745.

Walking into the air-conditioned club, Brad and Russ saw the sign that read "Leave Guns Here." The rungs were full of handguns, along with one M-16 rifle. Austin and Lunsford had left their .38-caliber revolvers in the Phantom with their other gear.

The two men sat down at the bar and ordered beers. Lunsford insisted that the beers be ice-cold. A comely young Vietnamese waitress opened the bottles and smiled when she set them down.

"Thanks," Brad said, drinking half the contents in one gulp. He took another sip, then spread his elbows on the smooth bar. Looking around the club, he waited a few seconds before turning to his RIO. "What's eating you? The war, or my flying?"

Tipping his bottle up, Lunsford took a long swig and set the bottle back on the bar. He turned to face Brad. "A little of both, I guess. Actually, it isn't you. I wanted to be a pilot, but I washed out in the last phase of training . . . at Kingsville."

Taken aback, Brad turned to his friend. "Jesus, Russ, I had no idea. I'm sorry."

"Don't worry about it," Lunsford replied, picking up his beer. "At any rate, I thought that being an RIO would be the next best thing."

Brad sat quietly while Russ took another drink, then continued. "Sitting in the backseat, after having flown jets, is more difficult than I had thought it would be. It drives me crazy, not having any control. Especially when I get the shit scared out of me."

Nodding in agreement, Brad took a drink.

"It's like riding in the backseat of a race car," Lunsford continued. "You're going like a bat out of hell, but you don't have any control over the outcome . . . if the wheels come off."

Lunsford set his empty bottle on the bar. "Anyway, I guess it's cumulative in my case. It has really been getting to me."

Brad swiveled and leaned against the bar. "Russ, it scares the hell out of me, too. Now that I think about it, I see your point. I'm so busy physically controlling the airplane, I don't have time to think about all the things that might go wrong, or to worry about what the guy in the front seat is going to do."

They both ordered another beer and leaned on the bar. Brad understood Lunsford's feelings. "Russ, do you want to fly with someone else?"

The pause hung in the air. "No," Lunsford answered, turning his head to face Brad. "You're goddamn good— one of the best I've ever seen. I have a lot of confidence in you, you asshole, but I just go into hyper mode when the shit hits the fan, or you pull one of your stunts."

They looked at each other and both laughed, breaking the tension between them.

"Shit," Lunsford said, "you sank a goddamned patrol boat with an air-to-air missile, flew my ass through one of the worst storms I have ever seen, then landed in a downpour and flamed out. No, I don't want to fly with anyone else. With your kind of luck, you don't need to be good."

Brad laughed. "What d'ya mean?"

"God must have an entire committee assigned to keep your dumb ass out of trouble."

"Well," Brad said, grinning, "they aren't doing a very good job. Look who I have for a backseater."

Brad Austin awakened, startled from his nightmare. He looked at his watch, trying to focus his bloodshot eyes. It read 0540. He slumped back in the metal bunk bed, thinking about the frightening dream.

His Phantom had been spinning out of control, inverted, spewing flaming fuel over downtown Hanoi, and the ejection seat would not fire. He had been yanking at the face curtain when he woke. Brad ran his tongue around his stale mouth, tasting the onions in the fried rice that he had eaten at midnight.

His bladder suddenly reminded him of the number of beers he had consumed. Brad swung his legs over the side of the upper bunk, then jumped down, landing unsteadily on Lunsford's flight boots.

"Goddamnit," Austin swore as he lost his balance and fell on top of his RIO. "Sorry."

Lunsford only groaned as Brad regained his footing and headed for the latrine at the end of the Quonset hut.

Upon returning, Brad attempted to talk Lunsford awake. That effort had no effect on the inebriated RIO. Austin finally aroused Lunsford by pulling him up to a sitting position, then helping him to the latrine. Brad could see that he had to take command of the situation if they were going to make their overhead time at the carrier.

"Okay, Russ," Brad said, sitting the lethargic man in the single shower, "this is for your own good."

Lunsford leaned over, slumping against the corner of the stall, while Brad pointed the shower head away and adjusted the temperature of the water. Aiming the stream of luke-warm water a foot above his RIO's head, Brad stepped back.

"Jesus!" Lunsford spluttered, sitting upright. "You son of a bitch!" He crawled out of the shower and leaned against the side.

"It was either this," Brad said, turning off the water, "or

carry you to the airplane. We gotta be wheels in the well by oh seven hundred.''

"You're a complete asshole, Austin.''

"That may be,'' Brad said, reaching down to help Lunsford to his feet, "but we've got an overhead time to meet.''

Brad walked his hungover RIO back to his bunk, assisted him in getting his flight boots on, then lifted him back to his feet. "Can you walk?'' Brad asked, holding Lunsford by his arm.

Russ lurched forward two steps. "Yeah, I think so.''

Lunsford wobbled toward the entrance, stopping to kick the bunk bed of the two air-force fighter pilots they had met the night before. "Time to get up, girls. Don't you know there's a war on?''

Brad Austin taxied the Phantom behind two marine KC-130 Herculeses. The lumbering, four-engine giants were part of a four-plane detachment from VMGR-152 that provided aerial refueling for the strike aircraft.

Brad had carefully preflighted the Phantom, noting no safety or flight discrepancies. Without oxygen, the crew would fly below 10,000 feet. Brad had found four small holes in Joker 203, one of which had severed the oxygen line. The other three holes, along with the damaged refueling probe, would not pose any risk during the flight to the carrier.

The only concern had been the hole in the canopy. Brad had inspected the damage, concluding that the canopy would make it to the carrier, since it had survived a pounding hailstorm.

"You feeling any better?'' Brad asked as the tower cleared the tankers to take off.

"Yeah, a little better,'' Lunsford answered, almost dozing. "Could we, just this one time, fly straight and level . . . with no g's?''

Watching the first Hercules commence its takeoff roll, Brad chuckled over the intercom. "Hey, party-time guy, that wouldn't be any fun.''

"I had enough fun last night to last a lifetime."

Brad watched the second KC-130 start its roll. "Okay, granny, we'll do a little sight-seeing. Our overhead has been changed to zero eight hundred."

"Eight o'clock?"

"That's right," Brad answered, taxiing to the hold short line. "We also have a note in Ops thanking us for the hooch."

"Hooch?"

"Yes, that's what it said," Brad answered, checking his flight controls and engine instruments. "Sergeant Grevers extended an invitation to drop in anytime."

"Yeah," Lunsford replied, settling his helmet on the headrest. "This is the last goddamned hole I would visit."

Brad keyed his mike. "Da Nang tower, Navy Two Oh Three is ready to roll."

Three army helicopters clattered over the runway before the tower controller spoke. "Navy Two Zero Three, cleared for takeoff."

Taxiing onto the runway, Austin advanced the throttles to full military power. After rolling 100 feet, Brad selected afterburner and felt the combined kick of 34,000 pounds of thrust.

The Phantom lifted off smoothly as Brad started a gentle climb. He deselected afterburner and set the power at ninety-two percent.

"Navy Two Zero Three, contact departure."

"Wilco, Two Oh Three," Brad replied, setting the departure control frequency. "Departure, Navy Two Oh Three with you. I have a request."

"Two Zero Three," the deep, gravelly voice replied, "go ahead."

"I'd like to stay low," Brad said, leveling the fighter at 1,000 feet, "and take a look at the coastline before we depart for the boat."

"Cleared as requested. Recommend that you remain at least one mile offshore."

Brad gently walked the throttles back. "Wilco, Navy Two Oh Three."

The radar controller cleared them off the frequency and Austin set the power for a leisurely cruise at 260 knots. They could see smoke rising from the jungle canopy as marine F-4s and A-4 Skyhawks pounded two enemy locations.

Passing Vung Chon May, Brad keyed his intercom. "Russ, this area would be a great place to build a resort. I can picture hotels, condos, and golf courses."

Looking along the scenic shoreline, Lunsford could visualize the possibilities for development. "I don't think we'll ever see it in our lifetime. War is a way of life for these people, and I expect they will continue fighting far into the future."

Brad gazed at the city of Hue. "You're right, and it's pathetic. Hundreds of thousands of human beings down there blowing the shit out of each other, when they could be building resorts." Brad looked out at the rising pillars of smoke. "We all have to be somewhere."

Lunsford watched a marine Phantom roll in on a target, hurtle toward the ground, drop a load of bombs, and climb for safety. "Homo sapiens—we're the most intelligent species on the planet."

"Yeah," Brad replied, peering at Quang Tri. "Makes you wonder, doesn't it?"

Brad turned the Phantom toward the sea and started a climbing turn. Passing 3,000 feet, he spotted a navy destroyer on the horizon. The ship was moving slowly, barely leaving a wake. "Russ, you up for a little air show?"

"Ah, shit," Lunsford spat. "I knew it. I knew you couldn't go more than a couple of minutes without doing something stupid."

"Come on," Brad responded, lowering the nose. "Think how boring it must be for the guys stuck out here on these ships. They could use a little excitement."

Looking around the right side of Austin's helmet, Lunsford could see the destroyer. "What happened to my smooth, no-g flight back to the boat?"

"You can get a straight and level on an airliner."

Lunsford looked at Brad's canopy. "Let's not screw around with a hole in the canopy."

"It made it through the hailstorm," Brad responded, then added, "so I don't believe a tight turn and roll is going to have much effect."

"Bullshit . . ."

Brad shoved the throttles forward and leveled the Phantom at 100 feet above the water. He watched the destroyer rapidly fill his windshield. Brad waited until he was abeam the port side, then wrapped the screaming Phantom into a 450-knot circle around the ship.

Tilting his head back, Lunsford could see the sailors rushing to the starboard side of the destroyer. "They're waving . . . and pouring out on deck."

Concentrating on holding his altitude, Brad returned to his starting point, snapped the fighter wings level, raised the nose slightly, and executed a flawless four-point roll. The maneuver was immediately followed by a vertical rolling climb in afterburner.

Lunsford's stomach let him know that it was time for a serious talk with his pilot. "I'm about to toss that goddamn fried rice."

"Okay, nice and easy."

Lunsford breathed slowly, looking out at the hazy horizon. "Oh, the roar of the crowd and the smell of grease-paint. Why don't you put in a request for the Blue Angels?"

"Already have," Brad replied, easing the Phantom's nose down. He leveled off, checked his TACAN for the position of the carrier, then called the ship. "Checkerboard Strike, Joker Two Oh Three."

"Joker Two Zero Three, Strike. You are cleared for the break." The break was a pass up the starboard side of the carrier, followed by a high-g, knife-edged turn (break) to position the aircraft downwind on the port side of the ship.

"Strike, my RIO is not feeling well. How about a straight in?"

A slight pause followed.

"You didn't have to announce that to the whole goddamned world,'' Lunsford sighed. ''I'm going to be laughed out of the ready room.''

''Hey,'' Brad replied, slowing the Phantom. ''You're the one who requested no more yankin' and bankin'.''

''That's approved,'' the controller radioed. ''Switch to the LSO.''

''Wilco.''

Lunsford swore again, then remained quiet as they rapidly approached the carrier.

Brad chatted with the landing-signal officer, slowed the F-4, extended the flaps, then lowered the landing gear and tail hook. Spotting the lighted landing aid, Brad called the ball and flew a smooth pass to the number three wire.

Following the directions of the flight-deck petty officer, Brad taxied to a spot on the bow where the blue-shirted aircraft handlers checked the wheels and chained down the Phantom.

A number of deck personnel stared and pointed at the hole in the canopy. Brad shut down the engines and both men raised their canopies. Toby Kendall scrambled up the side of the fuselage as Nick Palmer and Harry Hutton approached the F-4.

Brad could see that both Palmer and Hutton were carrying miscellaneous items, but he could not make out what the objects were.

''Welcome back, Lieutenant,'' Kendall said, unable to conceal his grin.

''It's good to be back,'' Brad responded, taking off his helmet. ''Believe me.''

Kendall helped the two men unstrap, then stepped down one step. ''What happened to your canopy, sir?''

''We went through a SAM burst,'' Brad answered, wondering what Palmer and Hutton were doing next to the forward fuselage. ''The one that knocked down Commander Durham's airplane.''

''Well,'' Kendall responded as he grabbed Austin's helmet, ''we can use the canopy off of Two Oh Eight.''

''Yeah,'' Brad replied as he lifted himself from his seat, ''that's about the only thing I didn't destroy.'' He still had not been down to see the aircraft he had flown through the trees and into the barricade.

Kendall stepped down to the deck as Austin and Lunsford climbed over the side of the Phantom. A small crowd had gathered, gawking at the splitter plate in front of the left engine intake.

Reaching the flight deck, Brad looked at the focus of everyone's amusement. "Just what I needed," he said to Palmer and Hutton when he saw the patrol boat painted on the side of the Phantom.

Hutton laughed, then handed the stencil and spray can to Kendall. "Think about it, Brad. Four more boats and you'll be an ace."

Lunsford stepped back two paces and framed the boat with his hands. "Why don't you guys paint a tree next to the boat?"

12

Austin and Lunsford left their flight gear in the locker and went to the ready room. Bull Durham and Ernie Sheridan were there to greet the "boat blasters," as Austin and Lunsford had been tagged.

"We owe you one," Durham said, shaking hands with the two junior officers. "I didn't know what the hell you were doing when you rolled in and came screaming toward the boat. Man, I'm tellin' you, we were both amazed when that missile came off and plowed into that mother."

Lunsford shook his head. "So was I."

Sheridan, who was the spark of any party and enjoyed hanging around with the pilots, sat down in one of the high-backed chairs. "Seriously, we sure as hell appreciate what you guys did."

"Well," Brad replied self-consciously, "I just hope you don't have to return the favor."

"No shit," Durham laughed as he sat down on the armrest of one of the briefing chairs. "Have a seat, and we'll bring you up to date." Austin and Lunsford sat and gave him their full attention.

"Did you have any trouble getting into Da Nang?" Sheridan asked.

Lunsford cut off Austin before he could answer. "No, we didn't have any problems. The tree surgeon flew us through the most violent goddamn thunderstorm ever recorded in this hemisphere . . . with a hole in his canopy and no oxygen."

Durham and Sheridan, laughing out loud, were well

aware of Lunsford's uneasiness in the air. They, along with everyone else in the squadron, respected the RIO for sticking to it and doing a good job.

"Then," Lunsford continued as Brad rolled back his eyes, "we made an emergency fuel GCA to a miraculous landing. That's when it got ugly."

Durham looked puzzled. "What do you mean?"

"We flamed out on the taxiway."

"You're kidding," Durham said.

"Fact," Lunsford responded. "The marines must have sent him out here to save their own inventory of airplanes."

The four men laughed, then continued to discuss the events of the past twenty-four hours.

Durham and Sheridan explained about the F-4 crew who had inadvertently shot a Zuni air-to-ground rocket into an idling A-4. The explosion had ignited another Skyhawk and set the aft section of the flight deck on fire. With both A-4s engulfed in a blazing inferno, the pilots had ejected. The two aviators had been rescued from the drink, but one of the pilots had sustained a broken ankle when he hit the catwalk before impacting the water.

The carrier was standing down from air operations for the remainder of the day. An underway replenishment was scheduled to begin at 0930.

A cargo vessel and an ammunition ship were currently positioning themselves alongside the ship. The difficult and time-consuming operation, known as an UNREP, would restock the carrier with food, fuel, machinery parts, and ordnance.

Rumors had been circulating to the effect that major air strikes were in the planning stages. Brad was quite interested to hear that MiG airfields might be included in the attacks. Durham believed that some of the restrictive rules of engagement would be lifted, allowing the carrier crews to hit in-country sanctuaries.

Another item of interest that had filtered through the wardrooms concerned a problem with the carrier's number two shaft. The huge drive shaft that turned a monstrous propeller blade had developed a vibration. The rumors circulating through the ship indicated that the carrier would depart Yankee Station early and proceed to Subic Bay for repairs. Those familiar with such matters estimated the ship would be in port for ten to fourteen days.

"Brad," Sheridan chuckled, "what did you do to your RIO? He looks and smells awful."

Austin laughed. "Yeah, we could use a thorough scrubbing."

"After the animal act at the club," Lunsford said, feigning disgust, "we spent the night in a pigsty."

"By the way," Sheridan added, "the CO wants to see everyone in the ready room at eleven hundred."

Brad had shaved and showered in the communal latrine shared by the junior officers in his section of the ship. He had returned to his stateroom and was dressing when Harry Hutton walked into the room. "Did you hear that we may leave the line early?"

Brad grabbed his shoes. "Yes. Bull and Ernie mentioned that there was something wrong—I don't know what—with one of the propeller shafts."

Harry leaned against the bulkhead. "There is definitely something wrong with the shaft. I went down to the engineering spaces, just checking around, and a chief told me we had to return to port. Something about bearings, or whatever."

Smiling, Brad looked at Hutton. "That wouldn't hurt my feelings."

Harry displayed his lascivious grin. "Yeah, a little sack time with the sweethearts of Olongapo. How about that little dolly we met at the Black Rose?"

"If Big Ida is your idea of little," Brad laughed, "you need to see an optometrist."

Harry sat down, pondering the sexual attractions available in the liberty town of Olongapo.

Buffing his highly polished shoes, Brad looked up at the innocent, cherubic face. "Harry, let me propose something for our own good."

A quizzical look appeared on Hutton's face. "What,

chaplain? You don't mean a tour to historical sites, or something like that?''

''No, Harry,'' Brad laughed, ''nothing even remotely resembling a cultural experience. The last thing I want to do is influence your intellectual and artistic taste.''

''Good.''

''What I have in mind,'' Brad continued, ''is getting away from this shit for a week or so. Olongapo is a goddamn cesspool full of drunks and whores. A little of that goes a long way as far as I'm concerned.''

Harry smiled broadly. ''Manila. They've got women there who will reduce you to a whimpering pile of protoplasm. We can get a steam and cream, too.''

Looking at his watch, Brad stood. ''I'm talking about Hawaii . . . civilization. If we can't get a military hop, then we'll go to Manila and catch an airliner.''

Hutton's face lighted. ''Yeah, American women for a change.''

''Harry,'' Brad said, reaching for his hat, ''I'm talking about first cabin. Oceanfront at the Royal Hawaiian. Room service. Breakfast on the lanai. Afternoons at the Mai Tai Bar . . . the works.''

''Yeah,'' Harry responded, gleefully rubbing his hands together. ''Bikinis as far as you can see. Let's do it!''

Brad, Harry, Nick, and Russ sat in the third row, waiting for the skipper to speak. The executive officer, Frank Rockwood, had just concluded his remarks about the squadron spaces being inspected in two days. He walked to his seat and sat down next to the CO.

Dan Bailey spoke quietly with Rockwood, then stood and stepped behind the podium. ''Well, gents, we've got a lot of scuttlebutt going around that I intend to set straight. First, however, I want to say that we came very close to losing a crew yesterday.''

Everyone glanced at Bull Durham and Ernie Sheridan. They sat in the front row with Jack Carella.

''Our brother in green did something very extraordinary and saved the day.''

Hutton punched Brad in the arm as quiet laughter filtered through the room. Brad gazed at the floor, feeling the looks of the other crew members.

"I don't advocate shooting Sidewinders at patrol boats, but we obviously have to use our ingenuity. Austin used good headwork in a dicey situation. He is to be commended." Brad felt the redness creep up his neck. He raised his eyes, focusing on the CO.

"Now," Bailey continued, "three items. We are returning to Subic Bay day after tomorrow to have our propulsion system worked over."

Murmurs filled the room as the crews exchanged knowing smiles. A port call was second only to going home from a deployment.

"The reason we aren't leaving the line now is because tomorrow we are laying an Alpha Strike on two airfields." Cheers broke out as the CO motioned for the men to quiet down.

"We have received permission to attack the MiG bases at Kep and Kien An. This is not a lifting of restrictions, just a parcel doled out from Washington."

"Sir," Brad said, "what about Phuc Yen and Yen Bai?"

Bailey shook his head. "Still protected airspace. Our squadron has been tasked to supplement the A-4s in bombing the airfields." The CO paused, surveying the arched eyebrows and bewildered looks.

Nick Palmer leaned forward in his seat. "Sir, you mean we're going to be attack pukes?"

"That's right," Bailey smiled. "Some of us are going to be bomber pilots tomorrow."

"Christ almighty," Palmer said to no one in particular.

"Some of you people," Bailey emphasized with his index finger, "haven't dropped anything but your pants in a long time."

Palmer looked at Bailey. "Skipper, we're fighter pilots."

"That may be true technically, but tomorrow, Mister Palmer, you will be a bomber pilot."

Hutton snickered out loud. "Nick the Brick."

The crews, including the CO, laughed at the new nickname. Nick the Stick had been permanently retired.

"Okay," Bailey interjected, "everyone listen up. We are short three aircraft, but tomorrow we are going with a maximum effort. I am going to lead the first division, and Commander Rockwood is leading the second gaggle. Jocko is going as my section leader, and Austin—who happens to have the most recent attack experience—will be Commander Rockwood's section leader.

"We will have a two-plane TARCAP to cover us over the target. The flight leader," Bailey smiled, "is none other than Two-Cow O'Meara."

Lieutenant Jon O'Meara, who was slinking down in his seat, had added another chapter to his reputation when he had inadvertently tossed a bomb completely over a target range. The U.S. Navy had had to buy two cows who were unlucky enough to be grazing at the point of impact.

"Commander Carella will brief you at oh-four-thirty. We are going with a variety of ordnance, but the particulars haven't been worked out yet."

The CO scanned a note before looking around the room again. "The last item concerns the probable return of Maj. Nguyen Thanh Dao."

Bailey saw the recognition in the eyes of the men. The North Vietnamese fighter pilot, who had sported a distinctive white stripe across the tail of his MiG-17, had been responsible for downing seven American aircraft. After painting the seventh red star on the nose of his MiG, Nguyen Thanh Dao had disappeared from the skies around Hanoi.

"Our intelligence people," Bailey said with a degree of concern, "believe he is back . . . in a MiG-21. Sources on the ground have confirmed that a white stripe has been painted on the tail of a twenty-one with seven red stars on the nose.

"So," the CO continued, glancing at Austin and Palmer, "if anyone sees Major Dao, sing out. The admiral wants him bagged . . . a priority."

Bailey studied the faces looking at him. The eyes of his

audience reflected pure determination to destroy the North Vietnamese pilot. Nguyen Thanh Dao had killed five crew members from the seven American aircraft he had shot down. The goal of every crew in the ready room was to kill the fighter ace.

"That's all I have for now, so get some rest."

The men stood to attention as Bailey stepped away from the podium. He walked over to Austin and paused. "Brad, I'd like to see you in my stateroom."

"Yes, sir," Austin replied, turning to follow the CO.

The two men chatted amiably as they proceeded to Bailey's quarters below the hangar deck. The CO unlocked his door, turned on the light, and stepped inside.

"Is there something wrong, Skipper?" Brad asked, following Bailey into the cabin. The CO motioned for Austin to have a seat.

"I don't know," Bailey replied, opening his safe. "Is there?"

Brad was forming an answer when the CO extracted a small box from his safe and handed it to the marine.

"Open it," the CO said, leaning back.

Brad removed the top of the rectangular container, then stared at the pair of shiny silver captain's bars. "Congratulations, Captain Austin," Bailey said, extending his hand.

"I don't know what to say," Brad replied as he shook hands with his CO. "I wasn't anticipating making captain so soon."

Dan Bailey smiled. "You were deep-selected, so that's a feather in your cap. Actually, you're not supposed to pin them on for another two and a half weeks, but I figured—at the rate you're going through airplanes—you might as well put them on now."

"Thanks, Skipper," Brad said as he replaced the lid on the small container.

"We'll plan a wetting-down party," Bailey chuckled, "when we get to Subic."

"Great," Brad replied, placing the box in his shirt pocket. "Thanks again, sir."

"You earned it."

Austin opened the door and excused himself. He was elated by the fact that he had been promoted early. This would mean a salary increase, but more important, he understood the significance the early promotion would have on his longer term career.

As he approached his stateroom, Brad could hear raucous laughter, followed by a scurrilous remark from Harry Hutton. The ongoing junior-officers-only poker game was once again in progress.

Austin opened his door to the sound of poker chips being tossed on Hutton's wood footlocker. The small room was crowded. Besides Harry, there were Nick Palmer, Russ Lunsford, Jon O'Meara, Mario Russo, and Ernie Sheridan. Dirty Ernie, being a lieutenant commander, had been given a waiver based on the unanimous acceptance by the members of the at-sea poker club.

"Just in time," Hutton chuckled as he shuffled the cards with a flourish. "Throw your wallet on the table and grab a drink."

"What did the old man want?" Russ Lunsford asked while Hutton dealt a new hand of five card stud.

"I thought I was in some kind of trouble," Brad answered, tossing a five-dollar bill on the battered footlocker. "Instead, the skipper gave me a raise."

"What are you talking about?" Hutton questioned as he counted out five dollars in miscellaneous chips.

"I got promoted."

"Bullshit," Lunsford replied. "What did he want?"

Brad unbuttoned the flap on his pocket and handed the small box to his RIO. "Open it."

The noisy game came to a halt as all eyes took in the container. Lunsford gently lifted the top off and set the box on the footlocker.

Hutton picked up one of the silver rank insignias. "I'll be a son of a bitch. I knew the marines were screwed, but this is unbelievable . . . making you a captain."

Everyone congratulated Austin as Hutton closed the box and handed it back to the new captain. Harry got up and fixed Brad a tall scotch and water. "Here you go, Your Lordship."

"Jesus," Austin replied, sitting down at the corner of the battered footlocker, "it's a bit early in the day to be hitting the sauce, isn't it?"

"Naw," Nick Palmer responded, tossing in his well-worn cards. "Dirty Ernie authorized it . . . and he's a heavy."

"Yeah," Ernie Sheridan added. "We have to turn in early for an oh-dark-thirty wake up, so we'll just pretend it's the five o'clock cocktail hour."

"Ante up," Harry reminded the group while he again shuffled the cards. The poker club had appointed Harry permanent dealer for the duration of the deployment.

The game continued another three hours before Sheridan, O'Meara, and Russo left. Each man was five dollars poorer than he had been at the beginning of the poker game.

Palmer and Lunsford helped clean the cluttered state-room, then started to leave.

"Hey," Hutton said, rinsing his glass. "Stick around a minute. Our nugget captain has come up with a brilliant idea, and we thought you guys might want to pitch in with us."

Palmer looked at Austin. "What's up?"

"Well," Brad replied, sipping the last of his drink, "Harry and I plan to go to Hawaii for a week or ten days . . . as soon as we get to Subic. Thought you two might want to go with us."

Lunsford and Palmer looked at each other and smiled. "It sounds great," Palmer said, "but do you think the old man will let us go that far away while we're in the middle of a cruise?"

"Sure," Brad answered, opening the small, portable refrigerator. He extracted a chilled soda and opened the can. "Care for a Pepsi, anyone?"

Nick and Russ declined.

"Rocky told me that we would have to put in regular leave papers, and that the old man would go for it. He said that after we got back—and he encouraged us to go—they'd tear up the papers and chalk it up to basket leave.''

"Shit hot," Lunsford said, enthused by the idea. "I could use some R and R in Hawaii."

"If we can't hop a military flight," Brad explained, "then we'll run over to Manila and go commercial. I'll arrange a suite at the Royal Hawaiian . . . one that will accommodate all of us."

"It's only money," Hutton chimed in, grinning. "Brad's going to take care of the details. Besides, he's a rich captain now, so we know where to get a loan."

"Count us in," Palmer said, undulating in a poor imitation of a hula dancer.

"I'm glad you don't fly like you dance," Hutton said with a disgusted look.

13

Brad Austin closely monitored his engine instruments as the starboard turbojet ignited and steadied at idle. The strike brief had been clear and concise. The eight Phantoms assigned to accompany the A-4 Skyhawk attack aircraft had various loads of bombs and Zuni rockets. The bomber-configured F-4s also carried two Sidewinders and two Sparrow air-to-air missiles.

Both combat air patrol Phantoms had full loads of four Sparrows and four Sidewinder missiles. Two additional F-4s, one loaded for the bombing mission and the other the spare CAP, were chained to the flight deck near the fantail.

Four F-8 Crusader fighters from another carrier air group would hit the target first to suppress the ground fire and antiaircraft weapons. They would make a strafing and rocket pass, followed seconds later by the Skyhawks and Phantom fighter-bombers.

The F-4s carrying 500-pound Mark-82 bombs and 1,000-pound Mark-83 bombs had been tasked with hitting the runway at Kep Air Base, thirty-seven miles northeast of Hanoi. The F-4s and Skyhawks carrying 250-pound Mark-81 bombs would hit the flight line and support buildings.

Brad taxied forward, the third aircraft in his four-plane flight. Each of the Phantoms in the flight carried twelve 250-pound Mark-81 bombs.

The first two heavily loaded aircraft taxied onto the port and starboard catapults, went to afterburner, then squatted down and roared off the bow of the carrier.

Brad gave the weight checker a thumbs-up, then looked at the windblown catapult officer. The yellow-shirted man wearing the Mickey Mouse headset gave Austin the signal to apply full power. Brad advanced the throttles to afterburner, said a silent prayer, rechecked his engine instruments, then saluted the catapult officer.

After a short pause, Austin and Lunsford were crushed into their seatbacks by the cat shot. As usual, Lunsford swore loudly as the Phantom hurtled off the bow.

Snapping the landing gear up, Brad looked at the aircraft rendezvousing in the distance. He raised the flaps and climbed another 500 feet before deselecting afterburner. Two and a half minutes after leaving the carrier, Brad joined the F-4s piloted by the executive officer, Frank Rockwood, and Bull Durham. Shortly thereafter, Nick Palmer glided into the number four position.

The flight rendezvoused with the tankers, topped off their tanks, checked in with the strike leader, then proceeded to their designated coast-in point north of Haiphong harbor. Kep was reported to be heavily defended by both antiaircraft emplacements and SA-2 Guideline surface-to-air missiles.

The A-4s would approach the air base from over MiG Ridge to the south, hitting the field as the last F-8 Crusader pulled off target. The Phantoms would approach from the northwest, turning at the last second to align with the runway and flight line.

Austin and Lunsford went through their usual combat routine. They covered the checklist, snugged their restraint harnesses as tight as they could yank them, then concentrated on getting the mental picture of the mission. Situational awareness was extremely important, and the aircrews had to conjure a vivid image of the positions and activities of the other flights by listening to the radios. Once all the strike aircraft were in sight, the task of sorting out priorities would become easier.

The Phantoms crossed the beach in loose formation.

"Okay, Jokers," Dan Bailey radioed, "check in."

"Two."

"Three."

"Four."

"Spade check," Rocky Rockwood ordered. He used a different call sign to avoid confusion between the two Phantom flights.

"Two."

"Three."

"Four."

Bailey keyed his mike again. "Jokers and Spades come port three three zero."

The Phantoms continued on their northwesterly course, passing Kep to the north, then turned west.

"This is Red Crown on guard. I hold MiG activity coming off Kep and Phuc Yen . . . showing four flights."

"Joker, copy," Bailey responded, then called Jon O'Meara, the flight leader of the target combat air patrol Phantoms. "Diamonds, we need some MiG protection."

"Diamonds just stroked the burners," O'Meara answered, feeling the aircraft shudder as the F-4 went supersonic. "We're at your eight o'clock, four miles."

"Roger," Bailey repeated. "Jokers and Spades, we go on stage in one minute. Check switches hot."

"Joker Two."

"Three."

"Four."

Frank Rockwood keyed his mike. "Spade One hot."

"Two."

"Three."

"Four."

Brad could see the four F-8 Crusaders, far below, streaking in from the southeast. "I see the gunfighters . . . the Crusaders," he said to Lunsford. "Goin' at the speed of heat. We should be right on the mark."

"Yeah," Lunsford responded, watching the F-8s make a turn to their final run-in heading. "Gomerville is going to be shit city in about thirty seconds."

Brad saw the eight A-4 Skyhawks start their roll in. He could see that the Crusaders were blasting the base in an almost line-abreast pass.

"Jokers and Spades in hot," Bailey ordered, rolling the Phantom into a steep dive.

Rockwood offset his four aircraft to the left of Joker Flight. Spade Flight had the responsibility for decimating the flight line and support structures.

Rechecking his master arm ON, Austin turned his gunsight to bright and looked at his warning lights. All systems appeared normal.

"MiGs! MiGs!" Frank Rockwood warned as he wheeled into his bombing run. "Four at three o'clock, coming around behind. Diamonds, we need cover."

"Diamonds are engaged with three bogies," Jon O'Meara groaned under punishing g forces.

Brad rolled his F-4 to follow Rockwood and Durham, then darted a look at the A-4s. The lead Skyhawk pilot had just released his ordnance and was pulling up and snapping into a tight right turn.

Moving out one wing length from Durham's F-4, Brad keyed his intercom. "Russ, watch the MiGs that are turning behind us. They're setting up a shot."

"I've got 'em."

Austin increased power to maintain his position as the Phantom rushed toward the ground at 510 knots. He watched the last two A-4s fire Zuni rockets into three parked aircraft. Two of the MiG-17 fighters blew apart, burning furiously as the Skyhawks clawed for altitude.

The Phantoms were diving through 6,000 feet when the sky lighted with antiaircraft fire. Four SAMs lifted off from emplacements surrounding the airfield. The Skyhawk pilots were hugging the ground and jinking all over the sky as they headed for the coastline.

Watching the altimeter unwind in a thirty-degree dive, Brad made a last-second wind correction, then released his bomb load passing 3,000 feet. Brad and Russ felt the Phantom wobble as the twelve Mark-81 bombs were kicked off the ejector racks.

The 250-pound explosives walked the length of the flight line, destroying one MiG-17 and damaging two other fighters, along with a lone transport aircraft.

Brad pulled 5½ g's as he raced for the security of altitude. Lunsford remained quiet, straining to breathe during the punishing maneuver. He was trying to locate the camouflaged MiGs chasing them.

Three more surface-to-air missiles rocketed aloft as Nick Palmer pulled off the target. "SAMs! Break, Rocky!"

Rockwood slapped his Phantom into a ninety-degree turn, bending the F-4 around in a grueling 8-g attempt to evade the missiles. Bull Durham followed his flight leader as Brad rolled inverted and pulled toward the ground. Palmer chased Austin in an effort to get below the SAMs. The radio chatter became unintelligible during the evasive maneuvers.

Diving through 1,500 feet, Brad whipped the Phantom right side up and slammed the throttles into afterburner. He yanked his head from side to side in an attempt to locate his flight leader.

The sky was full of twisting, turning aircraft when Austin saw Rockwood and Durham trying to escape from the four MiG-17s. Brad turned into the engagement and raised the Phantom's nose.

"Let's get out of here—take it down!" Austin heard over the radio as he and Palmer closed on the MiGs. He next heard the voice of Dan Bailey order Joker Flight to join up and head for the beach.

"Spade Four," Austin radioed Palmer as he selected HEAT on his armament panel, "let's drag 'em off."

Palmer clicked his mike twice.

A SAM flashed by Austin's left wing as he banked inside the four MiGs. The last aircraft in the North Vietnamese formation, seeing the rapidly closing Phantoms, broke away and dove for the deck. The pilot headed straight for the security of Phuc Yen.

The MiG flight leader and his two remaining wingmen opened fire with their 23mm cannons at the same instant that Austin heard his Sidewinder annunciator growl.

Brad, who could not shoot with two F-4s in the missile zone, watched in horror as the red tracer rounds slashed by Durham's aircraft and impacted Frank Rockwood's Phantom. The stricken F-4, spewing a white vapor trail, continued to fly straight and level for a few seconds, then burst into bright orange flames.

"Frank!" Durham shouted, casting a glance at the diving MiGs. "You're on fire! Get out!"

"Negative," Rockwood replied as he turned the flaming Phantom toward the coast. "Where are the MiGs?"

Durham rolled his F-4 and glimpsed the MiGs unloading and disengaging. "Running out to Phuc Yen."

"Spades," Rockwood said in a tight voice, "get out of here and form up over the water."

Sliding into a loose formation on Bull Durham, Austin checked the area for MiGs and SAMs. He heard Jon O'Meara, five miles to the south, announce that Diamond Flight was engaging two new adversaries. The radio calls were clipped and frantic.

Keying his mike, Brad was about to suggest that he and Palmer go to the aid of O'Meara and his wingman. Before Austin could speak, Rockwood's Phantom was enveloped in a brilliant ball of fire. A nanosecond later, the F-4 blew apart in a powerful blast that severed the tail and part of the wings from the fuselage.

The remains of the Phantom yawned to the right and went into an inverted flat spin, streaming flaming jet fuel as it fell toward the earth

"Get out, Frank!" Durham shouted while he pulled up in a high wingover. "Get out!"

Austin and Palmer pulled up to follow Durham. They watched the spinning fighter rotate through three complete turns, then saw a parachute pop open. The first parachute was followed by the opening of Rockwood's chute seconds before the F-4 plunged into a wooded hillside.

Bull Durham called the search-and-rescue coordinator at the north SAR station, giving him the exact location of the downed crewmen. The coordinator quickly radioed the information to the on-scene SAR commander orbiting over the gulf in his A-1 Skyraider.

"Spade Lead," Austin radioed during a sudden pause, "Spade Three and Four need to help Diamond Flight."

"Roger," Durham shot back, then briefed the SAR personnel about the terrain below him.

Brad and Nick banked sharply to the left and lighted their afterburners. The two aircraft quickly accelerated beyond the speed of sound. Brad could see that the two Diamond Phantoms, both holding maximum sustained turn rates, were surrounded by four fighters. Two additional MiG-17s were diving at the cornered F-4s.

Austin, with his radar in boresight mode, told Lunsford to go boresight and lock up the lead MiG that was about to open fire on the hapless Phantoms.

"Got him locked," Lunsford shouted. "Shoot! Shoot him!"

"Diamonds," Austin radioed, pulling the throttles back. "Spade Three. Reverse, unload, and go for separation. NOW!"

Feeling the F-4 go through Mach tuck, Austin finessed the stick as the aircraft came back through the sonic barrier. He watched O'Meara and his wingman snap their fighters hard-over and dive for speed. Austin popped the speed brakes, pulled a few degrees of lead on the first MiG fighter, then squeezed off two AIM-7 Sparrow missiles.

The big weapons dropped out of the wells, trailing thick plumes of smoke, and shot toward the Communist aircraft at Mach 3.

The MiG flight leader, unaware that Austin had fired missiles at him, rolled to follow the accelerating Phantoms. The enemy fighter stabilized a split second before it was blown apart in a violent explosion.

"You did it!" Lunsford exclaimed, listening to Palmer congratulate them. "You knocked the shit out of him! You got a MiG!"

The blazing fighter detonated again, raining debris across the sky. The cockpit spun crazily until it plunged into the hills below. Incapacitated by the first explosion, the North Vietnamese pilot had been unable to pull his ejection handle.

"Diamonds are reengaging," Jon O'Meara radioed

breathlessly as he and his wingman began pulling into a supersonic, gut-wrenching, vertical climb.

Mario Russo, O'Meara's RIO, was on the radio providing a constant update on the MiGs.

Retracting his speed brakes and adding power, Austin watched the remaining five MiGs go into steep dives and turn toward Phuc Yen. "Diamonds, the gomers are running out to Phuc Yen."

"Copy, copy," O'Meara replied. "What's your posit?"

Brad watched Diamond Flight top out and roll wings level. "We're at your twelve o'clock, low."

"Gotcha," O'Meara radioed. "Good kill . . . thanks. We'll form on you to cover Rocky and Ed."

Ed was Lt (jg) Edgardo Zapata, a nugget RIO who had been with the squadron less than two months. Frank Rockwood had assumed the responsibility of bringing the young officer up to operational qualification as quickly as possible. The fighter squadron, like many other front-line units, had suffered a chronic shortage of aviators and RIOs since the beginning of the deployment.

"Roger, Diamond," Brad responded, glancing around the sky. The MiGs, low to the ground, had distanced themselves from the American fighters. "Come starboard three five zero, and join on our right wing."

Two clicks acknowledged the call.

Suddenly, Frank Rockwood's distinct voice sounded over the radio. He was on the ground and transmitting over his emergency radio.

"Spade One is okay," Rockwood panted, "but I think they shot Ed during the descent."

Bull Durham took command. "Lay low, Rocky. We've got a SAR effort under way."

A minute passed while the four Phantoms led by Brad Austin coasted into loose formation with Bull Durham.

Brad glanced down at the cratered and scorched hillside where Rockwood's Phantom had crashed. He could see a line of soldiers working their way along a trail sixty meters below the burning wreckage.

The North Vietnamese regulars had already reached Ed

Zapata's parachute. The RIO's lifeless body, three feet above the ground, was hanging from the branches of two tall trees.

Zapata, who had fired every round from his .38-caliber revolver, had been shot through the head, chest, and thigh as he descended above the soldiers.

"Spade One," the A-1 Skyraider flight leader radioed, "Lifeguard is inbound with four Spads. We'll be over your position in twelve minutes."

Frank Rockwood watched the soldiers as they examined Ed Zapata's body. "Lifeguard, I've got company just below me. Twenty-five to thirty regulars."

"Copy," the Skyraider pilot replied. "We'll be there as soon as possible."

Austin slid out to a loose-formation position. He cautiously watched the sky while glancing down at Rockwood's conspicuous parachute.

"Spade One," Brad radioed, "can you hide your chute?"

"Negative," Rockwood responded. "It's caught over some branches. I tried to pull it down . . . no luck."

Bull Durham observed the soldiers advancing up the hill in the direction of the downed flight leader. "Rocky, you need to get away from your chute. I think they've spotted it, 'cause they're going straight toward your position."

"Okay," Rockwood replied, crouching close to the ground. "Which way looks the best?"

Durham had to be careful in the event the North Vietnamese had a confiscated American survival radio. If there was an English-speaking member in the enemy patrol, the soldier could spell disaster for Frank Rockwood.

"Okay, Spade," Durham said, analyzing the best course for the XO to follow. "You are on third base, copy?"

"Copy, third base."

Durham banked tighter. "The wreckage—the Phantom—is home plate. Go to second base and burrow in."

"Movin' out," Rockwood responded, then edged along the hillside to a thick stand of trees and undergrowth. He dropped down and crawled into the foliage.

Three minutes passed while the soldiers split into two sections. One group went directly toward the dangling parachute, while the others hurried along the trail below Rockwood. They quickly outflanked the downed aviator, surrounding him on two sides.

"Lifeguard One," Austin radioed as the soldiers moved steadily in the direction of the executive officer. "Say your ETA to Spade One."

"We've got you on the horizon," the pilot replied, adjusting his throttle, mixture, and propeller pitch for maximum power. "We'll be overhead in six minutes."

Brad swore to himself, then made a bold decision to help Frank Rockwood.

Lunsford, reading Austin's mind, tapped his intercom. "They're going to be on top of him before then."

Keying his radio, Brad glanced below. "Bull, we've got to keep their heads down."

"Roger," Durham replied, rolling his Phantom into a dive. "I'm ahead of you. Spades roll in at twenty-second intervals."

The North Vietnamese soldiers knew that the navy and marine F-4s were not equipped with cannons. The only thing the soldiers had to fear were bombs and Zuni rockets, and they could see that the five Phantoms had expended all of their air-to-ground ordnance.

Although the thundering F-4s were intimidating when they screamed low overhead, the riflemen felt safe firing with impunity at the powerful fighters.

"They're closing in on me," Rockwood whispered over his emergency radio. He wiped his sweat-soaked hands on his flight suit, grasped his .38-caliber revolver, and crawled between two trees.

"Hang in there," Durham responded, sweeping across the soldiers at 520 knots in afterburner.

Austin flicked his Phantom over. "Spade One," Brad calmly radioed, "get your head down and hang on."

Frank Rockwood recognized the steady voice of the marine aviator. He ducked his head and peered over the foliage at the advancing North Vietnamese platoon.

The F-4 streaked toward the ground while Austin lined up one group of soldiers in his windscreen. He bottomed out short of his mark and toggled the pylon jettison select switch. The ejector racks and Sidewinder missiles tumbled away from the Phantom's wings, then plowed into the soldiers with devastating accuracy.

"Bull," Austin groaned during the tight, high-g pull-up, "recommend we drop our racks and centerlines on the gomers."

"Spade Lead concurs," Durham responded, watching Palmer pull off the target area, "but keep your speed below four hundred seventy." The centerline tanks would occasionally drop off, then porpoise back into the Phantoms above 470 knots. "Diamonds copy?"

Click, click.

"Brad, Spade One," Rockwood broke in. "You mangled the bastards . . . killed a half dozen at least, but they're spreading out and taking cover."

Durham again rolled in when the fifth Phantom pulled off the target. He raced for the same spot that Austin had attacked. Durham pickled off his ejector racks and pulled up steeply. The heavy missile rails ripped through the soldiers, killing one man and injuring two others.

"Good drop!" Rockwood said, then turned to watch the group of men advancing from the trail. "You've got their attention, but the ones along the trail are only about eighty meters away."

Brad Austin keyed his mike. "Keep your head down. I'm makin' a run down the trail line."

"Bring it on," Rockwood replied, then added, "They're twenty to thirty meters northeast of the trail, seventy meters east of the last drop."

"Roger," Austin responded, wheeling into his second attack. "Can you move farther up the hill?"

"I can try," Rockwood answered cautiously, looking around the immediate area, "but I'll be exposed for twenty to thirty seconds."

Brad aimed for the spot the XO had described and punched off his 600-gallon centerline fuel tank. The large receptacle ripped through the scurrying North Vietnamese, injuring three of the soldiers.

"A little short," Rockwood radioed. "They're closing on me . . . about sixty meters away."

Nick Palmer was in his dive. "Grab hold, Dash One. I'm gonna drop 'em a goddamn load."

"Lifeguard," Brad pleaded, "we need cover. Say posit."

"We're two minutes out to the southeast. Hang on."

Rockwood's voice, faint and barely audible, came over the radio. "They're almost on me . . . ten to twelve of them at fifty meters."

"Okay," Bull Durham replied. "Spades and Diamonds, let's roll in in tight trail. Drop all your trash on this pass."

Jon O'Meara and his wingman charged downward while the soldiers fired at the fighters and advanced toward Rockwood. Durham dropped his centerline tank directly on top of two of the soldiers.

"Frank," Durham said, straining under the force of the pull-up, "haul ass up the slope. We'll place the last one between you and the gomers."

"Okay, but they're almost—" Rockwood's whisper stopped when he heard a sound thirty meters to his right. His heart pounded when he met the soldier's eyes. "They're on me . . . they see me!"

"Spades!" the Skyraider pilot shouted. "We have your target in sight. Rolling in hot." The prop-driven A-1s hurtled down toward the point of the debris settling to the ground.

Rockwood dropped to a prone position, aimed his revolver, then fired three rounds at the North Vietnamese soldier. The small man turned to dive for cover at the instant the first round hit him in the jaw.

Five more soldiers, crouching low and moving swiftly through the underbrush, approached their gravely wounded comrade. They had their rifles pointed in the general direction of the American pilot.

Rockwood aimed for their torsos and kept squeezing the trigger until the weapon was empty.

"I'm out of ammo," Rockwood radioed, breathing hard.

He heard a series of loud cracks, then felt searing pain when a rifle round tore into his right shoulder.

Pulling the emergency radio to his mouth with his left hand, the wounded aviator activated the transmitter. "It's too late . . . they've got me."

The next transmission was garbled, followed by a gasping plea. "I've . . . been hit again. Blow the tree line . . . to hell. That's an order."

A slight pause followed before the Skyraider leader keyed his mike. "We can't drop ordnance on one of our own people."

"Goddamnit!" Brad Austin swore loudly over the radio. "Lifeguard, you heard the commander. Vaporize his position."

"Roger," came the quiet reply. "Lifeguards in for a ripple pass. Drop it all on the tree line."

"So long, guys," Rockwood groaned, feeling the impact of another round.

Bull Durham, seething with anger and frustration, looked down at the point where Cdr. Frank Rockwood would lose his life. "Spades and Diamonds, light the burners and get over water ASAP."

"Roger."

Click, click.

Brad shoved the throttles to the stops and glanced at the executive officer's concealment. A moment later the entire area was pulverized by rockets and savage cannon fire.

Feeling the anguish of Rockwood's death, Brad was swept with revulsion. He let the Phantom accelerate well past the speed of sound as he tried to come to grips with the terrible tragedy.

Austin and Lunsford remained quiet as the coastline swept under the supersonic Phantom. There were no words to share the deep, personal pain of losing one of the best of the best.

14

The mammoth carrier steamed smoothly through the placid South China Sea. A steady rain fell, reducing visibility to a mile and a half under the 1,800-foot overcast. The damp, oppressive humidity contributed to a general feeling of malaise throughout the ship. The officers and men were anxious to dock at Subic Bay, and enjoy the freedom and pleasures of shore leave.

Standing alone at the aft end of the hangar bay, Brad Austin stared past the fantail at the churning wake. His mind was numbed by a lack of sleep, and by the emotional memorial service for Frank Rockwood.

The chaplain, a monotonous man, had droned about Rockwood's wife and three children for more than fifteen minutes. Dan Bailey, who had expected to hand the executive officer command of the squadron in less than three months, had finally stood and thanked the bewildered clergyman in mid-sentence.

The CO had immediately launched into a poignant eulogy that had left few dry eyes on the fo'c'sle. Losing Frank Rockwood, the skipper had choked, had been like losing a brother. Bailey had had to stop at that point, then uttered, "Tail winds always, Frank," and walked out drying his eyes.

The officers and men of the squadron had silently followed their commanding officer, each lost in his own thoughts about mortality.

Bailey, who had worked through the night packing his XO's personal belongings, had also finished a difficult letter

120

to Rockwood's wife. He had decided to send the letter of condolence to his own spouse, Karla, so that she could deliver it in person. The two families, who lived on the same street in base housing, had been close friends for seventeen years.

Brad looked at his watch, noting that it was time to change into his flight suit. Air Operations were scheduled to commence at 1530 for the Cubi Point flyoff. The majority of the air wing would launch for the fifty-minute flight to U.S. Naval Air Station Cubi Point, Philippine Islands. The airfield was adjacent to the sprawling Subic Bay Naval Station fifty miles west of Manila.

Cubi Point operations had been alerted to stand by for the steady stream of incoming carrier aircraft. The base personnel always looked forward to the air show that accompanied an air wing flyoff.

Brad had taken the initiative to talk to the commanding officer in private. The new marine captain had respectfully requested that he not have a congratulatory party under the circumstances. Dan Bailey had reluctantly agreed, feeling that the men needed to have a major blowout to purge the grief that hung over the squadron.

Austin had thanked the CO for respecting his wishes, then had asked permission to be included in the flyoff. Bailey had nodded and told him to see Jack Carella, the operations officer and acting executive officer, about flying Palmer's wing to Cubi Point. Bailey, who had approved the leave request from the two crews, knew that the men were eagerly looking forward to escaping the chaotic environment that surrounded them.

Brad listened to the shrill sound of the bosun's whistle, then tried to concentrate on the captain's daily announcement. Staring blankly at the whirlpools created in the carrier's turbulent wake, Brad was unaware that his roommate had walked up to his side.

"How are you feeling?" Harry Hutton asked, unsmiling. The usual confident grin was absent.

"Okay, I suppose," Austin answered, glancing at his friend. "How'd you know I was here?"

Hutton hinted at a smile. "When you're bothered by something—if it's daylight—you always come to the fantail and stare at the wake."

Brad smiled at Hutton's observation. Many of the pilots and radar-intercept officers occasionally needed quiet time to readjust their minds, especially after losing one of the brotherhood. Today was one of those days for Brad to try and get in touch with his feelings.

"If it's night," Harry continued, looking at the plane-guard destroyer, "you go forward in the port catwalk and watch the phosphorescence splash off the bow wave."

Austin turned sideways and leaned against the bulkhead leading to the hangar bay. "Eight."

"What?" Hutton asked, stepping inside the windswept hatchway.

"I've lost eight friends in aircraft accidents since I started flight training in Pensacola."

Both men remained quiet, reflecting on the tragic death of Cdr. Frank Rockwood.

"He was here with us," Brad paused, holding his emotions in check, "twenty-four hours ago. Now, he's lying in a goddamn dirthole . . . if the sorry bastards were humane enough to bury him."

"Come on," Hutton said gently, grasping Austin by the upper arm. "It's time to go jump in our zoom bags, pack our garbage, and go to the flyoff brief."

"Yeah, it is," Brad replied as he stepped over the hatch combing. "What a rotten day for flying."

"Who cares?" Hutton finally grinned his mischievous grin. "We're on our way to the real world."

The Cubi launch had gone smoothly and was completed in less than thirty-five minutes. One A-4 Skyhawk, leaking a steady stream of hydraulic fluid, had been downed on the catapult. Waiting for their catapult shot, Brad Austin and Russ Lunsford had watched the disappointed attack pilot grab his overnight bag and scramble aboard a KA-3B tanker.

After being catapulted off the carrier, Brad had joined on

Nick Palmer's right wing. Harry Hutton had taken pictures of Brad's Phantom as they rendezvoused under the clouds. The two F-4s had climbed rapidly, breaking out of the overcast at 11,000 feet. Palmer continued climbing, leveling the flight at 37,000 feet.

Austin flew a loose parade formation, relaxing and thinking about the misguided war effort, the traumatic death of Frank Rockwood, and the upcoming trip to Hawaii. Still gazing at the horizon, Brad tried to erase the mental image of the North Vietnamese soldiers who had died when his missile ejector racks ripped through them.

The emotion that he experienced was not one of elation or conquest. The visceral sensation Brad felt was that of a Pyrrhic victory. What was the purpose of all the senseless loss of life? What was the big picture? The situation was clearly evident to the military commanders and their charges. They were not being allowed to use their experience, training, and resources to win the war. Slowly shaking his head, Brad considered the obvious absurdity and incongruousness of the war effort. The word *ludicrous* stuck in his mind.

Brad shoved the unpleasant thoughts aside, thinking instead about enjoying a relaxing breakfast while he overlooked Waikiki Beach. A breakfast accompanied by hot tea and a morning paper.

Thirty-three minutes after takeoff, the F-4s flew out of the tropical weather system and dropped to 500 feet over the azure sea. Both crews flew in total silence until Harry Hutton came up on the radio.

"Jokers, come up two thirty point nothing."

The radio frequency 230.0 was not being used by other military pilots or air-traffic controllers at the particular moment.

"Two," Brad replied, glancing at the small plastic pineapple adorning Hutton's helmet. Just like a little kid going on vacation, Brad smiled to himself.

"When we get to Honolulu," Harry said with glee in his voice, "let's all get aloha shirts."

A pause followed. Lunsford pressed his mike. "Not all alike . . . we've got to have a little individuality."

"That's what I mean," Hutton explained. "Each of us will get a different colored shirt. We'll just be civilian tourists. The indulged and idle rich."

The discussion continued while the Phantoms thundered over three fishing vessels as the fighters approached the coast. Brad watched the shoreline of Zambales Province rapidly approach. The warm, pristine waters and lush green forest showcased the deserted snow white beach.

Palmer had the flight switch to Cubi Point approach control, then climbed to 2,000 feet as the shoreline passed under his Phantom.

Checking in with the approach controller, Palmer was given radar vectors to follow a flight of four A-4 Skyhawks. He scanned the afternoon sky, spotting the four attack jets screaming toward the runway. They were preparing to break from a tight echelon formation.

Rule one in naval aviation dictated that pilots had to look good over the air station. Formations had to be close and perfectly spaced. Every pitch-out break had to be performed with Blue Angel precision, especially if the flight was arriving at an air-force facility.

Palmer and Austin switched to the control tower as the flight circled over the luxuriant tropical forest. Both F-4 crews watched the Skyhawks flash over the runway and snap into knife-edge flight at three-second intervals. The four planes were nailed on altitude and spaced evenly.

"I give 'em a seven point five," Hutton said unabashedly over the radio. "Not bad for attack pukes."

Brad Austin slowly shook his head in embarrassment.

"Well, Norvel," the A-4 flight leader radioed, "if you're driving one of the clear air converters, how about a few pointers on arrival techniques."

The J-79 engines in the Phantoms produced two dark trails of jet exhaust. Going into afterburner was the only way to alleviate the highly visible gases.

Palmer thought about ignoring the challenge, but his ego

talked him out of it. He pushed the throttles forward and keyed his mike. "Joker, welded wing."

"Copy," Brad replied, wishing that he and Palmer had practiced the maneuver that they had discussed at length.

"Oh, shit," Lunsford said over the intercom as Austin increased power. "We're going to get our asses in deep kimchi . . . doing your dumb-shit stunts."

Brad tucked in close to Palmer's right wing, causing Lunsford to twinge and look down in his lap. "You're both crazy . . . goddamned idiots."

"Numbers for the break," Palmer said to the tower controller as he eased the Phantom's nose down. His indicated airspeed read 450 knots.

"Joker Two Zero Five cleared for the break," the tower chief replied calmly.

"Roger," Palmer acknowledged, flying as smoothly as his skills permitted.

The two F-4s, locked in tight formation, thundered across the end of the runway as the third Skyhawk was landing. Brad's left wing tip was three feet below the right wing of his flight leader, with three feet of overlap.

Palmer leveled at 400 feet for a moment, then smoothly pulled back on the stick and rolled the Phantom until the left wing tip pointed straight at the ground.

Brad Austin pulled up with his flight leader, then slid directly under Palmer's Phantom. He was working hard to remain eight feet under the belly of his leader's F-4. The two planes rolled wings level at 1,200 feet above the ground on the downwind leg of the landing pattern.

Austin looked up at the bottom of Nick Palmer's aircraft, concentrating on not moving an inch out of position. He inspected the rivets and UHF communications antenna, along with the hydraulic, oil, and grease stains.

Brad popped his flaps down at the same instant as the flight leader, then lowered his landing-gear lever when Palmer's main gear dropped out of the wheel wells on each side of his canopy.

Lunsford had his eyes closed, forcing his mind to think about Waikiki Beach. "Is it over?"

"Almost."

"Well," the A-4 flight leader radioed, taxiing to the flight line, "that's certainly a new one."

Hutton, having never experienced the delicate maneuver, chuckled when he keyed his radio mike. "Not bad for a couple of Fox-4 weenies."

The last A-4 was clearing the runway when Austin cracked his speed brakes to gain separation from Palmer.

Lunsford let out his breath. "Both of you morons should be in straitjackets."

Palmer touched down in a puff of white smoke, followed seven seconds later by his wingman. The Phantoms cleared the runway, called ground control, and taxied to the ramp near the carrier pier.

Opening their canopies, the four men were hit by the sweltering heat and humidity. They wiped their faces as the two F-4s came to a halt and chocks were placed around the main wheels.

After shutting down the engines, both crews hurried to secure their aircraft while Brad cadged a ride in the FOLLOW ME cart to Base Operations. He wanted to see if any flights were scheduled to Hawaii.

Nineteen more air-wing aircraft landed, causing the noise level on the parking apron to become unbearable.

Hauling four garment bags, Palmer, Hutton, and Lunsford started walking in the direction of Base Operations. A minute later, the trio was surprised to see Brad returning so soon. The little cart had not even come to a stop when Austin jumped out and thanked the sailor.

"They've got a flight, but we've got to move fast."

"What's the deal?" Hutton asked, handing Austin his canvas clothes bag.

"They've got a C-130 departing for Guam in ten to fifteen minutes," Brad answered, slinging the hang-up bag over his shoulder. He motioned down the ramp to three of the big Hercules transports. Sailors were busy placing containers on board the nearest airplane. "They're loading now."

"Guam?" Palmer inquired, slipping on his nonregulation Ray-Ban sunglasses.

"Yeah," Brad responded as he started toward the operations building. "They don't have anything on the board for Hawaii, but he said there are dozens of flights out of Guam for Hawaii. They operate around the clock."

"What about our leave papers?" Lunsford broke in. "We have to get them signed, and let them know where we're going to be staying."

Austin turned slightly. "The ops officer said he could sign them. Relax for a change."

Hutton started trotting toward the crowded operations building. "Let's get it on!"

15

Awakened by the sheer panic of his nightmare, Brad Austin felt the dampness of perspiration on the back of his neck. He looked around the Spartan interior of the capacious air-force C-141 StarLifter, relieved that no one had noticed his startled awakening. Only three of the forty-one military passengers were awake. Two men in civilian clothes were using their briefcases for lap-top desks. They had been working tirelessly on their project from the moment the transport had lifted off the runway at Guam.

Brad relaxed his head against the fabric seatback and inhaled deeply, then slowly let out his breath. The face of Frank Rockwood and the corpse of the MiG pilot he had killed had surfaced in the kaleidoscopic nightmare. What had awakened him, at least his last memory of the horrifying dream, had been the sight of the soldiers he had killed. They had been ripped apart and thrown into the air by the devastating impact of his centerline fuel tank.

He looked on both sides of his narrow seat. His three shipmates were sound asleep, snoring at various decibel levels. Lunsford's chin rested on his chest.

Checking his watch, Brad was pleased to see that the big Lockheed transport was scheduled to land at Hickam Air Force Base in less than an hour.

Harry Hutton, whose head had been resting on Brad's right shoulder, stirred awake when the pilot reset his watch. Hutton looked at Brad through swollen eyes. "Are we ever going to get there?"

"Patience," Brad answered, clearing his throat. "Fifty more minutes, according to our ETA."

Hutton yawned, rubbing his eyes. "Well, this sure as hell beats that sky pig we rode to Guam."

Brad rotated his head back and forth to loosen the stiff muscles. "First thing I want when we get on the ground is an ice cold beer."

"Ditto."

Austin and Hutton remained quiet, closing their eyes until the four-engine jet began the descent into Hickam. They roused Palmer and Lunsford when the flaps were lowered. Four minutes later, at 2:15 P.M. local time, the StarLifter's main gear rumbled onto the runway as the nose was gently lowered to the pavement.

When the jet taxied to a halt on the transient aircraft ramp, the foursome grabbed their bags and hurried to an air-force bus with a Honolulu placard on the front.

As soon as all the seats were occupied, the talkative Honolulu native shut the door, shifted into gear, and mashed the throttle.

The trip to downtown Honolulu had been punctuated by stops at the international airport, Hilton Hawaiian Village Hotel, and Fort DeRussy military reservation. Having donned khaki uniforms during the layover in Guam, the men were anxious to change into their civilian attire.

The four fliers stepped off the bus at the large military complex and walked along Kalakaua Avenue to the luxurious Royal Hawaiian Hotel.

The majestic structure, impressive in its fresh coat of coral pink paint, reflected a quiet grace and dignity. The manicured lawn was accentuated by colorful anthuriums, orchids, and red ginger. The scent of the flowers was all-pervasive.

Stopping to take in the elegant "Pink Palace of the Pacific," the four men were impressed by the unique architecture and Spanish-style cupolas. In the legendary lobby, they admired the Moorish ceilings and gleaming crystal chandeliers but ignored for the time being the exclusive shops lining the long hallway.

Quickly signing the guest registration, Brad accepted four keys to their two-bedroom quarters. Their suite overlooked the beach, and they had an unobstructed view of Diamond Head, the famous Waikiki landmark.

The spacious sitting room was flanked by large bedrooms on each side. Each room contained two queen-sized beds with tall headboards and overstuffed pillows. A large bath off the living room was stocked with extra towels and hand-milled soaps, along with four thick terry-cloth robes. A richly padded wet bar and a private lanai completed the opulent suite.

They took time only to shower and change before heading down Kalakaua Avenue to the bustling International Market Place. Hundreds of open-air cart vendors competed with shop owners for the attention of the tourists crowded into the narrow corridors. Children laughed and played while their mothers and grandmothers hawked everything from T-shirts to jewelry.

The foursome casually inspected the array of island goods, stopping at various stands before they retraced their steps. Each selected a colorful aloha shirt from a small shop at the entrance to the bazaar. Laughing at each other, the men walked back to their room and tossed their purchases on the coffee table between the matching pastel pink sofas.

"To the bar," Hutton declared emphatically.

"Lead on," Brad replied, holding the door open.

"Ah, yes," Nick Palmer sighed as a vivacious young cocktail waitress approached their table. "I could grow accustomed to this life-style without any formal training."

Seeing that Harry Hutton was about to deliver one of his infamous lines to the attractive waitress, Brad nudged him on the shin. "Don't even think about it."

Harry gave his roommate a go-to-hell look but remained calm and quiet while the group ordered a round of mai-tais. Feeling the weariness from the prolonged flight, Brad stretched his legs and took a deep breath. He was beginning to relax.

By the time the waitress returned with the tantalizing

drinks, Hutton had prepared his approach. He waited until she had set the drinks on the table. "You remind me of a movie star."

The young lady turned and smiled pleasantly. "Why, thank you. I'm sure my husband will be pleased to hear that."

Choking, Palmer blew a mouthful of his cocktail into the sand a foot from their table.

Shaking his head, Brad tipped the waitress. "I apologize. We left his muzzle in the room." The girl smiled knowingly and walked away.

Chagrined, Harry flushed deeply. "You're a bunch of goddamn assholes . . . every one of you."

Swallowing a big mouthful, Lunsford leaned close to Hutton's red face. "Harry, we can't take any more of your dumb-ass lines."

"Yeah, Harry," Palmer laughed, clearing his throat. "Why don't you just cut to the action, and ask them if they want to go jump in the rack?"

Hutton remained quiet, sipping his drink and ignoring the remarks. He removed the pale purple orchid from his glass and chewed on the stick of sugarcane.

Lunsford had ordered another round of cocktails when Brad noticed a striking young lady enter the lounge. She was accompanied by a well-dressed woman who appeared to be her mother.

Noticing that the table conversation had ceased, Brad became acutely aware that everyone else was looking at the captivating young lady.

Brad averted his eyes but quickly stole another glance, taking in the image of the petite brunette. The silky brown hair was enhanced by sparkling blue eyes and a radiant smile. She had an elegant face with perfectly sculpted features, and delicate hands and feet.

Her white tennis shorts accentuated her smooth, tanned legs. Brad guessed her height and weight to be five feet four inches and 110 pounds. She appeared to be in her early to mid-twenties. He could see that she was not wearing an engagement or a wedding ring.

"Bingo," Hutton laughed, nudging Brad's shoulder while looking at Palmer. "Now we get to see your acts."

Lifting his drink, Palmer chuckled. "Brad, I've got an idea how you can sweep her off her feet. She will be forever indebted to you, believe me."

Palmer glanced at Hutton and laughed. "We'll send Harry over to their table, then you rescue the women, and you'll be a knight in shining armor."

Hutton gave Palmer the middle-finger salute.

Brad looked again and caught the young lady's eye. They exchanged smiling glances.

After finishing their drinks, the older woman signed the check and they left. Brad got up, walked by the vacated table, glanced at the slip of paper, then continued down the hallway to the rest rooms. The check had been signed S. W. Ladasau.

Returning to the lounge, Brad saw that the bill had been removed from the table. He returned to his seat, tuning out one of Palmer's flying stories. Still thinking about the stunningly beautiful woman, Brad dreamily watched the surfers and outrigger canoes race along the tops of the sparkling waves.

His mind drifted back to the carrier, replaying his crash landing and the narrow escapes. The mental pictures of war and death were becoming impossible to obliterate from his thoughts. After a minute, his mind returned to the image of the beautiful brunette. He continued to gaze at the ocean, but his mind did not register the view.

After another round of drinks, the foursome went into the Surf Room and ordered dinner. They enjoyed a savory meal of fresh seafood and island cuisine. After Baked Alaska, freshly ground Kona coffee, and a snifter of brandy, the group had agreed that they were too tired to go out and pursue female companionship that evening. The flight had been grueling and uncomfortable, leaving them physically and mentally exhausted.

After returning to their suite, Palmer and Lunsford crashed on their beds and were asleep almost immediately. Brad walked into the living room and out to the lanai. Watching the bright moon, he sat down in a thickly padded lounge chair and replayed the scene in the Mai-Tai Bar. He could not erase the image of the stunning brunette.

Brad's last thought, before falling sound asleep, was about the young woman named Ladasau.

16

Austin awakened to the sound of waves gently washing ashore. The clear sky was beginning to show signs of sunrise. Listening to the chirping and singing of the birds, Brad squinted at his wristwatch lying on the nightstand. It read 5:35 A.M.

He closed his eyes for a few minutes, re-forming the image of the attractive girl he had seen in the cocktail lounge. Feeling restless, he prepared for an early walk on the beach.

Brad picked up a complimentary newspaper in the lobby, then leisurely walked out to the veranda. He watched the maintenance workers rake the powdery white sand smooth, and toss the debris left by the sun worshipers into three large plastic containers.

Feeling the tension flow from his body, Brad glanced at the front page of the paper, stopping occasionally to cast a look out over the tranquil ocean. He became engrossed in watching a navy cruiser that had just cleared the entrance to Pearl Harbor. A destroyer followed a minute later, increasing speed to match the larger vessel.

When the ships had sailed over the horizon, Brad started to open his paper, then froze in place. The woman of his dreams was walking up from the beach. She was wearing light green slacks and a loose-fitting green-and-white striped blouse. Carrying her white sandals, she was approaching the Royal Hawaiian from the Diamond Head end of Waikiki Beach.

Brad felt a fleeting moment of anxiety. What am I going

to say? he asked himself as the girl stepped onto the sidewalk. What the hell, he thought to himself, then got up. God never loved a coward.

The pretty woman looked at Brad when he stood. She smiled as she neared him. "Good morning."

"Good morning, Miss Ladasau," Brad responded, feeling slightly foolish.

"Pardon me," the woman replied, slightly tilting her head. "Have we met?"

Brad cleared his throat. "No, unfortunately, but now is as good a time as any." A quizzical look crossed her face.

"I'm Brad Austin."

The girl extended a slim hand. "Leigh Ann Ladasau."

"My pleasure," Brad replied, gently shaking her hand. "Do you prefer Leigh, or Leigh Ann?"

"Everyone calls me Leigh Ann."

"Spelled L-e-i-g-h?" Brad asked, releasing her hand. He was captivated by the soft, feminine voice.

"That's correct," she replied with just a trace of southern accent. Turning to leave, she looked over her shoulder. "Nice meeting you."

"Wait," Brad said, dropping the paper. "How about a cup of coffee, or some juice? The dining room will be open in a couple of minutes."

Leigh Ann contemplated the offer. "I'm sorry, but I'll have to decline. Thank you, anyway."

"We'll be in a public place," Brad appealed. "I won't attack you . . . I promise."

Letting out a sigh, Leigh Ann smiled. "You're a very persistent person. You must be in the military."

Brad hesitated, unsure of her reaction to the truth. "You're right."

"Which service?" she asked. "And what do you do?"

"Marine Corps . . . fighter pilot."

"Oh, well, that explains it," Leigh Ann laughed. "Okay, Brad, let's make it breakfast. I'm famished."

She dropped her sandals and stepped into them. "Your friends—the ones you were with yesterday afternoon—are they marine pilots too?"

''No. One of them is a pilot, but he's navy. The other two are navy radar-intercept officers. We fly—the four of us—as two teams in F-4 Phantoms.'' Brad could see a question on Leigh Ann's face. ''I'm on exchange duty with a navy fighter squadron based on board a carrier. We're on rest and relaxation while the ship is in port at Subic Bay . . . in the Philippines.''

''That must be exciting . . . flying from the deck of an aircraft carrier.''

''Yes,'' Brad replied, enthralled by Leigh Ann's blue eyes, ''it's a different world, believe me.''

The couple walked into the sheltered, open-air dining facility and chose a quiet table. Brad seated Leigh Ann as a waitress approached them. They both ordered a sumptuous breakfast and sipped fresh guava juice while they waited to be served.

''So,'' Brad said, ''tell me about yourself, now that I've kidnapped you right off the beach.''

She hesitated, smiling an acknowledgment before forming her response. ''I'm twenty-two, a recent graduate of Vanderbilt University, with a degree in English. I'm a resident of Memphis, Tennessee, and I'm on vacation with my parents, Doctor and Mrs. Simon Ladasau.''

''Interesting,'' Brad replied slowly. ''Have you had an opportunity to sightsee—drive around the island?''

''No, I'm afraid not,'' Leigh Ann answered as her breakfast was placed on the table. ''This is my second trip to the islands, and my father doesn't journey once we arrive. However, I have been on the Pearl Harbor cruise, which was very sobering.''

Brad thanked the waitress and looked into Leigh Ann's sparkling blue eyes. ''How much longer will you be here?''

She finished a bite of her eggs Benedict and dabbed her mouth with the linen napkin. ''We are leaving day after tomorrow. We've been here two weeks today.''

Brad felt a twinge of disappointment but decided not to be deterred. ''I've spent some time here at the Kaneohe Bay Marine Air Station, so I got to know Oahu fairly well.''

Brad pondered his next question. ''How about a tour of

the island? I know a great place to have lunch . . . a nice restaurant overlooking Kailua Bay.''

Leigh Ann swallowed discreetly. ''Brad, I do appreciate your offer—I sincerely mean that. We just met . . . and my parents have never met you.'' Leigh Ann smiled. ''You understand . . . I'm sure.''

Brad quietly placed his fork on the pink china. ''Why don't you introduce me, and we'll invite them along. I'll do the driving, and you and your parents can relax—have a guided tour.''

She remained quiet a moment, sipping the fresh guava juice. ''You are absolutely relentless, aren't you? Did they teach you that in the Marine Corps, or is it just your nature?''

Feeling slightly sheepish, Brad leaned toward her. ''Leigh Ann, I'd like to get to know you, and I'm being honest about taking your mother and father with us.''

She looked out at the ocean for a few moments, then turned to face Brad, gazing into his eyes. ''Why is it that I instinctively trust you?''

Caught off guard, Brad shrugged and smiled. He remembered what the CO had said about the oath the officers had taken. ''My commission states that I'm a gentleman, reposing of special trust and confidence.''

Smiling, Leigh Ann studied his face. ''I have two questions before I go gallivanting around the island with someone I barely know.''

With a degree of trepidation, Brad quickly said, ''Certainly.''

''How did you know my last name, and how did you know I would be walking on the beach this morning?''

Feeling an uneasiness in his throat, Brad swallowed the last of his juice. ''I looked at the name on the hotel check that your mother signed. I was fairly sure that you were her daughter.''

''Very clever,'' Leigh Ann remarked with a smile, then added, ''but what about this morning? Did you note our room number, then wait around the corner all night?''

Brad chuckled softly.

"What's so funny?"

"Well," he began, carefully choosing his words, "that wouldn't have been a bad idea, but the truth is that our encounter was pure dumb luck on my part."

She smiled serenely. "Your luck is still holding. My parents just walked in for breakfast."

Brad stood and shook hands with the handsome couple when he was introduced. Both parents were friendly and cordial as Brad seated Mrs. Ladasau and returned to his chair.

Leigh Ann explained who Brad was, how they had met on the beach, and then explained that he and his friends were on leave while their ship was being repaired. She also told her parents that Brad had been stationed on Oahu, and had offered to be a tour guide for the family.

Dr. Ladasau casually studied Brad. "Do you come from a family with a military tradition?"

"Yes, sir," Brad replied uncomfortably. "I am a third-generation graduate of the Naval Academy. My father is a vice admiral, and my grandfather is a retired rear admiral."

The doctor continued to quiz Brad. He was reserved, obviously scrutinizing this young man who had asked his daughter to breakfast and had offered a tour of the island.

When Brad reiterated his offer to drive the family around the island, Dr. Ladasau thanked him but declined the invitation, explaining that he had a tennis match with a colleague. Mrs. Ladasau also graciously declined, suggesting that Leigh Ann and Brad did not need to be dragging around old fogies.

Blushing, Brad stood when Leigh Ann neatly folded her napkin on the table and rose. Reaching for his check, Brad was unprepared when the doctor slid it to his side of the table.

"Please allow us, Captain," he said, casting a warning glance at his daughter. "You and Leigh Ann have a pleasant tour."

Catching the intimating look, Brad expressed his thanks and escorted Leigh Ann to the lobby. He suggested that she bring a bathing suit and a pair of sunglasses. They set a time to meet in the lobby, then Brad hurried across Kalakaua Avenue to a car-rental franchise. He selected a white Mustang convertible, and drove to the Royal Hawaiian.

Back in the suite, Palmer was showering while Lunsford was shaving. Dressed and ready to go, Hutton was lying peacefully on one of the sofas. He had donned his bright yellow-and-purple aloha shirt.

"Harry," Brad offered, trying to keep a straight face, "you look dashing."

Lunsford yelled from the bathroom. "I thought you couldn't be a RIO if you were color-blind. Guess Harry slipped through."

"Where the hell have you been?" Hutton asked, not waiting for an answer. "Better get your shit together, Your Captaincy, 'cause we're going trolling."

"I've already got a date," Brad replied, yanking open his section of the dresser drawer. He grabbed his swimming suit and his military-issue sunglasses. "I'm taking that brunette—the one who was in the lounge yesterday—on a tour of the island."

Hutton snickered. "Don't bullshit me."

"I'm serious."

"How'd you get a date with her?" Lunsford asked, wiping the shaving cream from his face.

"I met her on the beach. We had breakfast together."

Lunsford leaned around the corner. "You're talking about the knockout . . . the one who looks like a twenty-year-old version of Elizabeth Taylor?"

"One and the same," Brad replied as he grabbed two thick towels and hurried to the door. "Have a great day, boys."

17

With the trade winds tousling their hair, Brad and Leigh Ann motored along Diamond Head Road, taking in the sights of Kupikipikio Point and Maunalua Bay.

"Brad," Leigh Ann paused, looking back at the volcanic crater, "how did Diamond Head get its name?"

"Some of the pioneer sailors found glittering coral-encrusted crystals on the side of the crater, so they named the formation Diamond Head."

Leigh Ann turned slightly in her seat, facing Brad. "You are a good tour guide," she smiled.

Brad grinned. "It's my pleasure, I can assure you."

They continued past Hawaii Kai to the Koko Head Crater and stopped at Hanauma Bay. Brad pulled off the side of the main highway and parked near the scenic overlook.

Leigh Ann was mesmerized by the tranquility of the sparkling bay. "Brad, this is one of the most beautiful places I've ever seen."

"I thought you would like it," he answered, silently thinking that the woman next to him was every bit as lovely as the setting. "I think it's one of the most peaceful, serene locations on the island."

They watched the snorklers swimming among the thousands of brightly colored tropical fish in the warm, crystal-clear waters. Fishing had been prohibited in the cozy bay, turning the flooded volcanic crater into a giant seaquarium.

Leigh Ann smiled at him. "I had no idea the rest of Oahu was so . . . I don't know . . . dissimilar and beautiful."

"Yes, it would be a pity not to get beyond the Waikiki area, which is not representative of the entire island."

They passed Makapuu Point and Waimanalo Beach. When the reached the outskirts of Kailua, Brad pulled in front of a small restaurant overlooking Kailua Bay, where scores of colorful sailboats tacked back and forth across the placid, greenish blue water.

Brad got out of the convertible and walked around to open Leigh Ann's door. "This used to be one of my favorite restaurants when I was stationed at Kaneohe."

"For the food, or for the view?"

"Both," he replied, holding the door open. He examined the bay. "The view hasn't changed."

"I'm sure the food is still excellent, too." They sat on the open-air porch and ordered.

"Your father," Brad said, carefully selecting his words, "left me with the impression that he isn't very fond of the military, or perhaps he doesn't care for me."

"My father," she replied with a trace of frustration, "is a dyed-in-the-wool antiwar sentimentalist, especially the Vietnam War. I love him very much, but he sometimes embarrasses me." She glanced down. "I apologize for his . . . coolness."

"No apology needed," Brad chuckled. "I don't agree with the war either."

"You don't?"

"No," Brad replied, growing serious. "Our military commanders don't start wars, but when they are ordered to fight a war, they should be allowed to win . . . in minimum time, and with the least amount of casualties."

"I'm not sure I understand. Why would we be in Vietnam if we weren't trying to win?"

"Because," Brad replied, attempting to conceal his contempt, "the Johnson administration won't listen to their military commanders, or let them do their jobs. Johnson and McNamara dole out targets on a piecemeal basis, with the mistaken belief that the Communists will see the futility of their aggression and come to the peace table."

Leigh Ann's look registered her concern. "What's going to happen?"

"Well, I suspect that the administration will continue to bungle along, until someone faces the facts of war. The North Vietnamese won't give up until we destroy their capability to wage war."

"Aren't we doing that now?"

"To a degree," Brad answered uncomfortably, "under the current rules of engagement. But we aren't going to win the war until our military is allowed to attack all of the airfields, power plants, transportation systems, military installations, port facilities, war industries, and other targets in major population centers."

Leigh Ann frowned. "What a horrible thing . . . war."

"Yes, it is," he sighed, glancing at the bay.

Leigh Ann studied Brad. "What's it like to be a jet-fighter pilot, and fly from the decks of ships?"

Unprepared for the question, Brad searched for an answer that would not offend her sensitivity. "Leigh Ann, flying is fun for me, whether I'm in a fighter, or rolling and looping an aerobatic biplane. Flying from a carrier, especially at night, is the most exhilarating and terrifying experience I've ever had. The sensations and visceral fear are difficult to describe."

He paused, carefully phrasing his words. "You would have to ride through a cat shot and a one-hundred-fifty-mile-an-hour trap—arrested landing—to know what the brain and body experience."

"I'm sorry," Leigh Ann smiled, "but I don't believe I would care to experience the feeling."

Brad chuckled. "That's probably valid thinking."

Cautiously, Leigh Ann began to ask the questions that had piqued her curiosity since breakfast. "Where are you from . . . where do you call home?"

Without removing his eyes from Leigh Ann's delicate face, Brad thought about the past Christmas. Because of the animosity between his father and himself, which had developed into an unspoken estrangement, Brad had elected to forego future trips home. His mother, who had not been pleased with his decision, had understood the reason for Brad's resoluteness. His father was not accustomed to having people thwart his wishes.

"Well, I was born in San Diego, grew up all over the world, and would have to say that my home is the aircraft carrier."

Leigh Ann sensed that there was something more lying just below the surface. Something about his family that Brad Austin did not care to discuss.

He glanced at the sailboats and then looked up at a section of marine F-4s departing Kaneohe Bay Air Station. "That's what I fly."

Leigh Ann followed the thundering jets until the fighter pilots had deselected their afterburners. "What kind of airplanes are those?"

Brad turned back to Leigh Ann. "Fighter-bombers. It's officially called the F-4 Phantom, but it has earned various nicknames in the past couple of years."

"It sure is impressive . . . mean looking," she said, turning to watch the two fighters climb out of sight, "and loud."

"That it is," he replied as the luncheon appetizers were delivered to their table. "Would you care for a glass of wine with your lunch?"

"That would be nice."

Brad ordered a glass of the house white wine for each of them. They drank a toast to Hawaii and to the beautiful weather.

"This looks scrumptious," Leigh Ann said as she raised her fork. "Do you know what type of fish these are?"

"Sure," he replied, turning to look at her meal. "That's mahimahi at the top of your plate. To the left is ahi, which is a yellowfin tuna. On the right is opakapaka, a variety of snapper. Below is a king mackerel . . . and I'm sure you have the center section figured out."

"Yes," Leigh Ann laughed. "Shrimp."

Brad ate slowly and sipped his wine. He waited until she had finished a bite before asking a question. "What are your plans for the future?"

Leigh Ann placed her fork thoughtfully on her plate. "Well, I would like to pursue my master's, and, hopefully, find a good teaching position."

Brad nodded. "You seem to have a clear goal in mind."

"What about you?" she asked, raising her glass. "What are your plans for the future? Do you intend to make the Marine Corps a career?"

Brad looked into his wineglass. "I don't have any answers at the moment. Right now, due to our rudderless administration in Washington, I'm concentrating on getting through the next couple of months."

She detected a pronounced degree of antagonism in his normally affable voice. "So, do you have any brothers and sisters?"

"It's my turn to apologize," Brad said, realizing that he had let his hostilities invade the conversation. "I didn't mean to sound bitter."

"That's okay," Leigh Ann replied with a sincerity that surprised Brad. "I understand . . . I really do, Brad."

He smiled with a trace of embarrassment. "Yes, to answer your question, I have one older brother. He's in the navy, serving on a combat stores ship."

"Did he attend the academy, too?"

"Yes, he did," Brad said with obvious pride. "He is three years older, and helped me learn the ropes before he graduated. What about you? Any siblings to rival with?"

Leigh Ann grinned. "Yes, and we do have our moments of . . . let's say, misunderstandings."

Brad nodded.

"Eleanor, who is a senior in high school this year, is going through the rebellious stage." Leigh Ann smiled wryly. "That's why she stayed home . . . so the three of us could have some peace and quiet."

Brad laughed.

After lunch, they decided to save the swim for Waikiki Beach. Brad had suggested that they take the highway past the Nuuanu Pali. The drive through the Koolau Mountain Range would take them directly back to the outskirts of Honolulu.

Caught in an afternoon rain shower, they had to stop four miles from downtown Honolulu and raise the convertible top. They dove back into the shelter of the car, and Brad grabbed the towels from the backseat. He unfolded one of the thick pink towels and softly dried Leigh Ann's face.

"Thank you," she said laughingly, then reached for the other towel. "Your turn."

She patted his face dry, stopping when he took her hands and gently kissed her. Leigh Ann did not resist, returning the kiss with affection. "Is that part of your normal island tour?"

Brad grinned. "No . . . it's hard to schedule the rain."

She chuckled and softly kissed his cheek. "We better get back, before there's a cloudburst."

Brad nodded and placed the car in gear, then pulled back onto the highway. He reached for Leigh Ann's hand, gently folding her fingers in his. She smiled and moved closer to him.

Arriving back at the Royal Hawaiian, he walked Leigh Ann into the lobby.

"Brad," she said warmly, "I thoroughly enjoyed our outing . . . even the soaking."

"It was my pleasure," he replied, then laughed. "I don't mean getting you wet was a pleasure."

She shifted her beach bag. "I really do appreciate that wonderful drive."

"Well, Leigh Ann," Brad said with an impish look, "since I managed to get your hair wet, we might as well go for the swim we planned."

"Okay, but how about a ride in one of the outrigger canoes first?"

"Wonderful idea," he answered. "I'll meet you on the beach in fifteen minutes."

"You're on," she replied gaily. "See you in a few minutes."

Brad returned the automobile and hurried back to the hotel, thrilled to be spending more time with this beautiful woman.

Changing into his swimming suit, Brad thought about the

small amount of time he would have with Leigh Ann before she had to leave. Feeling an intense desire to be with her, he was considering the possibility of asking her to stay longer. He would be more than happy to pay for her room and associated expenses but doubted that her father would allow it.

Brad walked out to the beach just as Leigh Ann, wearing a provocative white bikini, came to join him. He found it difficult not to stare at her stunning figure. She was trim and shapely with beautifully tanned skin. Her scant top showed a hint of cleavage that accentuated her tiny waist and narrow hips. Her legs were the most beautiful he had ever seen.

Snapping himself out of his trance, Brad took Leigh Ann's hand and helped her board an outrigger canoe. They paddled out beyond the breakers, then turned and raced down the waves. After three more exhilarating round-trips they returned to the beachfront.

Weaving their way through the sunbathers, they walked hand in hand through the hot sand to the hotel. "Would you care for something to drink?" Brad asked, admiring Leigh Ann's tanned face.

"Sure," she smiled demurely. "A Blue Hawaii sounds good to me."

Brad ordered two of the specialty drinks. The day was going so well, he thought he would try to keep it going longer. He caught Leigh Ann's eyes. "At the risk of pushing my luck, will you have dinner with me this evening?"

Leigh Ann turned to face Brad. "I would be pleased to have dinner with you."

"Great."

"However," Leigh Ann continued, "I have an obligation I have to fulfill first. My parents are expecting me to attend a small dinner party with friends of theirs from medical school."

"That's fine," Brad said as the tropical drinks were placed on the table. "We'll have a late dinner."

She laughed softly. "Better than that. I'll have a glass of

wine, a few hors d'oeuvres, then explain that I have a dinner date with an irresistible pilot.''

Sipping his drink, Brad swallowed wrong, almost choking at the unexpected comment. He coughed twice, then excused himself.

''Are you okay?'' Leigh Ann asked with genuine concern.

Brad nodded and took a long pull on his straw. ''I'm fine.'' He swallowed again, clearing his throat. He hoped the redness on his face would also clear. ''You're really amazing.''

Leigh Ann looked at him over the top of her tall drink. ''Amazing?''

''Yes,'' Brad answered, reaching for her hand. ''You appear to be reserved and unapproachable, but you're really the most down-to-earth, uncomplicated person I've met in a long time.''

''Why, thank you, Captain Austin.''

18

Brad waited in the hotel lobby, trying to pass the time reading a lengthy article about the history of the Hawaiian Islands. Nick Palmer, Russ Lunsford, and an obviously inebriated Harry Hutton had stumbled in at a quarter past five. They had met three United Airlines stewardesses who were going to a luau with them. Harry talked incessantly about the virtues of the blonde "trophy" he had snared. He said they were going to a Polynesian feast of food, drink, and wild sex. And off they went, guiding Harry down the hallway.

Brad was startled when Leigh Ann walked up to the side of his high-backed chair.

"Expecting someone, flyboy?" she asked as Brad leaped to his feet. Perfectly coiffed, Leigh Ann was wearing a pale yellow spaghetti-strap dress and off-white sandals.

"You look beautiful," said Brad, reaching down for the plumeria leis he had purchased in the hotel flower shop. "I thought you might enjoy some fresh flowers."

"Brad, they're gorgeous. Thank you."

"You're welcome," he replied, carefully slipping one of the leis over Leigh Ann's head. Her fragrance was stimulating. He kissed her lightly on the cheek.

Placing the other wreath of flowers over Brad's head, she hesitated a moment, then returned the kiss. "You're a nice guy, Brad Austin."

"I'll bet you say that to all the guys," he replied, taking her hand as they walked out of the lobby. "How was the dinner party?"

"It was fine, but I was anxious to leave."

Brad arched his eyebrow. "You were?"

"Yes." She squeezed his hand and captured his eye. "I wanted to be with you."

Feeling elated, Brad mentally pinched himself. He was with one of the most attractive women he had ever seen, and she seemed to genuinely like him.

"Where are we going for dinner?" she inquired when they reached busy Kalakaua Avenue.

Brad's thoughts returned to the moment, stepping around Leigh Ann to the concrete curb. "I thought we would stroll down to the Moana, and have a slow, relaxing dinner."

"That sounds wonderful."

Brad glanced at Leigh Ann. "I reserved a quiet table with a view over the Banyan Courtyard."

"You must have some influence."

"Not actually." Brad squirmed.

She gave him a suspicious look. "You just called the Moana, and requested prime seating at the height of the dinner hour?"

"I told the maître d'," Brad responded, averting his eyes, "that we're on our honeymoon."

"Our honeymoon?" Leigh Ann asked, wide-eyed.

Brad chuckled. "Well, there are two definitions. One includes a period of harmony in a new relationship."

Smiling, she shook her head. "Did you reserve a honeymoon suite, too?"

"I thought about it."

Leigh Ann laughed out loud. "Incredible."

They walked up to the elegant "First Lady of Waikiki" and entered the hotel lobby. Feeling a little awkward, Brad led Leigh Ann to the main dining room. The Ship's Tavern was one of his favorite restaurants on the island.

"Austin," Brad announced nervously to the maître d'. "Eight fifteen."

"Ah, yes," the pleasant man replied. "Mister and Missus Austin. Right this way, please."

Leigh Ann darted a look at Brad but remained quiet as they proceeded to their table. After being seated, the maître d' congratulated the couple on their marriage, then returned to his station.

She tilted her head and smiled. "Let me hear your explanation as to the reason we aren't wearing wedding rings."

Brad took in the view of the spectacular sunset. "I haven't thought of one . . . yet."

She tried not to laugh. "Okay, Captain Austin, it's your turn to tell me all about yourself, and how many other wives you have."

Relieved when a cocktail waitress arrived, Brad ordered an aperitif for each of them.

"Well, I had a normal childhood, if you describe normal as going to seven different schools in twelve years. I enjoyed attending Annapolis, after the first year." Brad paused. "Are you sure you want to hear all this?"

"Yes, I'm positive."

"My degree is in aeronautical engineering, which helped me when I went through flight school." He stopped talking while their drinks were served.

Remembering that Brad had avoided discussing his family, Leigh Ann cautiously approached a question. "Brad, why did you join the marines when you come from a navy background?"

He closed his eyes for a second, thinking about the number of times he had had to answer the same question. "I had watched the relationships of other fathers and sons who served in the same service. Many times—too many times—it's like working in your father's business. I wanted to be in a separate service, so no one could infer that my father had any influence on my career."

Brad stopped again when their waiter arrived. After ordering dinner, Brad captured Leigh Ann's eyes. "May I ask you a personal question?"

She looked wary. "You can ask anything you like, but I may elect not to answer."

Brad set his glass down. "With your looks, intelligence, and personality, there must be a man in your life."

"There was," Leigh Ann responded, turning serious, "but that episode in my life is over."

"Episode?"

Leigh Ann was silent a moment, blocking out an extremely painful experience. "Brad," she began, "I was engaged to a medical student. A handsome, romantic, witty guy . . . and now I'm not engaged, thank God."

Confused, Brad remained quiet while he sipped his drink.

"That's why," Leigh Ann continued, holding her emotions in check, "I came to Hawaii with my parents. They wanted me to get away . . . and let my pride heal. That's why my father scrutinized you so closely this morning."

"Obviously, I am curious," Brad said in a gentle tone. "What happened?"

Their dinner arrived, taking the edge off the uncomfortable conversation. After selecting a bottle of chardonnay to accompany the truffled Bresse poultry and fillet of turbot in champagne sauce, Brad paused while the waiter opened the bottle.

After sampling the wine, Brad waited until their glasses were filled and they were alone again. "A toast," he said cheerily, raising his glass.

Leigh Ann smiled, lifting her wine.

"To a special evening," Brad said, reaching out to clasp Leigh Ann's left hand, "with a very special lady."

She squeezed his fingers when their glasses met. "To a special man . . . who made it all possible."

Brad touched her glass again and released her hand. They ate quietly, exchanging small talk. After dessert, Brad settled the check and they repaired to the Banyan Veranda for an after-dinner drink.

Brad seated Leigh Ann at a corner table and took a seat with his back against the wall. It was his natural instinct to sit in a position to observe everyone around him. His six was protected.

Brad ordered a Grand Marnier for Leigh Ann and a Drambuie for himself as they viewed the twinkling stars and the moonlight silvering the calm ocean. Their cordials arrived almost immediately.

He tasted his drink and gazed at Leigh Ann. The yellow spaghetti-strap dress accentuated her soft, round shoulders. "Well," Brad began cautiously, "do you want to tell me what happened to your engagement?"

Leigh Ann turned to Brad. "Not really . . . but I might as well face the humiliation."

Brad hoped he looked as sympathetic as he felt.

"His name is Tyler," she said in a small voice, "and he comes from a privileged background. So much so, that he believes that moral values and ethical conduct do not apply to him. He is above the masses."

Brad frowned in confusion. "You've lost me."

"He," Leigh Ann blurted, "was engaged to two people at the same time . . . and seeing a third woman on the side."

"Jesus Christ," Brad said, astonished that anyone could do that to someone so beautiful and wonderful. He reached for Leigh Ann's small hands.

She extended her hands to meet his. "That is the story of my engagement . . . and it's over—finished."

Inhaling deeply, Brad winked at her. "Let's take a walk on the beach, okay?"

She smiled in return, feeling a lump in her throat. Her eyes were wet, but she did not shed a tear. Brad paid the check and handed Leigh Ann a fresh cocktail napkin to dry her eyes.

"I'm okay," she said, regaining her composure. "I really am . . . I promise."

Hand in hand, they walked across the veranda, under the immense banyan tree, past the swimming pool, and then stopped at the edge of the beach. They removed their shoes and stepped on the cool sand. Brad carried Leigh Ann's sandals while she waded a short distance in the gentle surf.

When she returned to his side, Brad placed an arm around her shoulders. He was filled with warmth when Leigh Ann slid an arm around his waist.

They walked in silence until Brad spotted a wide, covered lifeguard structure. "Leigh Ann," Brad said with a hint of excitement, "let's sit in the lifeguard stand."

She had regained her humor. "Uh, oh. I think I'm in trouble now."

Brad laughed, then preceded her up the short ladder to the bench seat. He helped her up the steep steps, then leaned against the back support.

"Leigh Ann," Brad began as they squeezed close to each other, "I have something I want to discuss with you."

She turned to him, only inches from his face. "You're not going to propose, are you? We haven't even known each other twenty-four hours."

Brad was surprised that she had even broached the subject that had been so painful for her. "In my world, twenty-four hours can be a lifetime."

"I know," Leigh Ann replied, resting her head on Brad's shoulder. "I was only kidding."

"Well, I'm not kidding," Brad said with unusual gravity. "I would like for you to stay in Hawaii for the remainder of my leave period . . . if you can."

Smiling, she lifted her head and turned to him. "I've already thought about extending my vacation."

Brad was astounded that Leigh Ann had even considered staying longer. He twisted sideways and cupped her delicate face in his hands. He tilted his head slightly and met her lips, kissing passionately while she held him to her.

He released her, gently biting her lower lip. "This isn't a dream, is it? I'm not going to wake up and be alone, am I?"

"No, Brad," Leigh Ann purred, kissing him again. "I'm going to stay in Hawaii with you." They embraced, holding each other with an emotional intensity that quickened their pulses.

"Can't you tell," Leigh Ann whispered, brushing her lips against his ear, "when a woman has fallen head over heels for you?"

"Like I said," Brad responded, kissing her neck, then her shoulder, "you are amazing."

She leaned back, smiling broadly. "Well, flyboy, how about a nightcap at our hotel? My treat."

"Sure," Brad replied, reaching for their shoes. "I suppose it's in my best interest to have you in your room at a respectable hour.''

''Yes,'' Leigh Ann grinned. ''Appearances are important . . . my dad doesn't like warriors.''

He managed a small laugh. ''Yes, I'm painfully aware of that.''

Brad lightly kissed Leigh Ann, then helped her down from their perch. Feeling as though he was walking on air, he expressed it out loud.

''What?'' Leigh Ann asked when she reached the cool sand.

''I said,'' Brad chuckled, ''I think I've died and gone to heaven.''

Leigh Ann wrapped her arm around his waist, silently inviting Brad to reciprocate. ''Is that another line you use often?'' She hugged his waist a second.

''I don't have any lines,'' Brad replied, falling in step with her. ''Will I ever live down the tactics I've had to use to get to know you?''

Leigh Ann laughed softly as they approached the beachfront of the Royal Hawaiian. ''You're forgiven. Just don't ever hurt me.''

Feeling a glowing excitement, Brad stopped and turned to Leigh Ann. He held her shoulders. ''Leigh Ann, I don't have a wife, fiancée, or even a girlfriend. There aren't any skeletons in my closet.''

She gave him a hint of a smile. ''I notice the way women look at you, and I'm supposed to believe that there isn't another woman in your life?''

Brad glanced at the array of torches lighting the hotel grounds, then back to Leigh Ann. ''There was a woman in my life, but she found a meal ticket and married him while I was going to flight school.''

''It sounds to me,'' Leigh Ann said softly, ''as if you're still bitter.''

Brad gazed into her eyes, clear and blue in the luminescent moonlight. ''No, not bitter. I'm just embarrassed by my poor judgment of her character. I guess we have both made similar mistakes.''

"Well," she replied, pulling him to her, "you didn't make a mistake that might have made you miserable."

Brad could smell the pleasant fragrance of her smooth, dark hair. "That's true, but it was still a no-brainer relationship. My hormones and libido made all the decisions . . . and I am lucky to have escaped."

Leigh Ann met his lips, holding him close a few seconds. "Brad," she breathed, "I'm the lucky one. I found you."

They could hear the sounds of Hawaiian music drifting from the oceanfront Monarch Room. "Leigh Ann," Brad said, wrapping her in his arms, "isn't that a beautiful song?"

She placed her forehead against his. "The Hawaiian Wedding Song."

He kissed her, then said the name of the song in the Hawaiian language. "Ke Kali Nei Au."

Entwined, Brad and Leigh Ann walked to the Mai-Tai Bar, ordered exotic tropical coolers, then pulled two lounge chairs together on the beach and reclined. Leigh Ann tucked her dress under her legs.

Taking her hand in his, Brad listened to the soothing music, and basked in the warmth of Leigh Ann's touch. Her face was radiant in the soft glow of the torchlights.

"Tomorrow morning," Brad suggested, turning to look at her, "let's have the hotel prepare a picnic basket, then we'll rent a light plane and fly to Kauai."

"Could we?"

"Sure," Brad smiled. "I flew to most of the small airstrips on the islands when I was stationed at Kaneohe. I know a great place to land for lunch, after we tour the island and see the sights by air."

"How exciting," Leigh Ann exclaimed, then added, "Being involved with you, I have a feeling, is going to be an adventure."

Brad laughed out loud, feeling invigorated. "Involved? Do you consider our relationship to be more than just a fling in Hawaii?"

Leigh Ann carefully placed her drink in the sand next to

her lounge chair, then moved to sit next to Brad. She put her arms around his neck, kissing him ardently.

"God . . . damn," he wheezed, catching his breath. His heart pounded. "I've been at sea too long."

"Brad," Leigh Ann said, stretching out in his arms, "I've never felt like this before . . . not in two weeks, or two months. I thought about what you said—living a lifetime in twenty-four hours—and I've always been a lady who has gone by the rules."

"Of a civilized society," Brad interjected, holding her head in the crook of his neck.

"Yes," she replied in a low, muted voice. "Now, I want to express my feelings, say what I really mean, and trust and love again."

"Leigh Ann," Brad said, gently kissing her soft hair, "my feelings for you are genuine, even though we've been together only a short time."

"Mine, too."

Brad's mind raced, ecstatic in the knowledge that the beautiful woman lying next to him wanted him in the same way he wanted her. "Leigh Ann," Brad ventured, "let's go for a swim in the ocean."

Her eyes widened when she raised her head. "Brad, I can't go swimming in this dress . . . and I'm not wearing a bra."

Brad pulled her next to him. "I hadn't planned for us to swim in our clothes."

She kissed him in the small of his throat. "You're incorrigible."

"Leigh Ann," Brad raised her chin, "this is happening faster than I had ever imagined." They remained quiet a moment, locked in their embrace. She could hear his heartbeat.

"We haven't even had an intimate relationship," Leigh Ann sighed.

Brad chuckled. "You have a quaint way with words."

"Okay, flyboy, we haven't been to bed together," she laughed, then poked him in the ribs, "but I have no doubt that you'll make the proper arrangements."

Brad started to respond, then glimpsed movement a few yards away. Startled, he snapped his head to the side. He saw a bright yellow aloha shirt.

"Sorry," a somber Harry Hutton said. "We've been trying to find you." Leigh Ann sat upright, gripping Brad's arm.

"What the hell is going on?" Brad asked, experiencing a sinking feeling in the pit of his stomach. He leaned forward to a sitting position.

"We've been recalled," Harry announced painfully, "to Subic . . . to the carrier."

"Oh, no," Leigh Ann gasped, then trembled once.

"Harry," Brad said icily, "if this is one of your practical jokes, I am going to kick your ass." He turned to Leigh Ann. "Pardon me."

"Brad," Hutton said, venturing closer, "I am not kidding. The ship is getting under way tomorrow. The word was sent to Barbers Point, where they had a record of where we're staying, and the base duty officer notified the hotel operator. The assistant manager had seen us make the luau reservations, so they knew where to find us."

"Goddamnit," Brad swore to himself. "What the hell happened to the ten-day to two-week estimate?"

"Nick called Subic," Harry answered, "and talked to Jocko. The problem wasn't as severe as they had anticipated. The yard people worked around the clock to replace whatever the hell was broken. They ran the engine with the ship tied to the dock, and they didn't have any vibration."

Brad turned to Leigh Ann. "I'm sorry, this is Harry Hutton, my roommate. Harry, Leigh Ann Ladasau."

They exchanged polite greetings.

"When do we have to leave?" Brad asked, placing a comforting hand on Leigh Ann's knee.

"As soon as possible," Harry answered gloomily. "They've got us scheduled on an air-force tanker—a KC-135—leaving for Guam at oh three hundred."

Brad looked at his watch. They had a little less than four hours to departure time. "Harry, you guys go ahead. I'll change, check out of our room, then take a cab to Hickam."

"Okay," Hutton replied, feeling like an intruder. "It was a pleasure meeting you, Leigh Ann."

"Nice meeting you, Harry. I hope I'll see you again, under more pleasant circumstances."

"I hope so, too," he responded, then hurried to leave a message at the front desk for Palmer and Lunsford.

"Brad, please hold me."

He took her in his arms, suffering the anguish of impending separation. The powers that be were going to tear him away from this beautiful, wonderful woman, and send him back to war. A war filled with senseless death and destruction.

"Darling," Leigh Ann said, misty-eyed, "I want to see you off . . . at the base."

Brad steeled himself and held her closer. "Leigh Ann, I'm not going to have you riding alone in a taxi at three in the morning."

"Brad, I'm twenty-two years old."

"Please," he said uncomfortably, "let me have my way on this one. I'm a little overprotective when I care for someone."

Leigh Ann choked back a sob. "Okay, I'll wait for you in the lobby."

Brad escorted her to the lobby, then hurried to the suite. He quickly changed into his uniform, packed his belongings, checked for items left behind, and returned to the front desk.

He was perplexed to find that Leigh Ann was nowhere in sight. Brad settled the room account, threw his overnight bag over his shoulder, and started for the entry.

Leigh Ann rushed into the lobby as Brad reached the entrance. "Brad," she called. "Wait."

He spun around and handed his bag to the bellhop. "I'll need a cab, please."

She stopped in front of Brad, tentatively extending a small hand. "Please accept these from me . . . so you'll have something tangible to remind you of me."

Brad took the small pendant and the wallet-sized photo of Leigh Ann. Her picture, in black and white, was stunning.

"I had to get the picture out of my father's wallet. I'll get him another one when we get home."

"Leigh Ann," Brad stammered, "I don't know what to say."

She stared into his eyes. "Tell me that you will write to me, and that you'll be true to me . . . and that you'll come back safely."

Brad walked her to a spot affording some privacy, then held her tightly. "Leigh Ann, I care deeply about you." They remained quiet, feeling the distress of separation.

"Brad, I need your address," she said as she handed him her home address. "I'll write every day, I promise."

Brad wrote his address on one of his calling cards and gave it to Leigh Ann. He unbuttoned his khaki shirt, removed his gold wings, replaced the snaps over the prongs, then held Leigh Ann.

"Come back to me," she said, wiping away a tear, "safely."

"Count on it," Brad replied, squeezing the gold wings into her small palm. "We belong together . . . forever."

"Oh, Brad, I'm scared."

Brad turned and walked to the taxi, not trusting his voice. His world had been shattered by the reality of leaving Leigh Ann, and the certainty of what he had to face over the skies of North Vietnam.

19

The KC-135 shrieked like a thousand banshees as it thundered down the long runway. The four Pratt & Whitney turbojets strained to propel the fully loaded tanker to takeoff speed. The noise was deafening.

Brad sat in a tip-down troop seat close to the darkened cockpit. He watched the pilots, then turned and looked the length of the long, windowless fuselage. Harry and Nick were already stretched out on the uncomfortable passenger seats.

After what seemed like an eternity, the heavy aircraft lifted smoothly off the pavement with 500 feet of runway to spare. Brad unclenched his sweaty palms, exercising his tense fingers.

The laboring tankers, fueled to maximum capacity, had to depart late at night or early in the morning. The pilots had to take advantage of the cooler temperatures in order to get the maximum thrust from their engines.

Letting out a sigh of relief, Brad opened his breast pocket and gently lifted out the pendant on a gold chain. Even in the drab lighting, he could distinguish the intricate design around the dove. He held the shiny ornament in his left hand and reached into his pocket agian, extracting the picture of Leigh Ann.

Brad stared at her image as if to keep her close even though they would soon be worlds apart—he in his chaotic world of aerial warfare, and Leigh Ann in her more civilized surroundings. They had had so little time together. He hoped that she was peacefully asleep.

Harry Hutton leaned over, studying the photo. "She is absolutely beautiful."

"Yeah," Brad replied, opening his palm to view the pendant. "She is a beautiful person inside, too."

"What's that?" Hutton asked, pointing to the ornament.

"Something Leigh Ann gave me," Brad answered, carefully handing the delicate pendant and chain to Hutton. "That's a dove on the front."

Hutton ran his thumb over the design before turning to Brad. "Are you going to wear this?"

"Damn right I'm going to wear it," Brad replied, accepting the ornament back. "I'm going to hook it around my dog tags."

"It's crazy," Hutton remarked, leaning against the fuselage.

"What's crazy?"

"Brad Austin," Harry said slowly, "carrying a symbol of peace while he blasts fighters out of the skies."

Brad placed the photo and pendant back in his shirt pocket, then turned to Hutton. "Harry, I'll tell you what's crazy." He paused a moment. "No, I'll tell you the solution. This planet needs a new, consolidated rule book."

Harry laughed. "Written by Brad Austin, terror of the skies."

"You're damn right," Brad replied, buttoning his pocket. "If I ran this planet, there wouldn't be any more goddamn wars. You can count on that."

"My boy," Hutton said, giving Brad a strange look, "you've had too many trips to Disneyland."

They both remained quiet for a couple of minutes before Brad turned to his shipmate. "Harry, I'm in love with Leigh Ann."

"You mean in lust."

Brad gave Harry a cold look.

Hutton raised his eyebrows. "You're serious."

"Serious as a ramp strike."

"Brad," Hutton counseled, glancing at the sleeping forms of Palmer and Lunsford, "you just met this girl . . . what, less than a day ago?"

"Harry," Brad responded irritably, "I may not be Einstein, but my primitive brain knows when a feeling registers."

"Okay," Harry replied, then watched Brad open his pocket again, extract the pendant, slip his dog tags over his head, then attach the gold memento to his chain.

The afternoon crowd was beginning to gather in the Cubi Point Officers' Club. Brad stood next to a row of phone booths, patiently waiting for the naval-base operator to place his call to Honolulu.

Nick Palmer, Russ Lunsford, and Harry Hutton were at the bar quaffing cold San Miguel beers. The four men had twenty-five minutes before they had to assemble at the carrier on-board delivery (COD) aircraft that would return them to their ship. Their two Phantoms had already been flown to the carrier.

Brad was listening to the clicks and hums emanating from the phone line when the Royal Hawaiian operator suddenly answered. She quickly connected him with the room occupied by Leigh Ann and her parents.

Mrs. Ladasau answered, expressing her regret that Brad had been called back to duty so unexpectedly. She wished him well, then called her daughter to the telephone.

"Hi, Brad!" Leigh Ann sounded excited. "Where are you?"

Covering his left ear, Brad spoke a little louder than normal. "I'm in the Philippines—at a naval air station. We're getting ready to fly out to the ship."

"Brad," she said, hearing the intermittent static in their connection, "I miss you . . . I really do. This just seems unbelievable."

"What do your parents think about our relationship?"

Leigh Ann laughed softly. "My father thinks it's one of those flash-in-the-pan romances."

Brad glanced at the bar. "And your mother?"

"Mother and I were discussing you when you called. She fully understands how we feel, and said that she fell in love with Dad the first time she met him."

Seeing Palmer and Lunsford point to the arriving crew bus, Brad nodded. "Leigh Ann, I have to go. Just remember that I love you . . . and I'll be in touch."

"Brad, I miss you," she said above the phone-line interference, "and I wrote a letter—a long one—to you this morning."

"I can't wait," he almost shouted. "Gotta run. Take care of yourself."

"You, too, flyboy. I'll be waiting for you."

"God . . . damn!" Russ Lunsford exclaimed, jolted awake by the solid impact of the carrier landing. The sudden stop threw him sideways toward the front of the aircraft. Also startled awake, Brad, Harry, and Nick were groggy and disoriented.

"Holy shit," Hutton blurted, rubbing his eyes. "I believe we just arrived."

Lunsford turned to the youngster who served as the COD crew member. "Jesus Christ, do you think it might be a good idea to wake people before a crash landing on a carrier?"

"Yes, sir," the third-class petty officer mumbled. "I forgot. I'm sorry."

After the C-1A Trader was chocked and the engines were shut down, the men climbed out and entered the carrier through the forward hatch in the superstructure. They went below deck to their staterooms, deposited their gear, stopped at the head, then walked to the squadron ready room.

Entering the briefing room, the late arrivals were greeted with catcalls and good-natured banter. Dan Bailey motioned for them to come to the front of the narrow compartment. "Sorry, gents, but we need every warm body we've got."

The four sat down, while the CO told them what he had explained earlier to the squadron. In less than forty-eight hours they would be working with the carrier *Intrepid* in a combined operation to increase the pressure on North Vietnam. The rules of engagement would remain the same, but the intensity of bombing would be expanded.

After Bailey pointed out the primary target areas, Brad had a question. "Skipper, why are we hitting the same worthless targets we bombed before, with a larger amount of ordnance?"

Bailey raised one hand. "Look, I know what you're saying, and I agree. We should pick out strategic targets and annihilate them, no question.

"However, referencing the discussion we had previously, the White House calls the shots. It's that simple . . . and not open for deliberation."

Brad strained to maintain his composure. His exposition of guiding principles found the meaningless and irrational bombings absurd. The message from Washington was clear. The civilian leadership, demonstrating no will to win in their policy of slow escalation, would drag the war on for an indeterminate period. The politicians, who were scrambling to cover their careers, could care less about the individuals they had sent to do battle.

"They believe," Bailey continued with a hint of disgust, "that a policy of gradualism . . . an intensified show of force will pressure Hanoi into capitulating."

"Sir," Brad said as silence filled the ready room, "with respect, we aren't going to make a dent in North Vietnam, or in the thinking of Ho Chi Minh, until we saturate bomb them around the clock with every airplane in the inventory—air force, navy, and marine."

"No question, Captain Austin," Bailey said, tight-lipped, "but the subject is not open for discussion."

"Yes, sir," Brad responded in a temperate voice. "I understand."

Inside, he was suffering agonies over the insanity of seeing more pilots and RIOs die in halfhearted strike efforts. That knowledge, along with the incomprehensible rules of aerial engagement, caused an enormous rift in his loyalties.

Bailey made a few more general remarks to the crew members, then left for the wardroom. Four of the junior officers resumed their acey-deucey games, while others followed the CO to the evening meal. Afterward, everyone would gather in the ready room for hot popcorn and the evening movie.

Brad walked out of the compartment and down to the air-conditioned passageway leading to his stateroom. He opened a soft drink, sat down at the desk, and listened to the sounds of the ship.

The ever-present creaks and groans of the massive hull were occasionally interrupted by bells ringing, whistles blowing, and announcements over the internal 1-MC loud-speakers. Letting his mind wander from the war to Leigh Ann, Brad tuned out all of the sounds in the carrier.

He started to write a letter to Leigh Ann, then dismissed the idea when he thought about his frustrations. He did not want his feelings about the war to come out on paper, especially not to Leigh Ann. She would probably agree with her father. The United States should not be bombing anyone.

Opening his shirt pocket, Brad pulled out Leigh Ann's picture. Looking at her smiling face helped erase the thoughts of the lunacy of the war. He placed the picture on the desk, vowing to have the ship's photo shop duplicate it. That way, Brad reasoned, he could keep one picture in his room and carry the other in the cockpit.

Harry Hutton walked in a minute later, happy as ever. "You hungry?"

"No, not really," Brad replied, setting down the cola can. "I don't have much of an appetite this evening."

Harry sat down on the bed and studied his friend. "Brad, this shit bag we're in is really getting to you."

Austin looked at his roommate and picked up the can of cola. "You want the rest of this?"

"You bet," Harry replied, accepting the cold can. Their portable refrigerator was worth its weight in gold.

"I'm going to take a walk," Brad said, reaching for his brown leather flight jacket.

Harry tilted up the can, finishing the last third of the cola, then tossed the can into their metal trash container. "Care for some company?" Harry said as he stood.

"Sure," Brad responded, slipping on his jacket. "Let's go up to the bow."

"I'm following you," Harry replied, reaching for his flight jacket.

They locked their stateroom door and walked through two passageways to the light trap and ladder leading up to the catwalk. They climbed the short stairs and stepped out onto the open grating that hugged the flight deck.

Brad looked down through the framework of the catwalk at the foamy bow wave. He felt the damp spray rushing up through the iron grating.

Harry inhaled the sea breeze, then let it out slowly. "If I close my eyes, and really work at it, I see ourselves on board a cruise ship, lolling away the hours with two sensuous nymphomaniacs."

Brad turned and smiled. "I think I know how you get by from day to day."

"Whatever works," Harry responded with a grin.

They walked forward to the port side of the bow. The sun had just dropped below the horizon when Brad and Harry reached their viewing spot.

Harry leaned on the edge of the railing. "After you left the ready room, Dirty Ernie told me that we're going into Yokosuka as soon as our relief is on station."

Brad turned around and leaned against the railing. His thoughts shifted to Leigh Ann. "When are we scheduled to be relieved?"

"It's up in the air right now. The Bonnie Dick," Harry said, referring to the aircraft carrier *Bon Homme Richard*, "is supposed to start warm-ups at Dixie Station in about a week or so."

Brad quickly calculated the number of days until the ship would leave the line. "Why are we going to Yokosuka?"

Hutton gave him a bewildered look. "Ernie said they have some kind of equipment in Yoko that they don't have at Subic . . . to work on the prop shafts, or something related to them. From what he said, they've got problems with the reduction gears on two of the shafts."

Brad gripped the rail. "I thought the reason we were

yanked back from Hawaii was because they had this tub fixed.''

''I don't know shafts from shit,'' Harry replied, staring at the destroyer escort off the port bow. ''All I know is that our bird farm needs some maintenance.''

''Yeah,'' Brad replied, gazing at the rows of aircraft chained to the flight deck, ''this baby needs a lot of work, especially the catapults.'' They watched the horizon grow dark, each lost in his thoughts. After the stars were clearly visible, they decided to grab a quick bite at the gedunk.

Brad and Harry descended to the hangar deck and walked through the throng of men and airplanes to the small store. They both consumed a cheeseburger and a Coke, then carried their strawberry ice-cream cones to the ready room.

Brad and Harry entered the noisy compartment and sat down in the back row of seats. Mario Russo, the squadron popcorn officer, was dispensing brown bags of freshly popped corn. As soon as he was finished with the nightly ritual, Jon O'Meara started the movie.

Nick Palmer kept up a running commentary during the low-budget horror movie, making his comments when there was no dialogue. He had always narrated the love scenes at all ready-room movies, cracking up the entire group at every opportunity.

''Hey, O'Meara,'' a loud voice called from the front of the compartment, ''can't the navy do any better than this horseshit?''

''Pipe down,'' Ernie Sheridan called out. ''Can't you appreciate the intellectual stimulation the rest of us are experiencing?'' The loud groans were audible throughout the room.

After a few minutes, Brad drifted back to the Hawaiian Islands. Forgetting the grisly movie, he formulated a plan to meet Leigh Ann after the carrier docked in Yokosuka, Japan.

Handing Harry the remainder of his popcorn, Brad quietly slipped out of the darkened compartment and walked to his stateroom. He took off his uniform and hung it in the small closet next to the washbasin. Donning a pair of gym shorts, Brad opened the desk and placed his stationery on top. He propped Leigh Ann's picture against the bulkhead in front of him and picked up his pen.

My Dear Leigh Ann,

   I am back on the carrier, missing you more than I can express in words. I will be anxiously looking forward to your first letter. Seeing our mail plane overhead is the highlight of our day.

   Leigh Ann, how would you like to meet me in San Francisco? Rumor has it that we are going to Japan for more extensive work on the ship, so I thought I would fly from Tokyo to San Francisco, if you can arrange to meet me. There are so many things to see and do in the city, and I would give anything to share the experience with you.

   I will take care of your airline ticket, and all related expenses, if you can join me in approximately three weeks. I will have to let you know the exact date a little later.

   We can stay at the Fairmont Hotel, ride the cable cars to Fisherman's Wharf, dine in Chinatown, and enjoy the sunset from the Fairmont Crown—a cocktail lounge on top of the hotel. Watching the sun settle below the Golden Gate Bridge is an unforgettable sight.

   I look forward to hearing from you.

Love,
Brad

   P.S. I will not leave a forwarding address this time!

   He carefully folded the letter and sealed it in an envelope, which he slid into a pocket on his flight jacket. Reclining on his bunk, Brad stared at the picture of the smiling brunette, then got up and began his daily calisthenics.

20

Watching the TACAN, Brad waited until another nautical mile ticked over. He added power, then raised the nose and banked to the left. He continued the wide orbit until Nick Palmer coasted alongside in Joker 207. Harry Hutton waved from the backseat of the F-4.

When they passed over the carrier, Brad turned on course and scanned the sky for their tankers. Climbing through 16,000 feet, he spotted the two KA-3B Skywarriors four miles ahead. They were in loose formation in the standard refueling track.

Extending his fueling probe, he eased back on the twin throttles. The Phantoms flown by Jack Carella and Lincoln Durham had just plugged into the Whales. Brad would time his rendezvous with the tankers to coincide with the departure of the first two F-4s.

Brad and Nick would provide target combat air patrol on the left side of the strike group. Carella and Durham would patrol on the right flank. Fifteen miles in front of the formation, four additional Phantoms crisscrossed the hazy sky on their way to the targets around Haiphong.

"Joker Two Oh Seven," Brad radioed to Palmer, "come up tanker freq."

"Two Oh Seven."

The two F-4s closed to less than 100 yards behind Jocko Carella's aircraft. They held their position fifteen seconds while both squadron mates topped off their tanks. Carella dropped off the lower Whale, followed seconds later by Bull Durham from the other KA-3B.

"Snowball," Brad radioed, tweaking the throttles forward, "Jokers Two Oh Two and Two Oh Seven stabilized—Two left, Seven right."

"Copy," the lead tanker pilot responded, watching Carella and Durham accelerate out in front of the Skywarriors. "Jokers cleared to plug."

Brad clicked his radio twice, adding power as the probe entered the basket. He shoved the receptacle forward a few feet and steadied the Phantom.

"Fuel flow," came the call from the tanker pilot.

"Looks good here," Brad replied, thinking about the tremendous amount of fuel the F-4 consumed in afterburner. At a normal cruise speed of 575 miles per hour, the Phantom could travel approximately 1,500 miles. Close to sea level, in afterburner, the entire internal fuel load would be exhausted in a matter of minutes.

"You're unusually quiet this morning," Brad said over the intercom while he watched Nick Palmer smoothly plug the second Whale.

Russ Lunsford pulled his seat belt and shoulder harnesses as tightly as he could, then keyed his intercom. "That's because I'm praying that I'll still be alive this afternoon."

Brad did not respond. He had seen this kind of detached behavior from Lunsford many times when they had gone on a mission. Brad knew that if he attempted to ease Lunsford's anxiety, Russ would work himself into a frenzy.

"Jokers on the Whale," the strike leader radioed, "you about ready to join up?"

Brad keyed his mike. "Ninety seconds." Monitoring the fuel indicator, Brad waited until his tanks were full. A few seconds later, Palmer reported his tanks full.

Dropping off the Skywarriors, Brad and Nick added power to catch the strike group. They switched to Red Crown and heard the strike leader giving last-minute instructions. He was leading twelve A-4 Skyhawks. The entire group then switched to strike-flight frequency. As they crossed the coast of North Vietnam, the air-group commander commenced a slow turn to approach the petroleum storage tanks west of the city of Haiphong.

Below, fourteen A-1 Skyraiders skirted around known gun emplacements, then turned to their run-in heading. At that moment, Brad heard the radio come alive.

"Bandits!" someone warned. "We've got bandits . . . climbing twenty west!"

The sky suddenly filled with surface-to-air missiles and concentrated barrages of antiaircraft fire. Four Phantoms from the Jokers' sister squadron, fulfilling the role of flak suppressors, thundered across the target area. They dropped their Rockeye bombs seconds before the A-4s struck the petroleum storage tanks.

Brad watched in horror as a Skyhawk flew into the ground without any attempt to pull out of the dive. The pilot had been killed by the deadly antiaircraft rounds.

"Joker One is engaging!" Dan Bailey radioed from the forward fighter group. "Heads up, Jokers. Three MiGs at two o'clock."

Scanning the horizon, Brad darted a glance at the target area. Billowing clouds of black smoke mushroomed skyward as the A-1 Skyraiders pulverized the remaining fuel dumps.

"SAMs!" Hutton said over the wild radio chatter. "Comin' up at four o'clock."

Breaking hard to the right, Brad felt the violent g force shove him down in his seat. He glimpsed the ground, then saw two surface-to-air missiles flash by the side of his Phantom. He instinctively ducked, certain that the SAMs would detonate next to him.

It was impossible to interpret the ambiguous radio calls. Many of the urgent transmissions were blocked when a number of pilots tried to communicate at the same time.

Seeing Nick Palmer sliding into a loose trail position on his right wing, Brad reversed to the left and flinched again. Two A-4s snapped over to avoid a midair collision with the Phantoms.

"Oh . . . God in heaven," Lunsford groaned under the g load, "get us out of here."

The adrenaline shock had caused both F-4 crews to start

sucking oxygen. They frantically searched all quadrants of the sky for aircraft and missiles.

Brad saw an airplane explode at the same instant he saw three MiG-21s descend out of the clouds. He looked at Palmer, then back to the MiGs. He had not seen a MiG-21 before, but there was no mistaking the silver fighters. Two of the sleek aircraft were carrying external fuel tanks.

"Tally," someone said. "Break right! Break right!" Total confusion reigned. It was impossible to know whom the break right command was intended for.

Selecting HEAT, Brad pulled the Phantom into a modified high yo-yo. The gray sky and clouds blended with the ground. He saw Palmer's F-4, in perfect formation, slide out to the left side.

Looking back at the three MiGs, Brad was startled by a flash and jolting explosion between the two Phantoms. He quickly scanned the cockpit instruments, noting that the master caution light was glowing.

"We've been hit!" Lunsford shouted, staring at the shattered left wing. Four feet of the wing tip had been blown off by the unseen SAM. "So has Palmer! Palmer's been hit! He's drifting down!"

Brad's aircraft, with the right wing now providing more lift than the shortened left wing, rolled to the left. Lunsford snapped his head from side to side. "Our left wing . . . we've been hit in the left wing!"

"Come on . . . ," Brad coaxed, holding the control stick all the way to the right. He shoved on the right rudder, but the heavily damaged Phantom continued to roll out of control to the left.

"Have you got control?" Lunsford asked, watching a rail yard and power plant appear above the canopy. "Answer me, goddamnit!"

Inverted, Brad pushed the stick forward to hold the nose up, then cautiously moved the stick to the left. "Stay with me, you sonuvabitch . . . I'm working on it."

"Bullshit!" Lunsford swore, noticing a new problem. "Our left engine—we've lost the left engine! I've got circuit breakers out back here."

"Well, put 'em back in."

Lunsford quickly shoved the circuit breakers in and braced himself for an ejection. His mouth was dry and his heart pounded in his chest.

The Phantom rolled upright, then yawed to the left as Brad fought to control the aircraft. The airspeed was quickly bleeding off, which caused more control problems as the F-4 entered a second roll.

Brad looked for Palmer's Phantom, but it was nowhere in sight. His own fear was transmitted to the control stick. He tried to relax his viselike grip on the stick as the F-4 again rolled to the inverted position.

"Goddamnit, Austin," Lunsford shouted when the earth and sky rotated, "get us out over water!"

Checking the airspeed indicator, Brad saw that he was going to have to use afterburner on the right engine. "What do you think I'm tryin' to do?"

He entered another corkscrewing maneuver, tapping the afterburner through the inverted position.

His right leg, fully extended on the rudder pedal, was starting to shake from the continuous strain.

A MiG slashed by the F-4, prompting a harangue from Lunsford. "We're going the wrong goddamn way! Everyone is clearing the beach."

Brad muscled the Phantom upright again, watching the decaying airspeed. He could not use afterburner to accelerate the F-4. The thrust caused the aircraft to yaw out of control to the left.

"We're lucky," Brad labored under the strain, "to be going in any direction." He sensed that he was losing control authority. Any slower, Brad told himself, and the control stick would not hold the nose up during the period of inverted flight.

"Get on the horn," Brad ordered, wrestling the controls, "and get off a Mayday."

Lunsford had become disoriented during the wild ride. "Where are we?"

Brad saw the altimeter drop below 8,000 feet. "We're five to seven miles southwest of Haiphong." He had no sooner finished the statement when he glimpsed two Phantoms settle into a distant formation with them.

"Austin, where did you learn to fly?" Mario Russo asked from the backseat of Jon O'Meara's Phantom.

"We're going to have to get out," Brad replied, feeling the F-4 enter a prestall buffet. He saw 6,800 feet on the altimeter. "The nose is going to fall through when we go inverted again."

"Brad," O'Meara radioed, "we've got a SAR flight on the way. Red Crown has been notified."

Watching the horizon tilt, Brad shot a look at the rapidly unwinding altimeter, then keyed his mike. "Thanks. Have you seen Nick and Harry?"

"Negative," O'Meara answered, searching for Brad's wingman. "Maybe they cleared the beach."

Inverted and hanging from his restraints, Brad smoothly shoved the control stick all the way forward. "How far out are the SAR—"

His statement ended when the F-4 suddenly departed and entered a poststall gyration.

"EJECT! EJECT!"

Nick Palmer slumped in his seat, feeling the light-headed sensation of being semiconscious. He could hear Harry Hutton talking to him, but his reactions and thinking ability were in slow motion. His dazed mind could not comprehend what had happened to him.

Taking stock of the situation, Nick looked down at his control stick. He had a hold on the grip, reacting to a primordial instinct for survival.

The SAM shrapnel had penetrated the F-4 inches below the canopy rail. The high explosive had ripped into Palmer's right arm, shoulder, and chest. He could move his arm, but he was bleeding profusely from his gaping chest wound. Miraculously, his oxygen mask and hose had survived the blinding explosion.

"Nick," Harry soothed, "how are you doing?"

Palmer inhaled, then felt an excruciating pain. He ventured a few words. "Not so good. If I pass out, command eject us."

"Hang in there," Harry said, working the radios. "We're over the gulf, so you're doin' great."

"Yeah," Palmer gasped, trying to focus on the instrument panel. "Where's the boat?"

Harry looked out at Dan Bailey's Phantom. The CO was in the process of having the Air Boss erect the massive nylon barricade. "Straight ahead, eighty-three miles. The old man is escorting us in."

Palmer moved his eyes without moving his head. "I don't . . . see him."

"He's off our right wing," Hutton answered, prepared for an ejection, "in loose deuce."

The cockpit remained eerily quiet as the Phantoms cruised at 18,000 feet. The CO, fearing Palmer might have oxygen problems, did not want to climb any higher.

"Harry," Palmer gasped, staring at the altitude indicator, "we can't land. I can't focus my eyes."

Hutton inhaled and spoke reassuringly. "We're going into the barricade—piece of cake."

"Great," Palmer replied, then looked down again. He was sitting in a pool of blood. "I don't know, Harry."

"Come on, for Christ's sake," Hutton cajoled loudly. "You're a goddamned fighter pilot—a tail hooker. You can do anything."

Palmer instinctively flew the damaged Phantom straight and level at 240 knots. He blinked several times in a futile attempt to clear his vision. "You'll have to talk me down. I can't focus."

Harry closed his eyes a second, asking God for divine guidance, then opened them. "Shit, Palmer, I could give you a fifty-cent piece, then talk you out of a dollar's worth of change."

21

Brad saw the earth and sky spin a split second before the violent explosion rocketed him out of the cockpit. The windblast almost ripped his oxygen mask loose.

He tumbled through the cloudy sky, then snapped straight out when the main canopy popped open. He swung below his parachute and looked around. Russ Lunsford was slightly below him, seventy to eighty yards away.

Peering around and below, Brad was unnerved to see people staring and pointing up at them. He could see that they were Vietnamese farmers, but some of them were armed with rifles and scythes. He could also hear dogs barking amidst the shouting and clamoring on the ground.

Becoming aware of a screeching sound, Brad twisted his head in time to see his wounded Phantom hit next to the village. The thunderous explosion cartwheeled the F-4 through the village, setting the inhabitants and their dwellings on fire.

The gruesome scene was incomprehensible to the stunned pilot and his RIO. They watched in agony as people screamed in terror when the blazing jet fuel rained down on them.

In desperation, Brad surveyed an area to the east of the village. He steered his parachute toward the slight incline. If he and Lunsford could make it over the tree line, they might have a chance for rescue.

Dropping his survival gear on the cord attached to his parachute rigging, Brad pulled out one of his emergency radios. He had altered his personal equipment to carry two survival radios and a second revolver, complete with an extra clip of ammunition and a box of .38-caliber ammunition. He placed the radio securely in his torso harness and felt for his service revolver.

Watching the approaching trees rise to meet him, Brad heard the howl of an F-4 Phantom. He turned to see Jon O'Meara, who had dispatched his wingman to the carrier, streak low over the farmers who were crossing the field. They were running toward their burning village.

In the last few seconds of his descent, Brad could see that he was not going to clear the wide span of trees. He crossed his right arm under his chin, gripping his left shoulder. He placed his left arm under his crotch and crossed his legs.

Seconds later, Brad plummeted into the tall trees. The impact knocked the wind out of him. Gasping for air, Brad looked down. He estimated that he was twelve feet above the ground.

Recovering his breath, Brad hung suspended from his parachute canopy. His mind reeled from the sudden transition. Only a minute ago he had been in his plane; now he was dangling from a tree. He heard some of the shouting villagers racing toward the trees. He might as well have dropped a bomb on their families.

Harry Hutton could see the carrier in the distance. The strike group, far ahead of the two Phantoms, was recovering in an orderly flow. They had lost three aircraft during the attack, including the skipper of the A-4 Skyhawk squadron.

Weak from his massive loss of blood, Palmer heard Dan Bailey radio the carrier. The Air Boss confirmed that they would be able to take Palmer's damaged Phantom aboard in ten minutes. The barricade was almost in place.

"Okay, Nick," the CO said in a quiet, comforting voice, "let's dirty up. Power back . . . and I'll call for flaps and gear. You just keep the wings level."

"Copy," Harry Hutton answered for his wounded pilot, then keyed the intercom as Nick pulled the throttles back an inch. "Hang in there—we're going to make it." Palmer remained quiet, barely conscious.

Harry continued to give his pilot small heading changes as the two aircraft flew downwind toward the carrier. Abeam the ship, Dan Bailey radioed for Nick to lower his flaps and landing gear. Palmer would not be using the tail hook for the barricade arrestment.

The Air Boss called when the flight was three miles astern of the carrier. "Joker Two Zero Seven is cleared for a barricade arrestment."

"Roger," Hutton replied, coaching Palmer into a left turn. The gravely wounded pilot let the nose drop too far as he initiated the turn.

"Back pressure," Harry reminded. "Get the nose up."

"Joker Lead," the commander in Pri-fly radioed, "we're shooting a tanker. Should have you on board in twenty minutes or less."

"Copy," Bailey replied, nervously watching Palmer lose altitude in the turn. "Nick, keep your nose up . . . doing fine, but get your nose up."

Brad released his Koch fittings, dropping twelve feet to the dense undergrowth. He hit hard, then staggered sideways to regain his balance. He raised the tinted visor on his helmet and looked for Lunsford. "Russ, can you hear me?"

There was no answer.

Hearing the approaching villagers, Brad crashed through the thick foliage toward the incline at the edge of the trees. He saw something move to his left. Dropping to his knees, Brad drew his .38-caliber revolver, then glimpsed Russ Lunsford thrashing through the undergrowth. "Russ, I'm over here!"

Limping, Lunsford stumbled through the foliage, meeting his pilot at the edge of the trees. "They're right on our asses," Lunsford heaved, feeling the deep scratches on his neck and face. His ankle would barely support him.

"Come on," Brad ordered, raising the radio antenna and turning on the power switch. "We gotta make it to the top of that knoll."

Breathing heavily, Lunsford followed Austin up the slight incline. There were several indentations on top of the long hill. Another small field lay on the other side of the pockmarked incline.

Out of breath, both men dropped into a large sunken area at the edge of the slope. The depression was not deep enough to conceal them completely, but it did provide some cover. Looking around the area, Brad raised the survival radio to his mouth.

"Joker," Brad panted, "we need cover. We're on top of a long hill separating the tree line and a narrow field."

O'Meara replied immediately, wrapping the Phantom into a tight turn. "I've got ya spotted. Stay put."

Brad glanced at the F-4 and keyed his radio. "We've got armed men coming through the tree line."

"Copy," O'Meara responded, settling into an orbit. "Help is on the way. Hold on."

"We're in deep shit," Lunsford gasped, hearing the yelling farmers. "They're going to kill us."

Brad snapped his head around. "Goddamnit, Lunsford, get your shit together. I'll do the firing, you do the loading. I've got another fifty rounds in my torso harness."

Lunsford nodded his head, then reluctantly handed Brad his revolver. They both heard Jon O'Meara talk to the A-1 Skyraider leader.

"Lifeguard One, Joker Two Hundred."

"Go, Joker," the metallic voice answered over the roar of the big radial engine.

"We're going to need some ordnance real soon," O'Meara said, looking at a truck full of soldiers racing down a narrow trail by the side of the tree line. "We've got troops moving in on our guys."

"Roger that," the detached voice replied, then added, "we've got a Jolly Green and a Seasprite en route." The Jolly Green was an air-force HH-53 helicopter; the Seasprite was an armed Kaman HH-2C rescue helicopter.

Brad saw the first villagers emerge from the trees. Fear had dried the saliva in his mouth. He counted seven men and four youngsters. Barking wildly, two dogs ran out of the dense undergrowth. Every one of the Vietnamese was armed, including the teenage boys. Two of the men held AK-47s; the rest had assorted rifles and handguns.

Licking his dry lips, Brad raised his radio. "Joker, they're coming out of the tree line."

"I'm in," O'Meara replied calmly.

Brad watched the sleek Phantom flick over on its side and hurtle toward the villagers. Leveling at fifty feet, Jon O'Meara boomed right over the Vietnamese, tapping the afterburners three times.

The villagers ducked back into the undergrowth as the howling Phantom blasted over them. They emerged again when the F-4 shot skyward. The group spread out and again started up the incline.

Slipping off his flight gloves, Brad reached into a specially sewn pocket in his survival gear. He extracted a small metal box containing fifty rounds of .38-caliber ammunition. He placed the box between them, then felt Lunsford tap him. He looked up, petrified. "Oh, shit."

"Okay, Nick," Harry coached, "wings level. We're lined up in the groove."

"Okay," Palmer whispered, trying to keep his head up.

Bailey crossed under Palmer, moving off to the left side of the damaged Phantom. He listened to the landing-signal officer, who had trained Palmer to be an LSO, talk his friend down.

"You're going a little flat. Watch your altitude."

Locking his shoulder harness, Harry felt a tightness in his stomach. "Have you got the deck?"

"Blurry" was the only response.

Bailey added power and turned away, climbing steeply to the orbiting tanker.

"You're a quarter of a mile," Harry reported, feeling his pulse throb in his neck.

The LSO held his mike button down. "Line up. You're drifting right."

"Nick," Harry said, breathing rapidly, "come left just a hair. Get the left wing down." On their present heading, they would hit the island superstructure. Palmer corrected to the left, then let the nose drop too low. They were about to cross the stern of the ship.

"Get your nose up! Power!" the LSO shouted, preparing to dive into the crash net. "Get the nose up!"

Palmer hauled back on the stick as the Phantom slammed into the steel deck. Hutton braced himself for the violent barricade engagement.

The speeding fighter slammed into the nylon webbing, stopping far left of the landing-zone centerline. The left main mount was only two feet from the port catwalk. Nick Palmer brought the throttles to idle, then slumped unconscious against his shoulder harness.

"Joker," Brad whispered, watching the dogs and villagers inch up the incline, "there's a troop truck two hundred meters from us."

The Phantom flicked over again, diving steeply at the army vehicle. The soldiers opened fire with every weapon they had available.

Transfixed, Brad and Russ watched Jon O'Meara punch off his missile ejector racks at point-blank range. The left rack, with one Sidewinder attached, plowed into the cab of the truck. The direct hit knocked the vehicle sideways into a shallow ditch.

The stunned soldiers clambered out of the wrecked truck and rushed for cover in the trees. They left their dead officer and his driver in the mutilated cab.

With renewed caution, the angry villagers stalked the two Americans. They fanned out to the right side of the trapped airmen. One of the men stopped and took aim.

"Keep your head down," Brad warned.

A shot rang out, kicking up dirt next to Brad's head. The farmers were shouting at the soldiers, gesturing for them to hurry to their position. They had two war criminals cornered on the hill. Two more shots ricocheted between Austin and Lunsford.

"Goddamnit," Brad swore, gripping the .38 with both hands. He extended his arms and raised his head, remembering the rifle and pistol instruction at the Officers' Basic School in Quantico.

Brad fired three quick shots, then carefully aimed at one of the men brandishing an AK-47. He squeezed the revolver twice, sending the villager staggering backward. He waited a couple of seconds, then fired again, missing the fleeing Vietnamese. The man he had shot was crawling toward the trees, but he collapsed on his face after traveling three meters.

"Reload," Brad ordered tersely, then accepted the other .38 revolver. He grabbed the radio and slid it to his mouth. "Jon, where's Lifeguard?"

The radio became garbled when Jon O'Meara and the Skyraider pilot attempted to transmit at the same time.

"This is Lifeguard Lead. We've got a tally on the Fox-4. We're almost there."

Brad could barely hear the roar of the approaching A-1s. Glancing to the east, he spotted the descending RESCAP Skyraiders. Looking back at the tree line, he could see that the soldiers had joined the villagers. They moved forward, crouching at the edge of the trees. A barrage of concentrated fire erupted from the soldiers, forcing Brad and Russ to hug the ground.

"Tell Jon to make a pass," Brad said, placing the revolver over the edge of their depression. He rapidly fired all six rounds, then grabbed the other .38.

Brad heard O'Meara's voice as he fired another six rounds at the advancing soldiers. He grabbed his standby .45-caliber pistol and squeezed the trigger until the gun was empty.

Lunsford struggled to reload the empty .38s while O'Meara thundered over the line of soldiers and farmers. He was so low, Brad thought he was going to hit the ground. The Vietnamese flattened out on their stomachs.

The soldiers crept forward, firing in short bursts. If they rushed the Americans, Austin and Lunsford would die quickly. Brad fired another six rounds, then reached for the second .38. Watching the North Vietnamese soldiers prepare to race toward them, Brad and Russ fired wildly over the edge of their concealment. They heard Jon O'Meara and Mario Russo give the Spad drivers the location to hit.

"Oh, mother of Jesus," Lunsford said, fumbling to reload. His hands were shaking so hard he could not load the rounds in the chambers.

Brad spotted the A-1 Skyraiders rolling in for their first pass. The four Spads, each carrying four 20mm guns, rocket pods, and two 500-pound bombs, plunged straight at the soldiers.

"Come on," Brad ordered when the first rockets and gunfire swept over the soldiers, "follow me!"

Limping, Lunsford felt a sharp pain in his right ankle as he raced after Brad. They ran across an open area to a small irrigation dike and stumbled through the muddy water. Both spread out on the far side, trying to catch their breath. They watched the A-1s pound their former position, then heard the sweet sounds of a navy Seasprite.

The helicopter hugged the tops of the distant trees as it raced toward them. As the pilot flared to land, a door gunner opened fire at the advancing soldiers.

Brad and Russ got up and charged for the Seasprite, leaping through the door before the pilot could land. As the helicopter turned and accelerated, Brad caught a glimpse of Jon O'Meara's Phantom climbing away in afterburner. It was a sight that he would never forget.

A medic helped them to a secure position, then gave Russ and Brad containers of water. Between gasps, they gulped the warm liquid.

"We made it," Russ shouted over the beating rotor blades. "Sweet Jesus, we made it. Thank you, God." He dropped the plastic water bottle next to his seat and clasped his hands in a silent prayer.

Brad sat motionless, drained of all energy. He sagged against the fuselage, enjoying the comforting vibrations flowing through the helicopter. He drank another four swallows of water, then closed his eyes and gave thanks that he was still alive.

The medic, who had seen that they were relatively unscathed, waited until the Seasprite was over water to offer the two men a cigarette. Both declined but shared a third container of water.

Closing his eyes again, Brad let his mind drift. He desperately wanted to enjoy an icy-cold beer, and go waterskiing.

Sensing a change in the pitch of the rotor blades, Brad swung around and looked forward through the cockpit. He saw the carrier steaming off the starboard side of the helicopter. He watched the white wake as the pilot slowed, then approached the side of the flight deck.

Once the Seasprite was stabilized at the same speed as the ship, the pilot eased over the flight deck and gently lowered the helicopter.

Russ and Brad waited until the bouncing, vibrating machine had been chocked and secured to the deck, then moved to the entrance. They thanked the two pilots and medic before jumping out of the door.

They were both shocked to see Jon O'Meara and Mario Russo waiting for them. The four men hugged each other in an emotional embrace. The bond of the brotherhood was readily apparent to everyone who witnessed the union.

22

Brad walked into the quiet, antiseptically clean sick bay. Scary McCary was examining Russ Lunsford's swollen right ankle. Brad sat down in a chair next to McCary's cluttered desk and watched him manipulate Lunsford's foot.

"You're going to be fine," the flight surgeon said, writing a paragraph in Lunsford's medical file. "You've got a severe sprain, but it will heal rapidly. I want you to stay off your feet for forty-eight hours, and use the crutches I'm going to get you."

Lunsford looked at Brad before he spoke. "Doc, if Austin flies, I fly."

McCary sat back in his chair and wearily removed his glasses. "I'm grounding both of you for a while."

Brad and Russ registered their surprise. "Why?" they said in unison.

McCary handed each of them a government-issue fountain pen. "Both of you sign your full names on the back of this lab report . . . right here."

Brad set down his pen. "I get the point, but we—"

"No," McCary said, again handing him the black pen. "Sign your name."

Lunsford wrote his name on the report and slid the paper to Austin. Brad attempted to neatly sign his name. His hand trembled uncontrollably.

McCary pulled out Brad's medical file and placed it next to Lunsford's file. "Compare your signatures when you first reported to the squadron with that scrawl you call writing."

Brad and Russ looked at the comparisons. The graphic difference was evident to both of them.

"Lunsford," McCary said, placing his glasses on, "deals with the tension—and it is cumulative—by getting it out of his system. He yells and swears to relieve the anxiety and fear."

McCary paused, tapping a pen against the edge of his desk. He looked at Brad, focusing on his eyes. "You, on the other hand, keep stuffing it down. The fear, the tension, the killing, your hostility toward the rules of engagement. All of it is shoved down, creating a tremendous amount of internal pressure."

Brad looked perplexed. "Doc, that is the nature of this business. We are not horticulturists."

McCary smiled and turned to their medical files. "Both of you are grounded because of stress. I will let you know when I feel you're ready to fly again." He opened his lower drawer and removed several small bottles of bourbon. "I want the two of you to go to your room and get drunk, cuss me . . . whatever you want to do. I'll see both of you in three days—Friday—at fifteen hundred."

"Yes, sir," Brad replied, accepting his fate. "May we see Nick?"

"Sure," McCary replied, then turned in his chair and motioned to a corpsman. The third class petty officer stepped inside the office. "Rinehart, get a pair of crutches for Lieutenant Lunsford."

"Yessir."

McCary turned back to Austin and Lunsford. "Kick Hutton's ass out when you leave. Palmer is heavily sedated and needs to rest, so you have five minutes."

Brad and Russ stood when the corpsman reappeared with the metal crutches.

McCary pulled back the green curtain separating his office from the ward. "He's in the room at the end of the compartment."

Lunsford hobbled along after Austin as they made their way between the rows of beds. When they reached Palmer's compartment, Brad quietly knocked on the side of the entrance, then pulled the curtain to the side.

Harry Hutton was sitting on a chair next to Palmer's bed. A freckle-faced corpsman was adjusting a bottle connected to an intravenous tube in the pilot's left arm.

Brad and Russ stepped inside and closed the curtain. They both noticed that Harry looked pale and drawn. Brad looked at Nick Palmer. The injured aviator opened his eyes, acknowledging their presence. They remained quiet until the corpsman left the room.

Moving next to his wingman, Brad gently grasped Palmer's left wrist. "Partner, you just about took the last ride on that one."

Palmer smiled weakly, speaking in a pained whisper. "I never . . . saw it coming."

"We didn't either," Lunsford said, leaning against the bulkhead. "Someone may have called it, but we sure as hell never heard anything during all the confusion."

Palmer looked up at Brad. "Harry said that you guys had to jump out."

"Yeah, I lost it," Brad replied, releasing Palmer's wrist. "McCary says that you are going to be as good as new when they get finished."

Palmer gave a slight nod. He started to speak, but fell silent when his eyelids drooped closed.

Harry stood quietly. "They're flying him to Japan as soon as he stabilizes."

Brad looked at Palmer. His chest and right arm were swathed in bandages. His complexion was pale and chalky, with a sheen of perspiration on his forehead.

"Let's let him rest," Brad suggested, stepping out of the small compartment. "Harry, you don't look well."

The normally effervescent RIO waited for Russ Lunsford, then pulled the curtain closed. "I'll be okay. Scary grounded me, so—as Chief Flaven says—I'm gonna get plumb blowed slick."

"We're grounded, too," Brad replied as they made their way between the rows of impeccably clean beds. "How about if I get some ice and food from the wardroom, and we'll camp in our pit?''

"Good idea," Hutton responded, stepping out of sick bay.

Lunsford swore when he stumbled over a hatch combing. "They made this difficult enough. Now I have to negotiate these sonuvabitchin' knee knockers on crutches."

The three men made their way up to the hangar deck, then weaved through the parked planes to the ladder leading to their staterooms. The berthing compartments for some of the air-wing officers were midship, below the flight deck.

Climbing the steep ladder, Lunsford had to forego the crutches and hop one rung at a time to the next level. Brad carried the crutches and followed his RIO up the ladder. He gazed out across the huge hangar bay. Men were working in every available space. Bombs, rockets, fuel tanks, wheels, engines, and various other supplies were stacked everywhere. The maintenance crews were swarming over the array of aircraft, fixing mechanical problems and patching recent battle scars.

When the trio reached the next deck, Brad handed Russ his metal crutches. Lunsford turned to go to his stateroom. "I'll grab my good-time kit and meet you at your room."

"No," Brad said, looking at Hutton. "Harry can get your booze while I go to the wardroom. You need to get off your feet and relax."

"Thanks," Lunsford replied as he entered the passageway leading to the junior officers' quarters.

Stretched out on the lower bunk, Russ Lunsford accepted his second drink from Brad. Harry had made his nest on the deck. After folding two blankets together, he had placed his pillow against the bulkhead and pulled his footlocker next to him.

Fixing his second drink, Brad was about to ask Hutton a question when they heard a knock on the door.

"Shit," Lunsford exclaimed, propping himself up.

Brad opened the door to find Dan Bailey and Jack Carella looking at him.

"Gents," the CO said from the passageway, "we're not going to interrupt you for long. Doc McCary told us that he has grounded the three of you, and I don't question his decisions. You've been through a hell of a lot, and we think he is right."

Jocko Carella appeared to be more intense than usual. He played his new roll as the executive officer perfectly. "That's the good news. The bad news is that we expect all of you to have up chits Friday afternoon, and be ready to man up the next morning."

"Sir," Brad responded, thoroughly miffed at the implication that they were goldbricking, "we didn't ask to be grounded, and I'd be happy to go blast the bastards to oblivion right now."

"Calm down," Bailey said in a pleasant tone. "That's why you need some time-out—let off the steam. You're spring-loaded to the kill mode."

"We should be, sir," Brad responded, regretting his words as soon as he had uttered them. This mess was not the CO's fault. "I apologize, Skipper."

Bailey placed his hand on Brad's shoulder. "No apology needed, okay?" The CO met Brad's eyes. "Get as drunk as you want. We don't want to see you until the Saturday morning brief."

"Yes, sir," Brad replied, feeling some of the tension dissipate. "That is our first priority."

Bailey chuckled and pulled the door shut.

"Holy Christ," Lunsford said, lying down again. "You better take it easy, or the old man is going to have you down for a psychiatric evaluation."

Brad opened his desk drawer and pulled out a *Wall Street Journal*. "Let me show you something, Doctor Lunsford."

Placing the newspaper faceup on Lunsford's lap, Brad sat down. "I've highlighted the significant parts, so you don't have to wade through all of it."

Harry Hutton gave Brad a quizzical look, then remained quiet while Lunsford skimmed through the article. Harry's curiosity was aroused when Lunsford called the President a son of a bitch. Harry tossed down his vodka in two quick gulps. "What the hell are you reading?"

"Tell him," Brad said, propping his feet on the end of the bunk. "The *Journal* has a reputation for getting their facts straight."

Lunsford cleared his throat. "It says that the final decisions on aerial targets in Vietnam—including the targets to be authorized, the ordnance to be dropped, the number of sorties allowed, and, most disturbingly, the tactics to be employed— are made once a week at a luncheon in the goddamn White House."

Harry digested the information, unsure of its significance in relation to them.

"Tell him the part," Brad said evenly, "that is driving me to the brink of insanity."

Lunsford glanced again at the fourth underlined paragraph. "The luncheons are attended by the President, the secretary of defense, the secretary of state, the presidential assistant, and the press secretary."

"What's more important," Brad interjected, reaching for an ice cube, "is the fact that no military personnel are present, not even the chairman of the Joint Chiefs."

Harry sat quiet a moment, thinking about all the illogical things the air wing had been tasked to do. Now it made sense how the missions were formulated. "Jesus H. Christ. That's crazy."

"Oh, yeah," Brad continued, removing his shirt. "The White House will not accept a partnership with the military, so we're paying the price for having amateurs and politi- cians run a goddamn war that they are unqualified to direct, and don't have the will to win. They're sitting up in the palace with their blinders on, methodically screwing up this half-assed effort even worse."

Lunsford folded the paper. "It says that a lot of the brass—four-star types—are becoming very vocal."

"They damn sure ought to be," Brad snapped. "This goes against everything they've ever been taught. Any military commander worth his salt wants to protect his troops and accomplish the mission. The generals and admirals are as frustrated as we are.''

Brad placed the newspaper back in his desk. ''Those geniuses at the White House garden parties have got the military sending out eight planes with half bomb loads instead of four planes with full loads. They want more goddamn sorties, so let's risk four extra pilots and RIOs.''

The veins in Brad's neck were protruding. ''I'll volunteer to fly every mission, but why risk extra people in a half-assed effort to placate both the hawks and doves? They're covering their asses, because they don't have a clue what to do next, and we're paying for their gutless indecisiveness.''

Brad looked at Lunsford. ''You think *I* need a psychiatric evaluation? They need to send an entire goddamn bus load of psychiatrists over to the White House.''

Harry braced himself and got up from his corner. He reached for Brad's glass. ''Let me fix you a drink.''

Brad looked up. ''Thanks.'' The room remained quiet while Hutton refreshed Brad's drink, then his own.

''Why don't we,'' Harry suggested, handing Brad's glass to him, ''discuss Leigh Ann.''

Brad nodded his head. ''I get the message. Just one thing and I'll shut up. Those people in the White House who thought they would intimidate Ho Chi Minh with a piss-in-the-wind effort miscalculated so badly that they might as well have been looking through a telescope at another planet. Now, they don't know what in hell to do, and more of us are going to get our asses blown off.''

Brad exhaled, feeling the warmth of the alcohol. ''If they don't believe enough in this cause to give it one hundred percent, then they should step away and admit that they shit themselves.''

Brad remained quiet, then raised his glass. ''A salute to Nick Palmer, another victim of the cranial-rectal inversion in the White House.''

23

The wind whipped Brad Austin's collar when he stepped through the hatch leading to Vulture's Row. The narrow deck high on the side of the island superstructure afforded an unrestricted view of the entire flight deck.

Nursing a hangover, complete with a throbbing headache, Brad walked forward to the sheltered area next to the bridge. He leaned against the bulkhead and looked up at the top of the island, breathing in the refreshing sea air as he studied the mast and radar antennas. The tall structure sprouted reflectors, catwalks, booms, cables, crossbeams, and a myriad of ropes.

He looked down the walkway to the glass-walled obstruction known as Pri-Fly. Brad could make out the Air Boss and his assistant, who was talking on two telephones. In another seven minutes, they would be busy with the second multiplane recovery of the day.

Hearing the C-1A Trader's engines go to full power, Brad turned to watch the COD on the starboard catapult. The daily mail and supply-delivery flight was staggered between air-strike launches and recoveries.

The big radial engines, revving at full military power, produced a throaty roar. Brad watched the catapult officer twirl his fingers, then thrust toward the bow like a fencer. The tired-looking aircraft squatted down and raced off the end of the deck.

Stepping back out of the wind, Brad opened his shirt pocket and extracted the first letter Leigh Ann had written to him. Holding the pages tightly Brad slowly reread it. He cherished every word, feeling her presence next to him.

The letter ended,

I can only imagine how dangerous it is to fly jets from an aircraft carrier. I know you must be very good at what you do, but just remember—someone cares (very much) about whether or not you return from a mission.

Your gold wings are prominently displayed on my dresser. A picture of the pilot who earned them would be nice. How is that for an overt hint?

Until tomorrow.

My love,
Leigh Ann

Brad was gazing at the fantail, remembering the delicate fragrance Leigh Ann had worn that night on the beach, when he heard the first group of returning aircraft.

He glanced up the flight deck. The duty combat air patrol Phantom had been towed to the number-one catapult. The pilot and RIO sat in their cockpits, passing the time reading paperbacks. Their wingman was positioned directly behind the F-4.

A KA-3B tanker sat on the port catapult, engines running in preparation to launch and intercept two stragglers who were low on fuel.

Watching the A-4 Skyhawks enter the landing pattern, Brad let his thoughts drift back to Waikiki Beach. He replayed the time he had had with Leigh Ann, absorbing the experience one special event at a time.

Brad looked up when one of the Skyhawks missed the four arresting-gear wires and bolted off the deck. Two things caught his attention. The aircraft appeared to have battle damage, and the pilot was well left of centerline when he went off the angle deck.

Deciding to visit Pri-Fly, Brad carefully folded Leigh Ann's letter and hurried to the ship's control tower. Two other Skyhawks landed before the damaged A-4 turned crosswind. Arriving in the confined space, Brad heard the voice of the A-4 pilot as he rolled in on final. He could also hear the landing-signal officer.

"Skyhawk, ball," the pilot radioed. "One point eight."

Brad could hear the wind howling above the LSO's response. He glanced down at the men leaning into the wind on the LSO platform, then concentrated on the damaged A-4.

"Roger, ball," the LSO said in a conversational tone. "Watch your lineup."

The Skyhawk pilot hesitated a moment, then answered in a tense voice. "I've got a control problem."

Watching the Air Boss pick up his telephone, Brad noticed that the Skyhawk pilot was slipping his aircraft. He was having to cross-control the rudder and ailerons to compensate for structural damage to his primary flight controls. The airplane was cocked over to the left, flying slightly sideways.

"Four fourteen," the Air Boss said calmly, "nice and easy. You've got a steady wind down the deck."

Click, click.

The A-4 pilot approached the round-down in a left wing low attitude. He was struggling to stay on speed and course as he neared the carrier's fantail.

"Lineup," the LSO cautioned. "Watch your lineup!"

The Skyhawk flew through the air turbulence caused by the ship's superstructure. The aircraft rolled to the left as the frantic pilot fought the controls.

"WAVE OFF! WAVE OFF!" the LSO shouted, hitting the bright red wave-off lights. Crossing the edge of the flight deck, the pilot applied full power, raised the nose, and leveled the wings.

Brad watched in horror when the A-4's tail hook caught the number-one wire as the aircraft started to climb. Clawing for altitude, the Skyhawk pulled the arresting-gear cable to the limit, then stopped in midair and crashed to the deck in a thunderous explosion.

Brad's mind had seen the accident in slow motion. Something had shot out of the aircraft at the same time the A-4 hit the steel deck.

"CRASH ON DECK! CRASH ON DECK!" The Air Boss was issuing orders and barking commands to the fire fighters swarming around the aircraft.

Seeing a parachute floating down, Brad realized that the pilot had ejected a fraction of a second before the Skyhawk had slammed into the deck. Brad watched the pilot disappear next to the LSO platform. He was astounded by the next call from the landing-signal officer.

"I need six men at the LSO platform! On the double!"

The Air Boss gave the order over the flight-deck PA system, then talked to the LSO. Brad could not hear the Air Boss because of the confusion in Pri-Fly, but he heard the reply from the LSO.

"The pilot is hanging over the side! His chute is caught on a stanchion next to the life-raft storage."

Brad watched fourteen flight-deck crew members race toward the fantail. While the fire fighters extinguished the blazing wreckage, the group of sailors by the LSO platform hauled the dazed pilot up by his parachute.

Once they had the bruised pilot on deck, they unhooked his parachute fittings. Then two medics rushed to his side, gently placed him on a stretcher, and hurried to sick bay.

Feeling emotionally drained by the accident, Brad left Pri-Fly and descended to the flight deck. The aircraft handlers had shoved the wreckage over the side, allowing the fire fighters an opportunity to hose down the deck.

Brad heard the tanker's engines go to full power. He watched the Skywarrior hurtle down the port catapult and climb gracefully into the sky. The carrier was ready to resume normal flight operations.

Descending to the 03 level directly below the flight deck, Brad went to the squadron ready room. When he walked through the hatch, the crash was being replayed on the pilot's landing-aid television (PLAT).

"Watch this," Lincoln Durham said, staring at the PLAT monitor. "In-flight engagement."

Brad watched the horrendous crash from the vantage point of the in-deck centerline camera, then from the island-mounted camera. The island cameraman had captured the accident squarely in the center of the picture. The view from the upper deck was replayed in slow motion.

"Right there," Ernie Sheridan gestured, "is when he pulled the handle."

Mario Russo whistled. "Quick draw. That son of a bitch was fast on the trigger." The accident was played again at normal speed.

"God almighty," Bull Durham exclaimed. "He came out when the aircraft was about three feet from striking the deck."

Absently watching the fire-fighting efforts after the crash, Brad sat down next to Durham. "Any word on Nick?"

The new operations officer grinned. "Scary said they're going to fly him off tomorrow. He thinks Nick will go to Tripler, or back to the States." Durham gave Brad a thumbs-up. "He's optimistic that Nick will be able to return to flight status in the near future."

"That's good news, for a change," Brad replied, looking at his watch. He had ten minutes until he had to be in sick bay for his flight physical. "What's the scoop on tomorrow?"

Durham reached in the right breast pocket of his flight suit and retrieved a planning form. "Tomorrow's mission has been pushed back a day. We're going to hit some bridges in the middle of the Iron Triangle. I've got you leading the TARCAP, with O'Meara as your wingman."

The Iron Triangle consisted of the area between Hanoi, Haiphong, and Thanh Hoa. The region was heavily defended by concentrated antiaircraft batteries, surface-to-air missiles, and numerous MiG fighters.

"That sounds interesting," Brad remarked, seeing Harry Hutton and Russ Lunsford enter the ready room. "What time is the go?"

Durham consulted his list. "You're on the second launch . . . at fourteen hundred. Thought I'd let you sleep in, since you've been on bankers' hours." Durham flashed his gleaming smile.

"Thanks, Bull."

"No sweat," the friendly pilot replied, turning serious.

"I'd like for you to train for squadron LSO, since Nick is going to be gone."

Brad had not even thought about the possibility of becoming a landing-signal officer, but the idea appealed to him. He was always anxious to learn new skills.

"Sure," he said, calculating the amount of time and training that would be required before he would be a qualified LSO. "When do I start?"

Lunsford, followed by Hutton, plopped down in two high-backed seats across the aisle. Each held a half-full mug of lukewarm coffee.

"What I'd like to do," Durham said enthusiastically, "is get you hooked up with the Ghostriders' LSO—Tag Elliot. He's a nice guy and he has a lot of experience."

"Tag?" Brad asked, unsure if he had heard the LSO's first name correctly.

"That's right," Durham replied, catching the looks from Hutton and Lunsford. "Our jarhead is going to become a squadron LSO."

Harry rolled his eyes back. "You're shitting us, Bull."

"No," Durham laughed. "You're going to have a marine waving your pilots aboard."

Lunsford and Hutton groaned in mock agony. Harry looked at his watch. "We better get down to Scary's. It's fifteen hundred, and you know how he is about punctuality." Both RIOs got up and went to the small sink to pour out their coffee.

Brad started to get up, then paused a moment. "How's Cordelia?"

Durham grinned again. "She's doing great, and feels fine. Her obstetrician has her on a strict regimen, and Cordy follows the rules to the letter."

"That's good to hear," Brad replied, rising from his seat. "Tell her hello from me."

"I'll do that this evening."

Brad turned to Hutton and Lunsford. "You boys ready to go down for a Scary finger wave?"

"Can't wait," Lunsford responded, limping toward the door. "I think he's sick."

24

Brad sat in the hot cockpit while his fully armed Phantom was towed to the bow of the ship and positioned on the starboard catapult. The carrier had turned downwind, eliminating the faint breeze that had been sweeping over the flight deck.

Sweltering under the blazing afternoon sun, Brad watched the aircraft handlers unhook the tow tractor and drive away. He carefully placed his helmet on the canopy bow and surveyed the relaxed catapult crews.

Brad and Russ were taking their turn standing the alert-five watch. A second Phantom sat on the port catapult, ready to launch in five minutes if inbound targets were spotted.

Two additional F-4s were airborne, orbiting between North Vietnam and the carrier. If the BARCAP Phantoms encountered MiG fighters or enemy surface vessels, Brad and his wingman would scramble to assist them.

Dark stack smoke drifted from the top of the island and engulfed the open cockpit. The foul-smelling fumes made Brad's eyes water and his nose burn.

Russ sat on the wing, talking to Toby Kendall and cursing the acrid smoke. "Christ," Lunsford said, squinting up at the top of the carrier's superstructure, "we might as well be working in a coal mine."

Turning to look back on the wing, Brad set his paperback on the corner of the instrument glare shield. "Why don't you climb in and suck some cool oxygen?"

"It's too goddamn hot in that pit."

Brad smiled at the plane captain and stared at his RIO. "My, aren't we in a good mood today."

Kendall looked away, embarrassed.

"Oh, yeah, I'm the happiest sonuvabitch in the world. I'm slow roasting out here, and if you don't end up killing me, I'll probably croak from black-lung disease."

Brad reached into the sleeve pocket of his flight suit and slipped out a dollar bill. "Toby, why don't you take a break and go get the three of us an ice-cold Coke. My treat."

One of the ship's snack bars was located under the flight deck aft of the number-one catapult. Kendall would be only thirty seconds away from their Phantom.

Toby beamed and leaped up to the cockpit. "Yes, sir."

After Kendall had rounded the Phantom's nose, Brad turned to Lunsford. "Russ, how about acting like an officer and a professional in front of the men."

"Launch the CAP!" the bullhorn blared before Lunsford could answer. "Launch the CAP!"

Kendall raced back and leaped up to assist Brad with his shoulder harness while Russ jumped into the backseat. The green-shirted catapult crews hustled around the Phantoms while the pilots started their engines. The carrier was heeled over, turning into the wind and gaining speed. The flight deck had erupted in frenzied activity.

Brad's hands flew around the cockpit, rechecking the multitude of instruments and switches. The catapult officer rushed to the center of the deck as Brad lowered his wing tips and shut his canopy.

"You up to speed?" Brad asked, watching the cat officer for the turn-up signal.

"All set," Lunsford replied, finishing the last items on his checklist.

The yellow-shirted officer pointed at Brad, then raised his arm and shook his fingers, giving Brad the full-power signal. Inching the throttles into afterburner, Brad was shocked to see the cat officer give him the catapult-suspend signal.

"Oh, shit," Lunsford spat, "here we go again."

Brad cautiously retarded the power levers to idle. "What

the hell . . . Does anyone have a clue as to what is going on?''

"Cancel the launch," a voice said over the radio. "Repeat, cancel the launch. Remain in condition one."

"This is pure bullshit," Lunsford hissed. "They scare the bejesus out of me, then cank the goddamn launch while we're comin' up on the power."

Brad chopped the throttles and smiled to himself. "The boss probably saw you sunning on the wing, and decided to teach you a lesson." The crews were supposed to remain in their cockpits for the duration of their alert-five duty.

Lunsford popped his oxygen mask loose. "He's a horse's ass, and so are you . . . Captain Professional."

Raising the canopy, Brad spied the paperback he had borrowed from his roommate. "Why don't you borrow one of Harry's crotch novels? The time goes by a lot faster."

Removing his helmet, Brad missed Lunsford's scathing response.

Brad turned the shower faucets, adjusting the temperature of the water, then stepped under the fine spray and soaked his skin. Adhering to the navy policy of conserving fresh water, Brad turned the faucets off and lathered his body. After shampooing his hair, he turned the water on and quickly rinsed off the suds.

Toweling himself dry, Brad thought about his narrow escape from death. Why am I doing this? Where are we headed with this miserable war?

He wrapped his towel around him and picked up his shaving kit, then started toward his stateroom. The more he thought about the rules of engagement and the protected military targets, the more angry he became.

Reaching his quarters, Brad tossed down the kit. "The stupid bastards . . ."

Harry looked over the top of his latest edition of *Playboy* magazine. "Do I detect a note of hostility?"

"Harry," Brad replied, yanking open the closet door, "do you see what's happening to us . . . to the morale of the flight crews?"

Turning in his bunk, Harry set the magazine aside. "At the risk of offending you, there isn't anything we can do, except try to survive."

Brad placed his uniform on his bunk. "Jesus Christ, what a complete disaster."

Waiting a few seconds, Hutton propped himself up. "Brad, we've got to ride it out the best we can. We don't have any choice, and you know it."

Brad gave his roommate a strange look. "Yeah, you're right. We're simply cannon fodder for the incompetent politicians."

"Don't get pissed at me."

Brad drew in a slow breath. "I'm not upset with you, Harry. I'm just frustrated, and so is the skipper. You can see it in his eyes. He knows the administration is full of horseshit, but he has to protect his own future."

"Brad, that's all we can do, and pray for a future."

Austin slumped on his chair. "The futility of this mess . . . all the senseless deaths." Brad's eyes narrowed. "Harry, those spineless bastards in the White House are going to burn in hell."

Taxiing behind Jon O'Meara, Brad stopped thirty feet from the jet blast deflector (JBD). When O'Meara's Phantom reached the starboard catapult track, the hydraulically actuated blast deflector was raised.

"Are you ready for this act?" Brad asked Lunsford, who was already breathing heavily.

Keying his intercom, Lunsford looked in Austin's canopy mirrors. "That's a dumb-ass question. Hell no, I'm not ready."

After the catapult crews scooted from under the howling F-4, O'Meara plugged in the afterburner. The twin fire storm sent a powerful blast of exhaust into the blackened JBD. Part of the forceful thrust slipped over the blast deflector, gently rocking Joker 201.

Brad rechecked the flap control panel and looked up in time to see O'Meara's Phantom rocket down the catapult. The F-4 cleared the flight deck, settled below the bow, then climbed smoothly away. Clouds of superheated steam swirled back over Austin's Phantom.

"Well," Brad observed, adding power to taxi up to the catapult, "he didn't blow any spray off the water today."

Lunsford lowered his helmet visor and tightened the friction knob. "He blows spray off the water—you fly through trees."

Brad felt the catapult take tension, looked at the catapult officer, waited for the turn-up signal, then smoothly shoved the throttles into afterburner. Checking the engine instruments, Brad popped a snappy salute to the cat officer and braced his head against the ejection-seat headrest.

The F-4 blasted down the catapult track, smashing the crew back into their seats. As the fighter cleared the bow, Austin's vision returned to normal. He snapped the landing-gear lever up, allowed the Phantom to accelerate, then raised the flaps.

Brad left the aircraft in afterburner in order to facilitate the running rendezvous. He and O'Meara had decided on a quick join-up, so they could tank and get to the target area a few minutes before the strike aircraft arrived.

Seeing O'Meara's Phantom at one o'clock, Brad kept the airspeed at 420 knots until he was almost abeam of his wingman. He chopped the throttles to idle and deployed the speed brakes.

"Goddamnit," Lunsford exclaimed, watching O'Meara's F-4 slide to the rear of Joker 201. "How about a heads-up when you're going to throw out the anchor."

"Put me down for another beer," Brad replied, thumbing the speed brakes closed. He added a handful of power to stabilize in front of his wingman.

Lunsford looked at the tick marks on his dented knee-board. "You already owe me over a case, you sorry bastard."

Although O'Meara had launched first, Brad was the flight leader. Joker 212 settled into a loose parade formation on Brad's right wing.

Slowly increasing speed, Brad gently raised the nose. To this point, he and Jon O'Meara had not exchanged any radio calls. Passing 12,000 feet, Brad heard Lunsford swear and say something indistinguishable.

"What are you mumbling about?"

Lunsford looked up at the ejection-seat handles over Brad's crash helmet. "I was just figuring my current life expectancy."

Brad gave O'Meara the sign to switch to the tanker frequency. "What'd you come up with?"

"Zilch point shit."

Austin ignored the complaining from the backseat and concentrated on refueling his F-4. After departing the tanker, the flight headed toward the coast-in point.

The Gulf of Tonkin looked like gray slate as the two Phantoms approached the shoreline. Four additional F-4s would provide barrier combat air patrol for the carrier task force.

Another group of aircraft from the second carrier was going to simultaneously strike the highway and railroad bridges at Hai Duong. Four F-8 Crusaders would provide target air combat patrol for twelve A-4 Skyhawks.

The midafternoon weather was unusually clear, with good visibility above and below the puffy white clouds. The pilots and RIOs would have an easier time spotting the surface-to-air missiles and antiaircraft fire.

Brad listened to Red Crown and the strike leaders. The A-4s reported that they would be feet dry in two minutes. Brad looked down to the left in an attempt to spot the A-4s in his attack group. They were 5,000 feet below the prowling Phantoms.

"They're at eight o'clock," Lunsford said, tightening his seat belt and shoulder straps.

"Got 'em," Brad acknowledged as he lowered the F-4's nose. O'Meara moved out to a combat spread position, then drifted behind Joker 201.

Glancing at the picture of Leigh Ann, Brad inched the throttles forward and scanned his engine instruments. He had again taped the copy of the original photo under the right fire-overheat warning light.

Keeping the strike group in sight, Brad leveled at 7,000

feet and 460 knots. He had two AIM-7D Sparrows in the rear missile wells and four AIM-9B Sidewinders, two attached to each inboard wing station.

Rolling into a left orbit, Brad was startled by the call from the ground-control intercept operator.

"This is Red Crown. We have MiG activity coming off Kep. Repeat—six to seven MiGs climbing out of Kep. Red Crown clear."

"Jokers, copy."

Brad rolled back to the right and pointed the F-4's nose toward the MiG base at Kep. The intelligence briefer had said that there were reported to be five MiG-17s and three MiG-21s at the airfield.

"This is Red Crown!" the voice said with renewed urgency. "MiG activity at Gia Lam and Phuc Yen . . . going south of Hanoi. Stand by."

Brad switched his master armament to the ON position and keyed his mike. "Jokers, arm 'em up."

"Joker Two," O'Meara replied, searching the sky for MiGs and SAMs. Mario Russo cinched his shoulder harnesses tight and checked the radar switches. The strike group was pulling up for their run-in when the GCI coordinator called again.

"This is Red Crown. Multiple bogies around the Hanoi area," the controller radioed, then paused. "We hold nine aircraft airborne, and intel confirms four waiting to take off from Phuc Yen."

Agents friendly to the United States maintained a constant surveillance on the North Vietnamese airfields. They sent coded radio messages to reconnaissance aircraft that passed the information to Red Crown.

Brad caught a glimpse of three surface-to-air missiles leaving their launching pads. A second later, three more missiles lifted off and shot skyward. The SAMs trailed clearly visible smoke as they accelerated toward the strike aircraft. The sky was filled with an incredible amount of antiaircraft fire when the A-4 leader rolled into his dive toward the target.

Two more SAMs rose from an emplacement next to a

bridge. In a matter of ten to twelve seconds, the sky had been saturated with lethal missiles and AAA fire. Hundreds of dark puffs exploded around the Skyhawks.

"SAMs!" an A-4 pilot warned.

"Red Crown, Red Crown," Brad radioed, feeling the sudden rush of adrenaline. "Joker Two Oh One." The reply was garbled, but it obviously came from the controller on board the GCI ship.

"We're going to need more fighters!" Brad radioed, then added, "We need the BARCAP, buster! Recommend the carrier launch the duty CAP." Buster was the code name to move out at top speed.

"Those intel morons," Lunsford hissed, referring to the intelligence briefers. "You can expect low MiG activity, my ass."

Leaving the strike group behind, Brad wrapped the Phantom around and flew toward the MiGs south of Hanoi. He wanted to scatter or engage the MiGs as far from the A-4s as possible. The strike aircraft, which were subsonic attack planes, needed time to get offshore safely.

Both Phantom RIOs picked up the MiGs on radar at thirteen miles. Closing to four miles, the pilots saw the trio of fighters crossing from right to left. When they reefed their Phantoms into a tight turn behind the bogies, the three MiG-21s reversed toward the F-4s.

"They've got us pegged," Brad said over the intercom. "We need to take out their GCIs." The ground-control intercept radars were portable Soviet-made P-35 units. The numerous installations provided the MiG pilots with vectors to the American aircraft.

"Jokers," Brad radioed, "three MiGs on the nose!"

"Got 'em," O'Meara shouted at the same time he fired a Sparrow missile.

Making small corrections, the radar-guided missile tracked straight to the number-three MiG. Brad watched the Sparrow explode beside the fighter, blowing off pieces of the right wing.

"I've got a lock!" Lunsford called as the number-three MiG trailed fire and black smoke, then pitched down and rolled inverted. The pilot ejected as the aircraft entered a puffy cloud.

Brad fired a Sparrow from a distance of 6,000 feet. The MiG flight leader snapped inverted and pulled hard for the deck. His wingman followed a half second later.

Rolling to chase their quarry, Brad swore when the Sparrow lost radar discrimination in the ground return. The errant missile flew over the savvy MiG flight leader, then nosed over and impacted the side of a wooded hill.

Brad keyed the radio. "Jokers, go HEAT! We may get a shot when they run out."

Both Phantom pilots selected their heat-seeking Sidewinder missiles. Brad led the flight down to 100 feet above the terrain. The F-4s were 5,000 feet behind the second MiG when the flight leader reversed toward the Phantoms. The experienced MiG pilot completed his knife-edge turn at 50 feet.

Brad had a sudden, strange feeling. He could hear his Sidewinders buzzing from the radiation heat rising from the ground. The heat-seeking missiles, along with the radar-guided Sparrows, could not lock up a target this low to the ground.

The MiG was completing the tight turn when Brad saw muzzle flashes from the fighter's 30mm cannon. The pilot was firing at Jon O'Meara.

Believing that the two MiG-21s would head directly for a sanctuary airfield, Brad had allowed himself and his wingman to fall into a trap.

"Son of a bitch!" Brad exclaimed to Lunsford. "I've been suckered in."

The MiG pilot had placed the F-4 crews in a position where they could not use their weapons. The MiG fighter pilot had the advantage with his powerful cannon.

"Hang onto my wing!" Brad radioed to Jon O'Meara.

The MiG was almost head-on when Brad banked into a deliberate collision course.

Lunsford keyed the intercom. "Let's go for separation!"

Concentrating on the blur of flashes emitting from the

MiG's cannon, Brad tweaked the nose down and pressed home his apparent suicidal charge.

"We've been hit!" O'Meara yelled, breaking Brad's concentration.

In full afterburner, the Phantom roared over the MiG, missing the canopy by twenty feet. Brad had sandwiched the aggressive fighter pilot between the F-4 and the ground fifty feet below the MiG.

After flashing over the aircraft, Brad replayed in his mind what he had seen. The MiG pilot had been wearing a brown leather helmet, large goggles, a bulky parachute, and a tan scarf. What caught Brad's attention were two blurs of color. There was no mistaking the red stars on the nose, along with the white line across the tail of the MiG-21.

"That's Major Dao!" Lunsford shouted at the same time that Brad snapped the F-4 into a vertical climb.

"I'm goin' for the beach!" O'Meara radioed, turning hard for the coastline.

"Go!" Brad shouted. "I'll cover you."

Rolling the Phantom in the vertical, Brad caught sight of the two MiGs. They were off his left wing, drifting behind the F-4. They would be in position to blast the Phantom in a matter of seconds.

"You better get inspired," Lunsford yelled, "or they're going to eat our lunch!"

In desperation, Brad rudder-rolled the Phantom toward his adversaries. He could see muzzle flashes from both MiGs as the nose of his F-4 fell through the horizon. He was committed to go for separation and disengage. Without a wingman to drag off the second MiG, Austin would soon be boxed in.

Brad unloaded the Phantom to zero g and selected full afterburner. "Have you got them?"

Gasping oxygen, Lunsford twisted around to his left. "They're going . . . turned toward Phuc Yen."

Brad bottomed out 800 feet above the ground, indicating Mach 1.1. He pulled the power back to ninety-seven percent and keyed his radio. "Joker Two Twelve, say posit."

"We're ten miles from the coast," Jon O'Meara replied, then added, "climbing through one one thousand."

Brad raised the nose and scanned the sky. "Jon, what's your status? Can you make the boat?"

"I think so. My starboard engine is surging, but everything else looks good."

Brad checked his fuel-quantity indicator, then thought about the encounter with Major Dao. Joker 201 had almost become the eight red star on the MiG-21.

Crossing the coastline, Brad soon spotted his wingman ahead and to the right. He slid smoothly into formation on O'Meara's right wing as the Phantoms passed over a group of small islands.

Lost in their thoughts, both crews remained quiet during the return flight to the carrier. They were acutely aware that Austin's tactical blunder had almost cost them their lives.

25

Brad and Russ remained in their cockpits while the Phantom was lowered to the hangar bay. Brad had secured the engines after the F-4 had been chained to the deck-edge elevator. The tail of the Phantom extended out over the water.

When the elevator stopped, the aircraft handlers hooked a tow tractor to the nose gear of Joker 201. They quickly unchained the big fighter and pulled the chocks from the main wheels.

Contemplating the almost fatal mistake he had made, Brad felt the aircraft move as the tug driver maneuvered the F-4 off the elevator. The blue shirt stopped the Phantom directly behind Jon O'Meara's airplane.

Toby Kendall scrambled up the side of the fuselage to Brad's cockpit. "Cap'n, we got the word that Lieutenant O'Meara got him a MiG."

Brad smiled weakly. "He sure did, Toby."

The plane captain helped Brad and Russ with their flight gear, then stepped down to the hangar deck. He noticed that one Sparrow had been fired, but Austin and Lunsford were certainly not exuberant. Kendall busied himself postflighting the Phantom while the two officers walked to O'Meara's airplane. Russ Lunsford still favored his right ankle.

Mario Russo and Jon O'Meara, along with three mainte- nance men, stood on the right wing. They were inspecting the four holes along the engine air duct. There was also a hole in the leading edge of the wing, and two ragged openings in the right stabilator.

"Congratulations," Brad said when they reached the back of the wing. The pilot and his RIO were elated about their first MiG kill.

"Thanks," O'Meara replied, dropping to one knee next to Brad and Russ. "Looks like we took a couple of rounds through the engine."

Brad placed his helmet on the top of the wing. "I really apologize for setting us up for target practice."

"I would have done the same thing," O'Meara said as Mario Russo kneeled beside him. "Nine out of ten times those little goat holers cut and run. Shit, I was shocked when that son of a bitch cranked into us."

"Yeah," Russo said, shaking his head. "Those guys were not your average MiG drivers."

Brad leaned against the flap. "You're right. The leader was Major Dao."

O'Meara's eyes registered his surprise. "No shit?"

"None other," Lunsford responded as he shoved up his sleeves. "We about got our asses waxed."

"Well," O'Meara said to Brad with a grin, "you damn sure scared the shit out of him. I honestly thought you were going to hit him."

"I'll bet," Russo laughed, "that the little bastard fodded his wears."

Brad managed a small grin, then noticed a group of squadron officers and men coming to congratulate the MiG killers.

Relaxing on his bunk, Brad read the latest letter he had received from Leigh Ann. He hadn't heard from her since he had extended the invitation to join him in San Francisco. Brad worried that Leigh Ann's parents might be unhappy at the idea of his inviting their daughter to meet him in a faraway city.

He was reading the second page when Harry Hutton opened the door and entered the cramped cubicle. After shutting the door, he sat down with a troubled expression on his face.

Brad glanced up at his roommate. "What's the matter?"

"You've got a new backseater," Harry answered with a crease of a smile.

Perplexed, Brad frowned and absently folded Leigh Ann's letter. "I've got a new RIO?"

"That's right, partner."

"Who?"

"You're looking at him."

Breaking into a grin, Brad was uncertain if Hutton was pulling his leg. "Harry, if you're jake legging me around, I don't think it's—"

"I'm not kidding you," Harry said in a convincing voice. "The skipper is going to talk to you later. I told him that you were asleep, which you were."

Sitting up, Brad mulled over a number of questions. Had Russ Lunsford thrown in the towel? Why the change? "What the hell is going on?"

"Well," Harry said with a concerned look on his face, "the old man and Jocko apparently believe that Russ is about to go off the deep end."

"What gives them that idea?" Brad asked, confused by the unexpected change. "Is it because of me?"

Harry looked pained. "I don't know the full story. I wasn't privy to their conversation."

"Damnit," Brad blurted, then looked at the overhead. "I feel really bad about this."

Harry felt tension in his neck muscles. "They—the CO and XO—have been observing Russ closely the past few days. They have noticed, and so have I, that his hands shake uncontrollably at times."

Brad looked Harry straight in the eyes. "Hell, so do mine at times, especially from the constant adrenaline shocks. There has to be more to this."

Harry paused, thinking about the incident that had triggered the reassignment. "This morning, before you came to the ready room, the skipper and Jocko watched Russ try to drink a cup of coffee."

Brad started to speak but remained quiet while Harry continued.

"That was this morning, before you flew the BARCAP. He wasn't under the influence of an adrenaline charge."

"What happened?" Brad asked impatiently.

"Russ sloshed over half the coffee on the deck before he could set the cup down. He scalded both hands."

"Jesus," Brad responded, remembering how quiet and reserved Lunsford had been during the flight that morning. "You know, he was unusually withdrawn today."

Brad analyzed Lunsford's behavior since the previous flight—the encounter with the North Vietnamese ace. "Russ didn't rant and rave, like normal, on the way back to the boat after Jon bagged the MiG."

Harry inhaled. "I think, from what I've heard, that the near midair with the MiG—right down in the dirt—flipped his switch."

Clenching his fists, Brad felt responsible for what had happened to his friend and flying companion. "What are they planning for Russ?"

"Well, from what I understand, the skipper is going to give Russ a collateral job—a project—to keep him busy for a week or so."

"Then what?" Brad asked, feeling a deep concern. "What about the long run?"

Harry shrugged. "I don't know. From what I gathered, they are going to have Russ fly with Bull Durham for a while, then evaluate the situation."

Brad and Harry reflected quietly on Russ Lunsford's future. Being grounded would probably be the kiss of death to his naval career.

Brad placed Leigh Ann's letter in his pocket. "Do we have to get new roommates?"

Harry shook his head. "No. The CO said since I don't have a pilot, then it's you and me, and we can stay put where we are."

Dropping his head, Brad worried about Lunsford. "I better go talk with Russ. I'm the one who is responsible for putting him into shock."

Harry raised his hand slightly. "I'd give it some time. He feels like he has failed you . . . let you down."

"Okay," Brad replied, knowing how he would feel under the same circumstances. "I understand."

Brad opened the refrigerator and pulled out two soft drinks. Handing one to Harry, Brad opened his can and leaned back. "Well, tell me the truth."

"I always do," Harry responded, wiping the corner of his mouth where a sip of Coke had spilled out.

Brad set down his can. "Do you have any qualms about flying with me?"

Harry chuckled, then downed a quick swallow. "Hell, no. You and Palmer—you're the best in the squadron."

Glancing at the bulkhead-mounted aeronautical chart of North Vietnam, Harry grew serious. "You know something, that asshole Carella has turned into a real shitbird since he took over as XO."

"How's that?"

Harry lifted his Coke can and held it a few inches from his mouth. "He inferred that since I don't have a brain, flying with you wouldn't scare me."

"Yeah," Brad replied, "a real prince."

Austin stood on the landing-signal officer's platform while the carrier turned into the wind. The afternoon strike group was inbound for the recovery scheduled at 1545. The rescue helicopter hovered off the starboard side of the stern of the carrier.

Brad looked out at the ship's churning wake, taking in the plane-guard destroyer. The smaller ship split the middle of the wake 5,000 feet behind the carrier.

He shared the platform on the aft port side of the ship with the controlling LSO, Lt. Tag Elliot, another LSO trainee, and two sound-powered telephone talkers. They were all aware of the safety net that would be their escape route if an aircraft appeared about to strike the ramp.

Terrell "Tag" Elliot, who was heralded as one of the best LSOs in the fleet, had warmly welcomed Brad to join his other trainee. Elliot was a quiet, studious man who had an air of melancholy about him. His curly blond hair was normally mussed, and he always had a cup of coffee in his hand. He had even been known to take a thermos bottle of the scalding liquid to the LSO platform.

Elliot held a telephone receiver that connected him to the controller in the Carrier Air Traffic Control Center, the Air Boss in Pri-Fly, and the inbound pilots. In the other hand, he held a pickle switch, which he used to energize the bright red wave-off lights if an approach looked unstable.

The LSO had total responsibility for getting the pilots safely aboard the carrier. He assigned a grade to each approach and landing, then critiqued the pilots in their ready room. His word was law at the ramp, without an appeal process.

A thirty-eight-knot wind whipped the cluster of men, making them continuously shift to maintain their balance. They had to shout to each other in order to be heard.

While they waited for the returning planes, Brad thought about the previous four days. He had had a lengthy, pleasant conversation with Russ Lunsford. Both men had felt comfortable after they had expressed their honest feelings, and reinforced their mutual respect for each other. Their friendship was not in jeopardy.

Lunsford had enthusiastically attacked the assignment involving revamping and updating the squadron personnel files. He had also expressed a strong desire to return to flight status as quickly as possible.

Doc McCary had initiated a combination of tranquilizers, vigorous workouts, and personal counseling to assist Lunsford in adjusting to his environment.

Scheduled together for the first time, Brad and Harry had gone down on the catapult when a hydraulic leak had been detected under their Phantom. They were not going to be scheduled to fly again until Brad completed his five-day familiarization course with their sister-squadron LSO.

The most stimulation for Brad had been the letter from Leigh Ann. She had been enthusiastic about meeting Brad in San Francisco, but had insisted on paying her own expenses.

After checking with Dan Bailey, who had readily agreed

to endorse Austin's leave papers, Brad had talked with an acquaintance on the staff of the task-force commander. The lieutenant commander had confirmed that *Bon Homme Richard* was about to complete warm-ups, providing the weather cooperated. The carrier was expected to depart Dixie Station in forty-four hours, and relieve Brad's troubled ship shortly thereafter.

Bringing his mind back to the present from more pleasant thoughts, Brad listened to the first pilot call the landing-signal officer.

"Skyhawk, ball, two point eight."

"Roger, ball," Elliot replied calmly. He watched the aircraft with a critical eye, ready to offer verbal encouragement if the pilot needed assistance.

"Green deck!" a talker shouted above the roar of the wind and jet engines. The A-4 Skyhawk continued the approach, seemingly nailed to the glide slope.

Seeing the aircraft settle in close, Tag Elliot spoke to the pilot. "Power—need a little power."

The seasoned aviator made a slight correction before crossing the round-down and thundering into the number-two arresting wire. The A-4 screeched to a wing-rocking halt, then rolled backward as the pilot pulled his throttle to idle. The hook runner yanked the arresting gear loose, allowing the Skyhawk pilot to quickly taxi out of the landing area.

Brad turned and looked forward on the flight deck, checking to see that nothing was protruding over the foul-deck line. He noted that a KA-3B tanker was preparing to launch off the port-bow catapult. The jet blast deflector had been raised and the Skywarrior was being hooked to the catapult shuttle.

Returning his attention to the next aircraft in the landing pattern, Brad listened to the pilot call the ball.

"Skyhawk, ball, two point nine."

Brad could hear the approaching aircraft. The pilot constantly jockeyed his throttle, causing the engine to spool up and down. The continuous power adjustments were necessary to maintain a perfect descent profile down the glide slope to the arresting wires.

Noticing that the attack jet had started a left-to-right drift, Brad peered at Elliot. The LSO tilted his phone receiver next to his mouth.

"Line up. Back to the left."

The pilot of the Skywarrior tanker went to full power, checking his controls. Brad stole a glance up the deck, then returned his attention to the A-4. The Skyhawk dipped to the left and rolled wings level as it passed over the round-down.

Sensing trouble, Brad watched the attack jet continue to drift to the right. The aircraft slammed into the flight deck far to the right of the centerline, blowing the right tire. The tail hook impacted between the number-three and -four cables, skipping over the last arresting-gear wire. The damaged right landing gear pulled the Skyhawk even farther to the right of centerline.

"Bolter, bolter!" Elliot exclaimed, using body language to will the aircraft airborne. He also felt a sense of impending disaster.

The KA-3B thundered down the forward port catapult as the Skyhawk pilot pushed his throttle to the stops. He frantically shoved on the left-rudder pedal and yanked the control stick into his lap.

As the A-4 rotated, the right wing smashed into the port blast deflector. Debris exploded from the shattered wing as the desperate pilot fought to control his severely damaged aircraft.

Momentarily paralyzed, Brad witnessed the Skyhawk climb a hundred feet before it began a slow roll to the right.

The captain of the ship, anticipating an imminent crash, had already ordered a turn to the left to go behind the crippled A-4. The Skyhawk continued to roll to the right, passing behind and below the KA-3B tanker.

"EJECT! EJECT!" Tag Elliot shouted as the aircraft passed in front of the carrier's bow in a sixty-degree bank to the right. The A-4 was 190 feet above the water, nose level with the horizon. When the angle of bank approached ninety degrees, the Air Boss and the LSO yelled in unison for the pilot to eject.

Brad watched the canopy jettison, followed by the rocket-powered ejection seat. The pilot shot out horizontally, then started to arc toward the water. His parachute was only partially open when he impacted the water with tremendous force.

The aircraft crashed abeam the bow, creating a huge geyser of water. Wreckage ricoheted across the water for more than 200 yards.

Brad felt the ship heel over as the captain turned back into the wind. Elliot instructed the returning pilots to orbit overhead the carrier.

The rescue helicopter was slowing over the downed aviator, and the plane-guard destroyer had maneuvered to the right of the carrier's wake. The support ship was slowing in preparation to lower a boat over the side if the helicopter developed any problems.

As the carrier prepared to continue to recover aircraft, Brad watched the SAR helicopter hover over the A-4 pilot. The rescue swimmer jumped into the water as the carrier passed the helicopter. The injured aviator was apparently not able to don the rescue collar on his own.

"Ready deck!" the talker shouted into the wind.

Brad looked forward to see the last of the Skyhawk's debris being thrown over the side of the carrier. A plane handler kicked a shred of metal off the deck and gave a thumbs-up indication.

Tag Elliot was talking to the Air Boss and the pilots. It was time to continue recovering aircraft, before they all had to tank from the Whale.

Brad heard the approaching Skyhawk pilot call the ball, then glanced at the rescue helicopter. The rotorcraft was falling far behind the carrier, but Brad could see that the A-4 pilot was being hoisted aboard the helicopter. The injured aviator would be back on the carrier deck in a matter of minutes.

26

Stepping into the main wardroom, Brad joined the line at the cafeteria-style counter, then looked for an empty seat in the crowded room.

Spotting Harry Hutton and Russ Lunsford, Brad walked to their table. "Hi, guys."

"Hi," Russ answered, reaching for his milk. Harry nodded, swallowing a bite of tuna-fish sandwich.

Lunsford appeared to be more relaxed than Brad had ever seen him. Russ held his milk with a steady hand, smiling easily and laughing.

Harry raised his sandwich. "You been LSOing this morning, or just sleeping in?"

"No," Brad replied, placing his cloth napkin across his lap. "I've been in the library, studying the history of the landing-signal officer. I get to wave the afternoon gaggle, with Tag coaching me."

Lunsford finished his milk. "Are you going to have to go to the formal LSO school?"

"I don't know what they plan to do. This is just an indoctrination to the art, and, as you know, we're short of aircrews."

Brad reached for his iced tea and looked at Russ. "How's the personnel business?"

Listening to Lunsford tell about the revamped personnel files, Brad peppered his meal and began eating. "What's next on your list?"

"Scary told me," Russ answered, putting his dessert

spoon down with a triumphant air, "that I am cleared to fly tomorrow."

Brad looked up, concealing his concern. Whatever his faults, Russ Lunsford was a good friend. "How do you feel about flying again?"

Lunsford waited while a steward removed his plates from the table. "At first—yesterday when he told me—I had a few butterflies in my stomach, but I'm looking forward to getting back in the groove."

Harry put down the remains of his sandwich. "We are scheduled to fly wing tomorrow for Bull and Russ."

"Great," Brad replied, turning to Lunsford. "What kind of hop did we draw?"

"A TARCAP," Russ answered, folding his napkin on the table. "We are on the early morning launch, then the Bonnie Dick will relieve us. Tomorrow at this time, we will be steaming for Yokosuka."

Brad immediately thought of Leigh Ann. "Who told you that we're going to Yokosuka tomorrow?"

"The old man," Lunsford answered, serenely folding his hands, "made the announcement about an hour ago."

Unable to contain his grin, Brad ordered dessert from a steward, then resumed the conversation. "Has anyone heard from Nick?"

"Yes," Harry replied. "I had a short note from him yesterday. He wrote it with his left hand, so it took a while to decipher his scratchings. At any rate, he is in sunny San Diego. He said that he is going to be in the hospital—Balboa—for about a month and a half. After that, he is going to be undergoing physical therapy, and whatever else they dream up."

"Then what?" Brad asked, leaning back to allow a steward to remove his dinner plate. He had eaten only a few bites.

"Who knows. Scary still thinks Nick will be flying in a couple of months."

Harry waited until Brad's ice cream had been served. "I heard that the A-4 jock—the guy who skipped across the water yesterday—is turning in his wings. Scary said he broke his right leg and three ribs. I guess he is just one huge bruise.''

Brad wiped his mouth. ''I think you heard wrong. I went through advanced training with the guy—Chargin' Charlie Nickerson. He is one tough son of a bitch, and a hell of a pilot. He'd probably be the last guy to toss his wings on the table.''

''Well,'' Harry shrugged, ''that's what I heard from a guy in his squadron.''

Brad ate slowly. The cold dessert caused his teeth to ache. ''What are you two planning to do in Yoko?''

An enthusiastic grin spread across Harry's face. ''I don't know about Russ, but I'm going to engage in my own kind of physical therapy, and it isn't touring shrines and temples.''

Lunsford chuckled, appearing to be completely relaxed. ''Since you're deserting us, I'm going to have to take charge of Harry.''

''Right, Bosco,'' Hutton responded, turning to Lunsford. ''The last time we were in Yoko, you got blown away on hot sake, and I had to drag your drunken carcass back to the hotel.''

Brad finished his ice cream. ''I still think the best Russ Lunsford story happened in Hong Kong.''

Lunsford sighed. ''Do we have to hear that again?''

''Yeah,'' Harry laughed, ''when he got shit-faced and bought that plaid suit with the three-inch cuffs.''

''After he fell out of the ricksha,'' Brad grinned.

Lunsford flushed. ''Could you all talk a little louder, so the whole wardroom can hear?''

''You had to wear sunglasses,'' Harry continued, ''to look at that goddamn suit. Christ, he looked like a California clap doctor.''

''I've got an idea,'' Brad said excitedly. ''Why don't you guys ride up to Tokyo with me, to see me off. If I have time before my flight departs, we can amuse ourselves in the Ginza district. How about it?'' Brad asked, looking at his watch. He had to be on the LSO platform in fifteen minutes.

"I'm game," Harry replied. "What else have I got to do?"

Russ paused a moment. "Count me in, if I can wear my plaid suit."

Tag Elliot stood directly behind Brad, watching the F-4 Phantom rolling into the groove. Elliot's chin was almost touching Brad's left shoulder. The LSO looked much like an umpire standing behind a baseball catcher. Each man held a telephone receiver to his ear. Elliot held the wave-off pickle over his head in his right hand.

Brad intently watched the descending Phantom, concentrating on the visual clues Elliot had taught him. Austin listened to the distinct whine of the F-4's engines as the pilot adjusted his throttles.

Detecting the aircraft going above the glide slope, Brad spoke into his telephone receiver. "Slightly high . . . ease it down a bit."

The pilot responded in a smooth, well-coordinated effort. He crossed the round-down on speed, on centerline, and caught the number-three arresting wire. A perfect trap.

Focusing on the next Phantom, Brad had a fleeting thought about the A-4 Skyhawk orbiting overhead. The attack jet had a single 250-pound Mark 81 bomb that had failed to release from under the right wing. The Air Boss wanted all the strike aircraft safely on deck before the Skyhawk with live ordnance would be allowed to land.

Watching the Phantom closely, Brad thought the approach looked stabilized. At the last second, the pilot pulled off too much power and caught the number-two wire.

Turning to watch the F-4 run out in the arresting-gear cable, Brad caught a glimpse of three members of the ship's explosive ordnance disposal (EOD) team. The EOD experts were standing at the forward hatch in the island. During the morning launch, they had had to disarm a 250-pound bomb that had broken loose from an A-4 during a catapult launch.

Seven more aircraft landed without a single bolter, clearing the deck for the Skyhawk. Complicating the A-4 pilot's problem was the fact that he also had an asymmetrical situation. The right wing, with the bomb attached, was carrying more weight than the left wing.

Brad and Tag Elliot heard the booming voice of the Air Boss over the flight-deck loudspeakers.

"The hung ordnance is descending downwind."

"Roger, Boss," Elliot replied in his hand-held transmitter, than tapped Brad on the shoulder. "I'll take this one."

Brad nodded and stepped behind the LSO. Searching for the A-4, he spotted it directly abeam of the carrier. Following the aircraft through the turn to final, Brad glanced forward on the flight deck. It was deserted, except for the EOD team.

Turning back to the A-4, Brad watched the Skyhawk and listened to Elliot. As the aircraft approached the ramp, Brad felt his muscles tense. He shot a quick look at the safety net, then discarded the thought of diving in the padded net. If the bomb went off, he would be blown over the side of the carrier.

Flying a steady approach, the A-4 pilot planted the airplane between the number-two and -three wires. The bomb jarred loose, hit the deck, bounced up and hit the underside of the wing, then skittered down the angle deck and dropped into the water.

Waiting for an explosion, Brad held his breath. When the stern of the ship had passed the impact point of the bomb, Brad realized he needed to breathe.

The relieved Skyhawk pilot rolled back, dropped the arresting-gear wire, and shut down the engine. He did not want to move the aircraft until the plane captain had had an opportunity to assess the damage.

Elliot turned to Brad. "With some experience, you're going to have this wired."

"Thanks," Brad replied, stowing their LSO gear. "I appreciate the introduction to your fraternity."

After dinner, Brad strolled forward through the crowded hangar bay, climbed a ladder to the flight deck, and walked the length of the carrier. Arriving at the round-down, Brad watched the phosphorescent wake churned up from the ship's propellers and daydreamed about Leigh Ann. What was she doing right now? Had she told her friends about him? Would she be in San Francisco when he arrived? He hoped she would meet him.

Brad computed the time difference between the Gulf of Tonkin and Memphis, Tennessee. Leigh Ann would most likely be asleep at 4:15 in the morning. She would be having her evening meal when he next launched into combat.

Watching the escort destroyers roll gently from side to side, Brad decided to write Leigh Ann a letter. If she agreed to meet him in San Francisco, she would not receive the letter until after she had returned home. He wanted Leigh Ann to know how he felt about her, regardless of whether or not she could join him in California.

Back in his stateroom, Brad placed a piece of paper on the desktop, then absently tapped his Naval Academy ring on the side of the counter. He picked up his pen, set it down, and gazed at the picture of Leigh Ann.

He wondered if the two of them would enjoy the same activities and share the same basic philosophy of life. She had seemed like a very flexible person who would most likely be equally at ease on a yacht at Cannes or nestled next to a warm fire in a mountain cabin. Lake Tahoe came to mind, then the San Juan Islands between Seattle and Vancouver. He felt certain that Leigh Ann would enjoy the quiet peacefulness that permeated the isolated islands—a pristine environment of forested land surrounded by water as clear and clean as a mountain lake.

Brad smiled inwardly, remembering his first trip to the archipelago. The rustic cabin without a television or telephone. The unspoiled wilderness and the deserted paths through the stately fir trees.

Yes, Brad thought, staring at the beautiful woman in the small frame. A log cabin, a warm fire, a bowl of soup, some French bread, a bottle of good wine, and Leigh Ann.

Reaching again for his pen, Brad stopped when Harry inserted his key in the door. "It's open."

"Thanks," Harry replied as he stepped in and closed the slightly warped door.

"How was the movie?"

"Lousy," Harry responded with a disgusted look. "I don't know what the hell has happened, but some of this crap we've seen three times, and shouldn't have seen the first time."

"Harry," Brad suggested, "why don't you take up a collection and buy some juicy movies in Tokyo?"

"Good idea," Harry beamed. "Some good old-fashioned raunchy flicks."

Harry opened the refrigerator. "Shit, we're outta Cokes."

"No we're not," Brad smiled. "Try my flight-gear locker. Seventeen, twenty-eight, twelve." Harry repeated the numbers to the combination lock and hurried to the equipment room.

Brad filled two glasses with ice cubes. After refilling the small ice tray, he slipped it back in the refrigerator and leaned against the bulkhead.

He carefully studied Harry's latest foldout of the Play-mate of the Month. What he viewed did not impress him. The porcelain face reflected a sullen, pouting young girl who did not look too happy.

When Harry returned with two six packs of Coke, they poured their drinks and relaxed. Brad remained at the desk while Harry flopped on his stomach across the lower bunk. Something was on his mind.

"Brad, I haven't flown with you yet, but you seem more cautious . . . sort of pensive, or something."

Glancing at the picture of Leigh Ann, Brad understood what his new RIO was saying. "You may be right," Brad offered. "We are hanging our asses out for nothing. Think about this goddamn mess. We are caught in a shifting, confused, obvious smoke screen to sustain the minimum appearance of a war." The veins in Austin's neck were beginning to protrude. "It's very simple, at least to me. You fight to win."

Harry propped himself up on his elbows. "Sorry. I didn't mean to set you off again."

"Harry, I'll give it a hundred and ten percent, if we're fighting to win."

Brad paused, calming himself. "This is the last place I want to be, along with every other person on this ship. I'd much rather be sitting on a boat next to Leigh Ann, anchored in a cove enjoying an evening cocktail, than dodging missiles and MiGs in an unwinnable war."

"Okay," Harry replied tentatively. "I was just thinking about what the skipper said yesterday."

"I know," Brad replied, inhaling deeply. "If you lose the fine edge, you're setting yourself up to bust your ass, or words to that effect."

Harry looked at his pilot. "Our asses."

27

The carrier vibrated as the four massive screws propelled the ship to flank speed. With only a slight breeze over the flight deck, the carrier had to create the necessary wind to safely launch aircraft.

Brad and Harry finished their before-takeoff checklists, paying special attention to critical items. As a new flying team, they had to smoothly blend their skills to maximize the capabilities of their Phantom.

Taxiing over the number-two catapult shuttle, Brad caught a glimpse of Jon O'Meara's F-4 as it hurtled off the waist catapult. The Phantom settled low over the water, then rotated skyward, blowing spray from the afterburners.

"That guy," Harry said over the intercom, "is going to drop one in the water one of these days."

Brad ignored the remark, concentrating on the catapult officer. When the final safety checker scrambled out from under the F-4, the cat officer gave Austin the two-finger turn-up signal.

Brad slowly advanced the throttles to full power, then into afterburner. He carefully checked the engine RPMs and cycled the flight controls while he glanced at the exhaust gas temperatures. Everything was in the green and stabilized for takeoff.

Bracing his helmet, Brad snapped off a salute and sucked in a lungful of cool oxygen. Five seconds later they were over water.

Brad rotated the nose higher and popped the landing-gear lever up. After the landing gear had retracted, he noticed the right main mount indicated unsafe. Brad pulled the throttles back to keep the airspeed below the maximum gear-extension speed. "Harry, we've got a little problem with the right gear."

Hutton raised his helmet visor. "We're off to an auspicious start."

Brad placed his left hand on the landing-gear control handle. "I'm going to recycle the gear."

He lowered the lever, let the wheels extend to the down-and-locked position, then firmly raised the handle again. Feeling the wheels bang into the wells, Brad cast a cautious look at the gear indicators. Three safe.

"Lookin' good," Brad announced, shoving the throttles to the stops and raising the flaps.

After rendezvousing with Lincoln Durham and Russ Lunsford, the two Phantoms refueled and circled off the North Vietnamese coast north of Thai Binh. They could see the strike group from *Bonne Homme Richard.* The Skyraiders and A-4 Skyhawks were pulverizing a rail yard and the rolling stock lining the tracks. A-6 Intruders from another carrier had previously demolished the outflowing rail lines, trapping the loaded railroad cars in the crowded switching yard.

Two flights of F-8 Crusaders were flying cover for the *Bonne Homme Richard* strike force. Brad could see the antiaircraft fire blossom across the hazy sky. Two surface-to-air missiles lifted off, followed by four more SAMs. The sky was saturated with rockets, bullets, and shrapnel.

Both Joker crews heard their strike-group leader check in on the strike frequency. Their target was a strongly defended industrial complex. A secondary target, consisting of a highway bridge and railroad bridge, would be bombed by the second strike group.

Loitering off the coastline, an unarmed reconnaissance aircraft waited to dash in and photograph the damage. Every crew wanted to obliterate their targets on the first pass. No one wanted to return and run the deadly risk twice.

Brad quickly rechecked his cockpit switches and armament panel. What are we doing here? This is crazy . . .

absolutely nuts. Hanging our asses out for what? Experiencing a sudden stab of fear, he listened to the continuous calls from Red Crown.

The first strike had attracted a swarm of MiGs. The GCI controller continued to report more MiGs taking off from Kep, Gia Lam, and Phuc Yen.

"Are you cinched in tight, Harry?"

"I'm set."

Brad heard the leader of the four Phantoms from their sister squadron. They were engaging the first group of MiGs en route to the first target area. The F-8 Crusaders would tackle any fighters that eluded the Phantoms.

"Okay," Harry announced, "I've got 'em at three o'clock, going feet dry."

Brad looked to his right and peered at the coastline 8,000 feet below. He could see the strike aircraft race over the beach.

When Bull Durham lowered his F-4's nose, Brad automatically moved out to a combat spread position. He preferred to be three-quarters of a mile to the right of his flight leader, stepped up 500 feet. The aerial combat formation provided both crews an opportunity to constantly scan around each other's aircraft.

Descending through 6,000 feet, Lunsford locked up a MiG on his radar. Turning twenty degrees to the right, Durham headed straight for the Communist fighter. Brad stepped down 1,000 feet, crossed under his leader, then moved back into position on the left side of Durham.

"You got anything, Harry?"

There was a slight pause. "Yeah. The shakes."

Brad increased power to stay even with Durham. "Lock him up, Harry. We have to make it count."

"It's intermittent. The box won't lock on."

At four miles from their target, Brad spotted the lead MiG. A second later he saw three more in trail formation. He keyed his radio. "Bull, we have four bogies at one o'clock, crossing right to left."

"Got 'em," Durham replied, firing a Sparrow missile a moment later.

Entranced, Brad watched the missile make slight corrections, then track to the third aircraft in the line-astern formation. The Sparrow detonated under the nose of the MiG-21, blowing the cockpit away from the fuselage. The remains of the fighter plummeted toward the ground, streaming fuel and shedding parts.

"I'm going HEAT," Brad said to Harry at the same instant the MiGs turned hard into the two Phantoms.

Seeing the muzzle flashes from the first MiG's cannon, Brad unconsciously lowered his head a couple of inches. The MiG flight leader had selected Brad as his prey. The opposing aircraft were closing head-on with a closure rate of more than 1,000 miles per hour.

Slightly lower than the Phantoms, the MiGs were climbing toward Brad's F-4. Timing his move, Brad waited until the first MiG was seconds from passing under his fighter, then punched off his centerline tank. The Communist flight leader banked hard to the left, missing the tumbling external fuel tank. His wingman broke right, followed by the third MiG.

"Vertical reverse!" Durham ordered, pulling hard on his stick. "Kick off the tanks." He had not seen the fuel tank fall away from Brad's Phantom.

"Two."

Brad mirrored Durham's maneuver, jamming the throttles into afterburner. Passing forty-five degrees nose up, both pilots banked toward each other.

The MiG flight leader snapped his aircraft into the vertical and turned toward Durham's F-4. The white stripe across the camouflaged tail was easy to recognize.

"That's Major Dao!" Lunsford shouted over the radio.

Brad could hear the edge of panic in his friend's voice. The Phantoms passed nose to nose with thirty feet of separation. Both pilots twisted their necks as far as possible in an effort to see who the MiG flight leader would challenge.

"He's jumping Bull!" Harry said, straining to find the other two MiGs. "He's staying on Bull."

"Joker One," Brad shouted into his damp mask, "break hard port—go for separation!"

Durham unloaded the g forces and accelerated away from the MiG-21. Approaching the speed of sound, the American flight leader reversed to reengage the MiGs.

Catching sight of the two MiGs closing from eight o'clock, Brad pulled hard into a displacement roll. His conversation with Nick Palmer, in regard to aerial combat maneuvers, flashed through his mind. He righted the F-4 and started a turn to the right, allowing the MiGs to turn inside his Phantom.

"Do you see Dao?" Brad asked over the intercom. For the first time in his combat tour, Austin was beginning to taste fear and desperation. "Have you got him?"

Harry thrashed from side to side, frantic to locate the MiG ace. "No! He's got to be on our six—below us . . . I think."

Brad waited until the MiGs were inside his radius of turn before he unloaded the Phantom. In the same profile, the American fighter floated away from the MiG pilots. They instinctively snap rolled their aircraft to follow the F-4.

Brad gritted his teeth and yanked on the stick, pulling an instant 7 g's as he executed a barrel roll to the left. The MiGs flashed by under him, allowing Brad a narrow window of escape.

He shoved the nose down and caught sight of Major Dao tracking him from above and behind. The MiG pilot fired a missile that shot over the Phantom, disappearing in the morning haze.

"Joker Two," Durham yelled, "go vertical!"

"Two," Brad groaned under the g forces he exerted on the fighter. He could barely breathe, sensing the onslaught of grayout. His g suit felt as though it would explode if he pulled any harder. Harry appeared to be a lifeless rag doll in the rear cockpit.

When Brad's F-4 rocketed straight up in afterburner, the MiG ace turned his attention to Durham. The other two MiGs had maneuvered to gain the advantage on the American flight leader, causing Bull and Russ to concentrate on escaping from them.

When Brad reversed, he spotted the MiG leader setting up a shot at Durham. Hearing a momentary buzzing in his earphones, Brad punched off a Sidewinder. The angle off was too wide for the missile to track properly. It flew out of sight a second before two surface-to-air missiles blasted through the aerial combatants.

"Bull," Brad shouted, "reverse hard left!" Watching Durham's F-4 snap into knife-edge flight, Brad was startled when a third SAM exploded in front of the two MiG wingmen. One aircraft cartwheeled out of the sky in a blazing fireball. The other MiG pilot dove for the deck and raced toward Phuc Yen.

Seconds away from locking a Sidewinder on Major Dao, Brad was appalled to see a missile come off the MiG-21. The Atoll flew straight to Durham's Phantom, detonating over the right wing. The launch and explosion happened so fast that Brad did not have time to key his radio.

Durham's F-4 snap rolled three times, then tucked nose down and blew apart in a blinding flash.

"Oh . . . God," Brad said, tasting bile at the back of his throat. Stunned, he snatched the Phantom around while he searched for the MiG flight leader.

"They got out," Harry shouted. "Two chutes . . . I've got two good chutes!"

Without his two wingmen, Maj. Nguyen Dao did not want to go one on one with the superior Phantom. He lowered his nose and dove toward his base.

Spotting the MiG ace diving away, Brad pushed the stick forward and slammed the throttles into afterburner. "Call SAR. Get 'em the coordinates." A mile behind the fleeing MiG-21, Brad saw a vapor flash when the Communist fighter went supersonic.

Harry got the message to search and rescue, then keyed his intercom. "What the hell are you doing?"

"I'm going to get that sonuvabitch."

"Like shit you are," Harry said warily. "He's headed for Phuc Yen, and we aren't supposed to attack it."

"The rules," Brad replied, breathing rapidly, "as I understand them, say we can go over Phuc Yen as long as we are engaged in battle. We just can't hit anything on the ground."

Leveling at 200 feet and indicating Mach 1.15, Brad was not gaining on the wily MiG pilot. The two fighters were headed straight toward Phuc Yen, blasting the countryside with twin sonic booms.

"Goddamnit," Harry shouted, "we're almost out of fuel!"

Brad darted a glance at the Phantom's fuel-quantity indicator. "We've got twenty-nine hundred left. Call and have a tanker meet us offshore."

Harry gulped oxygen. "We're too low. We have to have some altitude to transmit that far."

Concentrating on the low-flying MiG, Brad felt certain that the pilot was being informed that the Phantom was on his tail. Ground-control intercept radar sites dotted the land in every direction. The two aircraft were rapidly approaching the protected air base. Phuc Yen was fourteen miles ahead.

"Brad, for Christ's sake, break it off!"

Seeing the MiG pull up a hundred feet, Brad instinctively followed. He hoped to get the Sidewinders to lock on for a split second. Just as suddenly, the MiG dropped down as tall power lines flashed under the F-4.

"We're here," Brad responded through clenched jaws, "and I'm going to nail that bastard."

Harry looked at Hanoi as the Phantom streaked over the outskirts of the city. He could see dozens of muzzle flashes from small-arms fire. He knew the entire area was heavily defended by 37mm, 57mm, and 85mm guns and numerous SAM sites.

"You're in protected airspace," Harry shouted, awed by the amount of ground fire aimed at their F-4. "We're violating the rules of engagement."

"No," Brad barked, "I'm *breaking* the rules of engagement!"

He saw that the MiG pilot was decelerating in preparation to land. Dao was maneuvering toward a left base for a left turn to final approach.

"Goddamnit, Brad, we're going to end up in Leavenworth . . . or dead. I'm not shitting you."

Snapping the Phantom into a left ninety-degree bank, Brad hugged the terrain while he paralleled the runway, bleeding off speed. Rolling wings level, he waited until the F-4 was at midfield, then slapped the throttles to idle and banked steeply to the right.

"Let's get the hell outta here," Harry pleaded, crushed down in his ejection seat. He had never flown this fast so close to the ground. Terrified, Harry braced his hands under the canopy and looked across the airfield. He glimpsed a group of men throwing themselves on the ground, while others were running for cover.

Three-quarters through the punishing turn, Brad shoved the throttles back into afterburner and leveled out a half mile from the end of the runway. He spotted Major Dao turning final at 300 feet above the ground. The MiG's landing gear was extended.

"Come on, Brad," Harry said, sliding down in his seat, "get us out of here!"

Crossing the edge of the airfield at thirty feet, Brad lowered the nose even farther and barreled down the runway. Ignoring the tracer rounds passing over his canopy, Brad concentrated on Dao's aircraft. A moment later the MiG-21 pulled up steeply as Brad blasted under the fighter.

"Ho . . . Christ," Harry uttered in sheer terror.

Simultaneously yanking the throttles to idle and deploying the speed brakes, Brad hauled the F-4 around in a face-sagging turn. The wing tip was fifteen feet above the ground.

"Oh . . . God," Harry moaned under the heavy g load. "Get him—bag him . . . and let's get the hell out of here!"

Brad rolled level after 180 degrees of turn, elated to see

the MiG turning and climbing for another approach to the airfield. Brad figured Dao must be out of fuel, or he would have raised the landing gear and attempted to engage the intruding Phantom.

"I'm pulling for a shot," Brad groaned, turning into his adversary. "Going to nail him."

Raising the nose, Brad banked the F-4 even farther, heard the Sidewinder tone, then fired a missile. He fired a second Sidewinder at the same moment the first missile blew the tail off the MiG. The second projectile exploded in the mushrooming fireball.

Slamming the throttles forward, Brad banked steeply. "We got him—he's going in!"

Brad witnessed the main fuselage of the MiG-21 hit the ground inverted, then explode again. He saw an additional MiG-21, but the pilot was departing the area low to the ground. Two MiG-17s taxied at high speed toward the takeoff point of the runway.

"Let's go, goddamnit!" Harry shouted, bracing himself for more violent maneuvers.

"Hang in there!" Brad replied, focusing on the two fighters about to take off. "We're on our way."

Reaching the middle of the base, Brad fired a Sidewinder at the two MiGs and pulled up in a victory roll, then dove for the deck again. His hands were shaking from the adrenaline boost.

Waiting until the Phantom had accelerated to 630 knots, Brad smoothly pulled the stick back and pointed the nose up fifty degrees. He pressed the stick forward just enough to achieve zero g load. The F-4 shot skyward in a hail of small-arms fire and antiaircraft rounds.

Harry held his breath until the Phantom had zoomed past 15,000 feet. "Do you know how much shit we're in? You blew one of the MiGs apart . . . on the ground. That's unauthorized."

"Can it, Harry."

Brad turned his radio to the tanker frequency and keyed his mike. "Snowball, Joker Two Oh Five."

"Joker, Snowball."

The afterburners had sucked the fuel level down to a critical state. Brad stared at the fuel-quantity indicator.

"Snowball, we're going to be feet wet in eight minutes with seven hundred pounds left. I need a big favor." The pilots of the unarmed KA-3B tankers did not care to venture too close to the coastline.

"We're on our way," the Skywarrior pilot radioed. "Go max conserve when you cross the beach."

"Wilco," Brad acknowledged, flinching at the unexpected SAM that slashed past the right wing. Puffs of antiaircraft fire filled the sky around the F-4.

"Harry," Brad said, trying to slow his breathing, "hook up with SAR while I work the tanker. If we can get enough fuel, we can help cover Bull and Russ."

Hutton's thoughts had converged on his immediate survival. "Haven't we pressed it far enough?"

"Goddamnit, Harry," Brad spat. "We aren't going to leave them down there—you saw two good chutes."

Harry checked in with the north search-and-rescue station, then monitored the SAR frequency. The news that he received sickened his stomach. He debated whether or not to tell his pilot until they had refueled.

Brad leveled at 23,000 feet and pulled back the power. Harry worked the radar, finally locking onto the Whale. The tanker pilot bent the KA-3B around like a fighter plane, positioning himself directly in front of the thirsty Phantom. Brad was down to 500 pounds of fuel.

Closing on the Skywarrior, Brad extended his fuel probe and flew the tip smoothly into the basket. His hands were still trembling, but he had dampened out his control inputs to fly with a high degree of finesse.

Breathing a collective sigh of relief, Brad and Harry relaxed while the F-4's fuel tanks were partially replenished.

"Brad," Harry said with unusual emotion in his voice, "there's no need to take on any extra fuel."

"What do you mean?"

Harry had difficulty speaking. "Bull and Russ were captured almost immediately after they hit the ground."

Brad's mouth quivered. "Who confirmed that?"

"Bull did . . . over his emergency radio. It was only seconds before they were captured by a gun crew."

28

Listening to the ship creak and groan, Brad Austin sat at his desk resting his forehead in the palms of his hands. His eyes were closed, sealing off the reminders of his environment. Why did it happen? Could he have done anything more to have prevented the MiG pilot from shooting down Bull and Russ?

Brad opened his eyes and focused on the stationery in front of him. He had made four attempts to draft a letter to Cordelia Durham, but he had discarded each attempt.

How could he tell her that as Lincoln Durham's wingman, he had allowed her husband to be shot down? What could he say to a woman who was pregnant, and might not ever see her husband again?

Brad drifted back to the debriefing. He and Harry had confirmed that Bull and Russ had a MiG to their credit. They had also explained that the North Vietnamese had shot down one of their own aircraft with a SAM. The glee that that information normally would have brought was nullified by the tragic loss of Bull and Russ.

Brad and Harry had not mentioned that Maj. Nguyen Thanh Dao had downed Bull and Russ. They also had not reported that the North Vietnamese ace would never shoot down another airplane.

Harry had been extremely nervous during the debriefing, deferring to Brad to supply the pertinent information about the engagements. Both men had answered every question truthfully. No one had asked if they had penetrated protected airspace and blasted an ace out of the air over Phuc Yen.

Brad picked up his pen and began to write.

Dear Cordelia,

I trust that you have been notified that Lincoln has become a prisoner of war. I was flying as his wingman at the time of the incident, and I can confirm that my RIO and I saw two parachutes. The search-and-rescue personnel have confirmed that Lincoln talked to them after he and his RIO were on the ground.

Even though I realize that words of comfort cannot dispel your grief, we have to be thankful that Lincoln landed alive. As you well know, your husband is a strong, courageous man of tremendous determination. I have every confidence that Lincoln will return to you.

If there is anything I can do—anything—please let me know. Please allow me to be responsible to you and your child until you and Lincoln are reunited.

With respect and warm regards,

Brad

Addressing the envelope, Brad also included his parents' address and phone number. He added a postscript to the letter, explaining that his mother would always have his current address.

He placed his pen on the desk and proceeded to his next task. What should he say to the parents of Russ Lunsford? They knew that their son had been Brad Austin's radar-intercept officer. How could he explain why Russ was incarcerated by the North Vietnamese while Brad was safely on board the carrier?

Brad was sealing the envelope to Cordelia Durham when Harry entered their stateroom and sat down. He looked somber and tired, with bags under his eyes.

Placing the letter down, Brad turned to his roommate. "Talk to me, Harry. Get it off your chest."

Hutton stared at the deck before facing Brad. "I've got a bad feeling about this deal."

"How so?" Brad asked, noting his friend's nervousness. He was concerned that everyone had noticed Harry's strange behavior.

Harry looked up. "We shouldn't have lied to them."

"Let me set the record straight," Brad said, leaning forward. "We did not lie to anyone. There is a distinct difference between a lie—an untrue remark made deliberately—and an omission."

Harry paused a moment, examining the sensitive issue. "Omission? How about just saying that we neglected to tell the whole story?"

"That would be good," Brad replied testily, thinking about Bull and Russ. "Oh, by the way, we overlooked a couple of minor points."

Hutton exhaled sharply. "It was wrong, and you know it was, for Christ's sake."

Absently squeezing his knees, Brad met Harry's eyes. "You're absolutely right, Harry. I admit both mistakes— violating the rules of engagement and not saying anything about what I did at Phuc Yen. It's a very humbling experience, and I'm damn sure not proud of what I did.

"However, I want to discuss your word—neglect. Neglect is when people in the White House allow our enemies to have protected airspace, and American pilots are free game anywhere, at any time."

Harry managed a slight smile. "I know what you're saying, and I agree with your frustration—all our frustrations—but I feel uncomfortable."

Brad looked at the pouting Playmate of the Month, then glanced at the calendar mounted on the bulkhead. "I'll bet Bull and Russ are a lot more uncomfortable than you are tonight."

A reddish tinge turned Hutton's face dark, "I didn't mean that we—"

"Harry, do whatever your conscience tells you to do, okay? According to the rules of engagement, which place us in great jeopardy, I was wrong." The two men remained quiet a moment, fully realizing the possible consequences of Brad's actions.

"If you want me to march in with you and 'fess up," Brad continued calmly, "I'll do it."

Harry shook his head. "No, I don't want to do that. It would destroy your career, and probably mine."

Brad inhaled deeply, then let his breath out slowly. "Harry, that is the least of my concerns. Think about Rocky, Ed, Nick, Bull, and Russ—all the people busting their asses in his obvious no-win boondoggle. Think about this goddamn travesty, and my career doesn't warrant consideration."

Hutton lowered his head and closed his eyes, then opened them and raised his head. "Jesus Christ, what a crock of shit . . . this whole goddamn mess."

"Harry, it's your choice. I'm the one who points the flying machine, so you didn't have much choice."

Jaw set, Brad faced his friend. "Well, you do have a choice now, and don't make your decision based on loyalty to me or my career aspirations."

Hutton's shoulders slumped. "Do we have any more booze around here?"

"Yes," Brad answered, glancing at the safe. "But I don't think it's a good idea to have liquor on our breath if we're going to see the skipper."

Harry sat up in his chair. "No. We'd only be digging our own graves. Let's forget about it, and think about the day after tomorrow." The carrier was scheduled to dock in Yokosuka in thirty-seven hours.

Brad stared blankly at the deck. "We avenged Bull and Russ, and Major Dao won't be adding any more stars to his airplane. If that's wrong, I was wrong."

Standing on the signal bridge, Brad watched the shoreline pass as the carrier steamed through the wide entrance to Tokyo Bay. The gray overcast, blended with the dark, leaden sea, made the morning seem like late afternoon.

Unable to sleep soundly, Brad had showered and shaved at 4 A.M., finished the difficult letter to Russ Lunsford's parents, then had a light breakfast in the main wardroom.

Propping one foot on the lower brace, Brad leaned on the

upper railing and gazed at the various ships maneuvering in the bay. He had been preoccupied with the fate of Bull and Russ. Were they being humiliated and tortured? Were they being subjected to brutal interrogations? His guilt was oppressive, hanging like a weight around his neck.

His emotions ran the gamut from deep depression over the well-being of Bull and Russ, to jubilation about his impending vacation with Leigh Ann. Forcing himself to erase the horrors of war from his mind, Brad concentrated on remembering every detail about her.

Harry had decided to remain on board the carrier. He, along with the majority of the squadron flight-crew members, were low in spirits. The deaths of Frank Rockwood and Ed Zapata, followed by the loss of Nick Palmer, and the capture of another crew, had demoralized the pilots and RIOs.

Brad remained on the single bridge while the mammoth ship was edged next to the pier. After the carrier had been gently docked, Brad went below to his stateroom to get his luggage, which he had packed the previous evening. Entering the cramped stateroom, Brad was surprised to see Harry sitting morosely at the desk.

"Hey, shipmate," Brad said cheerfully, "how about lunch and a beer at the club before I head for Tokyo?"

Harry turned without replying. Brad had never seen him so glum.

"Come on," Brad cajoled, tapping his friend on the shoulder. "I'm buying."

Harry displayed the hint of a smile. "Okay. I could use a beer." He stretched his arms back, yawning. "You still want me to go to Tokyo with you?"

Brad glanced at the packed overnight bag at the foot of Harry's locker. "Hell, yes. Who else is going to take care of me, and attract all the women for us?"

"Right," Harry replied, grinning his mischievous grin. "You need a keeper."

Brad and Harry sat at a dining table in the Yokosuka Officers' Club. The bar was full of ships' company and air-wing officers. The noise level was increasing in proportion to the rounds of drinks being consumed. The afternoon and evening promised to be a rowdy, no-holds-barred party full of sea stories and "almost killed" flying stories. The aviators referred to the tales as A-Kays. If a true story had an unbelievable air about it, the pilot or RIO would precede the anecdote with the word *TINS*—this is no shit.

After calling Japan Airlines, Brad had attempted to contact Leigh Ann. Her mother had answered, cool and polite as always. It was after 9 P.M. in Memphis. Mrs. Ladasau had explained that she expected her daughter home at any minute. She had not mentioned Leigh Ann's invitation to join him in San Francisco.

Brad had told her that he would call again, if it was not too late, at ten o'clock. She assured him that that would be fine.

Harry set down his empty mug and wiped his mouth. "So, when does your flight leave?"

Brad unfolded his hastily written notes. "They have a flight at six in the evening, so I figured we could make that one."

Frowning, Harry looked toward the noisy bar, then back to Brad. "Well, what the hell am I supposed to do? I thought you were leaving tomorrow."

Brad checked the time. "Harry, if there was an early morning flight, I'd stay over in Tokyo. There are only two flights a day—at three forty and six in the evening." Brad smiled and shrugged his shoulders. "Counting the travel time, I'm only going to have a few days with Leigh Ann."

Harry frowned again and signaled for another beer.

"Why don't you get a nice hotel room in the Ginza district?" Brad suggested, sliding his chair back. "I know you can provide your own entertainment in one of the hostess bars." Harry chuckled as Brad walked toward the telephones.

Brad picked up the receiver and worked his way from the local operator to an international operator. After two attempts to secure an open line, the phone rang in the elegant home in Memphis, Tennessee.

"Ladasau residence," Leigh Ann answered after the first ring.

"Hi, Leigh Ann. This is Brad."

"I've been waiting by the phone. How are you, and where are you?"

Brad looked at his watch again. "I'm fine. Harry, the guy you met in Hawaii, and I just finished lunch. We're in Yokosuka, Japan, where the ship is docked. Are you going to join me in San Francisco?"

Leigh Ann laughed softly. "My luggage has been packed for three days."

"Any problem with your parents?"

She paused, wondering if Brad was reading her thoughts. "Well, mother thinks it's fine—she likes you."

"What about your father?"

"We can talk about it later. I'm so excited about seeing you."

"Great," Brad replied, feeling his pulse quicken. "I'll be arriving in San Francisco late Tuesday morning—West Coast time. I hope you can catch a flight out in the morning."

"I've memorized all the flight times," she confessed. "I'll plan to leave early in the morning. My flight is scheduled to land in San Francisco at ten thirty-five."

"I can't wait," Brad replied, then added, "If you have any problems, or if you get delayed, please call the Fairmont and leave a message for me."

"Okay. Do you happen to have the telephone number?"

"Yes," Brad answered, struggling to free his wallet. He gave her the number, and she read it back to him.

"Oh, one other thing," Brad said, folding the confirmation notice from the Fairmont. "Your room is booked in your name, so please go ahead and check in, then relax and enjoy San Francisco."

"I'll do that."

"I should arrive in the early afternoon," Brad continued, returning his wallet to his back pocket. "If I encounter any delays, I'll leave a message for you."

"Oh, Brad, I can't wait to see you."

He could feel the excitement stirring inside of him. "I'm the one who can't wait."

"I'm going to call and confirm my airline reservations right now."

"Good idea, and get some rest, if you can."

"I don't think I can sleep," Leigh Ann laughed. "I'll see you tomorrow."

Brad tensed as the airliner lifted off the runway at the Haneda Airport and banked toward the Pacific Ocean. He had always been uncomfortable in an airplane, unless he had access to the flight controls. Looking around the sparsely filled jet, Brad was thankful that he had all three seats to himself. He stared blankly out the window, feeling a tinge of guilt about abandoning Harry.

Tilting his seat back, Brad felt the continuous bumps as the airliner climbed through the lower choppy air. A moment later, the flight suddenly became smooth as the jet gained altitude. Reaching into the oversized shopping bag in the center seat, Brad removed the box containing the beautiful kimono he had purchased in one of the stores at the airport.

He unfolded the soft garment and inspected the craftsmanship. The loose Japanese robe was a tasteful example of the traditional kimono. The luxuriously tailored silk gown featured wide sleeves and a broad sash.

Satisfied, he replaced the light beige and blue kimono in the box. He hoped Leigh Ann would be pleased with the gift.

Brad opened the latest copy of *Newsweek* and leafed through the magazine, skipping the articles having to do with the war. When the airliner leveled at cruising altitude, he placed the magazine in the seatback and thought about Leigh Ann. Would she really be as wonderful as he envisaged?

"Sir, would you care for a beverage?"

Lost in his thoughts, Brad had been unaware of the charming young Japanese woman standing next to him.

"Sure," Brad responded, folding the seatback tray into position. "I'll have a scotch and soda."

He gazed out the window at the setting sun, feeling the tension drain from his body. He pulled Leigh Ann's pendant from under his shirt and admired it.

His drink finished, Brad put the glass down and exhaled. A few minutes later, he drifted into a sound sleep.

29

HANOI

Jean-Paul Bouvier, the Hanoi correspondent for the French newspaper *L'Humanité,* held the Chevaliers magnifying glass over the black-and-white photographs.

He was a small man with a receding hairline and thick glasses. He studied the pictures for a minute with rapt attention. He had captured the unusual pictures of an American F-4 Phantom from a vantage point on the flight line at Phuc Yen Air Base.

The photographs clearly showed an American fighter plane flying down the runway a scant twenty feet above the surface. The Phantom had been showcased between the vertical stabilizers of two parked MiG-21s.

For Bouvier, the shocking sight of the F-4 and the thunderous sonic boom had temporarily unnerved him. After the American pilot had turned and fired two missiles, Bouvier had finally raised his camera. He had snapped a number of pictures of the fast-moving fighter, but only one photo showed recognizable elements of the airfield.

He had taken the time to extensively photograph the wreckage of Maj. Nguyen Thanh Dao's burned and twisted MiG-21. The second leading ace in the North Vietnamese Air Force had died a savage death at the feet of his comrades. Bouvier had also shot a number of pictures of the destroyed MiG-17 at the end of the runway.

Well aware of the American-imposed rules of engagement, Jean-Paul Bouvier knew that Phuc Yen had been declared an off-limits airfield. If the sanctuary status of Phuc Yen had been removed, the French correspondent had no doubt that the American pilots would have arrived en masse and bombed the base to oblivion.

Unsure of the current U.S. military position in regard to Phuc Yen, Bouvier had decided to wait a few days before he talked with anyone. If he supplied any information about the attack, he had to be absolutely positive that the American assault had been an unauthorized and premeditated strike.

Bouvier had already sent a release to *L'Humanité*, describing the circumstances surrounding the death of Major Dao. He had been careful to phrase his words so he would not sound accusatory.

Now, after the uproar from the North Vietnamese government and military officials, Bouvier was certain that the attack had been a rogue ambush. This was the type of incident that could provide great prestige for the timid correspondent. To expose the unlawful attack, Bouvier needed positive proof of the origin of the aircraft. Had the F-4 been an air-force plane or a navy aircraft?

Bouvier had his assistant print a larger picture of the trespassing Phantom. Using the enlarged magnifying glass, he was able to read the serial number and side number painted on the fuselage of the treacherous offender. He was surprised to see the name of an American aircraft carrier displayed on the side of the aft fuselage. The bold *NAVY* was partially obscured by the wing, but there was no question. The fighter was a navy F-4 Phantom.

Awakened by turbulence, Brad shifted in his seat and looked at his watch. Two hours and ten minutes to arrival time in San Francisco. He reset his watch to Pacific Coast time, then closed his eyes. Immediately, images of the war surfaced. He opened his eyes and stared at the seat in front of him, forcing himself to think back to Hawaii and Leigh

Ann. His mind kept returning to the war. What was happening to Bull and Russ?

Catching a glimpse of the approaching flight attendant, Brad looked up and smiled.

"You must have been very tired," she teased. "You slept through our two meal services."

"I apologize. I'm sure they were very good."

"I will be happy to warm a meal for you," she offered shyly. "You must be hungry."

Although not interested in eating, Brad did not want to appear ungrateful. "That's very thoughtful of you. Thanks."

After he had consumed a respectable amount of his Kobe beef, rice, and salad, he slid the tray to the table opened over the middle seat and watched the clouds until the airplane began the descent toward San Francisco International Airport.

FAIRMONT HOTEL

Leigh Ann stepped out of the taxi under the canopied entrance to the elegant hotel. Two bellhops eagerly gathered her luggage while she paid her cab fare.

Following the two red-jacketed men, Leigh Ann was fascinated by the marble columns in the richly appointed lobby.

"Miss Ladasau checking in," one of the bellmen said as they approached the desk.

"Yes, Miss Ladasau, we have your reservation right here," responded the portly gentleman behind the desk.

"Do you have any messages for me?" Leigh Ann asked, hoping that there had been no delays in Brad's travel itinerary.

"No, Miss Ladasau, no messages."

"Thank you," Leigh Ann replied as she placed her credit card on the marble counter.

The gentleman looked confused, then said in a very

discreet voice, "Miss Ladasau, your room has been arranged in advance."

"Oh . . . thank you," Leigh Ann responded, feeling the blood rush to her cheeks. She wondered if the elderly gentleman would approve of a young woman traveling alone to San Francisco to meet a man.

"Here is your room key, Miss Ladasau," the gentleman said, flashing a knowing smile. "The bellman will take you to your room. I hope your stay with us will be an enjoyable one."

After tipping the young bellman, Leigh Ann went directly to the window overlooking the bay. The view was exhilarating. She could see the Golden Gate Bridge, resplendent in its coat of red paint. She scanned the windswept bay dotted with sailboats, yachts, and ferryboats.

Turning to unpack her suitcase, Leigh Ann was startled by a knock at the door. She walked to the entrance and opened the wide door.

"Miss Ladasau?" the beaming Asian asked.

"Yes," she replied, glancing at the room-service cart in the middle of the hallway.

"Compliments of Captain Austin," he announced, stepping to the rear of the serving table.

Moving aside, Leigh Ann felt like Cinderella with a fairy godmother as she watched the man wheel in the cart, place a tray on the coffee table, followed by a champagne bucket, a bottle of white wine, and two stemmed glasses. Awed, Leigh Ann offered the waiter a gratuity, which he declined.

"Thank you," he replied, "but Captain Austin took care of everything."

When the man had gone, Leigh Ann stared in disbelief at the bountiful arrangement of hors d'oeuvres. The spread of assorted cheeses was surrounded by a variety of crackers, English tea biscuits, canapes, and cold fresh fruits. All thoughts of her father's disapproval vanished.

Forgetting about unpacking for the moment, Leigh Ann placed a selection of cheese, crackers, and melon on a plate. Turning to the wine, she was relieved to see that the bottle had already been opened. She carefully poured a glass of wine and pulled a chair and end table closer to the window.

Sitting down, Leigh Ann placed her plate on the end table and sampled the sauvignon blanc. The white wine had a distinct, deliciously crisp taste.

Leigh Ann smiled and gazed across the picturesque bay. She thought about Brad Austin, and realized that she had never been more excited in her life.

HANOI

Jean-Paul Bouvier had carefully drafted a release for his newspaper, detailing the facts surrounding the American attack at Phuc Yen. He had included a picture of the navy Phantom jet, along with photographs of the crashed MiG-21 and the MiG-17 on the taxiway.

After sending the evidence to *L'Humanité,* he had visited with his close friend and colleague, Marc Chauveron. After explaining the situation in detail, Bouvier asked Chauveron for his advice. The senior journalist for the prestigious Agence France Presse, Chauveron had a close rapport with the British consul general. Chauveron convinced Bouvier that they should enlist the support of the British consul general, and present the evidence of an American violation to the North Vietnamese.

The dignified Englishman had been uncomfortable about the accusation aimed at the Americans, but had agreed to accompany the journalists to the Communist party head-quarters.

Bouvier had shown copies of the incriminating photographs to a senior officer on the staff of President Ho Chi Minh. The aide-de-camp had rushed off, leaving the three civilians sitting alone for more than an hour.

When the officer returned, he had a statement to be issued through the international press corps. He had also insisted that Bouvier sign his name as a witness to the breach of rules by the Americans.

The general account of the unlawful incident, including a

formal protest and letter of condemnation aimed at the
United States government, would be distributed internation-
ally in twenty-four hours. The photograph of Brad Austin's
F-4 Phantom would be flashed around the globe.

30

Brad handed the bellboy a generous tip. "You can leave everything on the bed."

"Yes, sir."

When he knocked on Leigh Ann's door, Brad could feel his heart racing. Would they share the same emotions and passion they had felt in Hawaii?

Opening the door, Leigh Ann flashed her radiant smile, then threw her arms around Brad. He held her tightly, brushing her cheek with a kiss. They stood in the open door and embraced before either spoke.

"Brad," Leigh Ann said enthusiastically, "I thought you would never get here."

Brad held her at arm's length. "Well, I'm here, and we are going to enjoy San Francisco. May I come in?"

"Yes, of course," Leigh Ann replied as Brad stepped inside her room and she closed the door.

"Brad, you look great. Forgive me for staring, but I am so happy to see you." The vision of him that she had kept in her mind had not faded. He was as handsome as she had remembered.

"Where is your room?"

"Next door," he answered, gesturing to the door that connected the two adjoining rooms.

Leigh Ann looked at the door, then smiled and gave Brad a suspicious look. "How convenient . . ."

Brad chuckled, again feeling the exhilaration that had swept over him in Hawaii. "Would you like to begin our sight-seeing tour at Fisherman's Wharf?"

"That would be wonderful," Leigh Ann answered, embracing him again. "Let's take the cable car."

"Great idea."

Leigh Ann turned, remembering the bottle of wine and the tray of appetizers. "Before I forget, I want to thank you for your thoughtfulness. The wine and hors d'oeuvres were excellent. That was very kind of you."

"I'm glad you enjoyed them," Brad replied, mesmerized by Leigh Ann's delicate features. "One of my favorite diversions is sipping chenin blanc, with shrimp Louis and sourdough bread, while watching the ships and small boats in San Francisco Bay. That's why I enjoy going to Fisherman's Wharf."

She clasped her hands together. "I can't wait."

"It will be even more special, sharing the afternoon with you."

"Thank you," Leigh Ann said softly, still a little dazed at actually being in San Francisco with Brad. Was it really true? Was she really here, finally, with the man who had so overwhelmed her in Hawaii? She wondered if Brad felt the same way she did.

"Before we go," Brad stopped, remembering the gift he had purchased at the airport, "I've got a present for you."

"You do?" Leigh Ann replied with genuine surprise.

"Yes, all the way from Japan," he answered, walking to her doorway. Brad grasped the doorknob, then hesitated and turned around. "If you don't mind unlocking the door between our rooms, I'll close our front doors."

Leigh Ann winked. "You're pretty smooth, aren't you?"

Brad grinned. "Are you suggesting that beneath my cosmopolitan charm lies an ulterior motive?"

"I'm suggesting," Leigh Ann laughed softly, "that Cary Grant you are not."

"Thanks," Brad chuckled, pulling her door closed behind him. Entering his room, Brad closed the door and picked up the box containing the kimono.

When he walked into Leigh Ann's room, Brad found her at the window. He walked over and joined her. "I apologize for not having it gift wrapped, but there wasn't much time."

"Brad," Leigh Ann smiled as she accepted the box, "please don't apologize. You shouldn't have done this."

"Go ahead, open it."

Removing the top of the box, Leigh Ann's eyes widened. She carefully lifted the kimono and held it in front of her. "It's beautiful . . . absolutely beautiful!"

She kissed Brad on the cheek. "Thank you. Thank you very much."

"You're welcome," Brad responded, feeling a sense of pleasure as he watched Leigh Ann slowly run her slender fingers over the smooth silk fabric.

She walked to her closet, removed a satin hanger, and hung up the delicately beautiful robe. "I feel awful . . . I didn't get you a gift."

"Yes, you did."

"I did?" Leigh Ann asked, returning to the window and grasping Brad's hand.

"Yes," Brad responded, suppressing his desire to take her into his arms again. "You being here with me is the greatest gift I could possibly want."

"Well, I feel the same way, but I do appreciate my kimono," Leigh Ann smiled. "You must be exhausted after flying such a long distance. Would you like to freshen up before we go to Fisherman's Wharf?"

"Actually," Brad replied awkwardly, "I'd like to take a quick shower, and change into fresh clothes before we leave, if you don't mind."

"Not at all," Leigh Ann said, glancing at her luggage.

"Also," Brad said uncomfortably, "I've got to call a friend's wife. She's pregnant, and I want to see if she is getting along okay."

"Take your time. I need to unpack, and I want to try on my new kimono."

Hand in hand, Leigh Ann and Brad walked through the lobby. They emerged at the entrance in the midst of an arriving group of conventioneers. Working their way through the crowd, they rounded the corner and walked the length of the Fairmont Hotel to Powell Street. Brad and

Leigh Ann managed to hop a departing cable car just as it began to roll.

They took seats at the rear of the rumbling car. Laughing together, they rode north on Powell Street before turning west on Jackson Street.

"Brad," Leigh Ann said over the clanging bell, "this is fantastic . . . being here with you. San Francisco is wonderful!"

Brad smiled broadly as the cable car jolted and clanked through the turn to Hyde Street. Passing Greenwich Street, Brad suddenly turned to Leigh Ann. "Let's get off," he paused while the motorman loudly clanged the bell, "and take a look down Lombard Street."

"You're the tour guide," she smiled warmly. "Whatever you suggest."

"I think you'll enjoy this landmark," Brad replied as they hopped off the cable car. "This section of Lombard Street has been a tourist attraction for years."

They walked over to the top of the steep, winding street. The narrow thoroughfare twisted back and forth in sharp S-turns as the roadway dropped sharply toward the street below.

"This is astonishing," Leigh Ann commented as they watched a green van carefully navigate down the one-way brick lane.

The driver rode the brakes hard, twisting the steering wheel from side to side. Close to the curb, he narrowly missed a number of the ornate pots filled with bright flowers.

Watching the Volkswagen van grind to a halt near the bottom of Lombard, Leigh Ann pondered what would have happened if the brakes had failed. "What's the name of the street at the bottom?"

"Leavenworth," Brad replied automatically. His mind flashed back to what Harry Hutton had said when they chased Major Dao toward Phuc Yen. Was this an omen of things to come? If found out, would he spend time in the federal prison at Leavenworth, Kansas?

"Brad?" Leigh Ann asked, canting her head. "Are you all right?"

"What?" Brad brought his thoughts back to the present. "I'm fine."

"Are you sure?" Leigh Ann asked with genuine concern in her voice. "You turned pale for a moment."

"Yes, I'm fine," Brad responded, hearing the clanging of another cable car. "We'll continue on to Fisherman's Wharf, or walk for a while, if you like."

Leigh Ann laughed. "Actually, I'm anxious to see Fisherman's Wharf."

Brad and Leigh Ann stopped for a late lunch at a charming restaurant overlooking the bay. Leigh Ann moved her captain's chair closer to Brad. She slid her slender arm under his and clasped his fingers. "Isn't the bay beautiful?"

He looked into her eyes and smiled. "It sure is . . . and so are you."

"Brad," she responded, squeezing his hand, "you're making me blush."

"I'm sorry, but it's true. You are beautiful."

Leigh Ann lowered her head and withdrew her hand, obviously embarrassed. "Could we change the subject? Those people at the next table overheard you . . . and now they are staring."

"Okay," he grinned, "if you insist, but I would rather talk about you."

"I insist," Leigh Ann said in a low but firm voice.

Brad chuckled, "I'll abide by your wishes."

They sipped their wine and Leigh Ann became quite serious. "Brad Austin, what are you about?"

The unexpected question startled Brad, but he attempted to keep the conversation light. "What am I about? I'm not sure I understand the question."

"Who are you? What do you believe in? What do you think about the war?" She paused, then spoke quietly. "My dad thinks the war is unjustified and immoral. We had quite a talk before I left."

Leigh Ann noticed that Brad showed no emotion. She

wondered if he had even heard her. Leigh Ann decided not to make an issue of what her father had said just yet. Actually, he had been very outspoken about what he thought of Brad and his activity, and had made his daughter feel uncomfortable about meeting the pilot.

"What do you see in your future?" Leigh Ann asked, leaning forward to attract Brad's attention. "Who is Brad Austin?"

Grinning a bit uncertainly, Brad swallowed a sip of wine and placed his glass on the table. "Wow, it sounds as if you would like an account of my life history from birth to now, with a prediction for the future."

"Seriously," Leigh Ann said, tilting her head in her innocently provocative way. "I sense that Brad Austin doesn't let anyone get too far under the surface."

"Well," Brad furrowed his brow and shifted slightly in his chair, "generally speaking, the more shallow the wound, the less one bleeds."

"Does that mean you are not interested in a relationship that may require a commitment on your part?"

Suddenly uncomfortable, Brad turned slightly to face Leigh Ann. "I suppose it's my nature to be cautious."

Her eyes widened as she smiled. "Flying jet fighters off an aircraft carrier is your idea of cautious?"

Brad suppressed a grin. "I have confidence in what I do on board the carrier, or in aerial combat. If I had a single doubt about my capabilities, then I couldn't do what I do."

He hesitated, unsure if he should fully communicate his feelings. "Leigh Ann, in the air—in a combat engagement—I want the enemy pilot to commit first, so I can see what I have to do to kill . . . to defeat him."

"It really is a hostile environment, isn't it?"

Brad frowned again. "Sure it is. The guys slugging through the jungles and fighting from foxholes are under stress too. They live with it twenty-four hours a day. I, at least, have a hot meal and a clean bed to sleep in."

They both remained quiet a moment, contemplating their feelings about the war.

"Leigh Ann, whether a person is flying fighters or

fighting from a foxhole is immaterial in my mind. We have been sent to Vietnam to fight a war. There's only one hitch, however; our government won't let us win.''

She looked Brad in the eye. "My dad says that he believes in saving lives instead of killing people.''

Brad shrugged, then swirled his wine slowly. "I agree with your father's philosophy, but there are many factions, backed by huge armies, who do not subscribe to our standards of civilization.''

"Do you think,'' she paused while a waiter passed, "that we should be in Vietnam?''

"Leigh Ann, the concept of protecting our allies from being invaded is rightful, in my opinion. Wouldn't you defend a family member, or friend?''

"Yes, but there is so little support for the war here at home. You've seen the protesters and demonstrations. That's all we see, or read about.''

Brad shook his head slowly. "That's because this mess goes on month after month without any definable results. People are frustrated, Leigh Ann. They see the mounting American casualties—the hundreds of body bags on television every night—but they don't see any end to the war. We have the military capability to end the Communist aggression swiftly and decisively, and most people know that.''

"They why don't we?''

"Because,'' Brad answered, trying to speak calmly, "the Johnson administration doesn't have the courage to do what needs to be done. They've muddled the original goal into an illogical, vacillating war of slow escalation, hamstrung by countless restrictions.''

Leigh Ann looked frightened. "Your face is flushed.''

"Please don't be offended, but I would like to forget the war while we're here.''

"Me, too,'' she smiled, unsettled by Brad's anger. "May we talk about your future? What your plans are?''

Brad chuckled softly. "My future is anyone's guess. I put in a request to fly for the Blue Angels—the navy flight demonstration team. But, since I'm an academy grad who joined the marines, they'll probably shitcan—sorry—deep six my request. Who knows?''

"Yes," Leigh Ann laughed in a teasing way, "I can tell that you're definitely a cautious guy."

"My RIO—you met Harry in Hawaii—would certainly disagree with you." Brad thought about their flight to Phuc Yen. He swallowed his anxiety, glancing out the window at a catamaran. "How about a ferryboat ride around the bay, then we'll watch the sunset from the Fairmont Crown?"

"That sounds like fun," Leigh Ann exclaimed. "Will we have time to change for dinner?"

"Sure. Wear your favorite dress, and I'll wear a coat and tie, if I can remember how to tie a tie."

Leigh Ann beamed. "Brad, this is very special for me." She hesitated, wishing she had the nerve to tell him that she was falling helplessly in love with him. "I hope you know that."

Brad looked embarrassed, as if he had read her thoughts. "You are very special to me."

"I mean it, Brad. You have restored my confidence in men, and in myself . . . and I apologize if I grilled you."

"Forget it," Brad chuckled, not wishing to pursue the subject further. "By the way, tomorrow is your day."

"Excuse me?"

"Tomorrow," he smiled and placed his hand over hers, "I thought it would be nice to have you plan our day."

Leigh Ann started to speak, then stopped when Brad shrugged his shoulders in a questioning gesture. "What would you like to see?" he asked, picking up their check. "Where would you like to go?"

Leigh Ann looked a bit bewildered.

"Something wrong?"

"No," she laughed. "I'll give it some thought, and we'll discuss it over dinner."

31

YOKOSUKA, JAPAN

Commander Dan Bailey sat at the wardroom table, listening to three of his junior officers arguing about the lack of national objectives in the Vietnam War. Bailey was concerned about their collective sense of skepticism and their callous, cynical attitude toward the politicians in Washington.

The acting executive officer, Lt. Cdr. Jack Carella, walked briskly into the dining room. Spotting the CO, Carella walked over to his table.

"Sir," the XO said stiffly, "may I have a word with you?"

"Sure. Pull up a chair," Bailey replied, curious about the reason for Carella's serious look.

"Skipper, I need to speak with you in private." In unison, the three junior officers started to slide their chairs back.

"No," Bailey said, placing his napkin on the table. "Finish your meal, gentlemen. The XO and I will move to another table."

"Yessir," the three officers replied in chorus.

Bailey and Carella stepped a few feet away to a vacant table, then asked a steward for fresh cups of coffee. "What's up, Jocko?"

"Sir," Carella began, spreading a message on the tablecloth, "we just received this from Seventh Fleet."

Bailey read that the North Vietnamese had complained to the international press that an American navy F-4 Phantom had destroyed two MiGs at Phuc Yen, an airfield that had been declared a prohibited military target.

The message went on to say that the North Vietnamese government had lodged a formal complaint, which had been picked up by national newspapers and three major television networks. Excerpts from the *New York Times* and the *Chicago Tribune* had been included in the message.

Most startling to Bailey was the paragraph stating that the North Vietnamese were releasing a photograph of the intruding aircraft. The picture, taken by a foreign correspondent, indicated that the intruding aircraft was from their carrier.

Bailey grimaced. "What the hell are they trying to do?"

Carella talked in a low voice. "I don't know, but I can confirm this. The Pentagon is calling the accusations falsehoods and propaganda . . . and so is the White House."

Bailey studied Carella for a moment. "Then what's the flap about? What's bothering you?"

"Sir, I talked to a friend of mine at Pearl—he's on CINCPAC's staff."

Bailey arched his eyebrows, impatient for Carella to make his point. "And?"

"He said less than fifteen minutes ago that the aircraft is rumored to be from our squadron."

"What?" Bailey said loudly enough to attract the attention of nearby officers.

"That's what he told me, sir."

Bailey shook his head. "That's bullshit, Jocko. There's some new accusation every week."

"Sir, I'm not so sure about this . . . complaint."

"What do you mean?" Bailey asked, his mind quickly jumping to the possible ramifications if the story were true.

"The incident, as reported by the foreign correspondent, happened the morning we launched our last strike, just before we sailed for Yokosuka."

Picking up his coffee, Bailey paused. "Jocko, we don't need to borrow trouble."

"I'm just telling you what I heard, sir."

Bailey took a swig of the hot liquid, then placed the cup in his saucer. "I appreciate that, Jack. Let's just see what develops."

"Yes, sir," Carella replied, glancing around. "My friend said that the word is that Major Nguyen Thanh Dao was killed during the incident."

Dan Bailey entered the nearly empty ready room and spoke to Mario Russo, the squadron duty officer. "Where is Commander Carella?"

Russo detected an unusual intensity in the CO's voice. "He's in his stateroom, sir, doing paperwork."

"Have him report to the ready room."

"Yes, sir," Russo replied as he lifted the phone receiver.

Two first-tour pilots glanced at the CO, then quietly resumed their dice game. They instinctively knew that something was wrong.

Bailey walked to the coffee maker, then decided that he had had enough caffeine for the day. His nerves were already frayed by the conversation that he and the air-group commander had just concluded.

Sitting down in one of the high-backed briefing chairs, Bailey replayed the last strike mission in his mind. After less than a minute, he got up and walked back to Mario Russo's desk.

"Have mission planning bring me all the intel and debriefs for the last strike we flew, when we lost Bull and Russ."

Russo looked puzzled. "The classified info, too?"

"Everything." Bailey looked exasperated. "I need it as soon as they can get it here."

"Yes, sir."

Jocko Carella hurried through the door, then slowed as the CO approached him. "Jack, let's step out in the passageway."

Carella sensed trouble. "What's up, Skipper?"

The two stepped through the hatch, and dogged it tight. "I just came from CAG's stateroom," Bailey said in a tight voice. "We've got big trouble, according to him."

"The Phuc Yen deal?"

Bailey waited while two sailors excused themselves and walked past the two officers. He looked both ways down the long passageway, making sure that no one was approaching them.

"CAG and the admiral have been summoned to Pearl, to see CINCPAC."

"Oh, shit," Carella replied, letting his breath out slowly. "What does he think?"

"The only thing . . ." Bailey paused, seeing the mission-planning yeoman approaching the ready room.

"I'll take that," the CO said, extending his arm.

"Yessir," the petty officer replied, handing Bailey the package of classified strike information. The youngster quickly retraced his steps down the narrow corridor.

"CAG said the admiral is really pissed. Apparently, as you mentioned, they have a photograph of an F-4 flying over Phuc Yen."

"Uh, oh," Carella said, looking at the package of documents. "One of ours—our squadron?"

"He doesn't know," Bailey said disgustedly, "but the photo interpreters—the experts—are saying that the picture appears to be real. They said that the photo does not look contrived, according to what the admiral told CAG."

Carella let out a low whistle. "Any ideas, Skipper, who it might have been?"

Bailey considered the question carefully, rejecting a hasty judgment. From early childhood to fighter-squadron commander, he had been schooled to approach decisions with a pragmatic eye. "Let's take this info to my stateroom and replay every event during the strike. Maybe we can reconstruct what happened . . . see if anything out of the ordinary did take place."

FAIRMONT HOTEL

"My steak was absolutely delicious," Leigh Ann stated, dabbing her mouth with her napkin. "What an unusual charcoal flavor. I've never tasted it before."

Brad finished the last bite of his twice-baked potato, and reached for his wineglass. "They use Hawaiian kiawe wood for all their grilled entrees."

Leigh Ann smiled. "It really makes a difference."

Leigh Ann looked spectacular in a pastel blue dress with a trimly tailored, waist-length jacket accentuated by a short strand of lustrous pearls. Her earrings matched her elegant necklace perfectly.

He noticed the candlelight flickering in her sparkling eyes. Brad was obviously entranced by this woman sitting across from him. He felt a sudden, irresistible impulse to be alone with her.

"Would you care for dessert?"

She hesitated a moment, neatly folding her napkin. "No thank you, but please don't let me stop you."

Brad motioned for their waiter. "Actually, what I'd like to have is an after-dinner drink with you."

"That," Leigh Ann grinned while Brad thanked the waiter and signed the bill, "sounds like an excellent idea."

He reached for her hand. "Let's go to my room and have our drinks delivered."

Leigh Ann grew cautious. "Brad, I have to ask you a question, and I trust that you will be honest."

He released her hand and smiled. "Are you implying that I haven't been honest?"

"Brad, I'm serious."

"I can see that. What's the question?"

Leigh Ann folded her hands together, anticipating the worst. "Did you invite me here for the sole purpose of taking me to bed?"

Brad tried to hide his shock with characteristic humor. "Well, that wasn't the sole reason."

He immediately saw that his answer had not been well received. Tears glistened in Leigh Ann's eyes as she struggled to maintain her composure. "Leigh Ann, I'm sorry. I was only kidding."

The silence gnawed at Brad's conscience. "Look, I apologize, but allow me to express what I think, and how I feel."

She remained quiet, staring at her napkin.

"You and your father obviously had quite a conversation before you left. Did he convince you that that was my primary goal—to get his daughter in bed?"

Leigh Ann looked up. "We had a terrible argument," her mouth quivered, "and he forbade me to . . . to meet you here."

Brad glanced at the nearby couples. "Do you mind," he asked, feeling a rising anger, "if we go into the bar and find a quiet corner?"

Leigh Ann nodded yes and rose before Brad could reach her chair.

Brad sipped his scotch and soda, oblivious to the simulated tropical rainstorm pelting the lagoon in the bar.

"Leigh Ann, I can't do anything about your broken engagement, and your father has apparently categorized me as a . . . as being unsuitable for his daughter."

She inhaled deeply and let her breath out slowly. "My dad is concerned about me. He loves me, and he doesn't want to see me get hurt again."

Exasperated, Brad ordered another scotch. "What do you think, Leigh Ann? At some point in your life, you're going to have to make your own decisions. Your father isn't going—"

"I made a decision, and defied my father to see you. I also reminded him that he was the one who introduced me to the medical student who cheated on me during our engagement."

"Okay," he replied in a low voice. "What exactly does your father have against me?"

Leigh Ann sipped her drink before answering. "In his mind, you're the image of the wild, unstable, carousing playboy. A girl in every port, and so on. He just doesn't want me to become involved, then get hurt again."

Brad sat back in awe. "With respect to your father, we can't all be sedate and reserved doctors who go to the country club on Saturday night and play golf every Wednesday."

Her temper flared. "I will not listen to you run down my father."

"Time out," Brad said evenly. "I'm not running down your father. What I said is a fact. We can't all be just like your father. Some of us have to stand in harm's way, in order to protect his freedoms and life-style."

"Brad," she said with conviction, "he wants me to be happy, that's all."

Composing his thoughts, Brad glanced at the sultry lagoon, then back to Leigh Ann. "What's the real reason for his animosity toward me? Is my social level not good enough, being the rowdy, drunken military gypsy that I am?"

"Please, Brad, don't be defensive. That doesn't become you."

He finished the last of his drink. "What's the reason he doesn't want us to be together?"

"Brad, you're in the military, and you hold quite different views from my father."

"You're right," he replied, signaling for another scotch. "That's my job. I curse, drink, and shoot people for a living."

"That's not my dad's primary concern. He just cares about my welfare."

Brad exhaled sharply. "What's his primary concern? That I'm an abominable heathen—a warmonger?"

"No," Leigh Ann answered in a quiet voice. "He doesn't want me to fall in love with someone who has a high risk of being killed."

"And," Brad replied icily, "making you a widow before you're twenty-five. Right?"

"That's correct."

"On that point, your father is right. But life is full of risks, and rewards."

"Brad, I am not sure either that I am ready for that risk. Dad is right, and I don't think you have any idea how I feel. You just want what you want." Leigh Ann's lip trembled. "I'm going to my room."

He accepted his fresh drink. "I'll walk you."

"That won't be necessary, thank you."

Brad rose when she reached for her evening bag. "Leigh Ann, contrary to what your father thinks, life is not tied in a neat little package. Sometimes, we have to roll the dice."

"I'll take that under consideration," she said, then turned and walked away. Leigh Ann felt confused and angry. Brad's temper and passion scared her.

32

YOKOSUKA

Attired in civilian clothes, Harry Hutton, Jon O'Meara, and Mario Russo saluted and walked down the gangplank to the carrier pier. They had been granted three days off to go sight-seeing and souvenir hunting.

O'Meara and Russo had talked Harry into taking a train excursion to visit outlying cities. Jon wanted to see Kyoto, Japan's ancient capital; Mario was determined to explore Kobe and sample the distinctive flavor of the highly praised Kobe beef.

The threesome had agreed to stay in Kyoto the first night. Jon had made arrangements for them to stay at a traditional Japanese inn known as a *ryokan*. Harry had been reluctant when O'Meara had explained that they would be sleeping on the floor in rooms without furniture. Harry had acquiesced when Mario explained about the bathhouses close to the ryokan. Harry had liked the idea of having young women bathe him.

Carrying their compact overnight bags, the three men walked to the taxi stand, then patiently waited in line for a cab. Watching the cabs come and go, Harry had occasional thoughts of Phuc Yen, but dismissed the reflections as needless worry. Along with his traveling companions, Harry Hutton had not the slightest inkling of the brewing maelstrom.

SAN FRANCISCO

Brad listened to the Polynesian band and thought about Leigh Ann and her relationship with her father. He mentally kicked himself for not being more understanding and considerate to the woman he loved.

He shoved his half-finished drink across the table, paid his bill, then walked to the elevator. He wanted to apologize to Leigh Ann for getting angry, and set the record straight.

When the elevator stopped at his floor, Brad was startled to see Leigh Ann when the doors opened. "Are you okay?" he asked.

"Yes," she replied, stepping to the side. "I was on my way to talk to you."

Brad's hazel eyes smiled warmly, crinkling at the corners. "We think alike. I was heading for your room . . . to apologize."

"Brad, I'm the one who owes you an apology. I don't know what we were arguing about. I am here now and my father isn't. I have disobeyed him, so I really have made my decision."

He felt a surge of desire sweep through him. "Please, no apologies. Leigh Ann, I've been thinking about everything you told me."

She gave him a tiny smile. "Would you like to go to my room?"

"Sure, if you feel comfortable."

Leigh Ann slipped her hand through the crook of Brad's arm, squeezing him affectionately. "I've never felt more comfortable."

He gently pulled her closer to his side as they walked to their adjoining rooms. "I may be wrong, but I believe that your father, with all good intentions, is overcompensating where you're concerned."

Leigh Ann nodded. "He is, because of the way Tyler treated me."

"You're right," Brad responded as they reached the door

to Leigh Ann's room. "He is trying to make sure that you fall in love with the perfect mate." She inserted the key and allowed Brad to open the door.

He followed Leigh Ann through the entrance and closed the door. Brad was surprised to see a silver champagne bucket sitting on the coffee table. "When did you arrange to have the champagne sent up?"

Turning to him, Leigh Ann reached down to clasp both of his hands. She wanted to pull him to her, but hesitated for a moment. "I asked room service to deliver it," she smiled, linking his arms behind her back, "while we were at dinner."

Brad felt her body pressing against him as she raised her arms and encircled his neck. With a rush, repressed emotions were released as their lips met in a fervent hunger.

After what seemed like minutes, they separated to catch their breath. Leigh Ann gently cupped Brad's face in her hands. "I've missed you, darling . . . more than I can tell you."

He held Leigh Ann to his chest, resting her head next to his neck. A shudder ran through him. "I've been thinking about you every waking moment since Hawaii."

Leigh Ann brushed his neck and leaned back, looking up at the tanned face and sincere eyes. "What have you been thinking about me?"

Reaching for her shoulders, Brad's stare riveted Leigh Ann. "That I love you," he admitted hoarsely and drew her lips to his in a gentle, passionate kiss.

Leigh Ann responded with a crushing intensity that was intoxicating. She broke off their kiss and held him close. "I love you, too." She trembled and gazed into his eyes. "God, how I love you . . . Brad Austin."

He spoke with a huskiness in his voice. "Why don't I open the champagne," he breathed, "while you make yourself comfortable?"

Filled with longing, Leigh Ann smiled and slipped from his arms. "I'll only be a minute."

Brad tried unsuccessfully to collect himself while Leigh Ann stepped into the bedroom. He carefully opened the chilled bottle of champagne and turned out the lights on each side of the window. Looking across the moonlit bay, Brad felt a sensation that he had never experienced before. He was totally consumed, enraptured by his love for Leigh Ann Ladasau.

Staring blankly at the boat lights moving across the water, Brad sensed Leigh Ann's presence. He turned slightly as she approached him wearing only her kimono. She looked like a goddess in the soft light.

Brad stepped to the table and poured two glasses of champagne. He handed one to Leigh Ann. Placing his arm around her waist, Brad inhaled and raised his glass. "To us . . . and to our love."

They drank the toast and Leigh Ann set down her glass, turning to embrace Brad. "Hold me, darling," she murmured in a soft, wistful voice. "Please don't leave me tonight."

Brad unsteadily placed his glass down and scooped her into his arms. "I'll hold you all night," he said thickly as he carried her into the bedroom.

YOKOSUKA

Dan Bailey sat down in Jack Carella's stateroom. He had just returned from a meeting with the commanding officer of the other Phantom squadron on the carrier. An extreme weariness from prolonged stress swept over him. He rotated his head from side to side, then moved it up and down in an attempt to loosen his tense neck muscles.

"What did Commander Rooney have to say?" Jocko Carella asked, neatly stacking his pile of paperwork on the side of his desk.

Bailey ran a hand over his salt-and-pepper crew cut. He looked at his acting executive officer and moved his head in a wide arc. "He was uncomfortable, and didn't even want to discuss the subject. I've known him for a long time, and he hasn't changed. He'd rather avoid problems than investigate them."

Carella gave him a curious look. "I don't know him that well, but you'd think he would want to get to the bottom of the matter."

"Rooney has always been a keen political player who shies away from anything that might splatter mud on his dress whites."

The XO shifted in his chair, uncomfortable with the words *political player*.

"He said," Bailey continued, looking tired and grim, "that he wanted to keep his distance from the rumors until the accusations are proved, or dismissed."

Carella bit his lip thoughtfully. "Has he talked to the pilots who were involved in the strike?"

Bailey shook his head slowly.

"That's incredible," Carella responded, looking at the neatly penned notes on his desk pad. He had written three pages when he and the CO had first talked about the incident at Phuc Yen.

Dan Bailey examined the framed painting on the bulkhead next to Carella. The print showcased the aircraft carrier USS *Hornet* at the Battle of Santa Cruz. "His caution is directly proportional to his rank. He doesn't want any blemishes to impede his career."

"Skipper," Carella ventured, remembering what the CO had said in the passageway, "what do you think happened, if anything?"

Bailey glanced at the picture of the carrier again before looking directly at his XO. "I don't know. With Austin somewhere in California and the other guys out roaming the countryside, we're just going to have to wait until CAG and the admiral return."

Carella darted a look at his first page of notes. He had been convinced from the outset of their reconstruction of the events that Brad Austin had been the culprit. His intuition presupposed that the accusations were true.

"Sir, can't we contact Austin, and go ahead and get his statement?"

Bailey heaved a sigh. "No, because I allowed him to go without leaving an address, since we yanked him back from Hawaii. I'll get my ass fried for that if this can of worms turns out to be on the level."

Chewing the end of his pen, Carella grew more bold.

"Skipper, after going over the mission debriefing reports, I think we should at least try to get in touch with Austin. Everything points to him, even Hutton's reluctance to add anything of any significance to the action report."

Bailey studied Carella's piercing dark eyes, noting the intensity in his voice.

"Sir," Carella continued, placing his pen on his desk, "I believe that it is in our best interest to get straight answers from Austin and Hutton, before CAG and the admiral get back."

The CO rubbed his neck. If the accusations turned out to be true, the consequences could be serious. If Austin had indeed shot down a MiG over an off-limits airfield, Dan Bailey could toss his career off the fantail.

"I have a theory," Carella continued cautiously, "that Major Dao bagged Durham and Lunsford, and Austin went after him. Everything we've looked at points to that conclusion, at least in my mind."

Bailey weighed Carella's argument, wishing the matter would evaporate. "Jack, you may be right, but I want to get all the facts—all the information from CINCPAC—on the table before we confront anyone."

"Yes, sir," Carella replied, unsure if he should press the issue. "Skipper, I would suggest that we send Ernie Sheridan out to see if he can locate Hutton. At least, if the story is true, you'll have time to think about the problems we're going to have to face."

Bailey's shoulders sagged as he lowered his head, then raised it slowly. "Jack, I believe that sends the wrong signal. That type of approach would take on the appearance of a witch hunt. We have to trust one another, and wait to see what turns up from the investigation in Hawaii."

33

THE FAIRMONT

Brad felt the warm morning sunlight on his face. He blinked several times and turned his head toward Leigh Ann. She was entwined in his arms, her tangled dark hair partially covering her peaceful face. She stirred and nestled closer to him.

Reflecting on their shared ecstasy, Brad brushed her soft hair away from her face, then reached for the telephone on the bedside table.

Leigh Ann opened her eyes and smiled. "Good morning."

He returned her smile. "It is a good morning." Placing his hand on the telephone receiver, Brad kissed her on the forehead. "I thought I would have breakfast sent to our . . . your room."

They both laughed while Leigh Ann slid across the bed and reached for her kimono. "I believe we can dispense with the extra room at this point, if you're brave enough to share a bathroom with me."

"I believe I can handle that."

"Oh, you are a brave marine," she replied with a wink as she slipped on her silk robe.

Brad dialed the phone and looked at his wristwatch. Seven fifteen was a good start for a day of sight-seeing.

After ordering a generous breakfast for two, Brad gathered his clothes, which lay in a small pile beside the bed. He donned his wrinkled trousers and walked into his room. Ten minutes later, he emerged in a hotel robe and stretched out on the bed beside Leigh Ann.

She curled next to him and rested her head on his chest, laughing softly to herself.

"What's so funny?"

"Well, I'm not in the habit of traipsing around the country, meeting strange men in hotel rooms, but I finally did something I wanted to do, for a change."

He smoothed her hair. "You sure did."

She kissed his chest. "Dad would have a conniption."

"Your father," Brad chuckled, "would shoot me."

Propping herself up on one elbow, Leigh Ann turned to face Brad. Her smile was sultry. "No question about it. You're a scoundrel, but I love you anyway."

"I'm glad to know that," he yawned. "Sorry."

She laughed, then leaned back.

"Do you mind," Brad smiled, "if we watch the 'Today' show?"

"Not at all. I'll turn it on."

When she returned to the bed, Brad pulled her back to him, feeling her warmth. "I wonder how soon room service will be here?"

"Who cares," Leigh Ann sighed as her lips met his.

They propped their pillows against the headboard and turned their attention to the morning news program. Turning to face Leigh Ann, Brad leaned closer to her. He breathed the sweet fragrance of her hair.

Leigh Ann kissed him lightly on the forehead, then paused, transfixed by the photograph being shown on the screen. "Isn't that the kind of plane you fly?"

Brad turned his head and froze. There was his Phantom, Joker 205, banked steeply over Phuc Yen. He caught only a few key comments from the broadcaster, the words *State Department* and *investigation* among them. He stared at the photograph of his F-4, hearing the words *allegedly shot down a MiG* while a picture of a crashed airplane flashed on the screen. Two seconds later the dapper newsman switched to a different story, and the airplane wreckage disappeared from the screen.

Brad's mind spun, trying to comprehend the significance of the news report. *How much do they know? He could not believe that someone captured it on film. Will anyone else recognize that it was my airplane?*

Leigh Ann gripped his wrist. "Brad, what's wrong? Do you know the pilot of that plane?"

He stared in shock at the television. "Ah . . . yes."

Leigh Ann gave him a confused, frightened look. She had been startled by his strained voice.

"Leigh Ann . . ."

"Brad," she responded, reaching for his hand, "what's the matter?"

He shook his head slowly. "Jesus H. Christ . . ."

Leigh Ann felt a sudden pang of fear, frightened by the brittleness in his voice. "Please, Brad . . . I'm scared. What happened? Are you in some kind of trouble?"

"Yes," he answered in a flat, decisive voice. "I was flying that plane."

"Brad," Leigh Ann said tentatively, "what happened?"

He sighed and looked into her eyes. "I broke a rule—a big one—and destroyed a MiG taxiing at an off-limits military airfield. I also shot down their second-leading ace. I didn't report it, and, as we just saw, someone was taking pictures. It won't take the investigators long to figure out who did it, if they haven't found out already."

Leigh Ann remained silent, her mind racing in an attempt to assimilate all she had heard and seen. She thought about what her father had said, and what she had said to him. How could she face him now, and explain that Brad was not a renegade. *Or was he?* Leigh Ann stared at the screen, then glanced at Brad.

"Leigh Ann," he said dryly, "I'm going to have to go back, and turn myself in to my commanding officer." He felt her fingernails dig into the palm of his hand. "I'm facing a court-martial, and probably dismissal from the Marine Corps, if not a long prison term at Fort Leavenworth."

Leigh Ann gasped. "Brad, that makes you a criminal, doesn't it?"

"Yes, I'm afraid so."

"But you're an officer standing up for your country. You shot down an enemy pilot and destroyed another plane in the middle of a war. You're a hero."

A long silence followed.

"Leigh Ann, my good friends Bull Durham and Russ Lunsford were shot down by the MiG pilot I killed. Bull—that was his wife I called yesterday—and Russ were captured." Brad inhaled sharply. "But the main thing I did was violate the rules of engagement by attacking a MiG at an off-limits airfield.

"I have no excuse," he continued with dry cynicism, "except that my logic tells me that our civilian leadership is protecting their collective asses, while they place us in a position to fight with one hand tied behind us. Now, Bull and Russ are POWs, and I'm going to a court-martial."

"Brad, I don't understand what you mean by rules of engagement. Can you explain what the rules are . . . and what you did that was so bad that they would court-martial you? You were only doing what you were trained to do."

Brad rubbed the bridge of his nose. "The administration in the White House has established guidelines specifying where we can shoot and bomb, and where we can't. The quagmire would amaze you, but suffice it to say that I stepped over the boundary and violated a restriction."

Brad pondered his answer. "So, that won't make the pseudointelligentsia in the White House very pleased. I broke a rule, and I'll pay the penalty."

Leigh Ann released his hand and put her arms around him. "Brad, I truly love you, with all my heart, but I'm frightened."

Brad held her tightly, then gently kissed her. He tasted a salty tear and drew away.

YOKOSUKA

Dan Bailey, clad in boxer shorts and a T-shirt, propped his pillow behind his head and began reading the stack of officer fitness reports. His concentration was repeatedly broken by the pounding and banging on the deck below his stateroom. The noises, interrupted by periodic bursts from an air hammer, had been a continual irritation for more than fourteen hours.

In frustration, Bailey sat up and swung his legs over the side of his bunk. He dropped the fitness reports on the edge of his desk and walked to his small lavatory.

Bailey splashed cool water on his face and looked into his mirror. The reflection that met him was not the usual upbeat, energetic squadron commander. Bailey studied his red eyes, then the creases in his tanned face, concluding that he had aged ten years since the carrier had departed on the combat cruise.

Bailey dried his face, then stepped to his desk and sat down in his battered chair. He could not stop thinking about the incident at Phuc Yen. The more he thought about the accusations, the more convinced he became that the series of events could not have been coincidental.

He sat quietly, staring blankly at the opposite bulkhead. Hutton, who had been allowed to leave early on his jaunt, was due back to the carrier at approximately the same time as Austin. Then, Bailey thought, I'll have the answer.

"What a bag of shit," he said under his breath.

It was time for a stiff drink. He reached for his trousers, in preparation for a visit to the officers' club. Dan Bailey hoped the diversion, and a few laughs with his friends, would clear his mind.

KYOTO

The atmosphere in the Okutan restaurant was reserved. Harry Hutton gazed at the garden pond from a private tatami room. His attention centered on two young Japanese girls walking across a blanket of moss.

"What are you eyeballing?" Jon O'Meara asked, counting the handful of yen to pay for his share of the meal.

"Just taking in the local scenery," Harry answered, catching a glimpse of Mario Russo entering the room.

Russo dropped a folded newspaper on the low table, then squatted on his thin cushion and folded his legs. "The men's room looks like something from around the turn of the century."

Harry watched the teenage girls duck through a side gate and walk down a narrow path next to the garden.

O'Meara looked at the newspaper. "What the hell are you doing with a Japanese paper? You can't even read English."

"I saw this," Russo answered, unfolding the tattered newspaper to the front page, "and wondered what the headlines say."

O'Meara and Russo focused their attention on the large photograph of an F-4 Phantom in knife-edge flight. The wing tip looked like it was almost dragging the ground.

O'Meara gave his RIO a quizzical look and motioned for a nearby waitress. He handed the newspaper to her. "Would you mind telling us what that says?" he asked, pointing to the two bold lines of print.

She studied the headlines and handed the paper back to O'Meara. "Paper say," she hesitated, struggling with her English, "Hanoi protests American fighter over Phuc Yen."

Harry snapped around, knocking over his plum wine. His face turned ashen, prompting the surprised waitress to scurry away. Wide-eyed, he fixated on the photograph of his fighter-bomber.

Russo and O'Meara stared at Harry a moment before they both started to speak. "Harry," O'Meara said, darting a look at the Phantom, "what the shit is—"

"Oh, Jesus," Harry interrupted, oblivious to the cool wine dripping on his slacks. "Sonuvabitch—I knew it, goddamnit!"

Shocked, O'Meara and Russo looked at each other, then back to Hutton. "Is that you," Russo asked gingerly, "and Austin?"

Harry looked up and nodded. "Brad stepped over the line

when Dao shot down Bull and Russ. I tried to stop him, but he was determined to get Dao—to make up for letting them down."

"Major Dao," O'Meara leaned closer to Hutton, "shot down Bull and Russ?"

"Yes, goddamnit," Harry blurted, "and then Brad chased Dao to Phuc Yen, and blew his ass out of the air—killed him right over the runway, then blasted a MiG on the taxiway."

"Unbelievable," Russo said under his breath. "Does anyone know about this other than us?"

"Mario," Harry answered in anguish, "look at the picture, for Christ's sake. The whole world knows about it."

"Calm down, Harry," O'Meara soothed, nudging Russo. "I'm going over and have that waitress read the article to me, and we'll go from there, okay?" O'Meara squeezed from under the table, grabbed the newspaper, and walked over to the waitress.

"Where is Austin?" Russo asked in an even voice. He could see that the color was slowly returning to Harry's taut face.

"I don't know exactly. Some hotel in San Francisco."

"Well," Russo continued reasonably, "we better try to track him down, and let him know, if he hasn't found out already. We owe it to him."

Harry exhaled sharply. "How the hell do you expect to find him in the middle of San Francisco?"

"Harry, you know Brad. He doesn't stay in flophouses. We just need to call the better hotels."

With a grim look, O'Meara returned to the table and crouched down on his cushion. "The military and the State Department are denying the allegations, but unidentified sources in the Pentagon have admitted that an investigation is under way. The North Vietnamese called you guys Yankee air pirates, and murderers."

Russo expelled a sharp breath of air. "Brad is in some deep shit. All they have to do is look at the flight schedule for that date, including the Air Force, and interrogate the pilots and RIOs."

O'Meara looked skeptical, pointing to the picture. "I don't think so. Look closely at the fuselage. I'm sure they've enlarged the photograph, and that dark slash on the side of the fuselage, as you know, is the name of our carrier."

Harry sagged and leaned against the wall. "It's all over but the court-martial."

Russo examined Hutton's eyes. "You weren't flying the airplane. Harry, you didn't have any control over where Brad was going."

"True," Harry replied, "but I didn't report the incident—the goddamn violation."

"Listen," O'Meara interjected. "What RIO worth a pig's ass is going to rat on his pilot?"

Harry looked melancholy. "They aren't going to buy that. We're a team—we're supposed to follow orders."

Russo darted a look at O'Meara. "Any board of inquiry knows that we wouldn't sell out our pilots, even after all the dumb-shit stunts they pull."

Managing a faint smile, Harry shoved himself back and awkwardly got to his feet. "I'm going to find Brad, or at least get a message to him."

34

YOKOSUKA

The officers' club had grown quiet after the lunch crowd had returned to their duties. Harry Hutton sat at the bar, nursing a warm beer and looking remorseful. Next to him, Jon O'Meara and Mario Russo passed a dice cup back and forth in a game of Ship, Captain, and Crew.

The three men had decided to return to the base after several failed attempts to deal with the local telephone operators in Kyoto. One operator had mastered pidgin English but had not been successful in completing the information call to San Francisco.

After arriving at the club, Harry had located Brad after calling three other prominent hotels. He had been deeply disappointed when his pilot had not answered the call. Leaving a message, Harry had given the hotel operator the number of a pay phone in the officers' club.

"Come on, Harry," O'Meara invited. "We need some of your money in the game. You need to get your mind off this shit, and lighten up."

"Lighten up," Harry snorted. "They're going to hang our asses from the yardarm, and I'm supposed to lighten up? Jesus, give me a break."

Russo leaned around O'Meara. "Hey, you can't do anything about the deal at—"

Harry jumped when the pay phone rang. He leaped off his bar stool and raced for the row of telephones. Yanking up

282

the receiver, Harry turned his back to the room. "Lieutenant Hutton."

"Harry, Brad. I just got your message. What's the situation?"

Cupping the telephone, Harry stole a glance at the bar. "I don't know, except that our airplane is splattered on the front page of the goddamn newspapers—front page. We're in so much shit, we're going to need a snorkel."

"Yeah, I saw our aircraft on television. Have you been questioned yet, or said anything to anyone?"

Waiting for a senior officer to pass, Harry cleared his throat. "O'Meara and Russo know the whole story. They saw the picture in the paper—we were in Kyoto—and I told them what happened. I haven't been back aboard ship since the story broke, so I don't have a clue as to what the hell is happening, but it ain't good."

The line remained silent a moment before Brad responded. "Listen, Harry. I'm taking the next available flight, so I've got a suggestion."

"Suggestion?" Harry countered harshly. "You had better have some goddamn solutions."

"Harry, you're yelling. Calm down."

"I'm waiting."

"Get a room at the hotel—the one that's down the block from the Club Alliance, and I'll meet you there as soon as I can."

Hutton looked at his wristwatch, counting the remaining hours until he had to return to the carrier. "What are you planning to do?"

"I'm going to tell the skipper the truth, and try to keep you out of the firing line. I don't want them to get to you first. Don't go aboard ship until I get back."

Harry paused, seeing Jon O'Meara walking toward him. "I appreciate that, but I don't think any amount of damage control is going to keep us from getting keelhauled. Hang on a second."

O'Meara quietly told Harry what he and Russo had just overheard at the bar. Three of the air-wing officers had been discussing the incident.

Unconsciously gripping the phone more tightly, Harry watched O'Meara head for the lavatory. "Brad, the admiral and CAG were summoned to Hawaii to see CINCPAC, and they're due back tomorrow."

"I'll be there as soon as I can."

Harry placed the receiver down without responding. He walked back to his spot at the bar, glanced at Russo, then ordered a double scotch on the rocks.

SAN FRANCISCO INTERNATIONAL AIRPORT

Watching an airliner taxi to the adjacent gate, Leigh Ann brushed the wetness from her cheeks. Brad was talking to the gate agent, confirming her departure time.

The airliner moved steadily closer, trailing a shimmering stream of jet exhaust gases. The airplane stopped abruptly and the pilot shut down the whining engines.

Leigh Ann thought about Brad. Would he ever fly again? What would the military do to him? She choked back a sob when Brad walked to her side.

"Your flight is on time, and they're about to board. I'll call you as soon as I know something."

She nodded silently.

"Leigh Ann, I'm sorry about this."

"It's almost as if," she hesitated, looking into his eyes, "we aren't meant to be together. Maybe Dad was right in the first place."

Hearing the boarding announcement for Leigh Ann's flight to Memphis, Brad touched her face. "Don't you have any faith in me?"

"I don't know what I feel right now." She dabbed a tear. "I have such mixed emotions. First, Tyler humiliated me . . . and now this. Why can't anything turn out right for me?"

"I'm sorry if I embarrass you," Brad said, swallowing his irritation. "If your feelings are that shallow, it's better that I know now."

"My feelings aren't shallow." Her voice rose. "Why

didn't you explain to me that you were in trouble—serious trouble?''

''I didn't know I was in trouble. I knew the potential for a court-martial existed, but I found out about it at the same moment you did.''

Leigh Ann reached in her purse for a fresh tissue.

''Besides,'' Brad continued, ''what does that have to do with our relationship . . . if you truly love me? People who love each other stand side by side through all adversities.''

She glared at him. ''I understand that, but how am I going to explain this to my father?''

''What's he going to do—court-martial you? Why don't you think about me and stop worrying about your father? Make your own decisions.''

Her anger grew. ''You have no right to talk to me like that.''

''Leigh Ann,'' Brad countered, unable to quell his frustration, ''I do love you, but you need to step out of the shadow of your father, and develop some independence.''

''Brad, I'm a lot more independent than you or my father give me credit for. I can tell you what I intend to do. I'm going to give some serious thought to our relationship. My heart tells me that I love you, but maybe that isn't in my best interest. I just don't know right now.'' She turned and strode toward the jetway.

''Leigh Ann,'' Brad called after her, ''I do love you.''

YOKOSUKA

Brad dropped his luggage in front of Harry's room and knocked on the door. When the door opened, he examined Harry from head to foot, then looked at his swollen eyes. Brad grimaced, lifted his bags, and walked into the small, cluttered room. ''You look like dogmeat.''

''Good day to you, too,'' Hutton replied sarcastically, walking unsteadily to the messy writing table. He poured a liberal amount of scotch into a glass and drank two deep swallows. He cringed and sucked in a breath of air.

Brad spied a trash can full of beer bottles and take-out food containers. "Harry, what are you doing?"

"I'm celebrating my good fortune," he slurred before smothering a belch. "One goddamn flight with you and I'm headed for a court-martial, with my career flushed down the shitter."

Placing his baggage on the rumpled bed, Brad studied his friend's face. "We don't have time for games, Harry. Put the drink down, and get dressed."

"Aye, aye, Captain," Hutton responded, clumsily sitting down in the chair by the table. "Let me tell you something."

The silence was a palpable presence in the small room. "Go on. I'm waiting."

Harry placed his glass on the table. "Mario came by a few minutes ago to inform me that CAG and the admiral have returned from Hawaii. Everyone but us has been questioned by CAG and the admiral."

Brad's strained patience was wearing thin. "And?"

"Mario said that he and Jon claimed that they didn't know anything about an incident at Phuc Yen. He said our names were not mentioned, and that he and Jon kept their mouths shut. However, from what they have gleaned, Bailey has narrowed it down to us."

Brad sagged and sat down on the bed.

"I have to go back to the boat in a few hours," Harry continued, feeling suddenly nauseated, "and there's a standing order for me on the forward bow."

"Harry," Brad said with alarm, "you better go to the head."

Hutton pushed himself up and started for the bathroom. "I'm supposed to report . . . directly to the skipper," he managed before dropping to his knees in front of the toilet bowl.

After a long shower, Harry had dressed and taken three aspirins. With Brad's assistance, he had walked two miles in the fresh air before returning to the dingy hotel and checking out. They had taken a taxicab to the carrier pier an hour before Harry was due to report. They walked up the gangplank and requested permission to board the ship.

"Permission granted," the junior officer replied, adding, "Mister Hutton is to report immediately to his commanding officer."

"I'll do that," Harry responded, turning to enter the hangar bay. He noticed that the officer of the deck had picked up a phone receiver. He was certain that his arrival was being announced to Dan Bailey.

Brad and Harry went to their stateroom and changed into fresh uniforms. They were about to leave their cabin when the telephone rang. Harry answered the phone.

"Goddamnit, Hutton," Dan Bailey snarled, "when I say immediately, I mean it. And bring Austin with you." The duty officer had informed Bailey that Captain Austin had arrived with Lieutenant (jg) Hutton.

"Yessir, I'm—" Harry stopped, hearing the line go dead. "That was the skipper," he said quietly, "and he is pissed off to the max. He knows that you're on board."

"Let's go," Brad responded, centering his gleaming belt buckle. "Try to be calm, and let me do the talking."

"Yeah, you're a helluva sea lawyer."

Dan Bailey leaned back in his chair and read the hastily drafted message. He changed two sentences and propped a foot on the open lower drawer of his desk. He could not complete the secret message to CINCPAC until he had talked to Austin and Hutton.

The admiral had sent word, prior to departing Pearl Harbor, that he wanted every crew member who had participated in the air strike in question to be standing by on his arrival.

After interrogating the aircrews and listening to the tapes of the aircraft radio conversations, the admiral and the air-group commander had been convinced that Brad Austin was the only person who might have flown over Phuc Yen.

Seven minutes of radio silence from Joker 205 had made them suspicious.

That information, combined with the fact that no other aircrew had seen Brad's Phantom during that period of time, had convinced CAG that Austin had indeed shot down Major Dao over Phuc Yen. The possibility of an unauthorized attack on the taxiing MiG worried them most.

From the time that Hutton had radioed the north search-and-rescue coordinator, to the point when the RIO had again called the SAR station, was an unknown void.

Bailey glanced at the message. I'll soon have the answer, he thought, hearing steps outside his stateroom. "Enter," he barked when Brad rapped on the door.

Followed by Harry, Brad entered to find the CO smoking a cigar and tapping his fingers on the desk. Bailey's face reflected open hostility. Brad closed the door and stood at attention beside Hutton.

"How many MiGs have you shot down, Captain Austin?"

"Two, Commander," he replied without hesitation, eyes fixed on the bulkhead over Bailey's desk, "plus one on the ground at Phuc Yen."

"So, the truth is known."

"Yes, sir." Brad could hear Harry breathing quickly.

"Look at this," Bailey ordered, thrusting the incriminating photograph into Austin's hands. "Do you recognize your signature?" the CO asked, referring to the name of the carrier on the side of the Phantom.

"I've seen it, sir." Brad handed the picture back without looking at it.

"Goddamnit," Bailey bellowed, "if you had reported what you had done in the debrief and after-action report, we might have had a fighting chance to salvage this screwup. But now, Captain Austin, we are all in deep shit."

Brad swallowed hard and kept his eyes on the bulkhead. The silence hung in the air.

Dan Bailey savagely stubbed out his cigar. "Do either of you know who is on the way to visit our ship?"

"No, sir," Brad replied, clearing his throat.

Bailey scratched his head. "A senior captain from CINCPAC's staff, and a representative from the State Department."

Harry darted a glance at their skipper. Bailey's face was crimson.

"I am most likely," Bailey said more calmly, "going to be relieved as commanding officer of this squadron. But, the two of you are headed for a court-martial. That has already been discussed with the admiral."

"Commander," Brad said without moving his eyes from the bulkhead, "I am the one who is responsible for deviating from the rules. Harry tried to talk me out of going to Phuc Yen. He is not at fault, sir."

"Deviated?" Bailey responded, his voice rising again. "You broke the trust of the United States Navy, the marines, and our commander in chief." Bailey was exasperated. "We may have civilian leaders, including the President of the United States, who may not see the war our way, but you took an oath to obey them, and follow the orders of the officers appointed over you."

"Commander," Brad began as evenly as possible, "I will take whatever punishment I have coming, but Harry is not at fault. He did everything in his power to make me turn back."

Bailey sighed and slowly shook his head. "It's out of my hands at this point. Both of your fates will probably be decided at a court-martial. First, there will be a formal hearing, when they decide on a location. We can't go back and fix everything at this point.

"This whole thing," Bailey continued, looking tired, "has become a global embarrassment. The formal protest and letter of condemnation—including the goddamned photograph—have been flashed around the world. Our government is officially denying the allegations, but when you two confess, which you are going to do, there will be egg on a lot of faces."

Bailey paused a moment, trying to quell his growing frustration. "Jesus Christ, Austin, what was going through your mind, if anything?"

For the first time, Brad shot a look at the CO. "Sir, Major Dao shot down Commander Durham and Russ. I was determined to blow that sonuvabitch off the face of the—"

"Stand at ease," Bailey waved his hand, "both of you." Harry and Brad assumed the position of a relaxed parade rest.

Brad focused on Bailey's eyes. "I was initially in shock, sir, which turned to rage. I was consumed by the desire to kill Dao before he shot down another aircraft. I also felt responsible for letting my flight leader down, and I remembered what you had told us."

"What's that?" Bailey asked with a curious look.

"In the ready room, when you mentioned that the admiral wanted Major Dao bagged . . . that it was a priority."

Bailey's shoulders slumped. "Within the rules of engagement, Austin. Do I have to draw a goddamn picture for you?"

"Sir," Brad said emotionally, "Major Dao didn't have any rules-of-engagement restrictions. This entire war has been marked by political meanderings and flawed decisions, and there is going to be a backlash at some point. Sir, I fully understand about my oath, and following orders."

Wetting his dry lips, Brad continued in a pleasant, conversational manner. "Sir, I submit to you that there are times when we have to question the morality of orders that are not sound. This, in my logic, is not morally right— restrictions, stipulated by our civilian leadership, that place us in a corner and needlessly endanger more lives."

Bailey's look was almost a glare.

Brad paused, weighing his options. "Sir, those rules—the restrictions—have caused a lot of lives to be lost unnecessarily. You know that better than anyone. You have to write the letters to their families."

Seeing that he had hit a chord, Brad stopped talking. He knew that the skipper had the same doubts that he felt, but Bailey could not do anything about the situation.

"Captain, I am not going to debate with you. My job is to get to the bottom of this fiasco, and inform you and

Mister Hutton that you're to report to the flag bridge at zero eight hundred tomorrow morning.''

"Yes, sir.''

"Until then, you and Hutton are confined to quarters. Your meals will be brought to your stateroom, and you are not to talk with anyone.'' Bailey's voice rose. "Do I make myself perfectly clear?''

"Yessir,'' Brad answered in a respectful tone. "Your orders are perfectly clear.''

"Now,'' Bailey said, emotionally drained, "I have the unpleasant task of facing the admiral, and confirming that one of my crews set off this international incident. He may want to see you now.''

"Commander,'' Brad inhaled deeply, "if I submit my resignation, we can avoid a court-martial.''

Harry found his voice. "Sir, I will also submit my resignation.''

Bailey examined their faces. "I will talk to the admiral about that possibility.'' He glanced at the message to be endorsed by the admiral. "Dismissed.''

35

The music in the passageway was faint. Brad listened to the harmony and thought about Leigh Ann. What was she doing at this very moment? He glanced at his watch, computing the time in Memphis. He closed his eyes and pictured Leigh Ann lying next to him in San Francisco.

His thoughts suddenly shifted to defending his actions over Phuc Yen. Should he retain civilian legal counsel and go public? After all, he had shot down two MiGs, even though he had had to break the rules to down the second aircraft. How would the public react to knowing that a North Vietnamese ace would not shoot down a ninth American fighter?

Who was the enemy? If he played strictly by the rules of engagement, the chances were greater that he would be killed, or endure a long stay in a North Vietnamese prison. If he chose to take the fight to the enemy, he faced the possibility of a lengthy incarceration in a federal prison.

"You awake, Brad?" Harry asked, rolling on his side.

"Yes," he replied, sitting up.

Harry leaned over the top of his bunk. "What are we going to do? We're facing a court-martial."

Brad walked to the desk and sat down. "We're going to defend ourselves. The more I think about this crock of shit, the more incensed I become. If they want to play hardball, I'll reciprocate in kind."

"What about your father? He's a vice admiral who obviously has some pull."

Brad looked up with a wry grin. "He'd most likely be the

first volunteer for my firing squad. His fourth star just went down the tube.''

Harry sat up, crouched under the low overhead. "Do you think they'll let us resign?"

"Probably not. With something this juicy, I'm sure they'll want to make us examples for the rest of the team."

Brad opened the refrigerator and grabbed two soft drinks. "You may get off with a reprimand," he handed Harry a Coke, "but I'll probably get a dishonorable discharge, and a couple of years in Leavenworth."

Harry stared at a spot on the floor. "We really crapped in our mess kits."

"No, Harry. I did."

The silence was shattered when the telephone rang. Brad and Harry looked at each other, unsure if they should answer the phone. The CO had ordered them not to talk to anyone.

"I better answer it," Brad said, reaching for the receiver. "Captain Austin."

"Sir," the hollow voice replied, "you have a call from Vice Admiral Austin."

Brad let his head sag, feeling the tension grip his chest. "I'll connect you, sir."

Looking up at Harry, Brad covered the mouthpiece. "My father."

Harry closed his eyes and spoke in a whisper. "Oh, shit. How did he know we were talking about him?"

The seconds passed slowly.

"Brad, this is your father." The voice sounded controlled and steady.

"Yes, sir," Brad answered, mentally bracing himself for a broadside. "Good morning." It was late morning in Norfolk, Virginia.

Vice Admiral Carlyle Whitney Austin had always been an imposing figure. He was taller than Brad and twenty pounds heavier, with a no-nonsense personality. Carlyle Austin was a traditional, by-the-book naval officer, and a strict disciplinarian. "I have been informed about your incident."

"Yessir, Admiral," Brad replied cautiously.

A slight pause followed. "Son, you can drop the admiral and sir business. I'm your father, so let's keep it that way."

Harry caught the surprised look on his friend's face.

"Yes, sir—okay, Dad."

"Why don't you tell me precisely what happened, and don't leave anything out."

Brad explained, in detail, exactly what he had done, and why he had broken the rules. He outlined his frustrations and contempt for the restrictions, adding that he felt that the policies of the futile war effort were causing greater casualties than necessary. His father listened without interruption.

"Dad, I believe in our Constitution, and obeying orders. Our system is not the problem, as you well know. But the military and the American people are being shortchanged by their civilian leadership."

Harry looked askance, then frowned.

"I don't know if I have the right to disobey what I consider to be ridiculous orders, but the restrictions that have been forced on us are placing the crews in greater danger, and killing people who are trying to tiptoe through the rules. We're losing some of the best and brightest because of the constraints placed on them."

"Anything else, son?"

Brad's throat tightened. Why was his father being so calm? Was he going to explode at any second?

"Dad," he continued uncomfortably, "I feel that good leaders have to use excellent judgment in making their decisions, or we might as well be drones. I've had some of the best military training and discipline in the world, but I'm not going to march my men lockstep off a cliff because some unqualified bureaucrat orders me to."

"Brad, many people share your sentiments, including a number of my colleagues, but that's neither here nor there. You have always been reasonable, for the most part."

Brad felt the sting, but remained quiet.

"There isn't anything I can do on your behalf. If I attempt

to use my influence in any way, it would make things even more difficult for you. Do you understand?"

"Yes, I understand, and I wouldn't ask you to intervene. It's my problem, and I'll pay the consequences." Taking a deep breath, Brad steeled himself. "Dad, I'm sorry I've besmirched our name, and your career."

"Brad, you haven't tarnished our name, and don't worry about my career. I will be retiring two months from tomorrow."

Brad glanced at Harry before speaking. "Is your retirement because of me?"

"No, not at all. My papers went in six weeks ago, and I'm looking forward to sailing on the Chesapeake."

Feeling relief sweep over him, Brad smiled. "Congratulations, Dad. I hope we can go sailing together, if I can get myself out of this trouble."

"Son, you did what you had to do. Don't apologize for your actions. Stand up for them."

"Yes, sir," Brad replied, reverting to his military bearing. "I sincerely appreciate your call, and the words of advice."

"Well," the admiral paused, "you're my son, and you're not a loose cannon. Stubborn and determined," he chuckled softly, "but not a loose cannon."

Startled by the unexpected trace of humor, Brad laughed nervously. He felt closer to his father than he had felt in years. "Thanks, Dad. I'll keep you posted, and I'll call mother as soon as I have an opportunity."

"You do that. Get some rest."

"I'll try," Brad responded, noting the time. "Goodbye." He set the receiver down slowly and looked at Harry. "He took it calmly, and told me to stand up for my actions."

Brad and Harry climbed the steep series of ladders leading to the flag bridge. The last level of the gleaming staircase had white handholds with an engraved brass plaque mounted over the top of the stairwell. The highly polished plaque announced to the two visitors that they had arrived at the admiral's bridge. The marine corporal guarding the entrance snapped to attention.

"Captain Austin," Brad announced, "and Lieutenant Hutton, reporting to the admiral as requested." The young man in the spotless dress uniform opened the door and backed away.

Stepping through the entrance, Brad saw the admiral. Both Harry and Brad braced at attention. The commander of the task force was conferring with one of his staff members.

Brad had met Rear Adm. Warren Keuseman when the admiral had toured the air-group ready rooms. An engaging individual, Keuseman had a swarthy, rugged appearance. He had a faint scar on his right temple, accentuated by a shock of snow white hair. His freshly laundered khakis had been specially tailored for his fit, trim physique. His uniform sported shiny gold wings and gleaming silver stars.

Keuseman finished his conversation, signed a form, and turned to greet Brad and Harry. "At ease, gentlemen." The voice was pleasant, but there was no mistaking the somber look on Keuseman's face. The pale gray eyes briefly examined the pilot and his radar-intercept officer.

Brad and Harry, in unison, spread their feet and clasped their hands behind them.

"I'm going to be very frank with you." Keuseman paused to let the impact of his words register.

Brad felt a pang of trepidation. What the hell was going to ultimately happen to them? Harry cleared his throat, as he habitually did when he was nervous.

Keuseman walked to his cabin door. "Let's step inside." Brad and Harry followed the admiral into his quarters. Brad was awed by the furnishings. The cabin was richly decorated with cherrywood furniture and fine accessories. Two large original oil paintings of vintage aircraft carriers hung from the gleaming bulkheads.

"This meeting," Keuseman said, gesturing to a luxurious couch, "is informal, and off the record."

Harry and Brad sat down, stealing a quick, questioning glance at each other. Keuseman pulled his overstuffed chair from behind his desk and took a seat. The admiral remained quiet, letting the silence underscore the gravity of the situation.

"You two are in serious trouble."

"Admiral, excuse me, sir, but Lieutenant Hutton is not at fault, sir. I take full responsibility for my actions. He aggressively attempted to talk me out of violating the rules. My knocking down the MiG—Major Dao—was the entire focus of my life at that moment. Nothing else mattered."

Keuseman folded his arms across his chest. "Captain, I am aware of that. Your commanding officer and I had a long conversation after you talked with him. He believes that both of you are fine young officers who stepped over the line in the heat of battle. The main concern is hitting a ground target at an off-limits airfield."

Keuseman picked up the folders containing their military files. "Your records speak for themselves." He studied the pages in Brad's folder, glancing at the pilot, then returning to the service record. "I've known your father a long time, and I respect him very much."

Brad remained quiet.

"Frankly, I am elated that you shot down Dao, but we are caught in the spotlight of a State Department flap because of the unauthorized attack on a restricted airfield. I received word early yesterday morning that the under secretary of the navy has ordered an informal investigation. A representative of the State Department will be in attendance, so it doesn't look good at the moment."

Bolstering his courage, Brad raised his hand slightly. "Admiral, if I resign my commission, can we avoid the hearing, and possible court-martial?"

Unhurried, Keuseman placed the service records on his desk. "I mentioned that avenue to CINCPAC when he chewed me out early this morning. That is not an option."

Examining the admiral, Brad was amazed that he was so calm after having been reprimanded by the commander in chief of the Pacific Fleet.

"All of us," Keuseman continued, "have broken or bent the rules at times, including me. Hell, any fighter pilot worth his salt has gone over the line in combat. However, this incident has gotten the attention of the international press."

Dead silence filled the cabin.

"Personally, I'm proud that we have warriors like your-selves, and I'm extremely pleased that you dispatched Dao. He alone is responsible for downing eight of our aircraft, and I'm happy that you two made sure that he will never get a ninth one."

Keuseman paused, shifting his gaze to Austin. "The fact that you fired a missile at a MiG on the ground is a different story."

Brad cast a look at his RIO. Harry looked straight ahead.

"I told you I was going to be frank, and I am. After discussing this matter with your skipper, I advised CINC-PAC that we could have a real public-relations problem." Keuseman observed the reactions on the officers' faces.

Brad drew a breath. "I'm afraid I don't understand, sir."

A thin smile creased Keuseman's mouth. "Well, with public sentiment being what it is at the present time—not in our favor—it isn't going to be well received in many circles to ground a distinguished aviator who has shot down two MiGs and destroyed a third. The military has a public-relations problem because the media is reporting that we are killing innocent civilians. There won't be any doubt in anyone's mind that Dao was not a civilian. He was flying a fighter plane and shot down your flight leader."

Squeezing his fists tight, Brad felt a small ray of hope.

"CINCPAC doesn't buy it, though. He believes that we have to take steps to ensure that no one breaks the rules of engagement again."

Harry and Brad remained quiet, attempting to contain their fears. If the four-star admiral wanted them nailed to the cross, which he apparently did, they stood little chance of avoiding a court-martial.

"I also explained," Keuseman said, shifting his gaze from Brad to Harry, then back to Brad, "that our growing problem with aircrew morale is going to be exacerbated if we court-martial two MiG killers."

"Admiral," Brad ventured, "everyone is doing his level best, sir, but our hands are tied. Some guys are just trying to survive, while others, like me, are outraged that anyone would compromise us this way."

"Captain Austin, I understand. I really do. Your friends in the squadron, along with the rest of the air-wing troops, feel the same way. There is a general feeling spreading throughout the ship that morale is going to nosedive if you two are court-martialed."

Brad and Harry understood that Keuseman was attempting to comfort them. "Admiral," Brad said in a slow, deliberate manner, "I appreciate that, but we have to maintain discipline. If you like, I will speak to them, and explain that I was wrong and I'll take the consequences."

Keuseman smiled for the first time. "That won't be necessary. I'm going to speak to the aircrews this afternoon. When we are notified of the next step in this investigation, you'll be immediately informed. For the time being, I will remind you that this meeting has been off the record. You are to remain in your stateroom, and don't converse with anyone."

"Yes, sir," they responded, relieved to know that the admiral understood their feelings.

Keuseman stood, prompting Austin and Hutton to rise to attention. The admiral opened the door. "I'm proud of both of you. No matter what happens, I want to personally thank you for bagging Major Dao."

36

MEMPHIS, TENNESSEE

Leigh Ann walked through the trees in the common area behind her parents' home. She could hear the muted sounds of the golfers on the fairway adjacent to the common. A refreshing fall breeze stirred the trees, prompting her to look up at the tops of the swaying branches. A small bird was busy hopping about.

She continued a short distance, then stopped, sure of her decision. Leigh Ann had searched her soul during the long and painful flight home. She knew that Brad was right. It was time for her to take command of her life, and stop trying to fulfill her father's every desire. It was time to grow up, and become an independent woman.

She would confront her father about Brad, and explain that he was a decent, straightforward man who was following his conscience. Leigh Ann was going to explain that she loved Brad, and that he was in trouble and needed her support.

Leigh Ann had been surprised that Brad had not called. She fervently prayed that he had not decided to go his own way, and forget her. After a difficult self-analysis, Leigh Ann had realized that she had been somewhat of a spoiled brat. She longed for an opportunity to tell Brad that she had changed. But most important, she wanted to tell him that she loved him, and backed him, no matter what. She wished that he would call, because she wanted to tell him how she felt in her own words.

What could she do to help him? Leigh Ann considered every possibility. Who had enough power and influence to help Brad out of his predicament? After considerable thought, she concluded that she did not know anyone powerful enough to help the man she loved.

Growing more despondent, Leigh Ann suddenly had an idea. Her father was a close friend of a well-known and highly respected senator. Yes, of course, the chairman of the Armed Services Committee certainly had the necessary influence to help Brad. Besides, Senator Kerwin owed her father a debt of gratitude. Doctor Ladasau had saved the life of the senator's daughter after she had been in a terrible automobile accident.

Buoyed by the possibility of helping Brad, Leigh Ann hurried toward home. Halfway there, she slowed and thought about what Brad would say if she could discuss the matter with him.

She stopped, instinctively knowing what he would say. Brad was not the kind of man to accept favors, or have someone use influence to help him. Brad Austin would prefer to face whatever adversity was dealt to him.

In spite of what she knew would be Brad's objections, she felt an overpowering need to help him. He had not called her, and probably no longer believed in her love for him. Leigh Ann's plan of action was clear.

ON BOARD THE CARRIER

Harry weighed his options, then moved his plastic chess piece across the soiled board. "Checkmate."

Brad smiled and slid a quarter to his friend. "I guess my mind isn't on the game."

"That makes two of us."

Three days had passed without any information about the upcoming hearing. After talking with the task-force commander, their spirits had initially been raised. Now, waiting to find out their fate, Brad and Harry were growing more restless by the hour.

Harry rose and paced the cramped cabin like a caged animal. The strain and tension contorted his face. "God-damnit, I'm going crazy in here. Can't anyone make a decision?"

"Calm yourself, Harry. You're getting upset."

"You're damn right I'm upset," he snapped. "Keeping us confined in a shoe-box room with no windows is chicken shit."

"What do you suggest," Brad asked, trying to cheer his RIO, "a jailbreak?"

"Why don't you kiss my ass?"

Brad frowned. "Look, Harry, I'm sorry for getting you into this. I apologize. That's all I can do."

Harry sat down and sighed. "I'm sorry. Shit, you're my best friend," he managed a chuckle, "even if you are a dumb-ass pilot."

A knock interrupted Brad's reply. He got up and opened the door, then laughed. Harry turned to see Jon O'Meara and Mario Russo standing in the passageway. Jon silently handed Brad a bottle of scotch, while Mario held up a hastily prepared sign that read, "We know you can't talk to us. Cheers. The squadron is behind you guys!"

"Thanks," Brad said, shaking their hands.

Harry leaped up and hugged O'Meara while he shook hands with Russo. "You saved us!" He had a grin plastered across his face. "We owe you a big one."

Brad looked up and down the narrow passageway. "Have you heard any word?"

"Not a thing," O'Meara answered. "Just rumors. If we hear anything, we'll call and let the phone ring once, then call back in forty-five seconds."

"Thanks a million," Brad replied warmly. "We're going absolutely nuts in here."

"No shit," Harry said sarcastically. "You guys have time for a toddy?" He was craving companionship.

"Better not," O'Meara responded, observing the corridor. "If the skipper found out, he'd have us in hack, too."

"Tell everyone," Brad said, handing the bottle to Harry, "that we appreciate their support."

"Will do," Mario smiled. "Hang in there." O'Meara and Russo hurried down the passageway and disappeared around a corner.

Shutting the door, Brad walked to the lavatory and reached for two glasses while Harry opened the scotch. "That," Brad said, steadying his glass while Harry poured, "was damn good of them." They both had a sip before adding water.

"Brad, before we get totally screwed up, what do you think they'll do with us when the ship sails?" The carrier was scheduled to depart for Yankee Station in three days.

"I don't know. If nothing has been resolved, they could confine us to quarters here at Yokosuka, or send us to Pearl Harbor." He took a drink. "Who knows?"

Harry shook his head. "Amazing."

"What?"

"We blasted off this goddamned boat, got the shit shot out of us, downed a MiG flown by a leading ace, dodged the missiles and antiaircraft fire, landed on a pitching deck, and then got thrown in the slammer."

Brad started to speak, but Harry held up his hand. "Wait, that's not the best part."

Laughing out loud for the first time in days, Brad sat down on the lower bunk. The tension that had gripped both of them was suddenly shattered by the mental picture of their ludicrous situation.

"The best part is the fact that if we get out of this bucket of shit we're in," Harry paused to take a drink, "we get to take off and get the shit scared out of us again."

"I know," Brad replied, laughing uproariously. "It seems unfair for us to have all the fun." They looked at each other, then burst out laughing again.

Harry made himself comfortable. "Tell me about Leigh Ann, and your trip to San Francisco. Does she know about this?"

"Oh, yes, she knows the whole story," Brad answered with a pained expression.

"She must've been impressed."

Brad laughed at himself. "Harry, give me a break. I

already feel lower than a snake's belly in a wagon track.''

"Seriously," Harry said with a straight face, "what do you think about her?"

Brad stared into his glass. "I don't know. She has many wonderful traits, but she's difficult to reason with. I really do love her, but we have some complications, not the least of which is her father."

Harry cocked his head and swirled his drink. "You're saying that you didn't charm the hell out of him?"

"He's against the war," Brad replied bitterly, "and apparently not enamored with military people. He's off on the left page somewhere, and I'm certainly not what he has in mind for his daughter."

"Well, have another splash," Harry chuckled. "Things can only go downhill from here."

"Thanks, Harry," Brad responded, giving Hutton a caustic look. "You're a real comfort."

Brad lay awake, staring into the darkness while he listened to the hoarse breathing from the top bunk. Thinking about Bull Durham and Russ Lunsford made his situation seem relatively insignificant. How long would they be held captive? Would they survive the ordeal, or die from being tortured and malnourished? As hard as he tried, Brad could not shake the remorse that he felt for his friends in captivity.

He had received a pleasant letter from Cordelia Durham. She had included her mother's telephone number, and had requested that Brad call her again when he had an opportunity. She had told him about her move to her mother's home the day after Brad's previous call, and how well her pregnancy was progressing. Cordelia had avoided talking about her husband until the last sentence of the letter. She had simply said, "God, I miss Lincoln."

Suddenly, the waist catapult fired with a boom and slammed into the water brakes with a resounding thud. The impact caused the carrier to shudder.

"Holy Christ," Harry said, sleepily turning on his reading light. "What the hell is going on?"

Brad got out of bed and turned on the light. "They're exercising the cats."

"Well, the shitbirds picked a helluva time to do it."

After checking the time, Brad grabbed his soap, shampoo, and towel. "I'm going to take a shower before our breakfast is served."

Harry mumbled and closed his eyes, drifting in and out of sleep until Brad returned.

While Brad dressed, Harry crawled out of his bunk and ambled to the head. A few minutes later, a wardroom steward delivered their breakfast in containers covered with aluminum foil.

Brad waited for Harry to return before opening his meal. They were in the middle of their first bite when they heard a knock on the door. "Come in," Harry said after swallowing.

Commander Dan Bailey opened the door, startling the two men. Brad and Harry started to jump to their feet.

"As you were," Bailey ordered, taking a seat next to Brad on the lower bunk. He pulled a cigar from his pocket, lighting it while he observed Brad and Harry. Neither man said a word, quietly placing their forks on the paper plates.

"Well, gentlemen," he inhaled slowly, "your future is currently being discussed in the admiral's quarters."

The telephone rang, interrupting the CO. Brad and Harry looked at each other in alarm. Was it Jon and Mario? Bailey gave them a questioning look when neither of them made an attempt to answer the phone. Brad reached for it, removing his hand when it did not ring again.

Smiling, Bailey blew a ring of smoke. "You might as well answer next time. I'm sure your informer has some interesting news to pass along." Bailey watched the red creep into their faces. "It'll save me from being interrupted again."

Twelve seconds later the telephone rang again, shattering the quiet in the tension-filled room. "Give them my regards," Bailey said, watching Brad attempt to contain a laugh.

"Captain Austin," he answered, turning his face away

from the CO. "Hi. Hey, the skipper just stopped by . . . said to give you his regards."

Harry coughed and replaced the aluminum foil over his meal.

"I sure will. Thanks again," Brad said, hurriedly replacing the receiver.

Bailey turned serious. "The representative from the State Department, with his entourage in tow, just came aboard a few minutes ago. They're talking with the admiral as we speak."

Brad and Harry sat, unblinking, hanging on every word. This was it. The time to face the consequences had arrived with sudden finality.

"I don't know anything else at the moment," Bailey continued in a friendly, fatherly way, "but I'd advise you to be ready for inspection."

"Yes, sir," they answered, setting their meals aside.

"I can tell you this," Bailey said, glancing around their stateroom, "I put in all the good words I could, and the admiral is in your corner, believe me."

Bailey watched the happy reaction on their faces. "He's a fighter jock from the old school," Bailey paused and stood, "and you endeared yourselves to him by eliminating Nguyen Dao."

"Thanks, Skipper," Brad said, extending his hand, "no matter what happens."

Bailey shook both their hands. "Just tell your story, and don't bullshit anyone."

"Yes, sir."

Nodding his head, the CO left the room.

"Well, partner," Brad said, "put on your flak jacket, and stand by for action."

37

The flag bridge was unusually crowded when Brad and Harry were asked into the admiral's cabin. The commander who had invited them in told the two men to stand at ease.

Admiral Keuseman sat at his desk, flanked by a beefy civilian in a wrinkled seersucker suit and a navy captain in dress blues. The civilian, who had a sour look on his face, removed his thick glasses and slowly ran his eyes over the two fliers. His scrutiny made them even more uncomfortable.

"Good morning, gentlemen," the admiral said pleasantly, as the commander and another civilian stepped out of the cabin and closed the door.

"Good morning, Admiral," Brad replied while Harry nodded his head. Brad was familiar with the procedures involved in military hearings and investigations. He had studied the procedures at length, and had served as a member of an investigation board. This hearing was far different from anything he had read about or experienced.

Harry had the same unsettling feeling. Something strange was happening. The atmosphere in the spacious cabin was strained.

"Have a seat," Keuseman ordered, motioning toward the couch. "This is Mister Ogilvie, from the State Department, and Captain Emmett from CINCPAC."

Harry and Brad acknowledged the introductions. The captain sat stone still, examining Austin. The two strangers recognized the pilot and his RIO from the photographs that accompanied their service records.

The admiral shifted his chair. "I'm going to turn this over to Captain Emmett. John?"

The stern-looking man wearing the insignia of a submariner moved forward in his chair. "The first thing we have to establish," the former submarine commander paused, "is that the two of you did, in fact, commit a transgression by flying over an unauthorized air base and destroying an enemy fighter on the ground."

Emmett bore in on Brad. "Is that exactly what happened, Captain Austin"

"Not quite, sir."

The submariner's eyes narrowed. "Did you, or did you not, shoot down a MiG and attack a taxiing fighter at Phuc Yen? That's what I see in both the message and the report I'm holding."

"Yes, I shot down the fighter over Phuc Yen, and fired at an aircraft on the ground," Brad darted a look at the admiral, "but I trust you will give me an opportunity to explain the extenuating circumstances."

Emmett's facial expression reflected irritation. "Talk, Captain. Explain your breach of the regulations, and make it succinct. We are on a tight schedule."

Brad drew a quick breath. "Captain, the airborne MiG in question was flown by Major Dao, North Vietnam's second-leading ace. In the heat of the battle, my close friends—my flight leader and his RIO—were shot down by Major Dao."

"That fact, no matter how tragic," Emmett frowned, "did not give you license to attack a restricted area."

Harry shifted uncomfortably but contained his nervous cough. He focused on a plaque over the admiral's head.

"May I finish, Captain?" Brad asked, drawing a sharp look from Emmett.

"We're waiting."

Speaking clearly, Brad stared back at Emmett. "I would assume, sir, from seeing the dolphins on your chest, that you have never flown a fighter in combat."

Emmett gave him a cold, menacing look. "You're walking a fine line, Captain, and it would serve you well to remember that fact."

Admiral Keuseman arched his eyebrows, giving Brad a silent warning.

"Captain Emmett, this was not a premeditated act. I didn't go to Phuc Yen with the intent of shooting up the field or dropping ordnance on anyone. My intent was to kill a MiG ace. I reacted instantaneously, focused on one mission—to kill Major Dao before he added a ninth airplane and crew to his credit."

Harry finally coughed.

"Sir," Brad continued, trying to keep his emotions in check, "I was determined to destroy Dao, and I chased him down. I didn't have any control over where his airplane crashed." Brad took a deep breath. "I was wrong to shoot at the aircraft on the ground."

Silence filled the room. Emmett rolled a pencil back and forth between his palms. "Lieutenant Hutton, is that exactly what happened?"

Harry braced himself and spoke in a confident voice. "Yes, sir, that is precisely what happened."

"I understand," Emmett perused his notes, "from reading your statements in the report that you tried to talk Captain Austin out of breaking the rules and flying over a restricted airfield. Is that true?"

Taking his time, Harry formed an answer. "I pointed out various options in regard to the restrictions we have to deal with. Low to the ground, in the middle of a supersonic dogfight, is not the time to distract your pilot."

"Answer yes or no," Emmett spat. "Did you attempt to talk Captain Austin out of breaking the rules of engagement?"

"Yes, sir."

Emmett folded his hands and stared at Brad for what seemed an eternity. He had used the tactic many times to break the resolve of individuals whom he had investigated.

"Captain Austin," Emmett said, scribbling a hasty note. "We have established, by your own admission, that you did commit a breach of the rules of engagement."

Brad felt the tension increasing throughout his body. "That is correct, Captain. I broke the rules because we are warriors without competent civilian leadership. We the people of our country need clear objectives in this war. We're wasting a hell of a lot of lives because of the flawed policies emanating from the civilians in the White House.''

"You,'' Ogilvie shot back, pointing a pen at Brad, "are in deep trouble. I suggest that you keep that in mind, and conduct yourself accordingly.''

Austin remained silent, staring back at the State Department official.

"Brad,'' Admiral Keuseman said with a firm voice, "I understand your feelings, but you will cooperate fully.''

"Yes, sir.''

"Captain,'' Emmett continued, "have you broken the rules of engagement before this incident?''

"No, sir, I have not.''

Emmett turned to face Harry. "Is that correct, Lieutenant?''

"That,'' Harry stammered, "was my first flight with Captain Austin. I know him well, and he doesn't disregard rules.''

Emmett swiveled to ask Keuseman a question. "Admiral, I'd like to hear from Captain Austin's usual RIO.''

"John,'' Keuseman frowned, "his former RIO, Lieutenant Lunsford, was in the flight leader's aircraft. As you know, the crew was captured as soon as they landed.''

Emmett jotted another note. "Captain Austin, CINCPAC would like to hang your ass out to dry, but there are complications. I'll let Mister Ogilvie explain the situation, then we'll discuss your future.''

Harry gently tapped the sole of Brad's shoe. Neither man showed outwardly the glow of hope they felt inside.

The State Department representative opened his attaché case and removed a piece of paper. He gave Brad a frigid look. "Captain, for political reasons, the State Department has been directed to deny that the incident at Phuc Yen ever happened. The mandate originated in the White House.''

Wide-eyed, Harry and Brad glanced at each other. Washington was going to cover up the incident.

"The official stance,'' Ogilvie grunted, "is simply that

Phuc Yen was an attempt to discredit the United States. The matter is being regarded as a propaganda stunt in their disinformation campaign.'' He read from the top-secret message. '' 'An attempt to exploit the Communist doctrine, and tarnish the image of our government.' ''

Brad inwardly breathed a sigh of relief. What did Captain Hard-ass have up his sleeve?

Ogilvie placed the message back in his attaché case. ''I have been given explicit instructions to relay to both of you.''

Harry and Brad digested each word.

''The incident never happened. Do you both clearly understand?''

''Yes, sir,'' they answered, trying to contain their excitement. The State Department and the politicos in the White House were going to actually deny that Brad had shot down North Vietnam's second leading ace.

''The two of you,'' Ogilvie pointed his pen again, ''are not going to mention the incident, or this meeting, to anyone.'' He paused for effect. ''Is that crystal clear?''

''We understand,'' Brad answered for both of them. ''If someone asks us questions, how are we to respond?''

Ogilvie looked at Brad, then Harry. ''This didn't happen. Your names have not been divulged. They slammed a lid on this at the very top. If you are approached by anyone—the press or your associates—you had better keep your mouths shut, if you have any smattering of intelligence.''

Brad flared, but quickly controlled his emotions. This was not the time to enter into a skirmish. For whatever reason, they had been spared from a certain court-martial.

Emmett took his cue. ''The media is going to be scrutinizing this carrier until you put to sea. If you know what's good for you, you'll blend into obscurity and keep a low profile.''

Harry and Brad nodded understandingly.

''Nothing,'' Emmett emphasized, darting a cold look at Ogilvie, ''will be placed in your records. However, Captain Austin, you are going to be quietly transferred back to the marines near the completion of the next at-sea period.'' The contempt was evident on Emmett's face. "Any questions?"

"No, sir," Brad replied with relief.

Ogilvie and Emmett rose from their chairs. "Thank you, Admiral," Emmett said, shaking hands with Keuseman. "We appreciate your cooperation."

Harry and Brad stood to attention.

"You're certainly welcome, John. Please tell the admiral hello."

"Will do, sir."

Ogilvie shook hands with Keuseman, thanked him, then followed Emmett out of the cabin.

When the door closed, Keuseman walked to the coffee urn. "Have a seat."

Brad and Harry sat down, unsure of what was going to happen next. The only thing certain was the knowledge that they would not be facing a court-martial.

Keuseman poured a cup half full. "Coffee?"

"No thank you, sir," Brad replied, realizing that he was too nervous to hold a cup steady.

Harry responded with a negative gesture of his hand. "No thanks, sir."

The admiral returned to his chair. "Well, gentlemen, you dodged a big one." There was no indication of victory on Keuseman's serious face. "But that's water under the keel." He slid his cup to the side and folded his hands on his desk. "Now, we need to address your collective futures."

They sat in silence, waiting to know their fate.

"First, I want to tell you—as a crew—that I'm proud to have you in the air wing."

They both breathed easier.

"I know this has been a rough ordeal, but it could have been much worse, believe me." Keuseman measured the two officers. "Off the record, there are cabinet-level negotiations currently in progress, accompanied by the usual posturing. The White House is trying to get the Hanoi regime to the bargaining table, at any cost. There are a number of sensitive issues being discussed, and your incident set off a series of events that could have jeopardized those negotiations. There have been a number of accusations lobbed from both sides.

"That's all I know, but I agree with Mr. Ogilvie—the two of you had better keep a low profile."

The admiral tried his coffee. "Captain, I would suspect, provided everything blows over, that when you return to your marine squadron, your record will be clean. They will have no knowledge of this incident. That assumes, of course, that you keep your nose clean until we get through this next at-sea period."

Keuseman smiled for the first time. "Commander Bailey is a good man, and he thinks a lot of both of you."

"Thank you, Admiral," Brad and Harry said, feeling as though they had survived a plunge over Niagara Falls.

"Just play by the rules from here on out."

Keuseman read the smiles on their faces, remembering a time in the past when an admiral had gone to bat for him. Keuseman had flown an F-9F Panther jet into a restricted area over Korea in an effort to strafe a train. A ground officer had witnessed the strafing run and had reported the incident. Keuseman had barely escaped losing his wings.

"I believe your CO will want to visit with you," Keuseman said, reaching for his phone. "I'll let him know that you're on your way to his stateroom."

"Thank you, Admiral," Brad and Harry said in chorus as they stood to attention.

"Stay out of trouble," Keuseman chuckled.

Dan Bailey leaned back and took the unlighted cigar out of his mouth. "I'm going to make this short and sweet."

Harry and Brad remained standing just inside the CO's stateroom.

"I don't know all the particulars, but suffice it to say that no one knows about Phuc Yen and the two MiGs." Bailey clamped his hands together behind his neck. "You," he looked at Brad, "are very fortunate, and don't forget that fact. One more feat of unusual skill or daring—one more claim to notoriety—and you will be history."

Brad swallowed. "I understand, sir."

"When you return to your squadron, you can be as infamous as you want to be. Until then, you had better be as squeaky clean as a virgin in church."

Brad nodded but remained quiet. Harry was filled with excitement and relief, but he managed to keep the grin off his face and his emotions under control.

"Now," Bailey continued, reaching for his cigar, "we have a squadron party to attend."

Harry and Brad looked puzzled. They had just avoided a court-martial and now they were going to a party?

"Due to the media scrutiny about Phuc Yen, everyone has been encouraged to enjoy as much liberty as possible. There are only a handful of people who know the truth, so the media will get every conceivable rumor. That will help debunk the story."

Bailey studied their reaction. "The two of you don't know anything. You are directed not to discuss the incident with anyone." His voice rose in pitch. "That means don't even talk to each other about your screwup."

They both winced. "Yessir."

"When you get older, you'll have plenty of time to tell the story to your grandchildren. We shove off in less than seventy-two hours, so I figure we can take half of that time for a party."

Bailey, seeing the small smiles spreading on their faces, decided not to mention the upcoming missions. The air war was heating up, and enemy air defenses were proliferating at an alarming rate.

"Ernie Sheridan has commandeered a bus from special services, so we're going to Kamakura most rikky-tik."

"Kamakura?" Harry asked, vaguely remembering the name.

"It's a small village across the peninsula by Sagami Bay. Ernie has reserved a block of rooms at a hotel, and the entire dining room and bar is exclusively ours."

"What can we do to help, Skipper?" Brad asked, but without enthusiasm. He was happy about being out of hack but still worried that he might get the ax. He also was desperate to get to a telephone and call Leigh Ann. He wanted her to know that the court-martial threat had been removed.

"Not a thing, except show up in the ready room in an hour and twenty minutes."

"Yes, sir," Harry answered gleefully.

"One other thing," Bailey said, thinking about the excitement when he announced the party, "we're going for the purpose of having a great time. Plan to return tomorrow afternoon. One word of caution, however."

Brad and Harry stopped smiling.

"I've told everyone that I don't want the place destroyed, and if there is any damage, everyone is going to ante up to pay for it. Clear?"

"Yes, sir," they both said.

"Better go pack," Bailey smiled, getting to his feet. "You have time to grab a bite and a few beers at the club before we leave."

"Thanks, Skipper," Brad replied, reaching for the doorknob, "and thanks for sticking up for us."

"Hell, I had to," Bailey responded, clamping a hand on each of their shoulders. "Just think how boring my life would be if they carted you two off to the dungeon."

38

The Japanese bartender opened another beer and sat it in front of Harry. Absorbed in his thoughts, Harry ignored the man and casually dabbled with his eggs and corned-beef hash. They had made it. The threat of facing a court-martial had evaporated. For the next two days they were free from the military and the associated confinements. Free to get falling-down drunk and enjoy a good laugh.

Harry glanced at Brad when he returned from the row of pay telephones. "Did you get in touch with her?"

Brad signaled for a beer. "Yes. Her mother answered the phone and gave me Leigh Ann's new phone number."

Harry looked curious. "Her new number?"

"Yes," Brad sighed. "It seems that Leigh Ann and her father had a falling out, and she moved into an apartment."

"Harmony on the home front," Harry grinned. "What's her mother's temperature?"

Brad gave Harry a callous look, then reached for his beer. "Her mother is very nice, and we get along great."

Harry swiveled toward Brad. "Back to Leigh Ann."

"She wasn't home, so I'll try later."

Harry smiled, shoving his plate away. "Do you think the romance is still budding?"

Tilting his bottle up, Brad paused. "I don't know. I wish I could talk to her."

"Well," Harry said, "don't force the issue. If it happens, it happens."

Brad smiled, then slowly turned to Harry. "You have the

unmitigated gall to advise me on my love life when yours resembles a train wreck?''

''Just trying to help.''

Leaning on the bar, Brad turned serious. ''I also called Bull's wife, Cordelia.''

''Really? How is she?''

''Under the circumstances,'' Brad replied, lowering his head, ''she's doing okay. Cordy is staying with her mother for a while.'' He cringed inwardly, seeing the faces of Bull and Russ in his mind, and imagining what they were going through. ''She's pregnant.''

''You're kidding.''

''No. Bull told me about . . . '' Brad's voice trailed off as he felt his emotions boil to the surface. ''Cordy is a strong woman. She'll make it.''

Sensing Brad's moral anguish and regret, Harry finished his beer in two gulps. ''Come on, my front-seat chauffeur, and let's get our shit in one bag. We've got a bus to catch.''

Leigh Ann turned off the interstate highway and drove north toward a bend in the Tennessee River. She had called Senator Arlin Kerwin's residence near Nashville, only to be informed that he was at his lodge on the river.

The senator's housekeeper had relayed Leigh Ann's request, explaining that the lady was the daughter of Dr. Simon Ladasau.

After a suspenseful wait, the phone had rung in Leigh Ann's apartment. She had been ebullient when the senator had invited her to his lodge to discuss the urgent problem.

Slowing to enter the senator's compound, Leigh Ann realized that it had been twelve years since she had last been to the lodge. As her car passed the gate leading to the manicured grounds, it kicked up dried leaves, spinning them slowly back to the earth. Leigh Ann stopped near the double front doors, composed herself, then got out and walked toward the porch. When she was halfway up the steps, Sen. Arlin Kerwin opened one of the massive doors.

''Good to see you, young lady,'' he greeted in his

booming voice. Short and gruff, the statesman was the consummate politician.

"Hello, Senator," Leigh Ann replied tentatively. "I'm sorry to disturb you, but I need your assistance."

"Happy to give it," he laughed as Leigh Ann walked into the spacious living room. "It's been what—ten to twelve years since I've seen you? Why, you weren't any taller than this," he said, holding the palm of his hand four feet above the floor. "How are your folks?"

"They're fine," she answered, feeling uneasy. Kerwin's wife had recently passed away. "Dad's slowly retiring, and Mom's as busy as ever."

"Good. Have a seat, honey, and I'll get us some lemonade." He turned to go to the kitchen. "You still like lemonade?"

"Yes, I sure do," Leigh Ann answered, surprised that Kerwin had remembered her fondness for his special concoction. She sat on the overstuffed couch and looked around.

Leigh Ann examined the stone fireplace and thick animal skins arrayed on the highly polished wood floor. A moment later, Kerwin brought their drinks into the room.

"Now, tell me," Kerwin said as he sat in his favorite recliner, "what's bothering you?"

Suddenly unsure of herself, Leigh Ann began slowly, then told Kerwin the entire story. How she had met Brad, and what had happened at Phuc Yen. That he was a conscientious and courageous person who was facing a court-martial for standing up for his country.

Close to tears, Leigh Ann stopped. She felt an over-whelming guilt about turning her back to Brad when he had most needed her.

"Just a minute, honey," Kerwin interrupted, rising from his chair. "Let me get a pad and pen." He gave her an assuring smile. "At my age, I have to write everything down, or I'll forget some of the details."

Leigh Ann placed her lemonade on the coffee table and dabbed her eyes. She was beginning to wonder if she was doing the right thing. What if she caused Brad more trouble?

"Okay," Kerwin said, sitting down, "let's get all the facts, then I'll make some inquiries."

After Leigh Ann had given him the pertinent information, the senator had pledged to look into the matter. He had assured her that he would do everything in his power to right any injustice.

What Kerwin had not disclosed were his own political motives for disagreeing with the restrictions being put on the men fighting the war. He had an ongoing argument with members of the White House in regard to how the war was being handled.

When Austin and Hutton left the squadron ready room, their assignment was to stop at the dirty-shirt wardroom and get four large bags of ice.

Arriving at the navy bus, they dumped the ice into a canvas seabag containing five cases of beer. A poker game was already under way in the back of the cluttered vehicle. The mood was festive, reminding Brad of fraternity parties he had attended on civilian campuses.

After Dan Bailey and Jack Carella stepped aboard, the youthful Japanese driver adroitly turned the bus around and headed for the main roadway to Kamakura. Every time the driver let up on the gas pedal, the engine backfired, startling pedestrians along the side of the narrow road.

Brad and Harry sat together, joining in the boisterous party. They relaxed and left the air war behind them, concentrating on not spilling their beer when the bus rocked from side to side.

Halfway to Kamakura, Jon O'Meara nudged Hutton from the seat behind Brad and Harry. "You guys want to have a little excitement?"

"No," Harry replied, shaking his head, "you're not going to drive the bus."

O'Meara gripped Harry's shoulder. "Let's climb on the roof," he glanced at Brad, "and get some sun."

Wide-eyed, Harry belly-laughed. "Are you crazy? What if we fall off?"

Brad chuckled, looking forward to see what Dan Bailey and Jocko Carella were doing.

"We're not going to fall off. Just sit on the window, grab the luggage railing, and pull yourself up." O'Meara turned to his RIO. "Right, Mario?"

"Piece of cake."

Brad edged around in his seat. "We've had about all the excitement we need for a while. We're walking on ice so thin, if we sneeze, we'll fall straight through."

"Yeah," Harry said, "the skipper'll have a heart attack if he finds out you're on top of the bus."

"Okay," O'Meara smiled, checking to see if Bailey was engaged in conversation, "then at least keep us supplied with beer."

"We'll take care of it," Brad replied, reaching for their beers. "Don't bust your asses."

"We've got it under control."

Amid raucous laughter, O'Meara and Russo hoisted themselves on top of the vehicle, then reached down for their beers. Propped against the luggage retainers, Jon and Mario watched the scenery and waved at passing motorists.

Life was good again, the sun was warm, and the beer was cold. They had two days to recapture their youth, be totally irresponsible, and live life to the hilt. Harry and Brad kept Mario and Jon supplied with fresh beers, collecting the empty bottles for the trash container.

Approaching Kamakura, O'Meara and Russo heard their frollicking squadron mates break out in song. The morbid chorus was sung to the tune of the "Battle Hymn of the Republic." Mario and Jon sipped their beers and listened.

He rolled out on final and was just a little low.
He ignored the wave-off of the frantic LSO.
When he finally added power, he was just a little slow.
And he'll never fly home again.

Gory, gory, what a hell of a way to die.
Son of a gory, gory, what a hell of a way to die.
Gory, gory, what a hell of a way to die.

And he'll never fly home again.

He should have added power when he pulled back on the stick.
He should have flown it like a bird instead of like a brick.
Now all that's left of him is just a little oil slick.
And he'll never fly home again.

Brad and Harry joined in the loud singing, which went on for several verses. As the beer flowed, the noise level increased.

Harry punched Brad in the side. "This is certainly an uplifting little tune."

Brad turned and smiled. "Hey, in this business, you don't buy any green bananas."

Harry looked disgusted. "What a cheerful thought."

The bus rolled to a smooth stop as the last chorus was ending. Jon O'Meara looked at the small, pristine hotel, then turned to Mario.

"We'll just toss the skipper a salute."

A second later, the door squeaked open and Dan Baily stepped out. He walked a few feet, then turned to speak to Jack Carella. The first word was barely out of his mouth when he froze in place. "Christ almighty . . . ," he said, looking up at what had caught his eye.

Carella glanced at the roof of the bus. "Jesus."

Standing at attention, Jon and Mario clutched their beer bottles in their left hands, then snapped a salute to Bailey and Carella.

Shaking his head, Bailey ignored the salute and turned to his executive officer. "I need a tall drink."

Dressed in their party suits, the pilots and RIOs were finishing the last of the sushi and tempura. The custom-tailored navy blue flight suits were adorned with embroidered gold wings and the owner's name and rank. An American flag patch was sewn on the top of the left sleeve of each party suit. On the right sleeve, just below the shoulder, a round patch proclaimed that the flier was a member of the Tonkin Gulf Yacht Club.

The noisy conversation around the dining table came to an abrupt halt when Bailey stood and tapped his glass. "Gentlemen," he said with a straight face, "please rise for a toast."

He waited until everyone filled their sake cups, then raised his cup. "To the United States Navy," he paused, glancing at Brad, "and, God help them, the United States Marine Corps."

The men laughed, darting a look at Austin.

Drinking half of his sake, Brad raised his cup. "To Bull and Russ—to their freedom."

"To Bull and Russ," the group chimed in, downing their warm sake. Following Bailey's lead, the men sat down and continued with their conversations.

Brad had been relieved that no one, including O'Meara and Russo, had asked about the Phuc Yen incident. The CO had obviously instilled the fear of God in the squadron.

This outing, Brad thought, had been designed to serve many purposes. A squadron party was always a great diversion before going to battle. The evening of celebration, away from the officers' club and Yokosuka, also served another purpose. The CO could maintain close surveillance over the group, ensuring that no one conversed about the Phuc Yen and Major Dao rumors. Once the carrier was at sea, the stories would slowly drift into oblivion.

"Let the show begin," Dan Bailey ordered.

The flight crews, with the assistance of the four Japanese waitresses, cleared the tables and rearranged the furniture in the combination dining room and bar.

After everyone's drinks had been refilled, the first skit was performed. The funny parody of a day in the life of a squadron CO brought howls of laughter.

Next, Ernie Sheridan placed a record on the dilapidated squadron record player. When the bump and grind music started, Mario Russo stepped from behind the screen wearing a yellow raincoat and cowboy boots. His awkward attempt to imitate a striptease dancer made everyone groan. The room erupted in laughter when he whipped off the raincoat. The sight of him wearing purple underwear, supported by pink suspenders, sent the giggling waitresses scrambling from the smoke-filled room.

"Get the hook!" Dirty Ernie yelled over the whistles and laughter. "Get him off the stage!" Outbursts of laughter and catcalls accompanied the end of the pathetic performance.

After the animal acts were over, Ernie Sheridan cranked up the volume and placed another record on the ancient machine. When "Wild Thing" blasted from the speaker, the serious drinking started.

Brad slipped out of the noisy room and walked through the lobby to the entrance. Stepping outside, he looked up at the moon and thought about Leigh Ann. He reached for his dog tags and pulled out the pendant she had given him in Hawaii. He looked at the tiny ornament in the pale moon-light. Would he live to see her again? Would she care?

The ambulatory helped their shipmates to the waiting bus. A light mist fell from the low overcast as Dan Bailey addressed the men who had not fallen asleep in their seats.

"One thing," he grinned, slipping his sunglasses down to peer over the top. "There will be no riding on the roof of the bus. Got that?"

"Skipper," Dirty Ernie moaned, gesturing toward the inert bodies of O'Meara and Russo, "I don't think you'll have to worry about that."

Harry and Brad managed a weak chuckle. They were bone tired, dehydrated, and had splitting headaches from the quarts of hot sake they had consumed.

The trip back to the carrier was quiet and uneventful. After arriving at the dock, the scraggly looking group boarded the ship and headed for their staterooms.

Brad opened their cabin door and plopped his overnight bag on the desk. Harry closed the door and sagged into the desk chair.

"Care for a drink?" Brad asked cheerfully.

Harry gave him a cold look. "Don't ever let me do that again." He studied Brad's face for a moment. "You look like you're bleeding to death through your eyeballs."

"I feel like I am."

WASHINGTON, D.C.

As good as his word, the scrappy chairman of the Armed Services Committee had confronted the administration about the alleged incident at Phuc Yen. He had gone straight to the White House after his plane had landed at Washington National Airport.

Kerwin had threatened to initiate a hearing and call a press conference if the administration did not level with him.

After being rebuffed by the secretary of state, Kerwin had called for a hearing to discuss the rules of engagement, and to resolve the status of marine Capt. Brad Austin.

The secretary of state quickly confronted Kerwin, giving him a stern warning that his inquiry could jeopardize the ongoing peace negotiations. The secretary assured the senator that Captain Austin's record was clean and that the matter had been concluded to everyone's satisfaction.

Sensing a cover-up, Kerwin was more resolved than ever to get to the bottom of the matter. He had been outraged that a heroic fighter pilot who had laid his life on the line, and who had apparently been responsible for destroying at least three MiGs, was being penalized.

The most disturbing disclosure, Kerwin had told the secretary, was that the American people were being misinformed. The senator had explained that this was not an issue over one pilot's transgression. This was an issue dealing with continued implementation of a flawed war policy.

Kerwin had strongly reiterated his position on openness, and informed the secretary of his intention to convene a hearing at the earliest possible date. Phuc Yen was not to be forgotten.

39

The hazy sun was barely above the horizon when the mammoth flattop cleared the pier. After the tugboats had finished positioning the ship, the carrier got under way. The smaller craft in the bay steered well clear of the behemoth as she gathered speed.

An hour later the carrier cleared Tokyo Bay and rendezvoused with her escort ships. The destroyers spread out and quickly positioned themselves around the carrier. The task force turned southwest for the long journey to Yankee Station in the South China Sea.

The carrier was a beehive of activity as all hands prepared for the high intensity of combat operations. In the hangar bay, men crawled over and under the airplanes, cleaning canopies and conducting preventive maintenance.

On the flight deck, the catapult and arresting-gear crews worked tirelessly to prepare their equipment for air operations. Aircraft handlers shuffled airplanes in preparation for the first launch.

Brad walked through the enlisted men's chow hall, noting the activity. The men sat at their tables, calmly eating and talking, while ordnance personnel wheeled bombs through the center of the room.

After negotiating a series of staircases, Brad went to the ready room for the CO's operational brief. Taking a seat next to Jon O'Meara, Brad placed his notepad on his thigh and extracted a ballpoint pen from his pocket. ''I see that you survived.''

"If I make it through the next twenty-four hours," O'Meara yawned, "I think I'll live."

"Where's Mario?"

"He's hard down, so I told the skipper I would take copious notes and thoroughly brief him."

A group of men, including Harry Hutton, entered the room seconds before Dan Bailey walked in.

Bailey joked with a few men, then approached the podium. His pleasant look disappeared, replaced by a grim scowl. The crowded room became deathly quiet.

"I have just returned from a meeting with CAG," he announced uncomfortably. "We're going to have some tough duty for the foreseeable future."

Brad watched Bailey's gestures, absorbing the gist of his message. How could the air war get any worse?

"The situation is heating up," Bailey continued, looking at the sea of somber faces. "There has been a marked increase in the number of cargo ships entering Haiphong harbor. The shipping activity is going on around the clock. From what intelligence says, at least fifty to sixty percent of the vessels are off-loading huge quantities of SAMs and antiaircraft guns."

Bailey looked into the eyes of his charges. "We are going to make a concerted effort to obliterate certain strategic sites, because the White House wants to get the North Vietnamese to capitulate. If we allow the missile and triple-A emplacements to proliferate, our job is going to get a lot more difficult."

"And deadly," Brad stated in a matter-of-fact voice.

"You're right," Bailey replied, turning his attention to Austin, then back to the group. "I know what you want to ask. Why don't we bomb the cargo ships?"

Brad nodded affirmatively with the majority of the other men.

"I share your frustrations," Bailey said, looking around the room, "but they remain off-limits."

Brad indicated that he had a question.

"Yes, Captain."

"Skipper," he began, feeling Bailey's eyes boring into

him, "don't take me wrong. I just want to know something."

"Brad," the CO said patiently, "as long as our government guarantees safe passage to foreign vessels, Uncle Ho is going to conduct business with them, and some of the ships will obviously be hauling weapons."

Exasperated, Bailey took a deep breath and blew it out. "It's that simple, Brad."

The ready room remained silent for a few moments before the CO regained his composure. He ached inside, knowing that his men were right and he could not do anything to correct the abysmal situation. His responsibility was to train the crews and prepare them for aerial combat, then send them off the carrier and into battle.

"Okay," Bailey continued, blanking out his feelings of contempt, "here is what we're going to be facing. More missions and more SAMs, flak, and missiles. The heat is going to be turned on the North Vietnamese, and we're the ones who are going to increase the flames."

He looked at O'Meara and Austin, then scanned the entire room. "We're going to start warm-ups, back-in-the-saddle stuff, and get honed to a razor's edge before we hit Yankee Station."

The frown returned. "Any questions, gentlemen?"

No one spoke.

For three days the air wing had flown around the clock. The flight crews had conducted refresher training, along with day and night carrier qualifications. One KA-3B tanker had been damaged when the nose gear collapsed during a hard landing.

General quarters had sounded on two different nights, keeping the crew at the peak of readiness. There was a feeling of esprit de corps throughout the ship.

Fire drills and man-overboard drills had been practiced during flight operations. The ship's captain had been pleased with the results, and had rewarded the crew with a picnic on the flight deck prior to entering the Gulf of Tonkin.

Fourteen hours later, the task force had arrived on station, and the deadly business of war commenced.

Brad entered the cluttered locker room and opened his combination lock. The mood was somber as the crews went through their preflight ritual.

The mission brief and intelligence summarization had been depressing. Haiphong harbor was full of Soviet, Polish, Chinese, and North Vietnamese ships. Some were tied to the piers; others were moored to buoys in the harbor. Hundreds of dock laborers were unloading stockpiles of weapons, including Soviet-made SA-2 Guideline surface-to-air missiles.

The prohibited areas and sanctuaries around Hanoi and Haiphong were ringed with SAM and antiaircraft emplacements. The dams and dikes that had been declared prohibited targets were now stacked with petroleum supplies and lined with missiles and triple-A guns.

Hutton walked to the locker next to Brad and leaned against it. "Why are we doing this?"

"We, as in you and me, or we, as in the Tuesday luncheon group in the White House?"

Looking forlorn, Harry fixed Brad in his gaze.

"Harry," Brad said stoically, "I've got the mystery figured out. Came to me in a supernatural experience."

A slight grin changed Harry's sad look.

"McNamara and his whiz kids own construction companies in the Republic of North Vietnam."

Hutton closed his eyes and chuckled.

"No, think about it. We bomb the dog shit out of dozens of meaningless targets, then stand down for whatever period of time it takes to rebuild them."

Brad's voice rose slightly. "Then, after everything has been remodeled," he lightly poked Harry, "Mac and his stooges telegraph the gomers to get the hell out of the way, because the first team needs some target practice."

Harry stopped smiling. "Brad, are you okay?"

"Do I look okay?"

"I'm serious."

"So am I," Brad replied, checking his newly issued .38-caliber revolver. "I couldn't be happier if I'd just won the Irish Sweepstakes and the Nobel prize."

"Maybe," Harry said cautiously, "you should ground yourself for a few days."

"No, I don't need to ground myself. I need to permanently ground every MiG pilot in North Vietnam, then I'll take a day off."

"You're losing it, my friend."

Brad emptied his pockets and placed their contents on the top shelf of the locker. He removed his academy ring and dropped it in the sleeve pocket of his flight suit, along with fifty American dollars.

Feeling his dog tags and Leigh Ann's pendant, Brad reached for his g suit. "Are you going with me, or have you decided to sit this one out?"

"Yeah, I'm going," Harry replied, reluctantly opening his locker. "What choice do we have?"

Brad zipped his g suit tight and reached for his custom-made torso harness. The snug-fitting harness would be attached to fittings on the ejection seat.

Inspecting his locker, Brad examined the small red-and-gold box at the back of the shelf, making sure it was intact. Inside the box was a crisp one-hundred-dollar bill for his squadron mates to buy a round of drinks if he did not return from a mission.

Reaching for his helmet, Brad paused, then turned to his RIO. "Harry, we have to believe in ourselves. We're all we've got."

Harry rested his forehead on his locker door and sighed. "I know."

Brad placed a hand on Hutton's shoulder and gently squeezed him. "We're going to make it."

40

The massive flattop turned into the wind in preparation to launch the morning Alpha Strike. Since arriving on Yankee Station, the air wing had been hampered by the unseasonal monsoon conditions. A reconnaissance pilot had raced across the primary and secondary targets, reporting that the weather had lifted enough to strike the bridges.

Brad held the brakes and checked the engine instruments. Everything looked stabilized and normal. Exhaust gas temperatures matched; RPMs and hydraulic pressures were all steady. The F-4 carried a full complement of Sparrow and Sidewinder air-to-air missiles.

Waiting for Jack Carella to taxi in front of his Phantom, Brad looked around the flight deck. The crews, soaked to the skin by the frequent rain squalls, worked feverishly to ensure that the launch went as scheduled. The noise was deafening, forcing the men to communicate via radio headsets or hand signals.

Brad listened to the assistant air boss while the deck hands, leaning into the thirty-two-knot wind, fought to maintain their balance. Their pant legs whipped in the combination of wind and jet exhaust.

Peering through the drizzle on his canopy, Brad watched the carrier *Coral Sea* as the ship began to launch aircraft. The low overcast and reduced visibility made it difficult to see the airplanes leave the deck, but he could see them hurtle down the catapults.

Brad looked down at the kneeboard strapped to his right thigh. A chart, radio frequencies, and other mission information were clamped to the flat surface. The squadron had been assigned to fly cover for the A-4 Skyhawks and A-1 Skyraiders that were going to bomb the Haiphong rail and highway bridges.

If the strike was successful, the spans linking the city with the mainland would be destroyed. If not, the afternoon strike would attempt to complete the job.

Jack Carella, with Ernie Sheridan in the backseat, would be Brad's flight leader. They had the responsibility for rendezvousing with an RA-5C Vigilante, then escorting the sleek photoreconnaissance aircraft directly over the target after the strike. The reception would definitely not be friendly.

Brad keyed his intercom. "You got everything cooking back there?"

"No," Harry answered nervously, "I'm composing a goddamn sonata."

Brad grinned at the reply, then watched Carella and Sheridan taxi toward the starboard catapult. A few seconds later, the drenched flight-deck director gave Brad the signal to taxi forward.

"Here we go," Brad announced to Harry as he added a handful of power to get the fighter rolling.

The Phantom lumbered up the slippery deck to the port-bow catapult. Stopping behind the jet blast deflector, Brad was scanning his instruments when the F-4 on the catapult was fired. He instinctively looked out at the aircraft.

The heavily laden Phantom squatted and raced down the deck. Brad watched in disbelief as the right afterburner snuffed out halfway through the cat stroke.

"Uh, oh," Brad said as the F-4 staggered off the bow. The pilot overrotated, causing the nose to rise too high. The Phantom rudder walked across the water, kicking up spray as it yawed to the right.

"Jettison! Jettison!" the frantic Air Boss radioed to the pilot in an attempt to get him to drop his ordnance. "Eject! Eject! Eject!"

Brad watched in horror as the RIO ejected at the instant

the F-4 hit the water. The explosion caused debris to rain down as the carrier plunged through the floating aircraft parts.

"Did they get out?" Harry asked, stunned by the sudden tragedy. "Any chutes?"

"The backseater made it," Brad uttered, sick at the sight of death. "The pilot went in." The ejection seats had been sequenced to fire the RIO first.

"Was it one of ours?" Harry asked hesitantly.

Brad added power to taxi onto the catapult. "No, it was from the other squadron."

Harry turned as far to the right as possible. He could see the plane-guard helicopter settling over the downed crewman.

While their Phantom was being hooked to the catapult, Brad talked to Harry. "Remember our drill if we have any problems coming off the cat."

"I've got a grip on the loud handle."

They had briefed that if Brad gave the command to eject, Harry would initiate the ejection. Brad would have one hand on the control stick and the other on the throttles.

Carella's F-4 blasted off the starboard catapult and climbed gracefully away.

Brad felt the cat shuttle take tension on his Phantom. He observed the windswept cat officer talk into his Mickey Mouse headset, then give the turnup signal.

"Here we go," Brad announced as he shoved the throttles to full power, then into afterburner. He inhaled a deep breath of oxygen, quickly scanned the engine instruments, looked at the cat officer, and saluted.

The catapult fired, blasting the F-4 down the track and off the bow. The aircraft sank precariously low to the water before it started to climb.

Breathing rapidly, Brad raised the landing gear and flaps. "Is it okay," he said in an attempt to break the tension, "if I open my eyes now?"

"You're a smart-ass," Harry grunted as the Phantom entered the low, rain-filled overcast.

• • •

Brad skillfully maintained his position behind the tanker. They were cruising at 14,000 feet between two dark cloud layers. The refueling track had been altered to avoid the severe rainstorms closer to the carrier.

After sucking the last drop of jet fuel the Phantom could hold, Brad eased the throttles back and propped loose from the refueling basket.

A small ray of sunlight filtered through the upper cloud deck. Brad glanced at the thin break in the overcast before he guided Joker 207 into position on Carella's right wing.

They cruised serenely up the coast, rendezvousing with the RA-5C Vigilante close to Haiphong. Carella checked in with the photo pilot, who answered with a simple, "Roger."

The carrier-borne supersonic reconnaissance aircraft was long and thin, like a dart. Flying in a racetrack pattern, the two Phantoms followed the "Viggie" and waited for the strike to commence.

Brad reached forward and smoothed the tape holding Leigh Ann's picture to the instrument panel. He was not going to give up.

"Will you pay attention, for Christ's sake?"

Snapping his head up, Brad was startled to see that he was drifting perilously close to Carella's plane. "Sorry, Harry."

"Well, stay awake."

The three aircraft continued to circle in a holding pattern off the coast. Brad studied the Vigilante's sensor pod and the camera openings behind the nosewheel door. He looked at the small window behind the cockpit. Inside the fuselage, the observer-radar operator sat in a dark cocoon, preparing to dash across the Haiphong rail and highway bridges.

The radio calls began to increase as four Phantoms preceded the strike group over the main target. The F-4s were tasked to keep the area free of MiGs, then cover the strike aircraft out to sea.

Brad could barely see the two sections of fighters as they thundered over the target and pulled up in a climbing turn. The Vigilante pilot, remaining quiet on the radio, turned and flew closer to the target area. Carella and Austin spread out on each side of the reconnaissance plane.

"Lonestar," the Red Crown controller radioed with urgency, "vector three two zero for numerous bogies." Lonestar was the call sign for the four Phantoms.

Brad watched the Lonestar F-4s drop their centerline tanks and turn to the heading to intercept the MiGs. He glanced at Carella's aircraft. Ernie Sheridan had his arms up, resting them on the canopy rail. He appeared to be relaxed and unconcerned. Just another routine day at the office.

Watching the smoke trails disappear behind the four F-4s, Brad knew that the Lonestar flight had stroked their afterburners to accelerate past the speed of sound.

"Jokers," Carella ordered, "master arm on."

"Two," Brad responded, checking his armament panel. He keyed his intercom. "Harnesses . . ."

"I'm set." Harry caught sight of the strike group approaching the beach. "Here comes the wrecking crew."

"Yeah," Brad replied, following the fast-moving, low-flying Skyhawks. "They better close the tollbooth."

The slower A-1 Skyraiders were approaching from a different direction. The eight Spads would bomb and strafe petroleum storage facilities near Haiphong harbor, then provide air cover for any downed aircraft.

The sky erupted with streams of tracer rounds and dark smoke from the heavy concentration of flak. Rows of antiaircraft guns pumped thousands of 23mm and 37mm shells at the Skyhawks. A half dozen surface-to-air missiles shot off the launchers next to the bridges. Black and smudgy white patches of smoke surrounded the target area.

Three flak-suppression Phantoms dived across the menacing gun positions, dropping full loads of cluster bombs on the exposed emplacements.

Suddenly the radio transmissions became garbled as everyone attempted to talk at once. The Lonestar flight leader had visual contact with the approaching MiGs, and the Skyhawk leader was pulling up for his bombing run.

Brad watched the A-4 pilot roll into a dive and fly straight

through a flak trap. The predetermined airspace was where
the North Vietnamese believed the attack planes would have
to enter to hit the bridges. Fifty-two gunners concentrated
their fire to a deadly barrage of bursting shells. The
Skyhawk exploded in an orange-and-black fireball, tumbling through the air trailing a streak of flame.

"Oh, shit," Brad exclaimed, then saw the pilot blast out
of the fireball. His parachute popped open an instant later,
and he descended toward the bridges.

Shaken by what he had witnessed, Brad keyed the
intercom. "They got CAG." The air-group commander, a
veteran Skyhawk pilot and former A-4 squadron CO, had
been leading the strike group.

"I saw it," Harry replied solemnly. "Dash Two better
alter his run-in or they're going to bag his ass, too."

The Vigilante pilot steepened his angle of bank, making
it easier for Joker Flight to view the target area.

Austin dropped farther behind the photo aircraft. He did not
want to risk a collision while he was watching the bombing
and strafing runs. Brad stared in disbelief at the second
Skyhawk. The pilot pressed the attack on the same run-in line.
"He's going right down the same chute . . . they're about to
take him out."

The A-4 pilot flew through the flak barrage, released his
bombs, and limped away with smoke pouring from the tail
pipe.

"Come on, Three," Brad said through clenched teeth,
"break it off, and set up a different approach."

As if he had heard Brad's words, the third pilot snapped
into a tight turn and lowered his nose to hug the ground. The
remaining pilots followed the new leader as he repositioned
the flight for an attack from a different direction.

Lonestar Flight had engaged five MiG-17s. The enemy
fighter pilots, determined to attack the American bombers
over Haiphong, had shot straight through the flight of
Phantoms. Brad listened to the Lonestar leader curse and
shout orders to the other three pilots.

Austin searched the sky for the approaching MiGs, then
glanced at the bridges. The lead Skyhawk, diving from a

different angle, dodged a SAM, salvoed his bombs, and blasted over the target.

Looking at Carella's Phantom, Brad was tempted to key his radio. They needed to intercept the rapidly approaching MiGs before the fighters reached Haiphong.

The explosions and bright flashes over and around the bridges caught Austin's attention. One of the spans had collapsed, severing the bridge. A cloud of brown smoke and dust rose as the next Skyhawk pilot dropped his bombs on an adjacent span.

"Bandits! Bandits! Joker," Red Crown called from the ship lying off the coast. "Five bogies at three three zero, eleven miles. Lonestar is closing on them, but you better set up for an intercept. Come starboard to three—"

The urgent transmission was cut off by a frantic Mayday call from the second A-4 pilot who had flown through the flak trap. His smoking engine had seized and disintegrated, forcing him to bail out of the crippled Skyhawk. He was going down south of the city of Haiphong, and needed air cover and the RESCAP Skyraiders.

"White Lightning," Carella radioed to the Vigilante pilot. "Joker One."

The radio transmissions were chaotic, forcing the quiet reconnaissance pilot to try three times to answer his escort.

"Go, Joker."

"Jokers are going to engage the bogies. Recommend you orbit and wait for us."

The Vigilante pilot heard most of the message. "Copy, Joker. Lightning will orbit."

Carella banked steeply, lighted the afterburners, and raced toward their adversaries. "Jokers, punch off center-lines, and go combat spread."

Brad toggled the jettison switch and kicked off his 600-gallon fuel tank. His radar warning receiver was alive with chatter and groans. "Harry, heads up for SAMs."

"Shit!" Harry shouted an instant later. "We've got SAMs at two o'clock! Coming up fast!"

Brad quickly scanned to the right. What he saw made him freeze in terror. Two missiles, trailing plumes of smoke and fire, had them boresighted. They would impact the Phantoms in seconds.

"Joker One, break right! Jocko, break right!" Brad yelled, snapping the F-4 into a punishing 8-g turn. Carella whipped his Phantom over, pulling close to Brad's aircraft. Hutton was petrified, believing that they were going to have a collision with Joker 1.

The two SAMs detonated under the belly of Austin's F-4. The force of the twin explosions caused the Phantom to shudder and violently yaw to the left. Feeling his heart pounding, Brad fought the stick and darted a look at the annunciator panel. Thank God! The caution lights remained dark.

"Nine and ten o'clock, Jokers!" Ernie Sheridan shouted over the radios. "SAMs at nine and ten!"

Brad saw a streak of blazing fire rip past his canopy. He ducked instinctively, cursing out of fear as the SAM arced out of sight. How many more shots until they nailed him?

41

"Tallyho!" Carella yelled, reefing his thundering Phantom straight up. "Jokers engaging."

Brad spotted the MiGs as he pulled into the vertical and prepared to jump the five aircraft. Two of the MiG pilots raised their noses and turned into the Phantoms, while the other three continued toward Haiphong.

Brad completed a zero-airspeed reversal, then cringed when he almost collided with the Lonestar flight leader. Gulping oxygen, Austin unloaded the F-4 and hoped the MiGs would overshoot.

The Lonestar Phantoms raced after the three MiGs headed for the strike group. Brad saw one of the F-4s fire a missile at the same moment the two MiGs that he and Carella had engaged opened fire. The North Vietnamese pilots were taking advantage of their tighter turning radius to pull inside of the heavier F-4s.

Brad felt the Phantom stagger as the tracers penetrated the tip of his starboard wing. He pulled so hard that he momentarily grayed out. Harry groaned and shouted obscenities when Brad entered a vertical rolling scissors with the trailing MiG. He had lost sight of his flight leader in the swirling fight.

"Come on, goddamnit!" Harry shouted, gripping the sides of the canopy. "Shoot him. Lock him up!"

"Where's Carella?" Brad asked, straining under the punishing g forces.

Hutton swiveled his head, searching for Carella and Sheridan. "Jocko is low . . . seven o'clock. No factor."

"Keep an eye on him." Brad pulled the Phantom until it buffeted. "We don't want to midair."

One of the biggest fears was the possibility of hitting a friendly aircraft during a multiplane engagement. After every turn and twist, Brad gained more advantage on the MiG pilot. It was obvious that the Vietnamese pilot was not proficient at using his fighter in a vertical contest.

At fifty degrees nose off, Brad fired a Sidewinder. The missile tried to make the corner, but went ballistic and shot past the MiG. The narrow escape scared the MiG pilot into a hard break. The high-g maneuver caused the airplane to bleed off speed, giving Brad the advantage he needed.

After the MiG reversed, Brad punched off a second missile. The Sidewinder came off the rail, did a snake dance, then tracked straight for the MiG.

"Go! Go!" Harry yelled as the missile plowed into the tail of the fighter.

After the initial impact, the MiG flew out of the explosion and raced toward the ground. The aircraft was missing the upper portion of the vertical stabilizer, but flew away in controlled flight.

"Who makes these goddamn missiles?" Brad asked with tightened jaw muscles. "Mattel?"

Yanking his head from side to side, Brad searched for Carella and the other MiG. He pulled on the stick and entered a barrel roll.

Scanning the sky, Brad momentarily lost his situational awareness. Seeing the MiG and Carella flash past, he selected afterburner and snatched the control stick over into a nose low turn. The g forces slammed his helmet against the canopy.

"You're passing five hundred knots," Harry yelled as the Phantom rocketed toward the ground. "Bring the nose up! Get the nose up!"

Feeling the controls get stiff, Brad glanced at the attitude direction indicator and the altimeter as the F-4 plunged through a thin layer of clouds.

"We're supersonic!" Harry exclaimed in panic. "Pull up! Pull up!"

Brad snapped the throttles to idle, popped the speed brakes open, leveled the wings, and pulled as hard as he dared. "I've got it, Harry." The stressful 10-g maneuver broke two wing panels, bent a flap actuator, and popped seven rivets in the left wing.

Brad watched the altimeter bottom out at 800 feet before the Phantom, traveling faster than the speed of sound, zoomed back to 14,000 feet.

Catching sight of Carella's F-4, Brad retracted the speed brakes, slammed the throttles into afterburner, and keyed his mike. "Joker One, where's the MiG?"

"He's at my twelve," Carella grunted in an agonizing turn, "going for separation."

Brad turned inside Carella's aircraft in an attempt to fire a Sidewinder at the diving MiG. The enemy fighter was too close to the ground for the missile to get a clear tone and lock on.

"Joker Two," Carella shouted, "join up, and let's get back to the Vigilante."

"Roger," Brad heaved.

"Jokers," Red Crown radioed, "we're showing three bandits at your three five zero, fourteen miles. They're headed your direction."

"Joker One copies."

Scanning his instruments, Austin was startled to see a warning light illuminated. "Harry, we've got a low-fuel light."

"We can't have," Hutton replied anxiously. "Check the fuel dump switch."

"I have," Brad responded, verifying the readings from the fuel gauges. "We've got fuel in the wings, but it isn't transferring to the fuselage."

Brad toggled switches to no avail. They would soon run out of fuel. He jettisoned their missile racks to reduce the parasitic drag on the wings. With smooth wings, they could stretch their range.

"Harry, the SAMs that exploded under the belly must have caused a valve to stick."

"Or the high-g pull-up," Hutton offered, trying to think of a solution to their problem.

"Maybe," Brad replied as he closed in on his flight leader. "Hang on while I try something."

Harry braced himself a second before Brad snapped the Phantom down. The negative-g maneuver was followed by an instantaneous seven positive g's. The wing fuel remained trapped. Using the rudders, Brad violently yawed the aircraft back and forth. Still no success.

"Joker One," Brad radioed in frustration. "Dash Two has a fuel problem."

"Say again," Carella said over the garbled radio calls.

"Joker Two has a fuel-transfer problem. We're going to flameout any time now."

"Stick with me," Carella ordered, "and we'll escort you out over the water after the recon run."

Harry smacked the side of the canopy. "That sonuvabitch! Declare an emergency, and let's get the hell out of here, right now!"

Brad moved out to the left side of the RA-5C Vigilante while Carella positioned himself on the right side.

"Harry," Brad said, removing Leigh Ann's picture from the instrument panel, "we've got to maintain flight integrity, even if we can't do anything." He shoved the photo into his torso harness. "The appearance of two Phantoms may keep the MiGs away from the Viggie."

They both knew that the poststrike photographs were invaluable. Men's lives depended on the damage assessment. If the strike results were deemed unsatisfactory, more crews would have to return to the heavily defended bridges.

"White Lightning," Carella radioed in a strained voice, "Jokers ready when you are."

"Copy," the reconnaissance pilot answered. "We're rolling in now."

Brad could see the billowing clouds of smoke rising over the target area. He also saw the hundreds of puffs of flak filling the airspace over the bridges. Two MiGs shot past, going in the opposite direction. Brad wondered why Red Crown had not warned them about the fighters.

Heading toward Haiphong at an angle, the Vigilante pilot leveled at 3,800 feet. Brad heard the F-4 Lonestar flight leader call feet wet as the photo pilot banked steeply and commenced his run-in at 600 knots.

The clean Vigilante was pulling away from the Phantoms, forcing Carella and Austin to select afterburner. The increased thrust was rapidly draining the last few gallons of jet fuel from Brad's Phantom.

"SAMs!" Ernie Sheridan hollered. "Nine o'clock."

Brad glanced to his left in time to see a missile streak in front of him and explode over the Vigilante. The photo plane disappeared in the flash and cloud of smoke, then reappeared trailing fire.

The reconnaissance pilot turned sharply and darted for the coastline. Carella and Austin banked hard, following the blazing Vigilante.

"How much fuel?" Harry asked at the same instant the right engine flamed out.

"Mayday! Mayday!" Brad transmitted as the left engine quit. "Joker Two Oh Seven has flamed out."

"We'll coordinate RESCAP," Sheridan said, "then call the search-and-rescue station."

Brad lowered the Phantom's nose in an effort to glide as far as their speed and altitude would permit. He calculated their rate of descent against the distance to the shoreline. It would be close.

A flash caught Brad's eye. He looked out in front of his aircraft in time to see two parachutes pop open. The blazing Vigilante rolled inverted and plunged for the sea.

Feeling the thuds from small-arms bullets, Brad and Harry were stunned when a concussion buffeted the powerless Phantom.

"Don't do anything, Harry! I'm going to get us as far as I can. Just sit tight. This is our only chance."

Harry braced his back against the ejection seat. "Are we going to make the water?"

"I don't think so, but stay with me." Brad started easing back on the stick as the Phantom descended through 2,000 feet. Brad could feel the flight controls stiffen as the engine turbines wound down. The hydraulic pumps were failing, making control of the airplane more difficult.

Passing 1,000 feet, Brad pulled with brute force, but the nose continued to drop below the horizon. "Hold on! Hold on a few more seconds."

The stricken fighter passed over a small rise a quarter of a mile from the shore. Descending through 500 feet, Brad reached for the ejection handles over his helmet. "Eject! Eject!" Harry blasted out of the Phantom in a thunderclap of wind and debris.

Staring at the rapidly rising terrain, Brad grasped the primary ejection handle and yanked the face curtain down over his helmet. The blast propelled him clear of the Phantom four seconds before it exploded on the edge of the shore. The ball of flames and metal engulfed the beach and rained across the water.

Brad's parachute opened with a tremendous jolt, snapping him sideways. After three swings, he plowed into the wet, low-lying ground. The vicious impact wrenched his knee and knocked the wind out of him.

Gasping for breath, Brad tore at the Koch fittings in an attempt to release his parachute. After struggling to rid himself of the canopy, Brad ripped off his oxygen mask, then reached for his revolver and got to his knees. He looked up and down the shoreline, spotting Harry running toward him. Hutton had left his life raft with his parachute.

Quickly examining his knee, Brad was relieved to see that it moved freely. Harry dropped to his knees next to Brad. Hutton's nose was bleeding, and he was holding his left arm.

Hearing an F-4 overhead, Brad caught sight of Carella's Phantom circling a mile away. A secondary explosion from Brad's downed fighter shocked him into action. The main core of the burning wreckage was sending an enormous cloud of black smoke into the sky. They had to get away from the crash site before ground troops arrived.

"Come on, Harry," Brad urged, getting to his feet. "We've got to get as far offshore as we can, and fast."

"My arm's broken," Harry replied. His face was ashen and twisted in pain. "I can't swim."

"I'll tow you. Keep your helmet on."

Brad placed his revolver back in its holster and yanked loose his one-man raft. "Let's go." They raced for the water, splashing into the surf at the same moment three rifle rounds kicked up spray next to them.

Brad inflated the raft and Harry lunged over the side, landing on his back. With a surge of adrenaline, Brad grabbed the raft and began sidestroking as hard as he could. Having been a competitive swimmer at the Naval Academy, Brad had conditioned himself to swim long distances.

More shots ripped across the water, narrowly missing the bright yellow raft. Brad swam as hard as he could, straining to distance them from the beach.

"I see the sonuvabitches," Harry groaned in agony. "They're about a hundred yards to the right of the crash."

"Harry," Brad choked from a mouthful of seawater, "can you get some rounds off—keep their heads down?"

"I'll try."

Hutton released his arm, painfully extracted his revolver, then fired six rounds at the three men setting up a mortar. One of the soldiers was firing his rifle at the raft while the other two men were bracing the muzzle-loading mortar. Although he didn't have a prayer of hitting the North Vietnamese, Harry convinced them to drop to a prone position.

"Get on the radio," Brad paused, swallowing more of the salty water, "and see if you can get Jocko, or someone. We need help right now if—"

A geyser of water erupted thirty feet in front of the raft, showering them with spray. Brad altered course and stroked with all of his strength. The mortar crew would soon have them bracketed.

Hutton fumbled with his survival radio while another shell exploded next to them. "Joker," Harry shouted in desperation, "we need cover fire! There's a mortar firing at us north of the crash!"

"Copy," Carella replied. "Say mortar posit."

A third shell hit closer, stunning both of them. "North—a hundred yards north of the wreckage!"

"We're rolling in."

Gulping air, Brad changed direction again and kicked with the last ounce of energy in his body. He flinched when a fourth shell impacted in the position they had occupied only seconds before.

The Phantom plunged toward the mortar crew and fired an unguided Sparrow missile. It wiggled twice before exploding between the burning wreckage and the North Vietnamese soldiers.

Carella pulled up steeply and banked over the downed fliers. "I'm going to try again. Hang in."

Breathing a sigh of relief, Hutton watched the mortar team grab their weapons and scamper toward the marsh behind the burning Phantom. "They've retreated," Harry yelled, ignoring his pain. "They disappeared behind the crash site!"

"Joker copies. We've got help on the way."

Brad stopped swimming and held onto the side of the raft. His lungs heaved in an attempt to resupply oxygen to his exhausted body.

Hearing the Phantom overhead, Brad glanced up at the aircraft. His mind had trouble comprehending that he had been up there only minutes before. Now, he was in the sea, struggling to survive.

"Harry, Joker," Carella radioed. "We've got to tank, then we'll be back."

Hutton shaded his eyes and looked up at the Phantom. He, too, felt strange sitting in a raft while he talked to Carella and Sheridan in their jet. "How long till the helo gets here?"

"The SAR folks," Carella paused to confirm a radio call that Sheridan had made, "are on the way. The Vigilante crew is in the drink, too, so ten to fifteen minutes."

42

Brad heard Carella light the afterburners as they sped toward a rendezvous with the waiting tanker. "Harry," Brad said, handing Hutton his revolver, "reload yours and keep mine handy."

Repositioning his left arm, Harry turned to Brad. "I hope to Christ they get here before the mortar crew comes back."

"I'm going to tow us out as far as I can." Without warning, something bumped Brad's legs. "Holy shit," Brad uttered in panic.

"What?" Harry responded, frantically searching the shoreline. "What's wrong?"

"Something ran into my leg." Brad brought his legs up under the raft. "Something big." He inflated his life jacket to provide a cushion for his upper torso.

"I'll dump in the shark repellent," Harry offered, searching behind him for the packet. "If we're careful, you can crawl in on my legs."

Brad was tempted to get out of the water but thought about their close proximity to the shoreline. Harry dropped the shark repellent in the water.

"Thanks, but I better tow us out as far as I can. We're sitting ducks if the mortar team comes back."

Brad glanced out to sea. He did a double take when he saw the bridge and mast of a large ship. The vessel was approaching them at high speed.

"Harry, we've got company coming."

"Where?" Hutton responded, yanking his head around to see where Austin was looking. "I hope it's one of ours."

"If it isn't," Brad peered back toward the beach, "we can kiss it good-bye."

Harry grimaced, then turned his head to meet Brad's eyes. "I wish I could help you."

"You are helping. As soon as you hear the helos, toss out the dye marker and light a smoke flare."

"I've got 'em ready."

Hutton gingerly propped himself up. "Where are those goddamn helicopters?"

"I don't know, but things don't—sonuvabitch!"

"What?" Harry asked, wide-eyed with fear.

"Something just bounced off my right leg." Brad thrashed the water, towing the raft as fast as he could swim. His heart beat so hard he could feel constriction in his chest. Christ, am I going to have a heart attack?

After seventy yards, Brad slowed to a steady pace. "Harry," he gasped, "if you see anything break the surface—dorsal fin, anything—call it out but don't shoot it, and get ready for company in the raft."

"Okay," Harry replied, then froze in horror. "Shit! We've got big trouble."

Brad slowed and stared at two North Vietnamese patrol boats. They were accelerating from their concealment behind a fleet of fishing boats. At full speed, the Swatow-class gunboats were turning directly toward Brad and Harry.

Austin searched the skies, hearing the familiar sound of the big radial engines in the A-1 Skyraiders. "Call RESCAP and light the flare!"

He felt something strike his left leg. Brad churned the water while he quickly positioned himself at the rear of their raft. "I'm getting in!"

Harry grasped the air chamber and leaned back to balance the unstable dinghy. He braced his flight boots inside the aft section, locking his knees. Brad thrust his body upward, pulling himself into the raft. His helmet hit Hutton in the chest.

Aware of a deep, resonant sound in the distance, Austin and Hutton were startled by a thundering impact near them. A coastal battery had opened fire at their bobbing raft.

Brad heard another loud report. He looked over the front of the raft to see the ship that had been speeding toward them. He judged it to be two miles from the shore.

"Harry, a destroyer . . . thank God." Turning quickly to see the ship, Hutton almost tipped over the dinghy.

The American destroyer captain, risking his vessel in the shallow waters, was turning broadside to the beach and had commenced firing at the shore battery.

Brad clutched Harry's good arm and shifted to see the North Vietnamese patrol boats. The two craft were side by side, less than a mile away.

Brad and Harry both heard a whistling sound a second before another large shell exploded beside them. The concussion from the impact lifted the raft out of the water and tossed both men into the sea.

Stunned by the blast, Austin popped to the surface and grabbed Hutton in a lifeguard grip. "We've got to get away from the raft," Brad sputtered.

Coughing up brine, Harry moaned in agony. "We're not going to make it, are we?"

"Yes, goddamnit," Brad bellowed in pain and frustration, "we're going to make it."

Austin was fighting not to succumb to his overwhelming fear. Choking, he towed Harry twenty yards from the clearly visible dinghy. He looked around, desperate for assistance. He glimpsed a swarm of RESCAP Skyraiders in the distance, then heard the clattering of a Seasprite helicopter. He saw a second helicopter in the distance.

The A-1 Spads were circling the downed Vigilante crew, but the first rescue helicopter was racing toward their raft. Brad shouted with joy and looked back toward the gunboats. They were separating to set up a cross fire at the Seasprite.

"Is that a helo?" Harry gasped.

"Yes," Brad answered, glancing at the destroyer in the distance. The slowing ship was pounding the shore installation into oblivion.

"Come on," Brad coaxed the helicopter pilot. "The gunners are almost on us."

The Seasprite sped toward them, then slowed while a

door gunner began firing at one of the patrol boats. After stabilizing over the Phantom crew, the pilot lowered the helicopter near the water.

The spray lashed across Brad's face, stinging his eyes and making breathing difficult. He was having a hard time holding onto Hutton.

Hearing automatic weapons firing, Brad held Harry tightly and twisted to see which direction the gunboats were heading. Staring in shock, Brad watched the two craft charge toward the Seasprite. The North Vietnamese boats opened fire, walking the machine-gun shells across the water and into the Seasprite.

To his horror, Brad witnessed the pilots slump forward as a man in a wet suit leaped from the helicopter. Black smoke streamed out of the exhaust and whipped below the rotor blades.

The helicopter drifted sideways, tilted on its side, caught the whirling blades in the water, then violently crashed into the sea.

Petrified, Brad stared at the wreckage and renewed his grip around Harry. "Oh, God . . . no."

Aware of the shells slamming into the water, Brad darted a look at the closest gunboat. He felt a sledgehammer blow to his helmet, knocking him loose from his friend. Brad yanked the lanyard to inflate Harry's life preserver, then slumped facedown in the sea.

Three A-1 Skyraiders roared low over the water, firing pods of rockets at the North Vietnamese gunboats. One craft blew apart, sinking stern first; the other patrol boat turned and sped for shore.

The rescue swimmer, slightly injured when he had leaped from the crashing Seasprite, lifted Brad Austin's face out of the water. He tugged him next to Harry Hutton, hooking them together.

The swimmer, glancing at the second helicopter, checked on the pilot. The machine-gun shell that had ricocheted off Brad's helmet had temporarily knocked him unconscious.

Gagging, Brad expelled a mouthful of seawater, then coughed to clear his esophagus. Gasping, he sucked in air and stared, confused, at the young man who had saved his life.

The swimmer grabbed Brad's life preserver. "I'm on your side! You're going to be okay!"

The Spads pulled up in a wingover and rolled in on the fleeing vessel, strafing the boat with 20mm gunfire. After a third pass, the patrol boat slowed to a halt. The panicked crew jumped overboard when they saw the Skyraiders dive again. The lead RESCAP pilot sank the Swatow with two 500-pound bombs.

The second Seasprite moved into position and hovered over the three men. The swimmer unhooked the crew's life preservers as the rescue sling was lowered. Hindered by the turbulent rotor wash, the swimmer placed the sling under Brad's shoulders, then hooked the D ring on his torso harness to the cable.

After Brad had been hoisted aboard the helicopter, the swimmer hooked himself and Harry to the cable. As the hoist operator lifted the pair from the water, Jack Carella and Ernie Sheridan made a low pass, rocking the Phantom's wings.

43

Four days later, Brad and Harry had arrived in San Diego to convalesce at the Balboa Naval Hospital. After providing initial medical treatment for the crew, Doc McCary had approached Dan Bailey and Admiral Keuseman with a special request from Brad and Harry.

The admiral had been pleased to arrange the recuperative leave for the two men who had shot down Maj. Nguyen Thanh Dao.

Harry's arm had been encased in a cast, and Brad had the responsibility for carrying their bags.

Unbeknownst to Brad, Harry had called Nick Palmer at the hospital to let him know when they would be arriving. Nick, in turn, had made another call for Harry.

When Austin and Hutton walked through the main entrance at the hospital, Nick and Leigh Ann were waiting for them.

Brad dropped the luggage and embraced Leigh Ann when she rushed into his arms. She tilted her head back and kissed him. "Brad, I hope you're not upset that I'm here."

"Of course not," he replied, feeling awkward in front of his friends. "I'm just surprised . . . pleasantly surprised, I mean."

Palmer laughed. "Get your foot out of your mouth."

Brad turned to Nick and shook his hand. "You're looking great. When are they going to let you go?"

"I think that I've already overstayed my welcome, judging by the remarks the nurses have been making."

"Well, partner," Harry chuckled, "we're back together again."

"Yeah," Palmer sighed. "It's a dream come true."

"Excuse me," Brad said, reaching for Leigh Ann's hand, "but we're going to take a little stroll."

"Wait a second," Palmer said, turning serious. "I don't know what's up, but a Lieutenant Colonel Chastain has been trying to locate you since yesterday. The guy has called almost every hour."

Puzzled, Brad looked at Palmer for a moment. "I've never heard of him. Did he leave a number?"

"He sure did," Palmer responded with an emphasis on the word *sure*. "Every single time, as far as I know, including his home phone. They've got it over at admissions. Says he's calling on behalf of Senator Kerwin."

The senator had contacted Leigh Ann the day before she had left Memphis.

"Brad," Leigh Ann said in a small voice, "I need to tell you something."

He looked at her suspiciously. "What?"

Hutton and Palmer looked up expectantly.

"I had been worried about you, and the possibility of a court-martial when you are really a hero, so I talked to a friend of the family—"

"Court-martial?" Nick interrupted, thoroughly confused. "What court-martial?"

"Nick," Brad said, trying to find out what Leigh Ann had done, "Harry can fill you in on the details."

Turning back to Leigh Ann, Brad spoke in a measured voice. "Whom did you talk to?"

She looked toward the ceiling, then back to Brad. "Senator Kerwin."

"No shit," Harry exclaimed, quickly adding to Leigh Ann, "excuse me."

Stupefied, Brad considered the implications. "Arlin Kerwin, the head of the Senate Armed Services Committee? You talked to him?"

"Yes," she answered, feeling a sudden chill. "I wanted

to help you. I was so worried, and I didn't know to whom to turn.''

Brad collected his thoughts. ''Leigh Ann, it was supposed to be confidential, and anyway the matter has been dismissed. It's history, and everything is okay.''

Palmer was growing more inquisitive. ''What is going on?''

Clearly irritated, Brad looked at Hutton. ''It's a military secret. Harry, keep them amused until after I make this call.''

Ashen faced, Brad rejoined his friends. ''Well, folks, I've been invited to a hearing in Washington.''

Leigh Ann cringed. ''I'm sorry. I was . . . ,'' she cast her head down.

Brad put his arm around her shoulders and hugged her to him. ''I guess you blew it, but how could you know? It's okay. It really is. I have been asked—ordered, actually—to attend a hearing concerning what we were told never happened at Phuc Yen.'' Austin exhaled, then shook his head. ''So, it's time for another rug dance.''

''Are we in the frying pan again?'' Harry asked, changing his words out of respect for the lady who was present.

''I don't know anything at this point, except that I've got to report to Colonel Chastain tomorrow afternoon.'' Brad hugged Leigh Ann in an attempt to reassure her. ''I'm supposed to catch a flight out of North Island this evening.''

Taking a deep breath, Leigh Ann looked up at Brad. ''I want to go with you. Please.''

''Okay,'' Brad replied without hesitation. ''I'll let them know that I'm going to fly commercially.''

Harry frowned. ''You better watch your six.''

Brad nodded and faced Leigh Ann. ''Where are you staying?''

''In a motel near here, and I've got a rental car.''

''Okay,'' Brad replied with a smile, ''we'll grab your luggage, check out, and head for the airport.''

Brad turned to Hutton. ''Harry, will you call North

Island, and let them know that I'm taking an airliner to Washington?''

"Sure," he grinned. "Give 'em hell."

"Yeah," Brad chuckled. "What can they do? Make me a captain and send me to Yankee Station? You guys take care of each other."

WASHINGTON, D.C.

After the long flight, Brad and Leigh Ann checked into the Hotel Washington. They ate a late dinner, followed by a nightcap in the quiet cocktail lounge. Their relationship was on solid footing again, but the stress and uncertainty of Brad's difficult situation dulled the elation.

Exhausted by the tedious trip from San Diego, Leigh Ann and Brad succumbed to their weariness shortly after midnight. Collapsing on the ornate bed, they held each other, then fell asleep with Leigh Ann's head on Brad's chest.

After breakfast in the hotel restaurant, Brad and Leigh Ann walked down Pennsylvania Avenue to the White House.

Instead of experiencing pride, Brad had a gnawing feeling inside. His anguish was fueled by a mixture of sadness and loathing. The decisions that were being made in that building were causing untold lives to be lost in a protracted, senseless strategy of slow escalation.

He steered Leigh Ann back past the Treasury Building, crossing the street to enter Sherman Park.

"Brad," Leigh Ann said as they crossed another street and walked into Pershing Park, "what do you think will happen in the meeting?"

"Hearing," Brad squeezed her hand affectionately. "This is not a good-old-boy town meeting."

She tugged on his arm. "Okay, hearing. Will you be in any jeopardy?"

Brad thought about the various possibilities. "The way I understand this, your friend Senator Kerwin is basically using me as the kindling to start a roaring blaze."

Leigh Ann pulled Brad to a halt. "What do you mean? Arlin Kerwin is one of the most respected politicians in Washington. I don't think he would do anything to hurt you . . . or me."

"Leigh Ann," Brad replied, taking both of her hands. "My handler, the lieutenant colonel I called from San Diego, couldn't say much over an open phone line, but he painted a clear picture for me."

"What did he tell you?" Leigh Ann asked, motioning toward a park bench.

"I don't know the whole story," Brad answered, sitting beside Leigh Ann. "Apparently, there has been a lot of feuding between Capitol Hill and the White House about the direction the war has taken.

"It seems as if," he continued, lowering his voice as a couple walked past, "certain individuals, including Senator Kerwin, have been waiting for an opportunity to catch the administration with their shorts down."

"Brad, I am really sorry for getting you into this. I didn't know that everything had worked out so well for you and Harry."

Brad smiled and put his arm around her. "I told you not to worry. My incident, and the subsequent cover-up, is the catalyst Kerwin has been waiting for. If, in some small way, I can help expose the madness in the White House, the better off we'll all be."

Brad chuckled and shook his head. "Believe me, when Kerwin starts digging, he won't quit until he has all the answers, or he surfaces in China."

"That's what bothers me," Leigh Ann said with a hint of sadness. "I don't want to see you used, then discarded."

Leaning over, Brad tilted Leigh Ann's chin up and lightly kissed her. "Let's have some lunch before I have to report to the colonel."

Brad paid the taxi driver, then walked into the hotel lobby. Leigh Ann was sitting in a chair, looking radiant in a beige dress with brown accessories.

"How did it go?" she asked, rising to greet him.

"Fine. The colonel is a nice guy, and we had a cordial chat. He told me when and where I have to be tomorrow, then encouraged me to hold my ground and tell it like I see it."

"Is he going to be there with you?"

Brad gave Leigh Ann a wry smile. "I don't think so. I would imagine that anyone remotely connected with me will be hunkered down in a bunker tomorrow."

Leigh Ann impulsively kissed him on the cheek. "I'll be there."

Brad laughed out loud.

"What's so funny?"

"Ah . . . I'm not sure I can withstand any more of your help."

Leigh Ann looked hurt.

"I'm kidding . . . just a little humor."

She gave him a thin smile. "I am sorry, and I'd like to make it up to you. How about if I take you to dinner?"

Brad cocked his head. "You're going to take me out for dinner?"

"That's right, flyboy," she said with a look of determination. "I learned a lot about being independent from a guy I once met in Hawaii."

Brad raised his eyebrows. "Is that so?"

"Yes," she smiled demurely, "and afterward, I have a stimulating evening planned."

44

Brad donned his tunic and adjusted his tie, then glanced at his watch for the fourth time in ten minutes. He dreaded the next few hours more than he had ever feared anything.

Turning, he saw Leigh Ann smooth her conservative suit. She, too, looked nervous. How different from the sensuous, confident woman he had known in bed.

"Leigh Ann, you don't have to attend this hearing. It's closed door, and you may have to sit outside for who knows how long."

She walked to Brad, then kissed him, careful not to disturb his uniform. "I happen to be in love with you, and I want to be by your side, or as close as possible."

"Okay," Brad replied, looking at his watch. "It's time to go to the gallows."

Arriving fifteen minutes early, Brad and Leigh Ann walked up the steps to the imposing building. After Austin identified himself, he and Leigh Ann were allowed to go to the area outside of the room where the hearing would take place.

They took seats outside the room, and silently watched a number of people shuffle in and out of the hearing chamber.

Brad started to speak to Leigh Ann, then stopped abruptly. Ogilvie, from the State Department, accompanied by Captain Emmett from CINCPAC were approaching them.

"Great," Brad said quietly to Leigh Ann, "here come the two sweethearts who grilled me on the ship."

"Who are they?"

"I'll tell you later."

Emmett sat down without acknowledging Austin, while Ogilvie, wearing the same rumpled suit he had worn on the carrier, walked toward the couple. Brad rose to face him.

"Captain," Ogilvie said testily, "you've opened a real can of worms, and you're going to rue the day you blew the whistle."

Bristling, Brad thrust out his jaw but refrained from replying. Ogilvie spun around and rejoined Emmett.

Precisely at 10 A.M., the doors were closed. The waiting area became as quiet as a tomb. Ten minutes later, Brad was called into the hearing.

Ushered to a long table, Brad stated his full name, then remained standing and swore to tell the truth and nothing but the truth. He observed Arlin Kerwin, who reminded him of a simpleminded country humorist he had seen on television. Appearances, Brad thought, can be deceiving.

"Son," Kerwin said in a friendly, fatherly manner, "we're here today to establish exactly what happened at Phuc Yen, and why there is an ongoing attempt to conceal what happened."

Brad silently nodded.

"There aren't any members of the service present," Kerwin continued in a congenial tone, "so you needn't be intimidated. I want you to tell this committee precisely what happened, and what consequences you faced. We are going to get to the bottom of this matter, so don't leave anything out. I've got the dates, so just tell us the facts."

Clearing his throat, Brad fixed his eyes on the chairman of the Armed Services Committee. "Senator, I was flying as wingman in a two-plane section. We were providing combat air patrol for a strike group when we were attacked by three MiGs, one of which was flown by North Vietnam's second-leading ace, Major Nguyen Thanh Dao."

A lanky senator whom Brad recognized pointed a finger at him. "How could you tell who was flying the planes?"

Brad saw a look of irritation cross Kerwin's face, but he remained quiet.

"We had had briefs on the aircraft markings of various North Vietnamese pilots. Major Dao's aircraft was readily distinguishable by the white stripe on the tail, and the seven red stars on the fuselage, signifying seven American aircraft shot down. Plus, you could tell by the way he handled his aircraft. He was definitely one of the better pilots."

"Continue, Captain," Kerwin said, glancing at the tall senator.

Brad swallowed. "We engaged the MiGs, and during the battle, Major Dao shot down my flight leader, Lieutenant Commander Lincoln Durham. I was initially stunned, then outraged." Brad paused, carefully selecting his words. "I made an instantaneous decision to pursue Major Dao and destroy his aircraft before he could land at a restricted airfield."

The contentious senator leaned next to his microphone. "Can you define restricted airfield."

"Yessir, to the best of my understanding of the rules of engagement on that particular date."

Brad sensed the members of the committee staring at him. "If we were engaged in battle, we could overfly an off-limits airfield. However, we were not authorized to attack the airfield or the aircraft on the ground."

Kerwin wrote a note. "Please proceed."

Taking a deep breath, Brad concentrated on Kerwin. "I shot down Major Dao over the airfield at Phuc Yen, a designated off-limits airfield, and proceeded to destroy a MiG on the ground. I violated a restriction and did not report the fact."

The tall senator's eyes narrowed. "Why did you think that you had the authority to operate like a loose cannon?"

A hush settled over the large room.

"I didn't feel that I had the authority to operate on my own." Brad was boiling inside but showed little outwardly. "In the heat of battle, with my life on the line and my adrenaline pumping, I fired a missile at a MiG taxiing for takeoff without analyzing the ramifications of my actions."

"Perhaps, Captain Austin," the combative lawmaker said in a surly manner, "you should seek some other profession that will allow you the time to think before you act.''

Kerwin responded before Brad could form a civilized answer. "We are not here to discuss Captain Austin's qualifications, or question his actions. He has demonstrated his capabilities by destroying three MiGs. I think that tells it all.''

Brad was surprised that the chairman knew about all three MiGs, then realized that the senator probably knew his life history.

"What we are trying to do,'' Kerwin continued, "is find out why his actions were censored.

"Then what happened, Captain?'' the chairman asked, removing his glasses.

"After what I had done had been revealed, I was confined to quarters, along with my backseat radar operator. We were informed that an investigation would take place.''

Kerwin replaced his glasses. "And did an investigation take place?''

"Yes, Senator. On board the ship.''

"And what was the outcome?''

Brad steeled himself. "We were informed that we would not be court-martialed and that the matter was being shelved.''

Kerwin leaned back and folded his arms across his chest. "What were you told, and who told you?''

"We were informed,'' Brad said evenly, "that the incident had never happened, and that it would be in our best interest to keep it that way.''

Showing no emotion, Kerwin wrote another note. "Was there a reason given?''

"Yessir,'' Brad replied uncomfortably. "We were told that my incursion, if admitted, might compromise expected negotiations with the North Vietnamese.''

"Who informed you of that finding?''

Brad's stomach knotted. "The State Department representative waiting outside in the hall.'' A murmur filled the room.

Kerwin paused, consulting his notes. "A Mister Ogilvie?''

"Yes, sir."

"Did he give you a reason—tell you who initiated the cover-up?"

Brad hesitated, unsure how far he should go. "Mister Ogilvie explained that the decision had originated in the White House."

Kerwin locked Brad in an unblinking stare. "Is that unconditionally true?"

"Yes, it is, Senator, to the best of my recollection. I don't remember his exact wording, but he clearly stated that the decision came from the White House." The tension in the room was palpable.

"Okay, son," Kerwin said, smiling pleasantly, "tell us about your feelings, and those of your colleagues, about how the war is progressing—how it's being managed."

Throwing caution to the wind, Brad drew a breath and placed his folded hands on the table.

"Senator, I can only speak for myself, but I'm sure that the majority of the aircrews would express the same feelings. I feel that the air war is being micromanaged to the detriment of everyone. Targets are apparently considered for the effect they will have on the media, and what the general public will think. We are being forced to operate under restrictions and limitations that completely negate our efforts, while more aircrews are being sacrificed.

"We bomb, then back off while more restrictions are shoved down our throats. Every new sanctuary becomes a haven for North Vietnamese antiaircraft guns, surface-to-air missiles, and ground-controlled radar."

Brad slowed, keeping his emotions in check. "Senator, we have been shocked by the missions that we have been ordered to fly. It's obvious to all of the aircrews that the targets, weapons and aircraft used, and routes to and from the target areas are not being selected by military planners." The members of the committee were riveted by Brad's solemn testimony.

Brad looked from one end of the table to the other, then back to Arlin Kerwin. "Gentlemen, we are being sold down the river."

Kerwin removed his glasses and placed them in his pocket. "Captain Austin, this committee appreciates your cooperation, and your candid remarks."

Brad remained silent.

"We will take a ten-minute break," Kerwin announced, then rose, "and then reconvene."

Sliding his chair back, Brad saw the chairman approaching him. The senator motioned him to the side. "Son, I admire you for your forthrightness. You have been very helpful."

"Thank you, Senator. This has been one of the most difficult things I have ever faced."

Kerwin tilted his head and lowered his voice. "I don't want you to worry about anything. My job is to make sure that you can do your job."

"I appreciate that, Senator."

"I'll tell you something," Kerwin said with a knowing smile. "There is a young lady who thinks mighty highly of you."

Brad beamed. "The feeling is mutual, sir. She's right outside."

Kerwin's surprise showed on his face. "Is she?" He had a moment of doubt. "Well, I'm afraid, under the circumstances, that I'll just have to have you give her my best."

"I understand, sir."

Kerwin patted Brad on the shoulder. "Now, you get on out of here, and take good care of that young lady. She is a special little gal."

Brad shook Arlin Kerwin's hand. "Thank you, Senator Kerwin, on behalf of both of us."

Austin reached for his cap, then walked out the door. He remained expressionless as he and Leigh Ann silently walked past the State Department and CINCPAC representatives.

Once outside, Brad took Leigh Ann's hand as they walked down the steps. "Everything seems to be okay as far as my screwup is concerned."

"That's wonderful," she said gleefully. "I'm so happy for you."

"I think," Brad replied cautiously, "as far as I can tell, that I'm just a piece of the bait."

Leigh Ann looked perplexed. "What do you mean by that?"

As they reached the sidewalk, Brad stepped around her to be next to the curb. "I think," Brad said, saluting a navy lieutenant commander, "that Senator Kerwin is one of a number of influential people who are concerned about the prosecution of this war. How it's being managed or, more to the point, mismanaged." Brad glanced at Leigh Ann. "They're trying to sort out the lies that cover the duplicity that conceals the falsehoods."

Hugging his arm, Leigh Ann looked up. "Are you free to go—to leave town?"

"Absolutely. I was simply cannon fodder."

"You are not cannon fodder," she admonished, placing her arm around his waist. "Where shall we go?"

"Well," Brad chuckled, "technically, I should return to San Diego, but what the hell. My career is down the tube, and I'm probably a terminal captain."

She smiled coyly. "What are you suggesting, Captain Terminal?"

"How about if we stop at Lake Tahoe, en route to San Diego?"

"I'd love to," she laughed mischievously. "We could stop in Las Vegas, and get married."

Wide-eyed, Brad came to a halt and looked at Leigh Ann.

She burst out laughing. "I'm kidding. Just a little humor, flyboy."

Then they were both surprised to hear a voice behind them.

"Captain Austin, is that you?"

They turned around to see the lieutenant commander they had just passed. He was walking toward them.

Brad came to attention, saluted again, and said, "Yes, sir." A questioning look crossed Brad's face.

"You don't know me, but I'm Lou Metcalf of the Navy's Congressional Liaison staff. I was hoping to catch you before you left the hearing. I've been asked to tell you that the CNO, acting on Senator Kerwin's request, has directed the Marine Commandant to write you up for a Silver Star for your gallantry in combat. It will be presented to you in San Diego when you arrive there."

"Pardon me, Commander," Brad stammered, "but I'm confused. I wouldn't think that the navy would want me around after this debacle and the testimony I just gave."

"Not at all," Metcalf replied. "You are exactly the kind of aggressive aviator that the CNO and Commandant really want. You'll be reassigned to the Marines in Da Nang to complete your tour. After that, who knows?" Metcalf smiled. "But, I'll bet you can write your next orders after this tour in Vietnam. Just try not to get killed or captured."

Leigh Ann was listening intently. She looked straight at Metcalf. "What's the Silver Star?"

"Your guy just earned the nation's third-highest award for valor."

Brad shook Metcalf's hand, almost pulling his arm from its socket, then he engulfed Leigh Ann in an immense bear hug. "Leigh Ann, under the circumstances, we had better bypass Tahoe and go straight to San Diego."

Filled with pride and relief, Leigh Ann nodded yes.

"Things," Brad smiled, "have a different tint all of a sudden."

Metcalf grinned and shook his head as he watched the happy young couple rush hand in hand to the taxi stand.

Epilogue

Following extensive hearings during August 1967, the Senate Armed Services Committee came to the conclusion that the Vietnam air war had not achieved its objectives. The finding did not attribute the lack of success to the inability or impotence of air power.

The committee discovered that the fragmentation of our air might was caused by overly restrictive controls, limitations, and the doctrine of gradualism forced on our combined aviation resources.

The restrictions prevented the flight crews from waging the air campaign in the manner, and according to the timetable, which would have achieved the maximum results.

Shortly after the Senate Armed Services Committee arrived at its conclusion, Secretary of Defense Robert Strange McNamara left the Pentagon. President Lyndon Baines Johnson, on March 31, 1968, announced that he would neither seek nor accept renomination.

Glossary

AAA Antiaircraft artillery, also known as triple-A. Rapid-firing cannons or machine guns, often aimed by radar and computers.

ACM Air combat maneuvering. Two or more fighter pilots engaged in aerial combat.

Afterburner Also known as burner. Jet-thrust augmentation by injecting raw fuel into the engine.

Air Boss Air officer responsible for all hangar and flight-deck operations.

Alert Five Fighter aircraft armed, fueled, and manned. Ready to launch in five minutes.

Alpha Strike All-out carrier air-wing attack.

Annunciator Panel Display lights that warn a pilot about aircraft cautionary or emergency situations.

Atoll NATO code name for Soviet-manufactured heat-seeking air-to-air missile.

Ball The optical landing device on an aircraft carrier. Also referred to as ''meatball.''

Bandits Enemy aircraft.

BARCAP Barrier combat air patrol. Used to protect vessels at sea.

Barrel Roll Air combat maneuver for achieving an advantage over an adversary.

Barricade Safety net of nylon webbing used to stop aircraft unable to make a carrier-arrested landing.

Bingo The amount of fuel needed to divert to a shore base.

Blue Water Operations Carrier flight operations beyond the range of land bases.

Bogie Unidentified or enemy aircraft.

Bolter Carrier landing attempt in which the tail hook misses the arresting wire, necessitating a go-around.

Bow Front of the ship.

Break A hard turn to avoid a missile. Also known as pitch-out-break over an airfield or carrier (ninety-degree knife-edge turn to position the aircraft for landing).

Bridge Command post in the superstructure of a ship.

Bulkhead Naval terminology for a wall.

CAG Commander of the air group; oversees all aircraft squadrons embarked on a carrier.

CAP Combat air patrol.

CATCC Carrier Air Traffic Control Center (Cat-see).

Check Six Refers to visual observation behind an aircraft. Fighter pilots must check behind them constantly to ensure that enemy aircraft are not in an attack position.

CIC Combat Information Center. Central battle-management post in naval surface ships.

CINCPAC Commander in chief of Pacific Fleet.

COD Carrier on-board delivery aircraft. Used to transfer cargo and personnel to and from shore installations and the carrier.

Combat Spread Tactical fighter information, providing mutual support for the flight leader and the wingman.

Dash Two Second plane in a two-aircraft section; the wingman.

Departure Refers to an aircraft departing from controlled flight.

Dixie Station Position in the Gulf of Tonkin, off South Vietnam, used for carrier air strikes into North Vietnam, Cambodia, and Laos.

EOD Explosive ordnance detachment.

Feet Dry/Wet Pilot radio call indicating a position over land/water.

FOD Foreign-object damage to a jet engine.

Fox One/Two/Three Pilot radio calls indicating the firing of a Sparrow (One), Sidewinder (Two), or Phoenix (Three) missile.

Furball Multiaircraft fighter engagement.

GCA Ground-controlled approach. Radar guidance provided to a pilot in the process of landing his aircraft.

g Force Force pressed on a body by changes in velocity, measured in increments of earth gravity.

g-LOC g-Induced loss of consciousness.

Gomers Combat adversaries.

High Yo-Yo Air combat maneuver.

Hot Pump Refueling an aircraft while the engine is running.

ICS Intercom system in cockpits of multiseat aircraft.

Idle and Boards Throttles to idle and speed brakes extended.

IFF Identification or Identification Friend or Foe. Military transponder used to identify aircraft. The transponder sends a coded signal to the radar installation.

IFR Instrument flight rules.

JBD Jet blast deflector.

Jink Abrupt and irregular flight path designed to make it difficult for gunners to track the aircraft.

Knot One nautical mile per hour. A nautical mile equals approximately 1.15 statute miles.

Loose Deuce Navy and marine tactical fighter formation.

Loud Handle Slang for the ejection-seat handle.

LSO Landing-signal officer. Squadron pilot responsible for assisting other aviators onto the flight deck of an aircraft carrier; also called Paddles.

Mach Named for physicist Ernst Mach; term used to describe speed of an object in relation to the speed of sound.

Main mount Aircraft main landing gear.

Marshal Aircraft holding pattern behind the carrier.

NATOPS Naval aviation training-and-operations procedures. Provides rules and regulations for safe and proper operation of all navy and Marine Corps aircraft and helicopters.

Nugget Rookie naval aviator.

Overrotate Pull back too aggressively on the aircraft's control stick.

Plane Guard Helicopter assigned to search and rescue during carrier flight operations.

PLAT Pilot's landing-aid television. Closed-circuit television that monitors the flight deck.

Port Naval terminology for the left side.

Posit Position.

Pri-Fly Primary Fly. Control tower on aircraft carrier.

Push Time Designated time for a pilot to commence an approach to the carrier.

Radar Vector Heading given to pilot by radar operator.

Ramp Aft end of the flight deck; round-down.

Ready Room Squadron headquarters on board an aircraft carrier.

RESCAP Rescue combat air patrol.

RIO Radar-intercept officer. Naval flight officer in the backseat of F-14 Tomcat or F-4 Phantom aircraft.

ROE Rules of engagement.

SA-2 Guided Missile (SAM) Soviet-manufactured surface-to-air missile.

SAR Search and rescue.

Section Takeoff Two aircraft taking off in formation.

Sidewinder AIM-9 heat-seeking air-to-air missile.

Sparrow AIM-7 radar-guided air-to-air missile.

Split-S Aircraft is rolled inverted, then the nose is pulled toward the ground to rapidly reduce altitude.

Squawk Transponder code to ground- or air-based radar installations.

Starboard Naval terminology for right side.

Stern Naval terminology for the back (aft) end of ship.

TACAN Navigation aid that provides the pilot with bearing and distance to an aircraft carrier or air base.

Tally Derivative of tallyho; target in sight.

TARCAP Target combat air patrol.

Tone Sound that indicates a pilot's air-to-air missile has locked onto his adversary.

Torso Harness Snug-fitting flight clothing that attaches to the ejection seat.

Trap Arrested landing on an aircraft carrier.

Unload Release pressure on aircraft control stick to ease g load.

Vertical Reverse Air combat tactic.

VFR Visual flight rules.

Vulture's Row Observation deck on the superstructure (island) of an aircraft carrier.

Wardroom Officers' dining room.

Wave Off Landing-signal officer's order to abort the approach and go around for another try.

Winchester Out of ammunition and ordnance.

XO Executive officer.

Yankee Station Position in the Gulf of Tonkin south of Hainan Island. The point for carrier-launched strikes into North Vietnam.

Zuni Air-to-ground rocket.